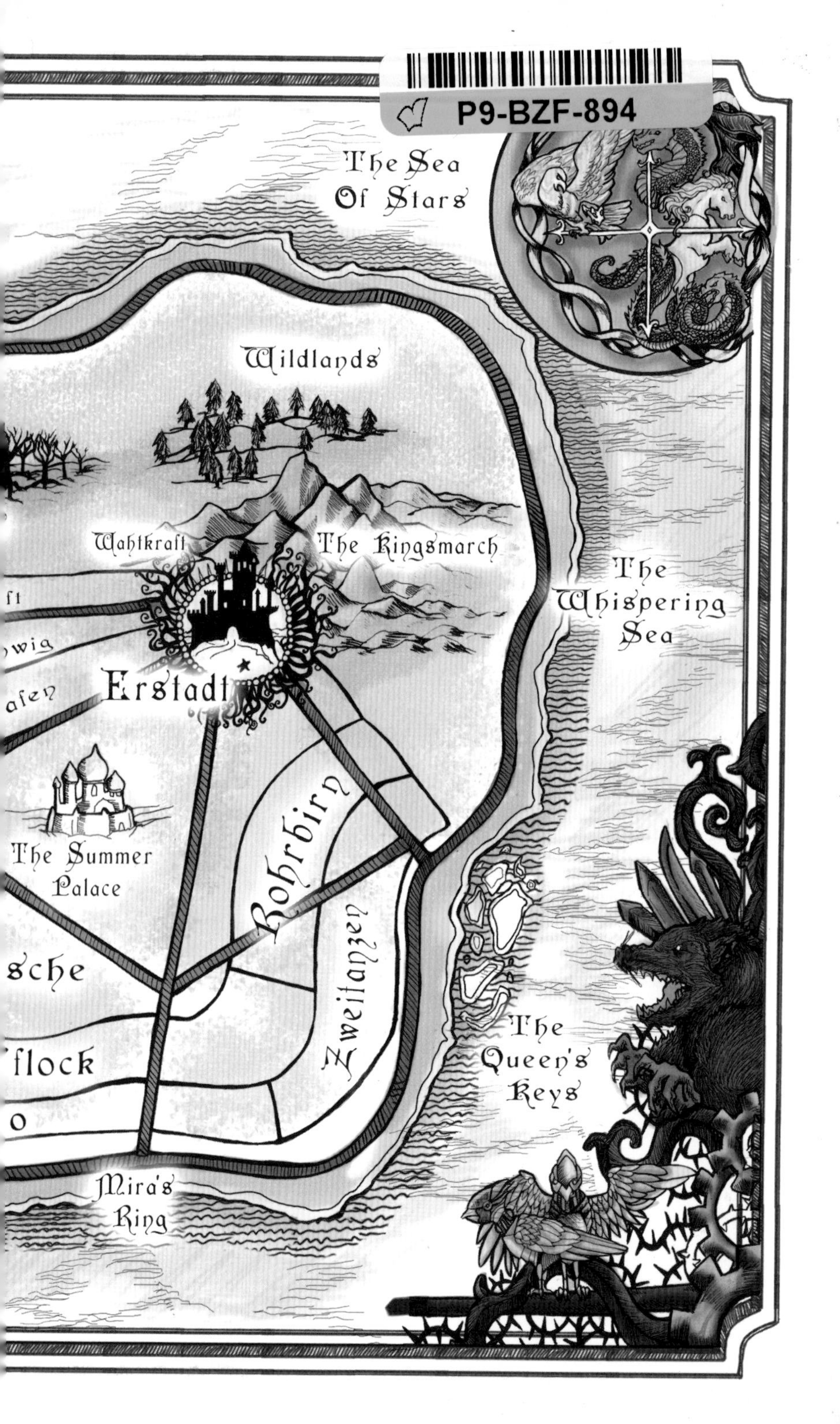
The Sea Of Stars
Wildlands
Wahtkraft
The Kingsmarch
Erstadt
The Whispering Sea
The Summer Palace
Rohrbirn
Zweitanzen
The Queen's Keys
Mira's Ring

OFFICIAL
DISCARD
peta

Also by Claire Legrand

The Cavendish Home for Boys and Girls

The Year of Shadows

WINTERSPELL

CLAIRE LEGRAND

SIMON & SCHUSTER BFYR

New York London Toronto Sydney New Delhi

SIMON & SCHUSTER BFYR
An imprint of Simon & Schuster Children's Publishing Division
1230 Avenue of the Americas, New York, New York 10020

For information about special discounts for bulk purchases, please contact
Simon & Schuster Special Sales at 1-866-506-1949 or business@simonandschuster.com.
The Simon & Schuster Speakers Bureau can bring authors to your live event. For more information or to book an event, contact the Simon & Schuster Speakers Bureau at 1-866-248-3049
or visit our website at www.simonspeakers.com.
Book design by Lucy Ruth Cummins
Sources of quotes at beginning of each section are from an edition of the Nutcracker fairy tale by E. T. A. Hoffman:
Hoffman, E. T. A. (1984). Nutcracker. (Ralph Manheim, Trans.) New York, NY: Crown.
(Original work published in 1816.)
The text for this book is set in Adobe Jenson Pro.
Map endpapers by Catherine Scully
Manufactured in the United States of America
10 9 8 7 6 5 4 3 2 1
Library of Congress Cataloging-in-Publication Data
Legrand, Claire, 1986–
Winterspell / Claire Legrand.—First edition.
pages cm
Summary: To find her abducted father and keep her sister safe from the lecherous politicians of 1899 New York City, seventeen-year-old Clara must journey to the wintry kingdom of Cane, where Anise, queen of the faeries, has ousted the royal family in favor of her own totalitarian, anti-human regime.
ISBN 978-1-4424-6598-5 (hardcover)
ISBN 978-1-4424-6600-5 (eBook)
[1. Magic—Fiction. 2. Fairies—Fiction.] I. Title.
PZ7.L521297Wi 2014
[Fic]—dc23
2013019385

For Diana, and Isabel, and Brynn: I could not have done this without you

and

for Stowell and Sendak, who inspired me

ACKNOWLEDGMENTS

Winterspell is a book many years in the making. From the moment I first sat down, tiny and wide-eyed, to watch *The Nutcracker* on PBS, I have been enchanted with this story. I have loved its pageantry and mystery, its bizarre dichotomy of holiday magic and something . . . *darker*, something secret and sly and sensual.

Helping this story grow from that early fascination to the book it is now has been a journey along which many people have helped me, and I thank them with all my heart:

First, my indomitable agent, Diana Fox—force of nature, fierce champion, friend—whose enthusiasm for this story and these characters was a constant encouragement.

My editor, Zareen Jaffery, whose insight, passion, and steadfast belief made it possible for me to mold *Winterspell* into what it needed to be.

Diana, Zareen—words are not enough to express my gratitude.

The entire team at Simon & Schuster Books for Young Readers, especially Justin Chanda, Julia Maguire, Rachel Stark, and Siena Koncsol.

Bara MacNeill and Brenna Franzitta, for their painstaking attention, patience, and care.

Lucy Ruth Cummins, art director extraordinaire and cover goddess, who gave *Winterspell* such a perfectly stunning design that I'm not sure I'll ever be able to stop staring at it.

Catherine Scully, who created the gorgeous map of Cane. I'm so glad this book brought us together.

The talented and kindhearted Marissa Meyer, for sharing your excitement about *Winterspell* with the world.

Writer friends and first readers Alison Cherry, Lindsay Ribar, Heidi Schulz, Kait Nolan, Susan Bischoff, Stefan Bachmann, Katherine Catmull, Emma Trevayne, and Ellen Wright—for your cheerleading, honesty, and friendship.

Brittany, Beth, Melissa, Jonathan, and Starr—for keeping me sane and for loving me even when I'm on deadline (or just generally stuck in a writer's headspace and therefore a bit dotty).

Matt, for the times I'm not at the computer, and for reminding me it's okay to step away. For believing in my stories, and for asking all the right questions. I love you.

My family, for the tireless support, and for reading, and for spreading the word. All my love to you, near and far (mostly far, but never in my heart).

And I must give special thanks to my mother, who shares my undying love for a certain one-eyed, eye-patch-wearing, mysterious, swirly-cloaked magician. You know who to picture when you read his scenes, Mom.

Lastly, to Kent Stowell and Maurice Sendak (to whom *Winterspell* is partially dedicated), and the past, present, and future companies of the Pacific Northwest Ballet, for their unique production of *The Nutcracker*—without which, it is safe to say, I might never have written this book.

Our stories say that when the human world was first made, not all of it fit.

Pieces fell off the whole, like too much dough being stuffed into a small pan, and those bits dropped into cracks and were forgotten. Our stories, the oldest ones, the ones most people no longer remember, say that my country, Cane, is one of those forgotten places, hidden away in some cosmic pocket of existence, for the most part separated from the human world, but not entirely. Tenuous links connect the two worlds—like certain traveling songs, and hidden doorways, and magic, if you're able to use it.

Not everyone in Cane believes that legend, though. Why would they? Their world is their world, and why would there be another? Most common folk don't like to think about unsettling things. Doing so disrupts their feeling that they are quite wise, thank you very much, or at least wise enough to get by, to have nice meals and a warm bed at the end of the day, and to know that there are no other worlds besides their own.

But I knew better.

The magic folk—the beings born, as our stories say, of the sea and the stars—knew better too. Once the magic folk fell from the skies and rose from the depths, they knew that we humans were from elsewhere, that the first of us had not been born here in Cane. But our blood surged with the land. We breathed, and it breathed. This connection, this kinship, was a gift from the great native creatures that had adopted us as their own, because before our arrival there had been only darkness. The dragons had been small, white, and blind, and the sea serpents had been writhing in frothy muck; the wild horses of the eastern flats had been frail and brittle-boned, and the nightbirds had had no wings.

When the humans stumbled into Cane, we brought the light. That is what our stories say.

So the magic folk pledged us allegiance in honor of our blood, our blood infused with the life force of the land itself, and for many years the country thrived. The dragons were strong, and the nightbirds soared; the eastern herds ran savage, and the sea serpents lured ships into storms. The forests whispered secrets and songs, for the magic folk brought it out of them. More humans arrived, by accident or by design, for the first four human families needed fresh blood. Over time the families grew and prospered—one in the capital, the other three ruling the outlying provinces as lesser equals. And after many ages Cane crawled with life—with us, the humans; and with the magic folk; and sometimes with creatures even stranger than that, who slipped through the secret cracks between worlds without meaning to.

But the peace did not last.

It ended, as so many things do, with betrayal.

With a glance. A whisper.

A kiss.

PART ONE
THE CROOKED CITY

An eerie feeling came over them when dusk fell and, as usual on Christmas Eve, no light was brought in.

1

One more hour and Clara Stole could turn criminal.

Could, that is, if she managed to stand her ground until then, for every eye in the crowd was watching her, waiting for her to say something impressive, something to commemorate the day. And she was so tired of fumbling through grand words that were never quite grand enough for such hungry, thirsty people. Hungry for food, thirsty for a numbing drink—but even hungrier, even thirstier, for hope.

Hope.

What *would* Hope Stole have thought of Clara, on this strange, wintry day? What would she have thought of her elder daughter? She would have been proud of Clara, surely, for the speech Clara was about to make, and for keeping the Bowery Hope Shelter project alive despite the gradual decrease in funding.

And, just as surely, she would have been angry at Clara for what would come after—the criminal part, the part that would involve sneaking, thievery, breaking and entering.

The part Godfather had unknowingly inspired.

Yes, Hope Stole would have been disappointed, and her eyes would have flashed in that famously fearsome way, and she would probably have railed at Godfather about responsibility this and safety that. She had always been worried about her daughters' safety, even more so than most mothers Clara knew, as if the world were full of dangers only she could see. Funny, that, as without her mother's influence, Godfather wouldn't have been brought into their lives, and without Godfather, Clara might not have ever thought of doing something like what she would do in—fifty-seven minutes, now?

And anyway, the daughter of a New York City gang lord is criminal by her very blood. Being *uncriminal,* Clara had decided—being good—would have been like snubbing her heritage.

Somehow she didn't think her mother would have been impressed with that line of reasoning.

But her mother was dead, and it was past time for Clara to find answers. If she could only, for this short while, manage to keep her head.

That was her credo these days, and an increasingly difficult one to follow: *Keep your head, Clara, while everyone around you loses theirs, or already has.*

And when you yourself are close to doing the same.

Beside her, Leo Wiley, her father's secretary, cleared his throat. Her cue.

Clara approached the edge of the stone steps, breathing deeply to calm her racing heart. Anxiety nipped at her insides; as always, she shoved past it. There was no place for it here, not when she was playing the good, glamorous mayor's daughter. A tangle of red hair came loose from its knot and fell across her eyes, as though it knew her true state of mind. Before her the crowd waited, shifting, eyeing her—blankly, skeptically, and, a few, with hope.

"My mother loved this city," Clara began, "and the people in it." Her voice wanted to shrink and crack, and her hands were shaking. She wasn't good at this, but she had to be, so she pretended. She didn't like wearing this fine gown; even with its many layers and her winter coat, she felt bare, exposed, too prettied up to feel safe. But she had to look the part, so she tolerated her raging discomfort. Not for the first time that day, she wished her father were up here instead. It should have been him dedicating this building in his wife's honor. But her father was different now; he had changed over the past year. Everything had.

"She, er . . ." Clara's voice trailed off. The crowd glanced around, uncertain. So many of them, so many mouths and fears and empty bellies, measuring her. Surely they could see through this lace and satin and velvet brocade to the shaking nakedness underneath.

Pull yourself together, Clara Stole. You can't afford not to.

"Pardon me." She dabbed her eyes with a handkerchief, fingered the ebony cross at her neck. "She would have loved to be here today, you see."

Ah. The crowd nodded sympathetically, shared knowing glances, shifted forward to better see the dear, tenderhearted, motherless girl. Clara felt Mr. Wiley puff up with pleasure; he would be proud of her performance. There would be a warm, supportive summary of the event in tomorrow's paper. It would be fantastic press for the mayor's office.

Clara clutched the worn wooden podium. It was the only thing preventing her from running away to hide, preferably in Godfather's shop. There, no one's eyes were ever on her except his solitary, sharp gray one—and the stern black ones of the statue in the corner.

"Again, pardon me." Clara cleared her throat; the sound of tears in her voice, at least, would be genuine. Fifty-five minutes now, perhaps. She clung to the estimate with slipping nerves. Only fifty-five more minutes. "My mother worked tirelessly for the betterment of our city," she continued, addressing the bare black branches in the park beyond, avoiding the eyes in the crowd. "She dreamed of a place where the less fortunate could turn for shelter, warmth, and rest."

Clara gestured at the narrow gray edifice behind her—the new Bowery Hope Shelter, the building stained here and there with ash from the 1879 fire that had left several east-side neighborhoods in ruins.

"My great hope is that this shelter will do justice to her memory, and help fulfill her dream of a city that provides a place for everyone."

Clara smiled at the crowd and stepped back, allowing Walter Higgins, the Commissioner for Human Health, to take the stage. A Concordia lord otherwise known as the Merry Butcher, his skill with a cleaver was legend—but today, he was all respectable reassurance. As he spoke, some of the crowd's tentative smiles grew. Perhaps they believed his words—that the new shelter would provide a spot of relief for the growing number of people forced to live on the streets, and boost city morale in time for Christmas. Clara sighed; she knew better. Inside the shelter would be warmer than outside, yes, but the building was shoddy and flea-ridden, and instead of beds, poorly constructed coffins halfheartedly disguised with tarpaulins lined the walls. It was the only thing Clara had been able to persuade her father to provide.

"There's no money, my sweet one," John Stole would tell her again and again while he smoked imported cigars and reeked of fine alcohol, and while the other lords of the underground syndicate-turned-empire that called itself Concordia attended the theater with their wives, in silk top hats and heavy furs.

No money, indeed.

Clara was not her mother; she could influence her father only so much. Concordia had chosen him for their figurehead two years before, when Boss Plum had helped her father become mayor, bribing and threatening John Stole's way to the top. But at what price? Her father's integrity, for one. John Stole had barely resisted the most heinous of Concordia's demands that first year in office. Clara had heard her parents' arguments through their cracked-open bedroom door—her father insisting he must bow to Concordia's wishes, her mother incredulous that he had gotten himself into this position.

But Hope's murder had weakened John Stole, destroyed in the space of a day the last vestiges of his crumbling fortitude. It was as though something had eaten away at him over the past year, transforming him into a powerless ghost. Sometimes Clara felt as though she had lost two parents instead of just the one—one to murder, the other to the snarls of Concordia's web.

She could still recall the headlines from that dreadful day, just after Christmas last year: HOPE IS DEAD!

"The headline writes itself, don't it?" Clara had heard one of the scandalized servants whisper to another outside her mother's parlor. There Clara had sat, sixteen years old and numb, her eleven-year-old sister, Felicity, sobbing in her arms, for once not worrying about her face turning blotchy.

The headline *should* have read, HOPE IS MURDERED: BLUDGEONED, SCALPED, MAIMED, AND HUNG LIKE A SPLIT-OPEN DOLL BY THE RIVERSIDE! Her father had not allowed her to see the photographs of her mother's body, but Clara had heard Concordia gentlemen whispering about the grisly details at the mayor's mansion when they'd slipped in through the underground entrance and thought no one was listening—especially not the mayor's quiet elder daughter, who, thanks to Godfather, knew how to sneak.

And in sneaking—through the mansion and throughout the city—she had learned many things. Though her mother had been officially declared a victim of the downtown gang wars, Police Chief Greeley had confided to a Concordia gentleman, "The way she was killed, the unnecessary, disfiguring violence . . . The Townies don't kill like that. None of the gangs do. I think it was something else entirely." And there had been similar killings, more and more of them, in the past few months—bad ones, violent ones, most of them by the water and all of them so shockingly gruesome that Concordia had ensured they were kept out of the papers, to prevent a citywide panic.

Clara had also learned that her father was losing favor. In recent months, during lunches and private meetings at the mayor's mansion, he had begun slandering his own people—Concordia people. He would accuse city council members, bought judges, even the chief of police, of unthinkable crimes. It was mutinous talk. Mutinous, anti-Concordia talk. Entrenched in every city department from sanitation and fire to law enforcement and the courts, the empire of Concordia had noticed John Stole's discontent. At first they had dismissed it graciously as the rantings of the recently bereaved. But their patience had worn thin now, almost a year after Hope's murder, and they were not happy. John Stole's efforts were largely ineffectual; Concordia could see, just as Clara could, that he was all froth and bluster, without any real power behind his words. But a loose tongue, even that of a grieving, weak-willed figurehead, could be dangerous, and John Stole knew too many secrets for his actions to go unpunished.

Clara had to act fast, before her family lost all credibility with Concordia, before she lost her chance to find out what had really happened to her mother. At least for tonight, she had to become the person Godfather seemed to think she could be—someone not trapped by circumstance and crippled by fear.

She had to be more like her mother.

Hope Stole had never let Concordia weaken her. She had looked its cruelest lords straight in the eye and lambasted them unflinchingly for their corruption.

Clara wondered if they'd had her killed for that.

Regardless, it seemed an unattainable goal. "I'm not my mother!" she had cried more than once during her training with Godfather, frustrated that he would expect such things of her, things so far out of her grasp—her mother's strength, her mother's courage.

"No, you are not," he would say each time, with the sort of conviction that had eluded Clara since her mother's death, "but you are her daughter. You have that same fire within you."

Godfather said it to encourage her, but his words served only to increase her fear. Yes, her mother had had a fire within—and look what had happened to her.

Mr. Wiley cleared his throat; the commissioner had finished his speech. Clara took the offered pair of shears and positioned the blades around the red satin ribbon stretched before her. She paused so the *Times* photographer could adjust the plates of his camera just so.

"Nice smile, Miss Stole, there we are," said Mr. Wiley. "Nice and bright."

Yes, a smile. A smile for the city still recovering from the recent depression, for the city thick with the rising violence of the downtown gangs and reeling from the unstable food prices, for the streets poisoned by a fear as rampant and deadly as disease.

She had to keep smiling, despite the many reasons not to. Concordia grew suspicious otherwise.

Clara pressed the shears' blades together and cut.

The bright red ribbon floated away on either side. Tepid applause came from the weary-eyed crowd.

Mr. Wiley directed her down into the press of people—to shake hands with Commissioner Higgins, whose fat, grinning face shone pink; to place a hand on the shoulder of a stooped old man who scowled up at the shelter. *Coffin house,* his expression seemed to say. He knew—he was not a fool—and yet what was there to do?

Clara swallowed, each brush of someone's arm against hers, each glance of every citizen she passed making her flinch. For there *was* nothing to do, except to pretend, and take what was given, and stay silent.

In this city Concordia had become law. And for the daughter of its figurehead, Concordia had become life.

So Clara stood beside the scowling old man and turned toward the photographer with a smile on her face. The old man's shoulders shook with cold against her arm. Above them a bedraggled cluster of ribboned holly hung limply from a streetlamp.

All things considered, the decoration looked ridiculous. Parodic. Cruel.

Clara stared up at it, the crowd dispersing around her.

Merry Christmas, indeed.

2

Clara hiked up her bustle, top-skirt, and petticoats, clipping their hems to her waist with the hook apparatus Godfather had fashioned. She could release the hook in an instant to cover herself if need be, but until then, she would need her legs free to move.

It was fifty minutes after her speech, thirty after she had slipped away from Mr. Wiley and lied once again to her poor maid, the unsuspecting Mrs. Hancock. Hope Stole would not have allowed someone so dim-witted to remain in her household's employ, but Clara was grateful for the maid's gullibility. It was what allowed Clara to so frequently disappear.

She took a moment, here in this quiet alleyway beside Rivington Hall, to close her eyes and forget who she was—fearful Clara, trembling, pretending Clara—to slip into that steady, hot, flinty place she only ever found after an hour of throwing punches at Godfather, when her hair clung to her skin and her body stung with bruises. She needed her wits about her if she was going to do this.

And she *was* going to do this.

Voices drifted out from one of the windows overhead, a white curtain fluttering in the chilled breeze. A bark of laughter and the jingle of harness bells came from nearby Essex Street. Fear seized her. She crouched low, hugging the wall as though it could do something to save her should she be discovered.

"Keep your head, Clara Stole," she whispered, fumbling to secure her petticoats, her fingers streaking them with street grit. Felicity would be appalled.

The thought gave Clara a fleeting smile—until her fingers brushed against the cotton breeches she hid under her gowns every morning. To feel the contours of her legs unimpeded by the usual layers of fabric made her shudder, as though she were touching some alien thing. The knobs of her knees, the curving lines of her thighs . . . She drew her hands away. She did not trust the tingling sensation her touch produced, and she was quite sure that the prospect of such a sensation, of such intimacy, was what made Dr. Victor watch her so hungrily.

She cringed to think of Dr. Victor, one of the more powerful men of Concordia. Elegant, handsome, and disgustingly rich, he had a disturbing preoccupation with Clara. He would threaten the perfectly nice young men who had attempted conversation since her debut, frightening them away forever; he would stare at her with that unholy light in his eyes that said he would like nothing more than to corner her and slide his hands, roughly, where he had no right to go.

In those moments it was not Clara's place to fight back. Dr. Victor was too powerful a man to defy, and her family could not afford to further upset anyone, especially Concordia's walking bank account. She needed to be seen as spineless, unthreatening, and most of the time that perception was the truth, a fact that filled her with relentless shame.

But it was not so today. Today she would dare to follow her mother's example. Hope Stole deserved for *someone* out here in the world of the living to know the truth about her death.

Clara forced her mind back into its fraught compartments and traded her lace gloves for dark leather ones that molded to her fingers like a second, sleek skin. Wearing them transported her into a sturdier state of mind, made her feel deadly and capable, as did the boots encasing her legs. Godfather had modified them for her months ago as a birthday gift—simple and cream-colored with plain laces to anyone who glimpsed them peeking out below her hem, but underneath her skirts they stretched above her knees, generously supple, blades hidden in the heels and ready to detach with the release of a concealed spring-loaded mechanism.

"The city is dangerous," Godfather had told her upon gifting them. And then, tenderly, tilting up her chin to kiss her brow: "I won't let the same thing happen to you."

The unspoken word had lingered between them like a bad dream: "murder."

Clara grabbed her parasol from where it leaned against the grimy brick wall, and scowled as she felt it bend in her grip. Unforgivably ridiculous, cumbersome frippery. A man would have his cane, his pocketknife, his gun, perhaps. He would not be weighed down by useless lace and handkerchiefs. It was as though society wanted its females to be at risk. Were it not for Godfather, Clara would not have had the tiny automatic blade in her bodice and the dagger in the holster buckled around her thigh, to say nothing of the skill to use them.

She had imagined it, desperately, over and over—driving the jagged blade into Dr. Victor's handsome face. But when she saw him in the light of day, her fear melted away any thoughts of bloody justice, leaving her feeling helpless and wretched.

Sometimes she would catch him looking at her in *that way*, as though she were his already. She tried as best as current fashions allowed to cover the curves she'd been developing over the past few years, but that did nothing to dissuade him. And whenever he saw her alone, he would sidle close and whisper, "It's your fault, you know, for being so beautiful, so wanton." His voice would slither across the words. "I can't help myself, Clara Stole." And Clara would want to gag because the chemical stench of him was so near, and she would believe him.

Thinking of it, Clara wiped angry tears from her eyes. She *was* weak, as he always said, pathetically so. She couldn't banish these thoughts from her mind, couldn't stop her hands from shaking at the thought of Dr. Victor's cold white fingers upon her.

Fighting for calm, torn between the comfort of her boots and breeches and the terror of what Dr. Victor would say if he saw her in such a state, Clara slipped the lock pick from her parasol's shaft and crouched down to work. Years of haunting Godfather's shop had taught her many things—how to replace the gears of a broken clock, how to bake clay figurines in a kiln, how to pick a lock.

How to incapacitate someone with a kick to the head.

Not, of course, that Clara had ever found the courage for that. Opportunity, yes, loads of times. But *courage?* That was something else entirely.

The lock gave way, and Clara slipped inside before she could convince herself not to. She waited for her eyes to adjust to the corridor before her, lined with plush carpet as dark as blood, and polished wood-paneled walls. Down the corridor to her left, the wall opened to reveal a small staircase and curling banisters.

Clara crept toward the stairs and then up them, each footfall measured, each breath a risk. If she were caught by a Concordia gentleman, if she couldn't release her skirts in time, if they saw her here, unescorted . . . *If, if, if.* The word infected her thoughts, a hissed refrain. Pausing every few steps to listen for sounds of approach, she mentally recited her planned excuses if caught—simpering apologies and manufactured coquettishness that still might do her no good. Despite being raised in a political household, she was a terrible liar, as Godfather always said. "You wear your heart on your face," he would tell her, and smile his sad smile.

As she progressed through Rivington Hall, the muscles of her legs and arms, strengthened over the past year of Godfather's training into lithe, combat-ready limbs, knotted with apprehension. At every hint of noise her fingers itched to release the daggers from her heels. Paintings of Concordia members past and present watched her progress with cold black eyes.

She paused before the landing of the grand staircase. This would be the tricky part—sneaking across the landing and into Patricia Plum's private office without anyone seeing her. According to the whispers Clara had caught, Plum herself was uptown for a luncheon, Dr. Victor was at Harrod House for the afternoon, and anyone else loitering in the Hall at this time would be drinking brandy, smoking, and fondling girls brought in from Allen Street.

But without Patricia Plum around, smelling of sweets and poppies, gliding silently in her silks with gentlemen hanging off her arms, Clara hoped to sneak into the woman's office without trouble. The air of Concordia's headquarters was always more relaxed with its widowed queen elsewhere, and with relaxation came inattention. Clara was counting on it.

From the corridor behind her drifted the sweet bite of cigar smoke and the trill of soft laughter, the slam of a door. The sounds jarred her, shaking her resolve. She wished suddenly that Godfather were here; the last time she had been to Rivington Hall, he had been beside her, and the danger had therefore not felt quite so dire.

That particular exercise had been one of Godfather's most exhilarating, a true test of her sneaking skills—both of them, cloaked in shadow and slinking through Rivington Hall's empty corridors in the last hours before dawn. Together they had mapped each twist and turn, Clara struggling to memorize each room, each staircase. Godfather's silent presence had never been far away, and it had felt like a terrific game. Each time Clara had successfully picked a lock or disappeared into silence beside him, Godfather had squeezed her hand in approval.

Tonight, however, she was alone, and the game was much more treacherous. In fact, Godfather would probably rage at her in his dear, protective way, were he to find out she had returned here on her own. He would call it "an unnecessary risk, my dear Clara."

Risk, yes. Unnecessary? Hardly. Standing on the steps of the homeless shelter her mother should have been alive to commemorate, struggling to breathe through the pangs of memory as the anniversary of her mother's death approached, had confirmed the need for this today—the need for action.

She could not bear another year of grief without explanation.

Clara stepped out onto the landing, body humming with readiness. Across from her stood a heavy wooden set of double doors, black in the dim lamplight. Plum's office. If Clara weren't careful, the Concordia gentlemen lounging in the lobby below could glance up the stairs and easily see her fiddling with the lock.

At the beginning of her training, shortly after the murder, Godfather had taught Clara how to turn feline when the situation necessitated it—how to slink and prowl, how to press oneself to a wall's contours and slide along it like a sigh.

"Like you would to a lover," Godfather had instructed, before clamping his lips shut. His pale cheeks had grayed. It was an odd quirk of his, one of many—his blush, unlike most people's, tinged his sharp cheeks not with pink but with silver and shadows.

Reflexively, Clara's eyes had flitted to the hulking statue in the corner of the workshop's cluttered main room—a silent, solemn figure amid piles of half-finished dolls and skeletons of clocks. The forest of lanterns that hung from the rafters dropped soft slices of amber light onto the statue's face, illuminating its regal profile.

"I— Godfather, I know nothing about lovers."

"Of course, yes. Forgive me, Clara. I didn't mean—" He'd sworn under his breath, awkward and irritated. "For a moment I forgot to whom I was speaking."

They had stared at each other and then looked away, and Godfather had fiddled with the strap of his eye patch and ruffled his graying brown hair. When they resumed their lesson at last, Godfather dimmed every lamp but one and demonstrated from across the room.

"Do you see?" As he slid through the shadows, moving in silence across the gear-strewn floor, Clara watched intently. "You must move as though through water. The room is yours to know, to possess. The energy within you subsumes its energy. You *are* the room. You *are* the shadows. Try it."

She did, awkwardly at first, knocking into tables and stumbling over a pile of discarded doll parts on the floor. Godfather snuck up beside her with instructions from the dark: "Slowly, my Clara. You are no longer a girl; you are not even a person. You are a cat, you are darkness, you are a storm too distant to hear. Try again."

After two hours the lamp gave out. Her muscles aching, sweat dripping down her back, Clara lost Godfather. She lost Dr. Victor and Concordia, and her dead mother, and her nerves—everything but the exhilaration of hiding not *from* someone, for once, but instead hiding with a purpose. Slipping so completely into the shadows that she knew nothing but the ache of her legs and the wall's texture beneath her palms, she was no longer Clara; she was shadow, and silence, and supple heat. Even the darkness on her cheeks seemed to tingle.

Then she knocked against the statue in the corner, and it was such a shock, such an awakening, that she had to gasp. Jolted out of her trance, her senses reeling, she used the statue to pull herself to her feet—and promptly forgot to breathe. The hard lines of the statue's thighs, belly, chest, scraped against her skin, snagging at the cotton of her chemise, and she found herself moving slowly so as to prolong the contact. Molding herself to the metal, she sighed. Her palms slick with sweat, she slid them up the statue's chest to cup the chiseled, handsome jaw, and pressed herself closer. She inhaled, shuddering, and tasted the tang of metal and the oils Godfather used to keep tarnish away. Curling into the crook of the statue's left arm, she let the sudden fancy overtake her. What would it feel like if that iron-muscled arm could come alive and pull her closer, its spikes digging into the back of her neck, its cold fingers threading through her hair . . . ?

The swipe of a match. The hiss of flame.

"That's enough." In the fresh lamplight Godfather's face was dark with fury, but his good eye was not on Clara; it was on the statue's face, as if . . . *admonishing* it.

Mortified, Clara peeled herself away. She stole a lingering glance at the statue's arm, muscled and savage, covered with spikes and foreign etchings. Her heart beat practically off its hinges. She had touched the statue many times, but never had there been such . . . *heat* to it.

In their sparring that night, Godfather's blows had stung as sharply as the glare of his eye. It was as if he had known her fevered thoughts and wanted to shock them out of her for reasons Clara couldn't fathom.

Now, as Clara crept toward Plum's office and went to work with her lock pick, she kept the reassuring presence of Godfather's odd little shop in her mind. Twice she thought she heard someone coming, and paused, her mind fumbling for the memorized excuses. When the lock gave, Clara almost laughed with relief, and cracked the door enough to slip inside.

She scanned Patricia Plum's office—the heavy oak desk drawers, the glass case in the corner, the cabinets by the walls, all with prominently displayed locks. But this did not discourage Clara; working quickly, she used her pick to open each case and cabinet. She inspected each book and trinket, felt along the walls and the backs of bookcases for something to give way, and found nothing until her gaze landed on the massive desk at the right of the room. She crawled beneath it, scooting past the legs of Plum's claw-footed chair. Even the carpet reeked of perfume and poppies, sweet, dangerous notes that sent Clara's head spinning.

With the blade of her dagger, she jimmied between each grooved edge in the desk's wooden panels until she found what she was looking for—a hidden catch, a tiny click as one of the panels gave way.

Clara closed her eyes and exhaled. Here, she hoped, lay the real treasures of Patricia Plum's office. It was a Concordia trick that Clara had observed over the years. The gentlemen thought themselves so clever, storing their important papers in secret cupboards and hidden compartments. Clara's own father did it: his sat behind a bookshelf, which, if you could find the catch, slid back to reveal a safe.

How easy it was, when pretending to fiddle with her skirts or read her book, to secretly observe those around her. How easy it was to excuse herself for a nap and instead hide outside her father's parlor as Patricia Plum murmured of bought judges and hushed murders.

For a few moments Clara dug through the narrow compartment, searching through wrapped envelopes and pages of correspondence. At every slight noise from outside, she froze, sweat beading on her forehead. Then, when she'd started to lose hope, Clara found something promising—several leather packets wound with ribbon and twine, the first marked DECEMBER 1898.

The month of Hope Stole's murder.

Risking the light, giddy with sudden nervousness, Clara turned up the desk lamp and rooted through her findings for what felt like hours. Each packet contained newspaper clippings, tiny paper booklets, and photographs—all documenting murder after brutal murder. Maulings, flayings, decapitations. It was terrible violence; it wasn't to be believed . . . but then Clara's eyes fell upon a particular photograph and a few familiar words, and the reality of the evidence before her hit her like a physical blow. Her hands flew to her mouth as she forced down the urge to be sick, to run, to return to her earlier ignorance and be happy about it.

Her mother, dead. Her mother, *torn apart.*

These were the photographs her father had never allowed her to see or to be printed in the papers. No, those photographs in the *Times* had been of Hope Stole alive, buttoned to the throat and wrists, her dark hair pinned up with mother-of-pearl combs, her hands on her husband's arm, and her *face*—full of light and mischief and a steady, solid strength—so unlike the faces of other women. Clara had often stood in front of her mirror and tried to imitate the look, putting up her chin and searching for the expression that would make her eyes light up with that same secret fire. Her father used to cup her mother's face when he thought no one was looking, whisper, "Your eyes are full of stars," and kiss her deeply, and from her hiding place in the shadows Clara would burn with embarrassment and curiosity.

But these photographs held nothing of the mother Clara had loved. Her body had been mutilated, clawed to pieces, torn limb from limb. Her scalp was missing, her face covered with blood; bits of dark hair clung to her neck and chest, where strange symbols marred her river-swollen skin. Her blood, strangely, seemed paler than it should have, gleaming in the grain of the photograph, moonlight turned viscous—but surely it was a trick of the lamplight.

Clara tried to detach herself from the horror of the moment and peered closer, drawn not by the blood but rather the markings carved into her mother's skin. None of the other bodies in these photos had sported such markings. A tiny alarm sounded in her mind, impossible to ignore. She peered more closely, struck by the markings' familiarity, for they looked almost like . . .

No. It cannot be.

She pulled out a folded-up sheet of paper from her stocking and Godfather's pen from her boot, and sketched everything she could—the number of wounds on her mother's body, the designs of those terrible markings. They were important, those symbols. What did they mean, and why were they there? And could it be true, this horrible thought?

A burst of laughter from down the hallway made Clara jump. *How dare they keep this from me?* she thought, her eyes stinging, her hands shaking. *How dare they? How* dare *you, Father?* But she continued until she had copied down everything she could. The investigation had gone cold, the case notes said. There had been no witnesses, nor reports of strange sounds or struggles by the crowded riverside. Hope Stole had last been seen on her way home from a luncheon on the Upper West Side, and she and her coachman and the pair of carriage horses had somehow disappeared in broad daylight with no one noticing, until their bodies had appeared the next day beneath the Brooklyn Bridge.

Hope had been the only one hanging from the steel rafters, symbols carved into her skin.

Trying not to imagine the stench of horse meat and river rot, Clara read over Chief Greeley's notes, about how they had no leads, how he did not understand this case, how the mayor himself had hired detectives and even cut deals with the downtown gangs' most disreputable figures, to no avail. The only thing anyone could say, after months of questioning, searching, and blackmail, was that there were beasts in New York City.

The word appeared several times in accounts of testimonies and interviews, in the notes of hired detectives who had abandoned the case and fled without even collecting their pay: "beasts."

One detective's report read: *There's talk everywhere since Mrs. Stole's murder, downtown and especially by the river, of bumps in the night, of humans and animals alike turning up maimed, of strange writing on the walls. These instances go unreported, for the common folk are too frightened of what it might mean. It's poppycock, if I may be so candid. It's the Townies, Gristlers, or Half-Hands, or one of the other gangs infesting the city's underbelly. They are playing tricks, striking fear into the hearts of the stupid and gullible for their own amusement.*

The detective's next entry said only: *I must leave this place. I have seen . . . I don't know what I have seen.*

Clara stared at the mess of information in her hands. She could not yet make sense of it, and she shook with fury and fear, but three things she did know—that her mother's murder, and the other murders as well, could not have been the work of the street gangs; that her mother's body had been the only one marked in that strange, savage way, and this was somehow significant; and that, yes, she had seen those symbols before.

In Godfather's shop.

3

Godfather Drosselmeyer was a man of clockwork: he used it in his creations, and he hated spontaneity. He would be distinctly bothered that Clara would dare to show up at his shop without advance notice. And the excuse she had given Mrs. Hancock about being out this afternoon was thin. If Clara was too long in getting home, she would have some explaining to do.

She did not care one bit.

She burst into Trifles & Trinkets at the corner of West Twenty-Third Street and Sixth Avenue ready to erupt with temper. Lucky for her—and unlucky for Godfather—this was the one place she did not have to stifle it.

"Godfather?" She locked the shop's door behind her and pulled the drapes down against the late afternoon light. "Are you decent?"

A metallic clatter, a spat curse, and Godfather emerged from the back room, mouth downturned irritably. Today he wore his most voluminous greatcoat, the one with unfashionable ruffles along the collar and falling down the back; under that, a dark frock coat, a fine red silk vest, and a tattered lavender cravat; faded striped trousers and beautiful square-toed boots that looked fit for a Concordia gentleman; and his "dress" eye patch, the one sewn of black silk.

The familiar sight of his mismatched eccentricity would normally warm Clara; obviously he had guessed she might visit today and had dressed for the occasion—never mind that, after a day of work, oil and grease spotted his once-fine garments and the end of his nose. But Clara felt no such warmth today. Had he known about the markings on her mother's body? And if he had, why hadn't he told her?

Since her mother's death, Godfather was the only one with whom she could speak honestly and without fear. From childhood he had always told her everything—even made-up things, which nevertheless entranced her. He'd told her about magic, and how it could sometimes hurt to use it, how you could soothe animals with it and use it to hide yourself, and even, though it was in poor taste, craft curses with it. Magic, he had warned her, should not be used to hurt. And she had listened to every word, rapt.

All of that fanciful talk, and nothing of real importance. Oh, how could she have tolerated him filling her head with such nonsense for so many years?

"Clara!" He smiled his crooked, unsettling smile—as though he knew secrets he not only would never tell you but would also use to play tricks on you, should you give him reason. That you could never be certain of what he would do next or what he was thinking was one of the things Clara loved about him—that and the fact that despite his unpredictable nature, she could always be sure of his love for her.

Or she had been, until today.

"You know, dear heart, that I prefer you to make appointments before coming to see me," he said, shaking out soot from his clothes as he approached her. "I was in the middle of a most precarious project."

She waited until he was close enough to touch—and then, giving in to the fury swelling within her, she turned on him, shoving him against the wall.

He nearly fell. His dragon-headed cane went flying, clattering against the stone floor as he stumbled to regain his footing. Normally, even with her extensive training, Clara would not have been able to knock her tall, lean Godfather off his feet, but she had surprised him, and her rage and confusion gave her unnatural strength.

The shelves behind him rattled; the figurine of a masked wolf dancing on its hind legs crashed to the ground and shattered; a clockwork soldier fell and cracked open, spilling his gears and shooting tiny pellets from his gun. Overhead, lanterns quivered like roosting bats. Godfather's birds—crows, pigeons, a tiny hawk; animals had always had an affinity for him—squawked and flapped on their perches near the thrumming back room, into which Clara had never been allowed. The familiar taste of spice, sweat, and tools flooded her mouth.

"Clara, what in God's name—?"

"I snuck into Patricia Plum's office today."

Godfather paused, blinking. "You mean you snuck into Rivington Hall?"

"That is the location of her office, yes."

"I have warned you—"

"Yes, you have warned me not to go there without you, even though the whole point of your teaching me how to do things like sneak into Rivington Hall is, I assume, so I can actually do things like sneak into Rivington Hall and not, in fact, to fill my head with useless covert skills." Her heart pounded in her ears. This wasn't the exhilaration of a nice, healthy evening of sparring; this was a new exhilaration, a furious one. "I was looking for answers, you see, because no one else would give me any."

Godfather interrupted her quietly. "The ribbon-cutting ceremony. It was today, wasn't it? That's why you did this."

She glared at him, irrationally cross that he should know her so well. "I snuck into her office and found something of great interest."

With that, Clara reached into her coat pocket, withdrew the paper onto which she had copied the markings on her mother's corpse, and thrust it into Godfather's face.

She watched his expression as he took in the sketched symbols—the symbols, Clara had realized in Plum's office, that covered the hard metal body of Godfather's statue by the hundreds. Godfather's skin, pale from too many days hunched indoors over his toys, grew even paler.

"Ah." Clara felt a terrible, grim satisfaction. "You recognize them, do you?"

His voice was steady, even cool, but he would not look at her. "Of course I do."

"As do I." She nodded toward the statue. Its markings repulsed her with their new, sinister meaning, yet the sight of the statue itself still heated her blood. It had always fascinated her, even at a young age; she had made a strange, secret game of talking to it and imagining how it would answer her. But in the months following that night, when she had learned against the planes of its body how to melt into the shadows, her fascination had evolved into something more, something she couldn't describe. Something, she often thought, alone in her bedroom, like *need*. She'd begun sending Godfather into the back room on pointless errands, to fetch her something or other for a project she was fiddling with, so that she could spend a private moment with the fearsome-looking thing. She would sneak over to it and press close, fancying it, in her more foolish moments, a stoic suitor who, with those hard arms as thick as her waist, would encircle her, bend her back, and whisper secrets into her hair.

The truly great thing was that no matter how shocking her fancies grew, the statue never did a thing. He stood there, unmoving, and he did not lick his lips or pin her with hot, uneasy stares.

But now, everything had changed. Now, Clara shoved such thoughts away, stalked over to the statue, and held up her sketches against it. Clusters of harsh lines, like the hieroglyphics of ancient Egypt gone utterly savage, echoed one another—some on the paper, some on the statue.

"Tell me what it means." Clara whipped her head around to glare at Godfather, who looked suddenly lost, ancient and small. "This was carved on Mother's throat, cut into her skin. And here it is on one of *your* possessions, as plain as daylight, and you never told me. They kept the photographs from me, but you . . . you know everything, Godfather. You must have known." She paused, feeling childish and tired. She could not meet his eye. "Did you? Did you know these were left on her body?"

Godfather watched her quietly for a moment. "I did."

A cruel, cruel punch to the gut. "*How* did you know?"

"I cannot tell you all of my secrets, Clara." That look crossed his face, that secret, sly look that sometimes overtook him at his most genius moments, and his most rageful. It never failed to frighten her. She took a step back, choosing her words carefully. She always felt far from him at these moments, never more aware of his . . . otherness. Godfather was not like normal people.

"Why didn't you tell me about them?"

His face closed, and he turned away. "Your mother wanted me to keep you and your sister safe from harm, and that is what I have chosen to do—obey her wishes."

"How does divulging one measly bit of information put me in harm's way?"

"Oh." He chuckled to himself. He retrieved his cane and studied the dragon's head. "Oh, it is anything but measly."

Now was the time to catch him. Now, when he was distracted.

Clara approached him. "Tell me, Godfather. What do the symbols mean? Why were they on Mother's body and not on the others'?" She put her hands on his, pressed her cheek to his arm. He loved her; he would not be able to refuse her. "Mother would want me to know."

He stepped away, his sharp face in profile, his eye gleaming in the lamplight. "You know very little of what your mother would want, my Clara."

An even crueler punch. She backed away, brittle and confused. "How dare you! I knew my mother well."

"I didn't mean that." Godfather came back to himself, as if the veneer of madness had been ripped away. "Of course you knew her. I only meant that there are things young girls oughtn't to know."

"That's rich, coming from you, who teaches me to fight and fashions me trousers."

"All right, then. There are things *as few people as possible* ought to know. Dangerous things that grow more dangerous as knowledge of them spreads. Will that explanation suffice?"

Such cryptic words. Even as Clara grew impatient with them, they made her think of Godfather's strange stories, stories he had often told her and Felicity when they were small, and then told Clara alone, for Felicity had grown frightened of "wicked old Godfather" and stopped accompanying Clara and her mother on their outings to the shop. And then, as John Stole had sunk further into Concordia, and Hope Stole had had to fight harder to keep him afloat, Clara had gone, with her mother's reluctant permission, to visit Godfather by herself.

And on those days—oh, on those days—his stories had grown in magnitude and frequency. He would wrap her in his coat as he had when she was little, or sit with her by the hearth with mugs of spiced coffee, and tell her one of his peculiar, dark stories in hushed tones. Afterward, at home, she would drift into dreamlands of blind dragons and singing palaces, and hooded men living in mountain clouds with the birds.

Clara frowned at him. "But she was my mother, not yours. I deserve to know why her corpse was desecrated in this way, even if it *is* dangerous to know."

Godfather was still for a moment, regarding her, and then he dropped into his rickety rocking chair, resigned.

Clara gave a halfhearted smile. He was cracking. She knelt before him. "Tell me what the symbols mean, Godfather. Why were they . . . They were *carved* . . ."

She paused, grief flooding her.

He took pity on her. "The statue was given to me, as I've always told you. You remember?"

It was all he would ever say when asked about it. "It was a gift," he would say, scowling, and he would stab whatever lay nearest him with whatever sharp tool he held at the time, promptly ending the conversation.

"Yes, I remember," she said, trying to be patient. Where Godfather was concerned, kernels of great, frightening truth were often buried in ramblings and dark fancies—if one had the persistence to listen through the nonsense and find them. "But you never told me who gave it to you."

His mouth twisted. "It was given to me by a mad queen. Or at least an angry one."

"I beg your pardon?"

"It was a punishment, a taunt. You see, we thought we had escaped, but then at the last moment—" He clapped his hands together, startling one of his sparrows off its perch. "And it's bound with a strange magic, a thick and twisty one. You don't know how diligently I have worked to find an answer, to understand what they mean, and how it has smarted—how it has *eaten* at me, Clara—but I think I've finally done it."

He rose to his feet and approached the statue. With one long finger he traced a symbol on the statue's chest, and then another on its shoulder. "I used to wonder, do the symbols tell a story? This particular piece of the queen's magic was unlike anything I had ever seen." He paused, smiling absently. "*Then*. But now—now I'm close."

Clara was barely keeping her temper. "Magic. You're telling me that those symbols are some sort of magic."

"Well, *they* aren't magic, no, but rather I've come to understand them as a sort of *manifestation* of magic. A cruel, vengeful one. I'm not sure the symbols themselves mean anything at all, actually. I think they are merely the remnants of what is left behind when terrible magic is performed." He gazed at the statue's face as though looking at something far away. "Terrible magic," he whispered. "Terrible. And I regret nothing I have done."

Clara went to him, slowly. Terrible magic, mad queens, vengeance. They were familiar words, ones Clara had heard in Godfather's stories since she was a small girl.

Hope Stole had brought Godfather—Drosselmeyer, he claimed was his name—in from the streets when Clara was still a baby. Hope had seen him performing on the road, a common street magician—but then, so much more than that. She had always said she sensed a talent in him, a diamond talent, and that she could not bear to leave him out there on the freezing streets without proper tools or work space. He would be part of the family, Clara's mother had said, as a sort of joke, but then she herself had started calling him Godfather Drosselmeyer, and the whole idea had stuck. To the Stole girls he was always Godfather; and to Clara he was all mystery and strangeness with his eye patch and his muttering, but perhaps she would not have grown to love him so much had he been more ordinary.

"You said you were close." Clara put a hand on his shoulder. "Close to . . . what, exactly?"

Godfather turned to smile at her, his wry, unnerving smile. "To undoing it, my Clara."

"Undoing *what?*"

For a moment he looked close to telling her. Then he shook his head and backed away. "Soon enough," she thought she heard him mutter. "She'll know soon enough."

Clara glanced at his wall of clocks. A hundred hands, approaching five. "But what does any of this have to do with Mother?"

A darkness flickered across Godfather's face. His hair, too long to be in fashion, had come loose from its ribbon.

"I think—I think they are—" But then it was as though something inside him switched off. He shook his head and moved about the workshop, lighting lamps. "I think," he said gaily, though to Clara it seemed strained, "that it's time we have a nice spar."

"But, Godfather," Clara insisted, watching in frustration as he threw off his greatcoat and rolled up his sleeves, revealing forearms as finely chiseled as the creations he crafted, "you haven't answered my questions."

"I've answered *some* of your questions. Not all, but some."

"All but one."

"Don't insist, Clara." He cleared a space for them on the floor, gestured for her to strip off her gown. "Don't insist I answer what I cannot answer."

"And don't insist I give up on an answer I must have." She hurried to him and caught his arms. "Godfather, please. What do you know? Are you telling me stories to amuse yourself? Or do you actually know what's going on with these markings, these killings? These *beasts*?"

At that, Godfather stilled. "Beasts?"

"The word fills the reports I found, from detectives investigating the murder."

"Beasts," he whispered. "Yes. Yes, I remember them."

Clara held her breath; she was close. Godfather's eyes were wide and distant, searching—through memory, through his own lunacy? Either way he would soon tell her, and maybe it would be nonsense, but at least it would be something, and she could mull it over in her bedroom that night.

But then, as quickly as the quiet had overtaken him, it was gone, and he gestured impatiently at her. "Well? Get on with it. Unless you're too tired from your many covert exertions."

Clara bit back her protests. Long ago she had learned it was better to indulge his moods, for a happy Godfather was a more generous Godfather. Perhaps if she wore him out thoroughly enough, he would be more likely to talk.

So, with a few flicks of her wrist, she stripped off her skirt and petticoats. Months ago Godfather had started ripping apart her dresses and fashioning them to be easily removable; it would not do to become entangled in one's own underthings during combat, if such a misfortune should befall her on the city streets. Clara therefore brought every fine new gown to him for dismemberment, and found immense pleasure in watching him remake them as more useful versions of themselves. Sometimes she found herself wishing he could do the same for her.

In her chemise, corset, breeches, and boots, Clara circled toward him with her fingers curled, her arms poised and steady. If this was what it would take to pry information out of him . . . well, there were worse sacrifices to make.

"Come, Godfather." She made herself sound playful, even though she felt far from it. *Indulge him, indulge him.* "Hit me."

He laughed, eye dancing, and lunged at her.

Clara met him halfway, throwing up her right arm to block his left jab. He grabbed her wrist and twisted, but he himself had taught Clara not to fight the attack but to move with it and turn it against itself. *Become one with the shadows when you sneak, my Clara. Become one with the blow when you fight.*

So she gritted her teeth as he jerked her arm around, pulling her into a tight hold, and then she elbowed him hard in the stomach. Gasping, he staggered back. Clara pulled free and whirled on her heel, smacking him hard on his right ear. Disoriented, furious, he let fly a sloppy left hook.

Clara dodged it with ease, grinning, enjoying this despite herself, for this—these moments flying about Godfather's shop, the spiced air hissing past her bare arms, her skin stinging from Godfather's strikes—was when she felt most unlike her usual self. She felt invincible, unencumbered by both fabric and anxiety. Bold. Brazen. Each blow she gave sent fire shooting up her arms; each blow she received, each stab of pain, stoked a strange pleasure within her. She was not nervous, fearful Clara here; she was shadow, fists and sweat and burning muscle.

Still fumbling for her to his right, Godfather leapt forward, but Clara had already moved right, kicking out with her left leg. His own legs would catch, and he would fall, and Clara would win. *So quick a match*, she thought, disappointed, but Godfather grabbed her booted foot and gave it a vicious turn.

Clara fell hard, turning to land on her arm and backside to save her knees. The stone floor jarred her, rattling her head. There would be yet another bruise on her body, which she would treasure; each purpling spot made her stronger, a talisman of pain and pride.

Thinking of this, she sprang up more quickly than Godfather had anticipated, with a roundhouse kick to his back that sent him stumbling into his workbench, tools flying. He rebounded quickly, coming back at her with sharp jabs to her arm, neck, belly. She blocked them—elbow, forearm. She dodged him—left, right. He was fast, and she was faster; she was leaving the world far below her, flying high, knuckles stinging, lungs burning.

Euphoric, she laughed and missed blocking the jab at her belly. Doubling over, she fell against the wall. Godfather followed with a body shot to her side, but Clara moved at the last second, and he clipped the stones.

"Damn," he gasped, clutching his hand, and Clara stopped. Hands were important to an artisan of his skill. She reached for his shoulder. "Are you all right?"

"Ha!" He spun around to grab her neck, but Clara had seen this trick before. She flung up her arm in time to catch his. They stood for a moment, panting, glaring at each other. Clara could smell the blood on Godfather's scraped knuckles, though he had thrust the wounded hand into his pocket.

"Very good," he breathed.

She smiled at him, and for a moment the worry in her heart

vanished; there were no gruesome photographs, no vile markings. There was only her, and Godfather, and the statue watching from the corner.

Then the door flew open.

It careened into the wall, sending Godfather's birds into a frenzy.

And Clara knew, before he even spoke, before turning around, who would be standing at the door.

"Why, Clara, here you are. Mrs. Hancock was beside herself when she realized you hadn't come home after your . . . Where did you tell her you would be? An outing in the park?" He scoffed, hardly more than an exhalation. "And all this time you were . . . Well. My, my. Clara, you appear to have lost your clothes."

Clara's horror was an arrow to the heart, swift and deadly; the elation of fighting vanished. She had taken too long getting home, and now—after a year of these sparring sessions with Godfather, a glorious year of successfully keeping their secret—he had found them:

Dr. Victor.

4

He stood at the shop's entrance, a tall, pale-haired whip of a man—leanly muscled, sharp eyed, with a smile of ice and eyes to match. In the sudden silence one of Godfather's crows ruffled its feathers and cawed.

"Good afternoon, Dr. Victor. We were . . ." But Clara's terror overwhelmed her, choking away any hope of excuses or lies. Dr. Victor was *here*, and she was dressed like . . .

"I can see that." Dr. Victor's gaze crawled over her body, lingering on the skin she was normally so careful to conceal.

Clara flinched, the sudden onslaught of shame a physical blow. She wished she were not breathing so hard, that she were not sweating and had not stripped off her clothes, come to Godfather for answers, or even broken into Rivington Hall. She should have gone home right after the ceremony, contented herself with reading or listening to Felicity natter on about a new gown freshly arrived from Paris. Mere seconds ago Clara had made Godfather bleed; now she was merely a girl, stupid, half-naked, and trembling, and she could not tell Dr. Victor to stop looking at her so greedily. The thought of what he could do in retaliation if Clara were to tell him what she truly thought of him, what he could make Concordia do to her family, kept her silent.

And besides, it was her fault, wasn't it, that he gazed at her so? She could have gone home; she could have stayed dressed. Instead here she stood, obscene, indecent, and as she stared at the floor, flushing miserably, she knew whatever Dr. Victor might do was what she deserved. A tiny spark of outrage cried out in protest, deep inside her, but she did not listen to it.

"Civilized people," Godfather began, tugging on his rumpled shirt, "knock on locked doors instead of kicking them in."

"A lunatic who has shut himself up with a young girl and proceeded to attack her," Dr. Victor said smoothly, "is in no place to make such statements. I'd watch yourself, old man. It would distress Clara so, were anything to happen to you. Come, Clara." He beckoned for her, a handsome devil in his immaculate vest and coat, pressed trousers, and gleaming boots. "I'll escort you home."

Clara ducked her head and began to dress. The shop around her had never been more silent, despite the chorus of ticking clocks and tinkling toy carousel chimes, the soft whir of machinery from the back room. As she reassembled her petticoats, Clara began to cry. She did not let the tears fall, for she guessed that would delight Dr. Victor, but her throat burned with them. A hard knot lodged itself in her chest, eclipsing all other sensation, leaving her feeling . . . shriveled. Raked open.

"Please, Dr. Victor," Clara said, hating the tremor in her voice but unable to steady it, "it was only a bit of fun. There's no need for alarm."

"I will decide what there is need for, Clara." The softer Dr. Victor's voice became, the greater stormed the fury underneath. Since her father's rise to the mayorship, Clara had heard this ominous softening many times. She shuddered from the lash of what he left unsaid, and from the horrible fear of when that buried malicious intent might erupt.

Godfather retrieved his cane from the floor. "The shop is closed, if you hadn't noticed. You are not welcome here."

"How long have you been doing this?" Dr. Victor whispered to Clara, ignoring him.

Clara couldn't meet his eyes. "I—I don't know."

"Your father has tolerated your coming here for too long, I see. I thought you'd have better judgment than this. Fighting like a heathen." He shifted where he stood. "Dressed like a whore."

Godfather was fuming. "You will not speak to my Clara like that, you—"

"*Your* Clara?" Dr. Victor said, the softest yet. "This 'Godfather' business has gone on far too long. You aren't her family. You'd be on the streets were it not for the gracious Mrs. Stole." He smiled; such handsome, practiced piety. "God rest her soul."

"How dare you speak of Hope!" Godfather shouted, surging forward, his cane raised.

Clara caught him by the arm. "No, Godfather!"

"Clara, I will not stand by and let him treat you this way."

"It's all right." She smiled at him. One word from Dr. Victor and he could ruin them—turn Godfather out onto the streets, or even have him killed, and unleash the Concordia dogs upon her father at last.

It was better, then, to smile. Better to lie and relent. And Godfather knew it as well as she did. She could see the resignation and fury warring on his face.

"Really. Don't worry." She almost embraced him—to reassure him, to reassure herself—but his arms around her might have destroyed her resolve. Instead she went to Dr. Victor's side and took his offered arm, letting the rough metal fingers of his glove—the mark of a Concordia gentleman—tuck her into place beside him. When he smirked at her, she granted him a demure smile; when he peered down her bodice, she ignored him.

"Clara," Godfather said, his voice rough. The earlier darkness shadowed his face, the darkness that had accompanied talk of her mother. "It will not always be like this. I swear to you, it won't."

"I don't know what you mean." She tried to sound careless, but she was sweating and trembling. Surely Dr. Victor could feel it.

Surely he was enjoying it.

He led her outside, his grip on her possessive. His perpetual perfume of medicine and chemicals and rot poisoned her breath. *What horrors has he committed at Harrod House today?* The thought filled Clara's mind with terrible images. She had heard rumors of the poor sick girls kept at Harrod House for Wayward Girls, and of Dr. Victor's highly experimental "cures."

As they stepped out into the dimming light, fresh snow crunching under their boots, Clara heard glass smash and birds screech, and Godfather roaring in fury.

"That will never do," Dr. Victor said later that evening, in the second-floor salon of the mayor's mansion. "Next."

The grand, twenty-room house at Fifth Avenue and Sixty-Sixth Street had not felt like home to Clara since her mother's murder, especially for the past few months. Dr. Victor had grown too comfortable, coming and going more frequently to keep an eye on her father, and also, Clara suspected, to keep an eye on her.

She was free of Dr. Victor almost nowhere and never now. After making her debut this past season, which John Stole had permitted to occur earlier than he would have liked because of Clara's frequent pleas, she had hoped to find more time *away* from Dr. Victor, if she were out dancing and being courted most nights of the week. But, no. He often insisted upon chaperoning her about town himself, whenever he could bear to leave the girls at Harrod House. Who, after all, would ever think anything of it? Dr. Victor was such a dear family friend. How nice, Clara supposed people thought—or pretended to think—for Dr. Victor to spend so much time with John Stole's motherless debutante daughter. How lovely, how perfectly convenient for her to snag such a man—established, handsome, wealthy enough to provide for her and her beleaguered family.

Clara Stole, they must have thought, *is truly a lucky girl.*

As Mrs. Hancock ushered her into the other room and stripped her once again, Clara stood, blank-eyed and still, refusing to look at her reflection in the mirror. She avoided it whenever possible, in fact. Such a hunched, twitchy, pathetic-looking figure. Who wanted to look upon that image and realize it was her own?

"I'm so sorry, miss," Mrs. Hancock whispered as she peeled away the last bit of heavy green velvet trimmed with gold. She added the gown to the stack of discards and retrieved the next one. "I'm trying to go as quickly as I can."

"Not to worry," Clara said brightly. Mrs. Hancock gave her a despairing look, and Clara flushed with shame at having to stand here so unclothed, even in the company of this perfectly harmless woman. Mrs. Hancock was looking upon Clara's bare legs; she could see the goose-flesh along Clara's skin. She could see the bruises on Clara's body, the scabbed-over cuts, and as ever she tactfully ignored them, even arranged the gown to better hide them, though her eyes were heavy with concern.

Clara's mortification overwhelmed her from all quarters. Withdrawing from the horror of it, her thoughts leapt wildly to Godfather's shop, to its warmth and oddness and safety. She thought of Godfather, crowing arrogantly after a successful clock repair; and she thought of the statue, tall and impassive in the shadowed corner—its full lips and narrow waist, its arms in their serrated armor. As she pictured this, the flush on her skin shifted from embarrassment to pleasure, despite the danger luxuriating in the next room.

Mrs. Hancock prodded her to step into another gown, jarring Clara from her reverie. Guilty tears pricked her eyes—such atrocious thoughts! Apparently she could not help herself. She was a slave to her wandering mind. She was hopeless, depraved.

Shameful, wanton, sinful girl.

Why was she so plagued by such wicked impulses?

A few more tugs, and Mrs. Hancock led her back before Dr.

Victor, who sipped lazily at his cognac. Winter seeped in through the windows, making Clara shiver as she stood there before him, being appraised. She tried not to wonder what he might be thinking. The neckline of this gown was far too low-cut, the frothy sleeves too coy, the bodice too perfectly snug. It left little of her form to the imagination, and Clara found herself frantic to get away. The sight of her body in this disgraceful display would affect Dr. Victor adversely, as it always did, turning his eyes dark and his cheeks hot.

"Is there anything wrong with this particular gown, Dr. Victor?" Clara struggled to speak, keeping her eyes on the floor. "These are such fine gowns, and this the finest yet. May we not choose it and be finished?"

Beside her Mrs. Hancock tensed, and Clara's stomach dropped like a stone. Dr. Victor's stillness was too swift, too complete. She could have heard the ash from Dr. Victor's cigar hit the plush rugs. Had her tone been discourteous? Had she somehow offended him?

"Leave us," Dr. Victor said at last.

Mrs. Hancock hesitated for only an instant before obeying. In the maid's absence Clara stood frozen by her own fear. Not for the first time in Dr. Victor's company, she considered calling for her father. She could do it; she could scream for him. He had no doubt returned from his afternoon outings. He would be downstairs greeting Concordia gentlemen as they arrived for the usual midweek coffee and brandy.

But then what would she do? Accuse Dr. Victor of . . . what, exactly? Looking at her? Smiling at her? And if she implied anything more, who would believe her? Her father would; even now, with his eyes always distant and cloudy and his breath smelling perpetually of drink, he loved her, and he would believe her. But the fury Concordia would turn upon them if John Stole accused the respected doctor of something so heinous would not be worth the relief Clara might feel.

So she remained silent, self-loathing souring her mouth. Dr.

Victor rose from his scarlet chaise in the corner, set down his drink, and approached her. He was a sinewy, looming man, the kind of man whose presence flooded a room with authority and menace. As he neared her, reaching for her arm with perfectly manicured fingernails, Clara thought he would not have to do anything else to hurt her. She would simply choke on the cancer of his existence; she would disintegrate beneath the eager heat of his eyes.

"Trying on party gowns, I see," murmured a voice from the door.

Dr. Victor stepped back at once. Clara moved away from him to the chair by the window, and gripped the high back to stay upright.

"My apologies, Mrs. Plum." The color flared high in Dr. Victor's cheeks. "I did not mean for you to witness Clara's indecency. She wanted to look her best for the party tomorrow evening. I was simply offering my advice on how best to appear . . . tasteful."

In her steadfast widow's black, fingers and neck shimmering with diamonds, Patricia Plum glided forward in rustling silks, leaving the door open behind her. Clara heard Plum say something about the gathering downstairs, but her relief was too great for her to listen more closely than that. Even when Dr. Victor had gone, Clara felt his eyes on her body. When Patricia Plum offered Clara a shawl, Clara took it without question, wrapping herself tightly away.

"I'm sorry," she whispered. "I didn't mean to."

Plum cocked her head, amused. "Sorry for what, exactly? Dr. Victor's perversions aren't your fault."

"Perversions?" Clara blinked at her. The habit of pretending his sins away took over. "He was simply helping me pick out a dress."

"Clara, don't pretend to be stupid. There's no need for it, not between you and me." Plum turned to check her own immaculate reflection in the mirror by the door. "We both know what kind of man Dr. Victor is. Unfortunately, we have to pretend that we don't."

Clara did not know what to say to that. "What . . . kind of man?"

Plum sighed irritably. "Will you be able to handle yourself now? It might be best to sequester yourself in your room for the night. The good doctor gets worse with drink, as well you know, and who's to say how long our coffee and brandy will last?" Her eyes cut to Clara's in the glass. "Concordia has much to discuss tonight. End-of-the-year business." She smirked to herself, tucking a dark coil of hair back into place. Her eyes were made of blue stone.

Clara tried to decipher Patricia Plum's face, without success. Godfather had taught her much about reading the faces of others—their expressions, their mannerisms. But Patricia Plum was a mystery. Since Boss Plum's murder a year and a half ago at the hands of the Eastside Delvers, Patricia Plum had headed Concordia with an assemblage of her late husband's most trusted advisors. How she had managed to maintain control and not lose the empire to one of them—Dr. Victor, Walter Higgins, or Hiram Proctor, no one knew. But no one knew much of anything when it came to Patricia Plum.

She, on the other hand, knew everyone and everything, from the schedule of the street performers on Broadway to what patrons sat in which boxes at the opera. She regularly met with bishops, university rectors, and glamorous foreign dignitaries, who would call upon her first, even before the mayor. What they talked about, no one knew, but one could sometimes catch glimpses of them in Plum's fine coach-and-four, jewels flashing through gaps in the curtained windows. People obeyed Patricia Plum when she spoke, without question, as if she were a sorceress of old, weaving spells with her eyes. Rumors of her origins ranged from witch to renegade European princess who had abandoned her birthright and made for America.

Some people said Patricia Plum had never loved her husband, that she had married Boss Plum to secure Concordia for herself. It was a laughable, unthinkable ambition for a woman, and yet when Clara met Plum's calculating eyes, she knew it was true. It was the one thing she knew for certain about Patricia Plum.

That, and how deeply Clara hated her.

Patricia Plum, Clara was convinced, was the mastermind behind this recent wave of discord, the suspicion about her father's loyalties, the spreading waves of antagonism against him. Clara's guess was that Plum knew a liability when she saw one and wanted to rid Concordia of John Stole's increasingly erratic behavior.

Thinking of this filled Clara with sudden defiance and cleared her head. "Why didn't you stop him?"

Patricia Plum turned. "I beg your pardon?"

"Dr. Victor." Clara clutched her shawl, horrified at her boldness. But she had to see it through now. "You see how he treats me. How he looks at me. I know you do. You see everything. You mentioned his 'perversions.' You send him away and tell me all will be well, yet you don't do anything to stop him. He goes unpunished, but you could punish him if you wanted. Why don't you? Why bother pretending to care if you truly care so little?"

A slow, cold smile. "Why don't *you* stop him?"

Clara stared at her. "I—I cannot . . ."

"And why can't you? Because you need him." Plum sat down opposite her, smoothing her skirts. "You need him to stay happy so he will go on protecting your father and sister, and so you can go on cavorting with your godfather. So things can stay as they are."

"We don't *cavort*—"

"And I need him too. I need to keep him happy so I can manage Concordia and he can still feel as though he's got a hand in things. I need him satisfied with being nothing but a counselor in the shadows, because our good doctor is not a good doctor at all." She leaned forward, her eyes hard. "If only you knew, Clara, the sorts of experiments Dr. Victor conducts in his laboratories . . . but perhaps you can imagine."

Oh, yes. Clara could imagine, and often did, based on the snippets of information she had gleaned over the years. The images were grotesque: skull-piercing metal tools, teeth plucked from their roots, girls screaming in terror while strapped to examination tables. Clara had smelled the formaldehyde and laudanum, had seen the bloody grime caked on Dr. Victor's Concordia glove after he'd spent a day out at Harrod House.

Plum's smile thinned. "You understand, then. I need him right where he is, happy and content. He's too dangerous, his tastes too extreme. Even the lowest of criminals would turn on us, should he gain too much power. Even the street gang lords have a moral code. But not him. And I'm tied to him, you see."

"You let him do it," Clara whispered, thinking of Harrod House, thinking, guiltily, of herself and what the future might hold.

"Yes, I let him. I would let him carve open the body of every pretty little orphan girl within a hundred miles if I had to. And I would do it for the good of our city, for *order*. Just as *you* must. We ladies must stick together, mustn't we?" Plum rose, shook out her skirts, and examined Clara, eyes cool. "Is that the gown you selected?"

Clara ignored the question. It was a dangerous move, but she had to make it. "Don't you want to change things? You could fight him, fight all of them. Make them follow *your* rules. You don't want to cower before people like Dr. Victor forever. Do you?"

Plum froze, her smile strained, and then laughed. "I'm no fool, Clara. Concordia is an empire. I won't lose years of work and blood and loyalty because of my pride. I won't risk losing what is mine, no matter the cost."

Terrible understanding overcame Clara. The widow would be no help; her father *could* be no help. She could not do much to protect him, but she could do this one thing—she could remain silent. And Godfather . . . Clara could not lose him. She would not risk his safety for her own. She would remain silent and small, she would care for her sister and father as best she could, and she would tolerate whatever of Dr. Victor her future might bring.

Patricia Plum must have seen Clara's comprehension. She smiled and straightened Clara's skirts—piles of white silk and taffeta edged with lace.

"Yes, that one will do marvelously, I think." Plum turned toward the door. "The neckline alone will drive Dr. Victor out of his mind."

5

Clara entered her father's study and shut the door quietly behind her. Her gown caught on the latch.

"Damn lace," she hissed, jerking the fabric half up her legs to free it. She was so close to crying—she'd been doing it for hours now, in unpredictable bouts—and her nerves stretched taut across waves of panic. Even now guests were arriving downstairs, and they would be expecting a flawless evening, a spectacular party. John Stole needed—they all needed—this night to go well.

So stop crying, in other words. Clara wiped her eyes viciously. Could she do anything but snivel these days?

"Clara." Felicity, scandalized, hurried over from her perch beside their father and fiddled with Clara's skirts, restlessly rearranging. "Don't show your legs like that. And don't move about so violently. You'll muss your hair. And don't say 'damn.'"

"You just said it."

Felicity pursed her lips, and Clara's breath caught. Those shining red curls, the impudent nose and stubborn jaw, those bright eyes—in Felicity's face whispered the echo of the vibrant man their father had once been. Everyone said the elder Stole girl looked like her mother, the younger, her father: red hair, the trademark freckles, one sharply jawed, the other softer.

Of course Clara was the softer. Of *course*.

"Yes, but I was saying it to reprove you," Felicity said primly. "That doesn't count."

Clara smiled, hoping that the sadness behind it did not show. She brushed her fingers over Felicity's perfectly coiffed curls. Her younger sister was so proper, so lovely, so concerned with whether or not they were serving the most fashionable cakes. Felicity had been conscientious about such things from an early age, and since their mother had died, she had thrown herself into the role of stylish aspiring hostess with a ferocious zeal. It was as though by doing so Felicity could capture a bit of the poised woman their mother had been—or maybe, by keeping her thoughts so firmly in the superficial, forget about her.

"Consider me reproved, then." Clara turned, clutching Felicity's hand in her own, and steeled herself. What would her father's mood be tonight?

"It's time," Clara said carefully, gauging him. "The guests have started arriving."

"You make it sound as though we're heading to an execution rather than to a party," Mayor Stole said from the shadows of his desk. He held his head in his hands.

So it was to be morose, then. Perfect. That was just what they needed, a drunken, weepy host for everyone to gossip about.

"Well, it's more similar to the former than the latter," Clara said, impatience getting the best of her. "We shouldn't be having it at all. I tried to tell you, and now we've spent money we don't have on a night no one will remember, except to say, 'How marvelous it must be for the mayor to hold parties for his friends while the rest of us starve on the streets.'"

"But Mother always held the Christmas party, every year," Felicity said in a small voice. She smiled bravely up at Clara. "It's tradition, and it's expected of us. We must"—Felicity took a deep breath, as if reciting something—"show a happy face to the public."

"Tradition," Mayor Stole mumbled. "We can't break with tradition. Hope would not approve."

Clara ignored how his voice broke on her mother's name, and tucked the pain of hearing his naked grief deep inside herself, with all the other broken pieces of her heart. "Father, are you drunk?"

"No."

"You're lying."

"Clara, please don't." Felicity clutched Clara's arm. "Father's not feeling well."

Clara laughed harshly. "Neither am I, and yet here I stand."

Mayor Stole reached for the glass beside him. "I can't do it, Clara. I cannot face them. I'm *tired* of facing them, of pretending loyalty I no longer feel."

"You perhaps should have thought of that years ago, when you first threw your lot in with them." Clara was on him in an instant, knocking the glass from his hand. It hit the floor and smashed into pieces. She had never said these things to him before, choosing instead to shelter him, in deference to his sorrow. But with the stress of yesterday heavy on her shoulders, she had no patience left for coddling. "And I don't care what you cannot do. I cannot get up every morning and lace myself into my dresses and try to cover for you, and yet I do. I cannot manage our household staff and attend charity functions you can't seem to bother with, and make calls to keep the few friends we have left from abandoning us completely, and yet I do."

"My aides do a fine job of that," the mayor said, staring after the fallen glass in dull shock. "And Dr. Victor."

"Dr. Victor," spat Clara, and though the damning words rose to her lips, she could not say them. Felicity's presence served as a reminder: She could not say anything, could not go whispering. And anyhow, what could her father do to help her? Concordia was beyond his control now. It had been for months.

"Yes, Dr. Victor does a fine job, indeed," Clara bit out. She would not break now, not tonight. "Get cleaned up and come to the ballroom. Your absence has already been noticed, and Mr. Krupin is asking after you."

"Krupin," repeated Mayor Stole slowly. "The banker."

"He is a rich banker, yes, and he sits on the city council, and he is not a patient man."

Mayor Stole blinked, rising to his feet. "I should speak with him."

"You should."

"And shave, as well." Mayor Stole rubbed his chin and straightened his waistcoat, and those tiny motions made him look so old—so suddenly, unsteadily dignified—that Clara could not help herself. Her impatience vanished; she went to him and put her arms around him. He stank of whiskey and unwashed hair, and it was an awkward embrace with Felicity still held tightly in one hand, but Clara latched on anyway, relishing the scent of him, stink and all. Her father's arms came around her, hesitant, and Felicity pressed her face into his side—delicately, so as not to muss her hair—and they stood there, a mass of fragile hope for the night. When Clara pulled away, she smoothed her father's hair and saw, for a brief moment, an echo on his face—the echo of his former, handsome self.

Her resolve hardened. It would be a good night, a fine night. She would make it so, and she would do it for him, for Felicity, for the family they used to be. Dr. Victor would try to frighten her, and she might never see Godfather again, but she was damned if they weren't about to have the most successful Christmas party there had ever been.

"Yes," she said, and kissed his cheek. "You should shave. Quickly, please, Father."

"Clara," whispered Felicity as Clara led her toward the door. "Are you angry? Please don't be angry. Everything's going to be wonderful, isn't it?"

Clara knelt before Felicity and pressed their foreheads together. "Of course, darling. You'll dazzle them tonight, won't you? You'll dance and dance?"

Felicity's distraught face blossomed into a smile that tore at Clara's heart. "Mother always liked to dance."

"Yes, do you remember those nights in her parlor?"

"Dancing in our nightgowns." Felicity hid her giggle with gloved fingers. "Putting feathers in our hair!"

"Princesses in bare feet. Now go on. Have some punch before the serving tables get crowded."

Clara stood for a moment, gathering herself, watching her sister rush gaily down the hallway toward the chatter of arriving guests.

"I'm sorry, Clara," her father whispered behind her. He squeezed her hand. "I know what you must think of me. But I am trying."

Clara blinked back tears. She could no longer look at him; doing so reminded her too dearly of what they had lost. "I know," she whispered, and left him in the dark.

From her hiding spot on the second-floor mezzanine overlooking the ballroom, partially concealed behind a red velvet curtain, Clara dreamed of murder.

Her nose stung with the echo of Dr. Victor's medicinal tang; he had hardly left her side all evening. If she had to endure one more moment with him . . . well, she would endure it, and do so without complaint. But she could *dream* about clawing his face to pieces; no one would ever know. She imagined the viscera of his eyeballs curdling beneath her nails. He would be afraid, the fear on his face reflecting what he must so often see on her own. And Godfather would stand beside her, nodding in approval, directing her how best to slice him to pieces.

Proper ladies don't think of such things.

She moved to a nearby window seat, closed her eyes, and breathed the violence away—as well as the sense of peace that accompanied it. When she opened her eyes once more, the frenzy had left her, and she was herself again—small, uncertain, naked in her many-layered dress.

From up here, she could see the steady flow of carriages and belled horses outside the mansion, as New York high society arrived to strut and dance and gossip. The frost-lined streets made an eerie, black-and-white world, as though the cold had sucked out everything but snow and shadows.

Inside, however, below the mezzanine with its private curtained sitting rooms, the ballroom swirled with color—satin and silk chiffon, handmade lace and puffed sleeves trimmed with ribbons, in blues, violets, forest green, and crimson. The men's dark coattails fluttered, their gloves flashing, clean and white. Ears, fingers, and waistcoats gleamed with baubles. Jeweled combs winked firelight at the ceiling like hundreds of mischievous eyes.

Godfather's electric lights had been strung from corner to corner across the molded ceiling amid clusters of holly and glittering gauze sashes of silver and gold. Piles of cakes and puddings, sausages and hams, soup and eggnog, and steaming spiced cider and berries with cream covered the serving tables in the refreshment room. Most prominent was the enormous fir tree in the corner, flickering with candles, silver bells, holiday poppers, angels, and poinsettias dipped in gold.

No money for the shelter to have proper beds, and yet there appears to be enough for a party, Clara thought gloomily.

As if on cue her father, settled by the grand marble hearth in a dark wingback chair, laughed. She found him at once by his hair.

Unbidden, Godfather flashed into her head—Godfather, caressing her hair wistfully, as if it reminded him of something precious and long lost. However inappropriate it may have been, Clara knew how Godfather had doted on her mother. It was, she supposed, natural for an artist to be so devoted to his patroness.

But it would not do to think of Godfather, who normally arrived at their Christmas parties fashionably late, with a grand flourish, and bearing many gifts for the attending children. That morning she had snuck off a note to him: *Stay at home tonight.* She hoped he would understand; Dr. Victor's mood had been decidedly black since finding her at the shop, and she could not chance him goading Godfather into one of his eccentric scenes in front of New York society. Dr. Victor would no doubt use such an opportunity to publicly lock him away, once and for all.

A life without Godfather was not a life Clara wanted to know—especially not before she wheedled some straight answers out of him.

Her father laughed again; the sound of it gave her pause. She left her hiding spot and made for the staircase, alert and wary.

Anyone else would perhaps not have noticed, but Clara had heard her father's genuine laughter often enough—he had been a joyous man once, laughing constantly at Hope Stole's scandalous jokes. But this was not a joyous sound. This was strained, and even frightened.

Something was wrong.

Dr. Victor laughed too, leaning against her father's chair, but his eyes restlessly roved until they found Clara at the top of the stairs. He pinned her in place with them. His gloved hand, white instead of silver at such a public event, beckoned. *Come here. Now. Or you will regret it.*

Clara recoiled, clinging to the sensation of the breeches beneath her skirts. Dr. Victor may have been able to leer at her breasts as they'd waltzed, but she would at least wear her trousers, wrapping her legs tightly away, and keep her dagger buckled to her thigh. He could not take that from her.

She approached them—her father and the Proctor brothers; the Merry Butcher; Reginald Winchester from the *Times*; the wealthy banker Pietr Krupin; and Mr. Mansfield, who ran the Garrick Theatre—downing glasses of champagne and chasing them with chocolate-covered cherry bonbons. But her father was on his feet now, agitated.

As she maneuvered through the crowded room, eyes danced at her, smiling faces nodded; guests conversed quietly, luxuriating over coffee and cakes. The lively strains of "Fiddle Me Lovely" seemed grating; the children by the Christmas tree, Felicity among them, opened their Christmas poppers to a shower of confetti, and the series of snaps made Clara jump.

"You look beautiful tonight, Clara," Patricia Plum murmured, gliding up alongside Clara to take her elbow. She smelled of cider and smoke. "Like a faery bride."

"I'm no one's bride," Clara blurted. They had arrived at her father's side, and she did not like the look in Dr. Victor's eyes at the word "bride."

The Merry Butcher laughed, his fat, pink face shining. So did Krupin, Winchester, and the Proctors. "A right modern woman, our Miss Stole!" said the Butcher.

But Dr. Victor did not laugh. Neither did her father. The tense remnants of a recently ended conversation lingered in the air. Clara tried to imagine what they could have been discussing; none of the possibilities were particularly cheering. Had her father gone ranting about Concordia's corruption again? Had he, heaven forbid, noticed Dr. Victor's fixation on her and reproved him? And why was the Butcher eyeing her father as though he were an unsatisfactory slab of meat?

"Clara," her father said, drawing her close for a kiss. He crushed her to his chest, his breath sour; Clara could hear his frantic heartbeat against her ear. She pulled away to find that his eyes were bloodshot.

"Father? What is it?"

"Pardon me, Mayor Stole." Dr. Victor cut between them. "I believe Clara has promised me a waltz."

Panic for her father made Clara daring. "You've had four already."

"And I will have as many more as I like." He grabbed her waist, turning her. People around them were beginning to notice, to whisper and point. It was unseemly for any man—even such a dear family friend—to handle Clara so, to watch her with such hard, hot eyes.

Patricia Plum hurried forward with a bright smile. "Now, Dr. Victor, that's quite enough."

"You will let go of my daughter," came Mayor Stole's voice—low, edged.

Dr. Victor was smugly incredulous. "Ah, Mayor Stole, that's where you're wrong."

"One too many glasses of champagne for these two, I'm afraid," joked Patricia Plum to those nearest them. "You know how men can be."

The crowd tittered nervously as Plum directed the nearest of them away, and Clara took the chance to wrench out of Dr. Victor's grasp—but then, from across the ballroom, came the sound of doors slamming open. A curious murmur rippled toward Clara, and she heard Felicity's small voice say, "Godfather?"

The fact that Godfather would enter at such a moment was so coincidentally terrible that Clara would have laughed, had she not been so afraid for him.

"Clara!" Godfather strode out from the ballroom's curtained entryway in a swirl of greatcoat and top hat and unkempt hair. Behind him a pair of wide-eyed street boys in patched jackets lugged a bulging velvet sack and a cloth-covered tower on wheels.

Clara escaped a distracted Dr. Victor and intercepted Godfather in the middle of the ballroom. The crowd had parted, the orchestra fallen silent. Over Godfather's shoulder Clara saw Felicity surrounded by a gaggle of other girls, eyeing Godfather's bundles with shining eyes. Clara knew they expected the traditional Christmas party toys, but the look on Godfather's face was the furthest thing from such frivolity.

"They've found me," Godfather whispered. He grabbed Clara's arms and left silver stains behind; shining liquid coated his fingers. It was in his hair, too, falling in tangles about his face.

Was it mercury? Clara wondered. *A soldering accident?*

"I told you I was close, didn't I?" he continued. "Closer than I knew, my Clara. I've had a *breakthrough*. But it must have alerted them, broken through my wards . . ."

"Hush, Godfather," Clara said automatically. "People can hear you." But propriety seemed foolish, with such an expression on Godfather's face; Clara had never seen him look so afraid.

"Let them hear. They need to leave." He threw up his arms, turning to face the room. His shirt gaped open, revealing a chest so white, it seemed carved of ice, marred with ugly blackened lacerations. "Leave, I tell you! It's safer that way. They'll come here; they're after me. And you, Clara." He bent over his bag, drawing out toys—soldiers in fur hats with wide, hinged mouths; clockwork falcons with snapping wings; wooden swords and porcelain jester dolls. "You'll help me, won't you? You'll help me fight? I had to come here. The shop has been compromised. My protection failed at last, and a scout found me. I managed to subdue him, but my abilities are patchy, and more will follow him straight to the shop, if they haven't already. Here, little one, have this." He shoved a shabby rat puppet into the hands of a girl who had dared to creep close. The child made a face at its ugliness. "It's not much use. Don't know how it slipped in here. But, oh, the delicious irony . . ."

"All right, I'll help you," Clara said, trying to piece together his cryptic words. "But we should go into another room, don't you think? The party—"

Godfather kissed her forehead, interrupting her. "My darling Clara, my *brave* Clara."

"Please, come sit with me quietly for a while." Clara turned to smile at the gaping crowd, mind racing. She trusted Godfather more than anyone else; if he said there was danger, he was right. But what to do with their guests? And what sort of danger was it? "Godfather's already done a bit too much celebrating, it would seem. Haven't you, Godfather?"

He stared at her. "Oh?"

She returned the look pointedly.

"Oh!" He forced a smile. "Yes. To be sure. I'm pissed as a pirate."

Some of the children, and not a few adults, giggled as Clara led Godfather toward the Christmas tree. The dirty street boys, eyeing the refreshments hungrily, followed them with the cloth-covered tower in tow. In their wake the orchestra resumed playing, and the murmuring crowd began drifting back to their party.

"Godfather—"

"Take your money and get far away, boys, as far as you can,"

Godfather said, shooing the boys away with a handful of coins. "It won't be safe here for much longer."

"*Godfather.*" Clara shook him. "You shouldn't be here. I told you not to come. Dr. Victor will try to ruin you."

"The good doctor is the least of our worries, my Clara." Godfather crouched by his towering bundle and pulled the cloth aside a little to reveal a chiseled metal thigh, the iron boot tipped with spikes, covered in those savage symbols.

Clara's skin flushed with sudden smoldering awareness.

The statue. As always, her hands itched to touch it. Her body swayed toward it. She had to fight the urge to sidle close to it, as she so often did, to whisper hello and tell it about her day in that embarrassing way she had of pretending that it cared, or even could. But her secrets were so safe, held tightly in the statue's metal crevices. How could she resist? And there had been moments, she swore there had been, when the statue's face had softened as she'd nestled near and chattered mindlessly about things too private to speak of to others, even to Godfather.

She swallowed hard, tore her gaze from the statue's armor-plated thigh. "Why is that here?"

"I told you, my breakthrough." Godfather raked silver fingers through his hair. "They've been after me for years, of course they have. *She* has. Trapping him wasn't enough; coming here wasn't enough. I've felt them jabbing"—he poked his fingers at her—"at the wards for years, but never getting any closer. Tonight, though . . . I've almost done it. *Almost.*" He punched his palm. "Unfortunately, my work disrupted the wards' protection."

"Godfather, for heaven's sake, speak plainly."

"Look. I've done it, I tell you. It's begun. *Look.*"

Clara followed his stained finger and saw it on the statue's leg—a thin, jagged crack in the metal, a seam ready to burst, and it glowed with a pale, blue light.

She stepped away, shaken. Years in its company, and she had never seen the statue do *that*. "You've got to get that out of here, Godfather. If Dr. Victor sees it, he'll brand you for a devil—"

Dr. Victor. In the chaos of Godfather's arrival, she had forgotten him, her father, Patricia Plum. With a sick lurch of her heart, she whirled to search for them in the crowd.

They were gone.

"Oh, God."

"I'm afraid that won't help in these matters," Godfather said, withdrawing a leather packet of tools from his greatcoat. "Believe me, I have tried."

Clara left him muttering and found Felicity's red curls in the sea of children picking over Godfather's toys.

"Felicity, watch Godfather for a moment, won't you?" Clara could hardly speak, her throat tight with fear. "Make sure he doesn't have one of his fits."

Felicity wrinkled her nose. "And how exactly am I supposed to do that?"

But Clara had already left her, weaving through the crowded ballroom toward the winding corridor on the mansion's north side—the heavy quiet of her mother's parlor, the swirling color of the music room, the kitchen stairs.

Father, where are you? She pressed close to the dark wood-paneled walls. The noise of the party faded, leaving Clara alone with her careful breathing.

At the hallway's end stood a set of grand wooden doors, slightly ajar—her father's private study. She hid among the shadows in the hallway's farthest corner.

". . . I'm through."

That was her father, hoarse, breathing hard.

"I'm afraid it's too late for that, John." Patricia Plum's voice, sickly sweet. "You can't just leave whenever you feel like it. What would we tell our citizens?"

"That I've resigned. Mayors resign."

Clara could not believe it. *Resign?*

Plum went on, ignoring him. "Besides, think of what you've seen, what you've done, what you've let happen."

"Yes, and I've had enough."

Dr. Victor laughed. "Had enough? Oh, now. John Stole, the face of Concordia, is taking the moral high ground?"

"I was a fool." Her father's voice cracked on the last word. Clara could not bear the sound and had to fight not to run to him. "For years I was a fool."

"That much is obvious, the way you've been acting. Spilling secrets to the *Times*, eh, John? Misplacing city funds?"

"You mean giving them back to the people they belong to."

"You self-righteous idiot. You're sabotaging Concordia. You think we haven't noticed?"

"Why, John?" Patricia Plum, disappointed. "You knew what we were when you joined us. You never had qualms."

"That was *before*."

Dr. Victor scoffed. "Oh, of course. Almighty Saint Hope."

Something heavy toppled over, glass crashing along with it. Clara reached under her skirt for her dagger, placing her palm atop it. Sweat trickled down her neck.

Her father was shouting, "You killed her, damn you. *Damn* you!"

"Get him off me," snarled Dr. Victor, and Clara heard scuffling, grunts, the sick thud of a punch.

"I've told you again and again," Plum said coldly, "Concordia had no part in Hope's murder."

"Oh, as we've had no part in the gang wars downtown? The opium trade, the depression?" John Stole laughed, a choked, crazed sound. "Harrod House, for God's sake?"

"My work there is entirely respectable," murmured Dr. Victor.

"Like hell it is, you sick bastard—"

"Tut, tut. Careful now."

"You didn't like the work Hope was doing, how she was helping people, making them think differently, upsetting your control."

Plum, derisively: "Your wife's work was never notable enough to concern us, John. Come now, let's not be naive."

"You meant '*our* control,' didn't you, John?" Dr. Victor's voice, perilously soft. "You are, after all, one of us."

"Not anymore."

Clara heard the thump of angry footsteps, Patricia Plum saying, "Let him go." A moment later her father emerged from the room, his tie undone and his face cloaked in shadow. He gulped down the glass of scotch in his hand and staggered around the corner.

Clara watched him leave, immobilized with panic. Resigning as mayor, leaving Concordia—were such things even possible? She moved to follow him, but then she heard Dr. Victor spit: "Enough's enough, Patricia. We've got to get rid of him."

"He's a liability," came the Merry Butcher's voice. "He's unpredictable and knows too much."

Clara froze, halfway out of her corner.

"And I had so hoped we wouldn't have to." Plum sighed delicately. "But he has allowed me no other choice. We'll proceed as planned. Have you found your man for Reginald Square, Hiram?"

Reginald Square. The New Year's Eve ceremony. Clara crept closer to the door.

Hiram Proctor wheezed in his distinctive rattle, "I have indeed. Rotten gent, clean shot. He'll be in the crowds that night, front and center. Once dear Johnny gets up to make his speech, auld lang syne, how do you do . . . *boom*."

"How tragic," Dr. Victor added, "that his wounds will be beyond even my skill to heal."

"And what if the shot's not fatal?" asked the Butcher.

"Never fear, my merry friend. A good doctor knows how to kill as well as heal."

Clara's knees gave out; she slid to the floor, clumsy and too distraught to care.

"A pity we can't kill him tonight," added Dr. Victor. "Poor Clara would be hysterical. She'd seek comfort in familiar arms, and I'd be forced to oblige." He hummed deep in his throat. "Merry Christmas to me."

"Speaking of Clara," said the widow, her voice floating like a song, closer now, "I know you're out there, sweet one."

7

They were on her immediately—the Butcher and Dr. Victor, yanking her into the room. Clara tried to scream, but Dr. Victor's arms were too strong, his stink too foul; it choked away her breath, sickened her with sudden terror.

"How long have you been hiding out there, girl?" the Merry Butcher demanded. Gone was the laughing, fat Commissioner of Human Health; this was the Butcher, whose hands reeked of blood. He shook her. "How long?"

She said nothing. Briefly she considered reaching for the dagger pressed against her thigh. Her mother, perhaps, would have been able to move as Godfather had taught her and skewer them all—but Clara's fear was too great. Her vision spun—the *world* spun. Dr. Victor's palm was tight over her mouth.

The Butcher scowled, pulled a pillbox from his jacket. "I'll make short work of this, Plum. It'll look like she had one too many. Easy, clean. Hold her mouth open, Doctor."

Dr. Victor laughed. "She's not yours to claim, Butcher, not even for death. She's mine."

"Really, Victor," said Hiram Proctor from the corner. "There are lots of other legs to get between, and some of them prettier than these."

Revolted, Clara twisted in Dr. Victor's arms, and his fingers tightened their grip on her face.

"Stop struggling, you wicked girl," he hissed. "Behave yourself."

"Gentlemen, that's enough." Patricia Plum's voice silenced them at once, and as she rustled toward Clara, even Dr. Victor backed away. She took Clara's chin in hand. "Eavesdropping is an unbecoming practice for a young lady, Clara."

"I—I didn't hear anything." Clara cringed at the sound of her own voice. It trembled like a child's, and was entirely unconvincing.

Plum studied her for a long moment. Clara dropped her eyes and bit her tongue, as though the pain of that could keep her standing upright, and she decided she was not sure whom she hated more—the widow or herself.

"I'd be angry at you for trying to lie to me," Plum said lightly, "if you weren't so terrible at it. I know you heard every word of our conversation."

Perhaps in Godfather's shop Clara could spin tales and turn tricks, but there was no use trying to fool anyone in this room. Her own fear had turned the air toxic, and it was impossible to think. "But . . . why can't he simply resign?"

Plum released her, disdainful. "Your father has been part of Concordia for years. He has seen much and knows even more. How am I to trust that he wouldn't use that knowledge against us?"

"He wouldn't betray you, Mrs. Plum. Concordia has been his life—"

Plum was unmoved. "A life he is all too willing to throw away, it would seem."

"So the only option is to kill him." Clara's words sounded hollow, heavy, as if her body refused to speak properly. She felt thrust into a fog of disbelief.

After a moment, Plum smiled a small, false smile. "Oh, Clara. I can see you're going to be difficult. Dr. Victor, would you please fetch the younger Miss Stole?"

"With pleasure," he said, his voice full of teeth.

Somewhere inside herself, somewhere hidden and furious, Clara was screaming. She was Godfather's creation there, a vengeful whirlwind, bloodying them with her blade and coloring the room red.

But externally she was close to sobbing, reaching for Plum like a beggar. "No, she's not a part of this. Don't bring her here. Don't hurt her. She knows nothing. I won't say anything about any of it, I swear to you. Leave us be, *please*."

"You're absolutely right. You won't say anything about it. I'll see to that."

"I don't like this, Plum," muttered the Butcher. "Let me dispose of the girl. No one need know what's happened here."

"No. That would arouse too much suspicion and upset Dr. Victor."

"Hang the doctor. He's mad as a hatter—"

"And he has done much for Concordia, as well as serve loyally as my personal lieutenant since my darling husband's death." Plum's expression had turned deadly, making the Butcher seem to shrink where he stood. "You would do well to remember that."

The door opened and shut with a swell of faint music. Dr. Victor had Felicity by the shoulders. An outsider might have thought him a kindly uncle shepherding his niece to bed, but Clara saw how his gaze roamed over Felicity's body.

Oh, for the courage to beat him senseless.

"Here you are, Clara!" Felicity hurried forward, curls slightly askew. "I've been looking everywhere for you. Godfather's acting so strangely. I hate when he's like this. It's humiliating. He keeps asking for you, and I said I could help him if he needed something, but he said, 'No, only Clara,' and he's taking the toys back from everyone, and . . . What is it? Clara, you're crying."

"We were talking about Mother." Clara turned away, meeting Patricia Plum's coldly amused gaze. "She loved these parties."

"God rest her soul," Dr. Victor added silkily.

Clara felt Felicity's slender arms about her waist and held her close, breathing in the smells of cinnamon and cake, and curls damp from dancing.

"Oh, Clara." Tenderly Felicity fiddled with Clara's skirts. "Mother wouldn't want you to be sad. She would want you to dance. Don't you like your gown? Come back to the party. You can dance with me, Clara."

Clara glanced at the Butcher, who glared at the fire, and at Dr. Victor, whose eyes gleamed. The sight paralyzed her. What were the right words to say? What was the right expression to assume? She could not have felt more helpless before them if she'd been peering out past the bars of a cage.

"Yes, I'll come dance," she whispered. "Will you wait for me by the stairs?"

Felicity smiled up at her. "Oh, yes. I'll even be the boy and lead, if you want. I dance better than any old boy."

"True enough. The boys here are cows with four left feet. Go on now."

Felicity stood on tiptoe to kiss Clara's cheek and left in a flutter of emerald-green skirts.

Clara kept her eyes on the door. Breathing—she must, impossibly, keep breathing.

"Why did you bring her here?"

"I wanted to remind you of how much you love your sister." Plum's voice was deceptively sweet. "She's a pretty creature, to be sure. Young and innocent. And if you utter one word of anything you've heard here to anyone, if you do anything to interfere with our plans regarding your father, I will kill her."

"You can't." Clara was sinking beneath waves of shock; they threatened to smother her. "You wouldn't. She's a *child*, twelve years old—"

"And I won't simply kill her, no." Plum advanced, perfectly glamorous, glittering. "I'll give her to Dr. Victor first. She's a bit younger than his usual patients, not to mention lovelier. I'm certain he'd relish the chance to experiment."

The study swirled about Clara, but Dr. Victor did not let her fall, catching her by the arm and whispering at her ear, "A pair—a lovely pair of girls for the good doctor. How sweet that would be."

"You've brought this upon yourself, Clara, with your deplorable behavior tonight." Plum slid close enough for Clara to smell the woman's breath against her face. "And really you should be thanking Dr. Victor. Without his, shall we say, *partiality* toward you, we would not be having this conversation. You should consider yourself lucky to have this choice at all: You can let us proceed as planned and save your sister's life, or you can watch her be mutilated at the hands of your fiancé."

Clara didn't understand at first. She could do nothing but turn the word over in her mind as though examining an unfamiliar artifact. *Fiancé*.

"Oh." Plum's hand, dripping with rings, stroked Clara's cheek. "I forgot to mention that, didn't I? How careless of me! Dr. Victor has requested your hand in marriage. I daresay your father wasn't too pleased with the idea, but soon enough . . ." Plum waved her hand dismissively. "It should work out nicely. With your father gone, you and your sister will fall to our care. He wants it that way. It says as much in his will."

The world had been reduced to a single, searing point, buried beneath Clara's breastbone. She longed to pluck it from her body, wield her own fury like a blade. But she could only stand there, reeling.

"I'll kill you," Clara whispered, frantic. "I'll kill you. I swear I will."

Patricia Plum burst out laughing.

Dr. Victor wrenched Clara's arms back, twisting them until she cried out in agony and fell to her knees. Pain pulsed through her in waves, and she discovered that she was sobbing, that numbness was giving way to grief and unstoppable horror. *Stop crying, Clara, you stupid girl,* the voice of her mind hissed. But she couldn't.

"Oh, you poor, foolish girl," Plum said, kneeling to cup her cheeks. "No, you won't. You'll do as you're told, stay quiet, and keep things as painless as possible for you and your sister. New Year's Eve is a week away, Clara. I'll be watching you closely. If I don't like what I see, your sister's blood will be on your hands. The choice is up to you."

Clara nodded, her vision a blur, and leaned back against Dr. Victor. She could not see a way out, not from this. The study's walls were folding her away into a tiny, pounding box, and she welcomed it. Dr. Victor's eyes tore off her clothes, and she let them.

You asked for this, the way you behaved.

"Then we're agreed," said Plum cheerily, and they left her.

Clara sat alone for long moments afterward, dizzy.

Perhaps she could take Felicity tonight and run. But run where, and what about Father? Yes, he had been more and more distant of late, to the point where the household staff came to Clara first with their questions, and Clara had to remind her father to attend his appointments, to go over his accounts, to comb his hair. Yes, he infuriated her—and saddened her—beyond expression.

But could she truly abandon him like that, even to save her sister?

I'm abandoning him regardless, came the inconceivable thought, *to assassination.*

"To save Felicity," she whispered to the empty room, but the reminder was no comfort. How was she to trust that Felicity would be safe, even if Clara did everything Concordia asked? Plum had said yesterday that she would do anything to keep Dr. Victor happy. Perhaps he would change his mind, decide that having Clara was not enough; perhaps he would eventually turn his attentions to Felicity. Clara would lie in her husband's bed at night and hear Felicity crying out for help, and be powerless to save her.

"Husband." The word sat heavy upon her, and so did the future it conjured—vowing to be his, a wife paraded around on his arm, catching the scent of dead girls upon him after a day at Harrod House.

Clara's thoughts spiraled to a dullness in her belly, a nausea she knew would never dissipate. There was nowhere to go, nowhere to hide or run. Plum had said she would be watching Clara, and Clara believed her. Concordia's tendrils snaked throughout the entire city; the empire's eyes were in the walls, on the streets, in the mansion itself. Patricia Plum's web had ensnared Clara as completely as had her gown's layers of lace and satin. She could only hope that staying as quiet as possible would keep

Felicity safe. If she could not save her father, she could save her sister. Or she could try.

Clara stumbled back toward the ballroom. She smelled of Dr. Victor; the stench kept her unsteady, but she strove to quell any outward signs of what had happened. She would return to the party and smile, dance, and play the gracious hostess until the last guest departed in the early hours of the morning, which seemed an impossibly long time from now. The ballroom's enormous grandfather clock—a present from Godfather—was chiming eleven o'clock.

She would also make Godfather go home and take his trinkets with him—including the statue. Distantly she wondered what he'd been on about—the blue light, the proclamation of danger, the silver liquid coating his hands—but such questions faded in the face of Patricia Plum's threat. So much for training, for excursions to the shop, for explanations; she might never know what those symbols on her mother's body meant, for she suspected Dr. Victor would now put a stop to that part of her life. Certainly now, after tonight. A selfish pang of loss overwhelmed her at the thought.

As Clara entered the ballroom, shouting erupted from above.

"Leave, all of you! Now!"

Clara's breath caught; that was her father's voice, slurred and hoarse.

Felicity rushed toward her. "Oh, Clara, stop him. Father's been drinking, and Godfather's frightening everyone, and—oh, what will they *think* of us?" She wrung her hands. "Do something, won't you? Hurry, Clara dear."

Guests had stopped dancing to stare—some with curiosity, others with horrified amusement—up at the mezzanine, where John Stole addressed the room, waving his drink.

"I've had *enough* of this ruckus," he bellowed, his eyes red and unfocused, his cheeks damp. "All you people eating my food, drinking my drink, pretending that you don't know what's going on around you. . . ."

Godfather hurried out from the crowd to Clara's side, his pack of tools in hand. "Well, this is unexpected but spectacularly convenient. I was about to tell them to leave—for their own sakes—and here comes your father, doing it for me." Godfather rubbed his face, leaving silver behind. In his other hand he held a black clockwork dragon to match the one atop his cane. Its eyes gleamed red, like rubied blood.

"Go home, Godfather," Clara said, feeling slightly unhinged. Her father's shouting, Godfather's ranting, Felicity's hands tugging fretfully at her skirts—couldn't they stop for one moment to see the disaster written on her face? "You can't be here anymore."

"But, Clara—"

"Don't argue with me. You should never have come here tonight." Without waiting for an answer, she took Felicity by the shoulders and tried not to imagine Dr. Victor doing the same, lifting her onto one of his surgical tables. "Go put Father to bed," she told her sister, "and hurry. Mention Mother's name. That will make him listen."

Felicity had begun to cry. "Clara, everyone's *staring* at us."

"I don't care. Now go."

"Yes, go. Go on!" Godfather waved his arms at everyone he passed, parading around like a deranged ringmaster. Guests began trickling out, frowning over their shoulders and chuckling to themselves.

"Off his rocker," she heard one guest mutter. "Gone mad. It's the murder that did it."

Patricia Plum floated toward the ballroom doors. "Yes, perhaps we had best call it a night? It seems Mayor Stole is eager for some peace and quiet."

"If peace and quiet come in a bottle," someone said, to relieved laughter.

Clara stood frozen. Her father continued shouting out curses from upstairs, and Godfather was bustling about, closing doors and hammering boards over them, nailing shut the windows. He even seemed to be muttering to the walls themselves, and was he actually painting them with whatever silver substance coated his hands?

Clara was aghast. *God help me, he* has *gone mad.*

"I do hope you'll remember everything we discussed tonight." Patricia Plum slipped past her with a light kiss to her cheek. "We'll talk again soon. Merry Christmas, Clara."

Clara watched her leave, Dr. Victor at her heels. He caught Clara's eye and bowed low, grinning devilishly.

When the last guest slipped out into the night, Clara stood alone in the empty ballroom littered with empty plates and glasses, and Godfather's abandoned creations. One of the electric light strings flickered. From outside on the street came laughter, spirited John Stole impressions, and the icy crunch of carriage wheels.

"Ah, Clara," Godfather said, hurrying over. "Finally we've a chance to speak alone."

If Clara looked at him, she would cry. She stared out the entryway after the departed guests. "Get out."

"I beg your pardon?"

"Take your things and get out."

"But, Clara, dearest . . ."

"Don't call me that," Clara whispered. Dr. Victor would call her that in their bed, a mockery of an endearment. She fled upstairs with that image in her mind, ignoring Godfather calling her name. Once in the safety of her bedroom she sat on the edge of her bed with her fists clenched in her lap, fighting for a calm that would not come. The sound of Felicity crying from down the hall pulled her mind into a noxious chorus:

It's your fault. You should have been braver. You should have been smarter. You should have taken better care of them.

It's your fault.

All of it is your fault.

8

Not half an hour later, minutes before midnight, Clara lay on her bed, restless and uncomfortable in her gown. Desperate thoughts raced through her mind, but none of them held a solution; her world had for so long been precarious, and now it would soon come crashing down around her—unless, *unless* . . .

But there was no *unless,* and just as the sob that had been building in her throat threatened to burst, Clara heard the sounds of smashing glass.

She sat up, listening to the pounding of her own heart until it came again—a crash from the ballroom.

They don't trust me, she thought at once. *They've come for Father, for Felicity.*

She quickly exchanged her dancing slippers for her boots and slipped out into the hallway, keeping close to the wall, the dagger from her thigh holster in hand. Winter crept around her, through window-panes and beneath closed bedroom doors, raising gooseflesh on her exposed skin. Her gown rustled, and she cursed it for the hundredth time that night, but there was no time to change. *Become one with the shadows when you sneak. Become one with the cold in winter. Become the shadows. Become the cold.*

Something brushed past her feet, and she jumped away, startled.

Half a dozen skinny black rats scurried along the baseboards, toward the window at the end of the hallway, where there was a slight crack in the plaster. Rats weren't new; she'd frequently seen them about the city. But she had never seen them upstairs like this, and how odd that they seemed so determined to leave, to return to the cold.

At the landing she crouched behind the banister and peered down into the ballroom, up from which came sounds of hammering. In one corner of the room stood the Christmas tree, dark and silent. At the ballroom's main entrance Godfather was nailing boards across the doors.

Clara sighed, light-headed with relief.

"Ah, Clara, good," Godfather said without looking up. "I was about to come fetch you."

She hurried down the staircase. "What on earth are you doing? I told you to leave."

"Reinforcements. They'll give us extra time."

"Time for what, precisely?"

He turned, his eyes wild. "They're coming, Clara. I can feel the wards giving way. I threw up hasty ones tonight when I arrived, but my work has taken so much out of me." He spat in disgust, "Can't even craft the simplest tricks, not anymore. . . ."

Clara had stopped listening. Towering above her in the center of the room, surrounded by a queer barricade of furniture and portraits taken down from the walls, was the statue. Its implacable face frowned down at her.

She approached it as she would a wild animal. The strangeness of the moment thrilled her. Yes, the statue was as familiar to her as Godfather; yes, she had projected onto its unmoving facade moods and a voice and an imagined history; but it had never been *here* before, never at her home. The symbols etched into its surface reminded her of her mother's mutilated body, but, horribly, that did not stop her.

"Hello, old friend," she said shyly, reaching for it.

She pulled her fingers away with a hiss; the faint crack of blue light on its left thigh had burned her. The statue trembled briefly on its pedestal. Something *inside* it screamed, low and in agony.

She backed away, thunderstruck. "Godfather?"

"Ah, you heard him, did you? My breakthrough." Godfather, gleaming with sweat, came up behind her. "For so many years I've worked, and now . . ."

"*Him?*" Fear and wonder rushed through Clara at the fevered look on Godfather's face. Images from the stories he'd told her—dragons and cursed fiddlers, lost lovers and tunnels carved between worlds—nibbled at the edges of her mind and seemed, here in the dark, as alive as Godfather. The statue's unearthly scream lingered against her skin—a pull, a thrum.

"Godfather, what's happening? Tell me."

"I've done what she hoped I never would. I've broken the curse, deciphered it. And she's sent them for me, of course she has. They're coming, even now. What it would mean for her, if I were to free him . . ."

He laughed, pushing back a lock of dark hair, and Clara saw him then as she did when he told her stories by candlelight, as more than some eccentric old toymaker. He was ancient, magnificent, and *other.*

"Who is *her*?"

"Anise."

He hissed the word, and the statue—*God help me,* Clara thought. *I'm hearing things*—cried out again. The sound seemed somehow enraged.

"Who is Anise? Who's *coming,* Godfather?"

In answer something clattered across the roof. A large weight fell onto the second-floor terrace.

Godfather took from the statue's side a long, slender sword with a hilt of black stones. "Here, Clara. You'll need this. I made it myself in one of my first experiments with their magic."

This elegant weapon was no wooden play sword of the sort she and Godfather had practiced with. As her hand curled around its hilt, the part of her that came alive in the safety of Godfather's shop thrilled at the weight of the sword; it felt as though she was meant to hold such power in her hand. Etchings along the blade echoed the markings carved into the statue, repulsing and fascinating her simultaneously. *How* were these elements connected, and what did it mean?

An inhuman scream sounded from the direction of the stables, followed by another, and then eerie silence. Godfather cursed.

"The horses," Clara whispered, the sword forgotten, replaced by dread. "Was that the horses?"

Godfather moved her toward the statue. "They're here."

"Who?"

Scratching sounded against the doors; a blunt force impacted the boarded-up windows.

"Loks," Godfather spat.

"Loks? What is that?"

"You'll see soon enough. I'm sorry, Clara, to request such a thing of you." He pressed a fierce kiss to her hand. "But you will be glorious, ferocious. This is what we've been working for, you and I. To fight whatever comes our way, and then . . ."

He paused, put his forehead against hers, chuckling under his breath.

She held his cheeks, forcing his gaze to hers. "And then what?"

"Stay still. Don't move." He withdrew three clockwork dragons from his coat and sliced open his palm with a serving knife.

Clara grabbed for his hand. "Godfather, you're—"

"Bleeding" was the word, but it would not come, for the liquid now coating his hand was not red.

It was silver.

"What is that?" She pointed at it stupidly. Things were clawing at the windows, smashing the glass, shredding the wood, but she could look only at his hand. "Godfather, your blood, it's—"

He ignored her, smearing his bloodied hand across the dragons and then throwing them across the ballroom floor. One went straight, the other two to the sides; they skittered along the floor with flapping clockwork wings and whirring jaws, chomping up the wooden slats beneath them. Each of them spit out behind them another, identical dragon, and another and another, until a black sea of them roiled across the entire room.

They scattered like crazed spiders, wings and talons snapping with a familiar whir of gears. *It sounds like the back room,* Clara realized. She had never been allowed there, and now she understood why.

In the wake of this dragon sea, the ballroom metamorphosed into a forest of black metal, iron, and glass. Staircases became jagged mountains, shining in the dim, wintry moonlight; strategically placed chairs became mazes of spindly towers. Godfather's toys, scattered across the room, grew into enormous versions of themselves—skeletal, winged horses; a squadron of clockwork soldiers, gears turning inside their gaping chests. Garishly painted bats and monstrous raptors darted up from the floor to perch on the chandeliers that now filled the entire room with drooping tangles of wire. Godfather's electric lights sizzled white. The grandfather clock in the corner tolled midnight, each chime lower and deeper than the last as the entire mechanism swelled to five times its normal size.

Likewise the Christmas tree grew until it reached the ceiling, where it erupted into a forest of iron needles. Oversize ornaments spun, throwing moonlight across the ceiling. The barricade surrounding the statue transformed into a maze of black mirrors until Clara was surrounded by a hundred versions of herself, peering out from behind a hundred laughing Godfathers, their bloody hands outstretched.

"It's working!" he cried. "I've done it—Clara, at last I've done it!"

The dragons, their work complete, settled silently at the edges of the room. Thousands of red eyes watched from the shadows and the ceiling; thousands of whirring metal wings glistened with silver blood. The air stung of salt and nearly choked her with its acridity.

"What have you done?" Clara turned to Godfather, torn between terror and awe. He was sweating, his cheeks pinched and gray; she hurried to him and held him up as he caught his breath.

"Godfather, can you hear me?" She slapped him lightly. The relentless clawing noises at the windows magnified tenfold. Fear swelled within her as she watched the boards over the windows bow under the pressure. They were everywhere, these phantom creatures, these loks, whatever that meant. "Are you hurt?"

He laughed, weak. "A bit. That magic's not meant for me, but I had no choice. I *have* no choice, not until things are as they should be once more. It wounds me every time." He straightened, glaring at the statue and swinging his fist through the air. "And yet still I triumph!"

Clara drew him back to her. "Godfather, pay attention. Something is breaking in. What are they? What shall we do?"

"We shall do as I've taught you," he said, turning her away and withdrawing his own sword, slender and unadorned, from where it leaned against the statue. "We shall fight."

The energy vibrating off Godfather was cold, as taut as silver wire. It frightened and energized her. She wondered if this was what being struck by lightning felt like, and she wondered why this was happening, and if it had something to do with the statue, which trembled furiously on its base.

At that moment several . . . *things*, hulking and black, burst through the windows on the mezzanine and crashed into the forest Godfather had made. Hellish screams filled the air, and against the backdrop of a broken window, Clara saw the silhouette of a long, fanged snout, a knotted back, a hulking, bearlike body covered in armor, and three naked tails.

Rats, Clara thought. The similarity was unmistakable.

But, no, not rats. What had Godfather called them? *Loks*.

Behind the loks, against the shattered window, a tall, lean figure stood, pale and clothed in ragged garments. The figure was decidedly male, and a light at his temple blinked mechanically, attached to some sort of wired apparatus. He called out a guttural command in an unfamiliar language, and the loks screamed in answer. They were approaching fast, crashing toward Clara through Godfather's wild maze.

"Keep them away from me," Godfather said, turning to the statue. "I'll help you as I can, but I must concentrate. Do you understand?"

He withdrew more dragons from his pocket, tinier ones, and sliced his unmarred palm above them. Silver dripped onto the dragon's serpentine necks. They came alive at the contact and scattered across the statue's surface, ripping at the metal, peeling it back bit by bit. They swarmed over the statue, biting and tearing, their spiderweb wings writhing. They seemed to follow Godfather's directions across the statue's body; he was coaxing them to life as a puppet master would, murmuring things under his breath and occasionally slicing open his forearm for fresh drops of blood. As the dragons moved, the statue began jerking violently, screaming something too inhuman to interpret. Blue light flashed along the seams of its metal plates, illuminating the etched symbols from within.

"Keep them away from you?" Clara backed away from the sight, sword in hand. Sounds of battle came from throughout the ballroom—shrieks and slashing claws, the clash of swords, and far too much of it to know where to train her attention. Memories of her sparring with Godfather, their evenings laughing over punches and swordplay, overwhelmed her with new significance. "You've been training me to fight not for me but for *you*."

"Clara, we haven't time for this. Please just—"

On the other side of the protective barricade, a gigantic weight crashed to the floor. Inside the statue something pounded furiously.

A massive clawed arm burst through the wall of mirrors behind Clara and yanked her through.

Choking on her own scream, Clara landed hard against a bristly body hot with blood. Black claws slashed across her arm and thigh. She saw yellow eyes, two sets of long black teeth in a mouth crusted with pus, and a distinctively ratlike snout. The beast smelled of sewage and grime. Around its head it wore an assemblage of gears and lenses that unfolded over its right eye. Clara struggled to break free, kicking and biting, but the lok's grip was iron. Angered, it reared back onto its hind legs.

Spots swam before her eyes as the lok's grip tightened. The creature roared unintelligible words, its stink washing over Clara's face. She had the impression that it had won a game and she was the prize. But she still had a sword somewhere. She had lost much of the feeling in her arms, but it was still in her hand—she had not dropped it. Desperation spurred her on past the frantic, impossible fear of being trapped in the arms of a monster. Any thoughts but those of survival fell away, leaving her mind sharp. She needed room to maneuver the blade into the lok's belly, but she could hardly breathe for the pain. The lens over the creature's eye flashed, catching her attention, and this seemed significant. The man at the window sported a similar light. Could he be controlling them? Were they somehow linked?

"Anise," she whispered. She didn't know who or what Anise was, but maybe that man upstairs knew, and maybe it would distract the lok long enough for Clara to make her move. She forced herself to stare at the blinking lens and infuse her voice with conviction she did not feel. Something sparked in her hair—from the swinging chandelier overhead, perhaps?

"Anise! I know you're there. And it's too late. Godfather's already done it."

Clara didn't even know what precisely Godfather was trying to do, but the words clearly meant something, for the lok's grip loosened. It cocked its head slightly in puzzlement, or, perhaps, to listen to something far away.

Clara did not wait to find out. Gathering her strength, crying out in pain as her bruised back twisted, she thrust her sword toward the lok's midsection and prayed that her blade would find a gap in the strange, corded harness wrapped around its middle. The lok jerked, putrid breath rushing over her face. Its steaming black blood spilled onto her leg.

The lok fell. Clara fell with it and rolled away from its flailing body. As she watched it die, shock settled in her mind. Her limbs were unsteady, and blood spotted her skin. *She had killed the thing that had attacked her.* The novelty of such a concept, the revelation of her own might, sent surety surging through her in a rush of heat.

She was invincible, ecstatic. For an instant the chaos around her fell away. She allowed herself to imagine slicing open Dr. Victor's own white belly, again and again, until he was nothing but a bloodied piece of meat, like the lok before her.

The main ballroom doors burst open with a great cracking sound, two loks bounding through, their tails like whips. Overhead, iron creaked and shadows swayed. Clara looked up to see a lok wrapped around one of the chandeliers, peering into the maze for a safe path down which to climb.

Something slammed into her unwounded side, and she fell hard against one of the long serving tables, now flung up on its side, a sheer, mountainous black wall. In the distorted reflection of the table's surface, Clara saw a lok rearing up to strike, but then one of Godfather's monstrous creations, a life-size clockwork soldier of metal and brass and meticulously crafted military finery, stalked forward and jerked its sword high. The blade whirred, separating into five smaller ones. When the soldier slashed, five dark ribbons appeared on the lok's belly.

A delirious thought occurred to her: Had each of Godfather's creations over the years been specifically crafted to someday come to gigantic life and defend against potential attackers?

The lok fell, but Clara did not wait to confirm its death. Three more were behind it, rushing toward her. She fled through the ballroom, dodging beasts of flesh and beasts of clockwork battling to the death. A pack of metal wolves pounced on a lok, their mechanized howls piercing the air. Another lok, its eyes clawed out, blindly snatched a dragon from the air and smashed it against the wall. It was as though this night had ripped everything from Godfather's shop and thrust it into a monstrous fever dream.

Another dragon dipped low, almost hitting Clara; one of the loks pursuing her knocked her across the floor, and shattered glass raked her skin. When she came to a stop, she looked up to see hundreds of shining daggers and the warped face of an angel.

The Christmas tree.

Clara staggered to her feet, slashing free of a tangle of light strings with her sword. The wires popped, catching one of the loks in the face. The creature fell with an abbreviated shriek, and the air smelled of charred flesh. Two remained, and as Clara ran, she held her sword up behind her, dragging it through the metal shards that had once been pine needles. Thin black daggers rained down in a luminous cascade as Clara covered her head and threw herself out into the open space beyond the Christmas tree. Behind her the loks had fallen, now no more than pincushions bleeding black.

From the center of the room came a terrible scream. It was unfamiliar and deep—not Godfather but someone else.

The image of the statue's handsome metal face sprang to Clara's mind. She searched for it desperately through the gaps in Godfather's barricade, but something higher up caught her eye.

Down the sheer slope of what had once been the staircase to the mezzanine crept the figure from the window—a man in torn clothes and covered with muck, as though he had been crawling on his belly through the bowels of the city. The man caught her eye and grinned horribly. He was pale and looked somehow . . . not right, the lines of his body not quite what they should be, though Clara couldn't pinpoint the wrongness more precisely than that. He shouted something to a nearby lok, and it turned toward Godfather's barricade, where the air thrummed blue.

Clara ran after it without thinking, too crazed for fear or strategy. A few loks broke away from their skirmishes to follow her. She reached the barricade and squeezed through a narrow gap in the glass, catching distorted glimpses of her reflection—bloodied, bruised, her gown shredded. Loks clawed through the glass after her, shrieking.

Godfather crouched at the statue's side, guiding the dragons in their work. They chewed between each of the statue's fingers and along each palm. Metal peeled away in curling strips and fell to the ground like rain. Blue sparks danced along the unfurling metal seams. The statue's handsome mouth twisted, emitting sizzling blue light, and cried out in pain.

Its voice was both human and not—rattling as a machine would, but as rich as a man's. Disbelief rooted Clara to the spot. She felt as though she had tumbled into a dream, fed by too much punch, too little food, and the weight of Concordia's threats.

"Clara!" Godfather shouted. This was followed by a vicious scream as a lok flew into her, knocking her back into a mirror. Her sword flew away, and she gasped for air, fighting to stay conscious. Stars danced in her vision—or perhaps they were the cascade of sparks now tumbling off the statue.

Godfather threw himself between the statue and the lok, blue fire singeing his hair.

"It's too late, Anise." He gestured at the statue, chuckling wearily. "You see? Not the king's fool anymore, am I?"

Clara searched through the sea of glass around her, desperate for her sword. Her hand landed on the heel of her left boot. "A handy place to keep a dagger, inside a boot," Godfather had said the day he'd presented them to her, beaming. "Everyone knows that. But I much prefer to use the boot itself."

Frantically she fumbled at the hidden mechanism on her heel until the blade fell free from inside it—a slender dagger, but it would suffice.

The lok raised his paw to strike, his eyepiece flashing. Godfather closed his eyes and murmured something that sounded like a prayer. Behind him the statue's blue sparks coalesced into a great tower of light. There was no more time; Clara ran at the lok with blood in her eyes and leapt, screaming with the effort as she thrust the dagger high.

The impact threw her back, blood splattering her. She flung herself to the side as the lok crashed to the ground. It did not move.

Godfather stared at her, astonished. "Clara . . ."

From the lok's left eye socket protruded her dagger's hilt. The creature's mouth dripped black.

Trembling, Clara put her boot on the lok's head and tugged, trying not to vomit at the sensation of her dagger's blade scraping bone. She rose to her feet, gripping the hilt like a tether. Her battered knees nearly buckled with the enormity of what she had done and how close Godfather had been to dying.

The other loks hissed in the shadows, slinking away. Ominously the man with the light at his temple had disappeared, which so frightened Clara that, weary as she was, she found her sword and held it up, at the ready.

"Well?" she shouted, shoving hair slick with sweat away from her eyes. "Are you finished with us, then?"

The only answer was reluctant lok chatter from the shadows as they dragged themselves out the shattered windows. Snow had been blowing in during the fight, leaving the ballroom a madhouse of black angles and white drifts.

The loks were leaving. Why were they leaving? And where had the man gone? Perhaps they were simply regrouping, or more were on their way.

Clara turned, wild-eyed, to ask these questions of Godfather—but he was on his knees.

Her heart turned cold and sank. She had not been fast enough. The lok had killed him, her precious, strange godfather, her dearest friend.

She dropped her weapons and ran for him, his name on her lips, but he was laughing; he was *crying.*

"Look," he whispered, pointing.

Where the statue had stood were shredded piles of metal, screaming quietly as each piece smoked to a crisp. In the middle of them, naked and glistening with sweat, lay a gasping, shivering man.

9

At once Godfather set to work putting the ballroom back in order. Clara watched, reeling from her own residual violence and the sight of the man on the floor, as Godfather refreshed the dragons with blood from his wrist. She wondered how many scars marked his body. Perhaps that was why he swathed himself in such unfathomable layers, even during the hot summer months. But there was no time to ponder, nor to examine the dragons' work as they fanned out across the glass-littered floor like a swarm of mechanical bees.

It would not be easy to carry the man outside to the stables—his body was a dead weight—but Godfather insisted they give the dragons room to work, and Clara didn't argue; the ballroom reeked of dead lok. She slid her dagger back into the heel of her boot and, once Godfather had clothed the man with his own coat, helped Godfather pull the man to his feet.

"No," the man whispered over and over as they struggled with him. He did not open his eyes, and Clara was glad. It was hard enough to feel his body so close to hers, this body that had once been a statue—*her* statue, her inexplicable friend—but that was ludicrous for her to even consider. They could not possibly be the same.

In the cobbled stable yard they found the bodies of one of the stable-boys and the horse he had been attending. The corpses' stomachs gaped open, slashed by monstrous claws that had left curdling, discolored pus behind. The stench made Clara gag, but once inside the stables Godfather shut the door. That offered some relief, although the walls vibrated with panic. The remaining horses pawed at the ground and pranced restlessly, bumping into their stall partitions, tossing their heads.

Irritably Godfather waved his hand at them, and then stumbled as though even that small motion had cost him precious energy. An unsteady chill jerked through the air, and the horses quieted. Though their necks gleamed with sweat, they seemed to calm, pressing closer with eager huffs, and the air smelled suddenly clearer.

Forgetting everything else, Clara stared in wonder. "Godfather, what did you do?"

He did not answer. He lay the naked man on the ground, rearranging his coat around him as best he could, but still Clara caught flashes of a hard white torso woven through with remnants of iron and marred by cruel tattoos—the echoes, she realized, of the symbols that had once been carved into the statue's armor. Metal plates capped his right shoulder and left thigh, their clasps digging into his skin. Thinner pieces wound around his forearms and calves, snaked down his belly and along his ribs like the lattice of a spider's web.

Hello, she almost said to him, almost reaching out to touch his arm. It was an automatic urge after a lifetime of doing so, but it was strange now, him no longer being *statue* and instead being *man*. What did that mean?

What had happened here tonight?

"Don't touch him." Godfather shoved Clara's hand away. The movement made her head spin. Her abused muscles ached, her skin stung from scattered cuts, and most disturbing, her blood felt . . . *electric*. It could have been, she supposed, an echo of the cold energy she had felt flowing off Godfather's outstretched arms before the loks had arrived; it was as though a storm had passed too closely overhead and left its echo in her veins. The sensation affected her perception strangely: the snow lacing the windows gleamed whiter than snow should gleam; Godfather's lantern shone more brightly; and the wind outside, even through the stable walls, blew with more definition, as though someone had taken a knife to it and carved strips of it loose from the sky.

She had hit her head. That was it. She had hit her head during the battle and had suffered a concussion.

Steeling herself, she knelt beside Godfather. "Tell me what's happened. Plum and Dr. Victor have Concordia gentlemen watching the mansion constantly. Someone will have heard the noise. They'll be coming, and the police, too—maybe *everyone*."

"Then we must hurry, mustn't we?"

She wanted to shake him. "Explain yourself!"

"Give me time, Clara, and I'll tell you everything you want to know. But it isn't safe here, not yet."

She whirled toward the house. "Father and Felicity—"

"They're fine. Barricaded in their rooms and sleeping." Godfather knelt beside the man and glanced up at her sheepishly. "I slipped a fairly potent sedative into the tea I had sent up to them from the kitchen. Anyway, it's not them we need to worry about."

"You *drugged* them? And the servants as well?"

He ignored her.

Clara fought for calm. This night was incomprehensible. "Will those—will the loks come back?"

"Probably. But when and how many, I can't say."

"Who was that man with them, the dirty one?"

Godfather's face darkened. "Borschalk. Apparently she could not be pained to come herself."

"She." Clara thought quickly. Always with Godfather it was a mighty task to keep up; he required constant deciphering. "Anise?"

Godfather grunted in answer, opening the greatcoat to the man's waist and examining him clinically. A thousand questions clamored for Clara's attention in the silence that followed, but she didn't know where to begin. Several options presented themselves, and they each sounded mad:

How did you make those dragons transform the ballroom?

Why did the loks invade the mansion?

Who is this man you're nursing, and why was he once a statue?

Why is your blood silver, Godfather?

She decided upon the least mad-sounding question. "Who is this man?"

Godfather had begun plucking metal pins and sharp-edged plates from the naked man's body with a set of pliers. The sight of it made Clara wince, but she forced herself to watch.

"Everything that happened tonight," she said. "The ballroom, the loks." She glanced at the man. "Him. Mother. These things are connected, aren't they?"

Godfather dragged his bloodied fingers through his hair and sighed.

"You've been hiding things from me. You lied about training me. You said it was to keep me safe here in the city, but you were actually training me for this, weren't you? For something else? You said there was something else, after tonight. You said, 'And then . . .'"

Godfather didn't look at her, focusing instead on his work. With each wrench of bone and iron, the naked man groaned.

"When I said I wanted you to be able to protect yourself, I was telling the truth," he muttered. "I just didn't say from what. Besides, the city is dangerous. Loks or no loks, I wanted you to be safe."

Clara clenched and unclenched her fists, fighting for patience. "Omitting important details is not much better than outright lying, Godfather."

He ignored her.

"And the rest of it?"

He continued to ignore her.

Frustration nettled angry tears from her eyes. "I deserve answers, Godfather!"

He paused then, and looked up at her. His eye was tender. "Yes, dear heart, you do. You deserve answers and so many other things. And, God willing, I will give them to you. But let me do this first, please, and when we're safe, you may ask me your questions."

He held her gaze for a long moment, and when she nodded, he returned to his work, using his pliers to pull a long, wire-thin pin from the man's shoulder. The sound rubbed metal against metal, and as Clara recoiled, the man awoke, lurching up with a roar that shook Clara's fragile calm. He clawed at his scalp, covered in shaggy black locks gone damp with sweat and blood, and tore at the seeping wounds marring his body. He began shouting nonsense, angry, throat-rattling words of another time or place. Even as Clara shrank back, reaching for her right boot heel in case he lunged at her, she tried to decipher it. What sort of language was this? For a moment she thought Russian, or German, or perhaps a demon's language. It sent cold feelings skipping down her arms. It was guttural, strident.

The man had torn Godfather's coat from his body and now stood completely naked before them. The remaining metal patchwork and faint tattoos were his only clothing, echoes of what had once been. Clara saw the lines of the familiar armored plates, chiseled muscle, and, of course, the accursed symbols.

She could not stop herself from looking lower than that, eyes sliding down the man's lean white belly—too hungry, too sharp—and down, a bit more . . .

Her eyes flew shut, her cheeks flaming.

"Nicholas, stop," Godfather shouted. Clara opened her eyes to see Godfather put up his hands, trying in vain to subdue this man, this . . .

Nicholas. Clara whispered it: "Nicholas." It sighed off her tongue.

Perhaps she had said it louder than she thought. His head whipped toward her, allowing her a glimpse of sharp, high cheekbones; a strong jaw; full lips chapped gray with cold and ash; and a mess of unruly black hair that fell around his cheeks.

"Now, you listen, boy," Godfather began.

Nicholas spat at Godfather's feet. His eyes were as dark as pitch, suspicious, searching. Clara looked away. Proper ladies, she was certain, were not meant to ogle strange, naked men. But even after she looked away she could feel Nicholas's eyes traveling her body, feet to face, where they paused.

"You." His voice was hoarse, unused . . . *other*. How long, Clara wondered, had he been trapped in there? And what was *in there?*

"Oh, help me, it's you," he whispered again in that Russian-German-demon accent, and Clara looked up to see him approaching her unsteadily. Godfather tried to stop him, but Nicholas shoved him back.

She should move. Proper ladies did not stand and stare when naked men walked toward them with eyes like that—full of wonder and amusement and curiosity, as if she were some miraculous thing.

She did not move.

His hands reached for her face and cupped it. As if searching for something, his thumbs traced her cheeks. The touch of his skin burned; Clara wondered if he would melt, and take her with him.

"I . . . I'm Godfather's friend. I'm sure you've seen me from—" It felt stupid to say "in there," so Clara didn't. "I mean, I go to his shop often. To visit him."

Nicholas was close enough for her to feel his breath on her face, to see the slender metal web hugging his right cheek. The blood spotting him was red, not silver, Clara was glad to see. He smelled of the seaside, of salt and brine. He was tall, with the sick paleness of no sun; his limbs were long and lean.

He would not stop searching her face—for what, Clara didn't know, nor did she care. The echoes of the statue sat upon him—*her* statue, which she had cherished and whispered to and pressed up against in the dark. And yet it was so different now, this nearness, this *real*ness. How embarrassing now to think she had pretended the statue were alive; and how frightening, to have such childhood familiarity ripped away, replaced with skin and muscle, and . . . Oh, if she had thought the statue's gaze piercing, it was nothing compared to the one inspecting her now.

He breathed her name: "Clara."

She would burst if she didn't break away from the dark eyes boring into hers, from the fingers caressing her skin—but she could not look away; she *would* not. "Yes."

He smiled crookedly, as if he were remembering how. "I know you."

The brokenness of his voice, the age of it, made Clara shudder. She leaned closer without thinking; her wrist brushed against his bare stomach.

"You do?"

Nicholas nodded, and beneath the wildness of his brow and the soft amusement in his eyes was something deeper, something hot and knowing. "I don't remember everything, but I remember you. I've seen you so many times. I've heard you speak to me. I've *felt* you."

"That's quite enough." Godfather pulled Nicholas away. "Cover yourself."

Even after Nicholas stepped away from her, Clara could feel the ghost of his touch on her skin. She wished she could capture the feeling before it faded—the fullness inside her, the sense of careful celebration. Her mind flooded with memories of countless stolen moments, when she had tiptoed to the statue and pressed her lips to its arm, traced her fingers down the chiseled slopes of its belly. Was it *truly* him? And if so, had he felt her do those things? Had he been aware of her all this time?

The look in his eyes, half in shadow as Godfather draped the coat over his body once more, seemed to answer *Yes.*

Clara looked away, heat flooding her.

As though Godfather knew the thoughts racing through her mind, he tugged at the metal embedded in Nicholas with a carelessness

Clara knew did not come naturally. When he withdrew another of the long pins, pulling it from Nicholas's spine as one would pull a thread through a needle, Nicholas screamed in pain, pounding his fist against the wall. The harsh words pouring from his mouth could not have been anything but curses.

Clara grabbed Godfather's arm. "You're hurting him."

The fury in his eye frightened her. "I have to get these filthy *drekk*'s tricks out of him."

Nicholas muttered something, his glare mutinous.

"So sorry, Your Highness." Godfather gave a mockery of a bow. "I did not mean to offend your exalted ears."

Drekk? Clara wondered. *Your Highness?*

"I want to clean him a bit more before we go." Godfather twisted his pliers hard and withdrew a metal shard from Nicholas's neck, prompting fresh blood and another scream. Godfather swiftly took a cloth from his pocket and pressed it to the wound. He smacked Nicholas's cheek, earning yet another glare. The resentment between them seemed practiced, surer than anything else on this uncertain night. "I need him to be able to keep up. You hear me, boy? I don't suffer stragglers."

A tiny fear deep inside Clara turned over and grew. "Go? Go where? What do you mean?"

"We can't stay in the city." Godfather's expression was incredulous. "Surely you realize that. We must leave, recover our strength. A Door would be the safest, swiftest way, but I can't possibly open one in my current condition."

Nicholas looked at him sharply.

Clara stepped away. Could he mean what she thought? "Are you actually suggesting—"

"I'm not *suggesting* anything. I'm saying it outright: we cannot stay here. We have to leave, tonight."

"Leave," Clara repeated. She could not understand what he meant by leaving through a door, but that was hardly the point. He wanted to *leave?*

Godfather nodded, rooting through a burlap sack hidden against a wall in the shadows; he must have left it there earlier that evening. "Don't worry, Clara. I've prepared everything." He pulled out wrapped packages of food; a leather purse stuffed with money, books, and papers; and one of the pocket-size electric lanterns he so loved. A tiny clockwork dragon skittered loose from his sleeve and fell into the open bag. "Here you are." He tossed a bundle of clothing at Nicholas. "Put them on, put them on. It's cold out, and getting colder."

As Clara watched him, it seemed as though she were stepping outside herself. A numbness enveloped her. Could it be as easy as this? Was this the escape she had been so desperately hoping for? It seemed too perfect to be trusted, naked Nicholas and nightmarish loks aside. Doubt sat uneasily in her belly.

"I can't leave my city," she murmured, more to herself than to him. And yet, why *wouldn't* she leave this miserable place, the sight of which poisoned her entire body with anxiety?

Godfather scoffed. "Your city. And why would you stay, Clara? For the shopping? For the theaters? For the coffin houses and poppy princes, the bodies in the streets? No, there's nothing for you here. How many times have you told me that you hate it, that you long for something better? I can give you that, if you'll let me. What, would you stay and bring death upon yourself?"

It was tempting, though a part of her protested—the part, she suspected, cultivated by her mother, who had, true to her name, never given up hope for this city, even with its many problems.

Godfather smiled, and the sudden shyness of it, the vulnerability, embarrassed her. It was too sweet a look on his face, too intimate. He took her hand. "We can leave this city behind, you and I, and leave Concordia, too. We have better things, grander things, in store for us now. And I'll keep you safe. I swear it."

Nicholas laughed, derision plain on his face. "Safe? You?"

Safe. The word sank into Clara's mind and settled there softly. What would it feel like to be safe?

"And Father and Felicity?" she said. "You'll keep them safe as well? You have enough supplies?" She turned toward the stable doors. "Perhaps I should gather some things before anyone else arrives. We should wake them now. How powerful was your drug? Will they be able to . . ."

She trailed off at the look on Godfather's face, a twisting, sour expression. He turned away, his voice bitter. "Your father is lost to his own empire, and has been for years. Why would you care about a man who, when his family most needed him, vanished? A man who leaves his daughter to fend for herself in a den of lions of his own creation—"

"*Daughters.* And it's been hard since Mother died. You know that. He's grieving."

"He's a coward, and it's time to leave. Help me sort through my bag. We can't forget anything."

"And Felicity?"

Godfather paused, turned away from her. "She isn't you. She would slow us down."

"Of course she isn't me. She's *Felicity*—"

"And when I look at her, I see your father in her face, and when I look at yours, I see your mother's." Godfather's eye glinted hotly at her. "We've always been close, Clara. We've understood each other, you and I."

Ah. There it was—the reason for the strange unease in her gut. It had been some kind of prescient instinct, trying to warn her. Clara backed away, shaking her head. Godfather had become someone else right in front of her eyes, telling her to leave her family behind, that her sister didn't deserve escape because she did not remind him of her mother.

Her mother.

The realization had been building throughout the entire conversation, and now it hit her with physical force. She stepped away from him, one hand on her chest.

"They came after you," she whispered. "They've been looking for you, for *him*"—she pointed at Nicholas—"for years now. Haven't they?"

Godfather was silent, still. Suddenly afraid?

"But they couldn't find you. You were hiding yourself, you said. Protecting him. So they went elsewhere to kill, found other victims. The killings by the water, the *beasts* . . ."

Mother.

She must have said it aloud, for she heard a strange, choked sound lingering in the air. Nicholas had turned away, and Godfather was distraught.

"They killed her because they couldn't find you," she whispered. "They tore her open."

"Clara, please . . ."

"She was innocent. She knew nothing of you and your statues and your secrets. And yet she took the death meant for you."

He reached for her, and she slapped him away.

"You as good as killed her." Her tears were making it hard to see. "When were you going to tell me? Or were you too ashamed? You *should* be ashamed. That you would keep such a thing from me . . . Oh, God." She turned away, leaning hard against the nearest stall, gulping for air. The horse inside whuffed gently at her shoulder.

"I thought," Godfather said, his voice small, "that you would no longer love me if I told you."

She stared at him, struck momentarily speechless. Even Nicholas looked incredulous.

"You selfish old man," Clara whispered, disgusted—at him, at herself for being so thoroughly fooled. He had broken her heart twice. Once with her mother's murder—which was his fault, *his fault*—and now again, tonight.

He looked wounded, but not nearly enough. So she stepped back and said quietly, "I hate you."

It was not true, of course, but she had to say *something* to ease this sickening fury mounting inside her, something that could inflict even a portion of the pain raking her insides raw. She did not wait to let the shock settle on his face. Instead she ran for the stable doors. Nicholas called out her name, and she ignored him. Godfather flung out his silver-stained arms toward the doors, and they, impossibly, flew shut in answer. But Clara could not be stopped; she needed to be as far away from Godfather as possible. With each step the awful truth of his betrayal grew between them, a great, impassable chasm. She reached for the doors, sobbing. She needed to see her father's face, feel Felicity's hand in hers; she needed to hold them close and then, somehow, get them out of this city—tomorrow, *tonight*. They would run from Concordia, run from Godfather and his deadly secrets, and Clara would lead the way, would keep them safe, as she had not been able to do for her mother. Heartbreak swelled inside her, giving her a desperate strength. She would claw the doors down if she had to.

There was no need. They burst open, wood snapping off and flying every which way. The ragged man from the ballroom stood there, the man who controlled the loks.

The horses shrieked, and both Nicholas and Godfather cried out a warning, but the man was too quick. He grabbed Clara by the arm and wrenched her out into the stable yard before she could even gasp. There, near the horse the loks had slaughtered, soft lights—nearly invisible, like dimming sunlight on calm water—flickered in midair.

The man was dragging her toward them.

"Clara, don't let him take you!" Godfather shouted. An invisible force, icy cold, hit Clara from behind, knocking the ragged man to his knees—but he was quick and lithe. His eyes snapped blue fire. He leapt to his feet and thrust his forearm back toward the stables, as though using it to bludgeon open a door. Another force ripped past

Clara in the opposite direction from the first, this one as hot as the previous had been frigid, and sent Godfather and Nicholas flying backward into the ground.

Clara reached toward them, but the man had pulled her to her feet. "I don't understand it," he said, his voice deep and sibilant. The hatred he turned her way was stunning in its ferocity. "I should be gutting you right now, leaving you to rot. But I obey my queen. Her wisdom is absolute." He spat in her face. He cursed her in words she did not understand. "Remember that, filth. You will never match her, no matter your blood."

She was blind with pain; he had her by her hair. "Who are you?" she gasped.

But he did not answer. He was pulling her on, dragging her across the frosted cobbles toward the strange lights in the air. Everything in Clara resisted, but it was no use; the man was too strong, his grip too relentless. She kicked at him, but it was like trying to fell a mountain. He laughed, lifting her by the waist, and Godfather was screaming behind her, and then Nicholas was there, somewhere in the chaos, naked but for Godfather's coat. He rushed at the man, arms raised to strike, but he was still so weak, and the man knocked him aside easily.

"You're next, *prince*," the man said, and then he was pushing Clara toward the lights, though her boots dragged on the stone and she reached for Godfather's limping figure. The lights were growing brighter; they were sizzling at her sides.

"Move!" The man shoved her hard toward the swirling brightness, and though Clara did not know what it was and what would happen to her if she passed through it, she knew it couldn't be anything good.

She screamed a wordless protest, clawing at the air.

The man cursed her and gave one final push.

Clara closed her eyes.

It threw her back. *Something* threw her back. It was as though she had hit a wall, as though her unwillingness to pass through the lights had manifested as some magnetic repulsion. The shock sent her staggering, sent the man flying into the stable wall.

The lights vanished.

For a moment everything was still. Nicholas lay crumpled beside Godfather, breathing hard, clutching his side, and Clara's eyes locked with his.

Then the man roared something furious and leapt to his feet. He bounded toward Clara, more beast than human. She tried to punch him and was easily subdued. He threw her over his shoulder and ran toward the mansion, kicked open the nearest door, and barreled through the wreckage of the ballroom and up the grand staircase—past Felicity's bedroom, past Clara's bedroom, and into her father's.

There he threw her to the floor and went to the great canopied bed her parents had once shared. With minimal effort he dragged her unconscious father from the pillows.

"Wait," Clara cried, struggling to her feet. "Don't hurt him!"

The man turned at the window, her father held brutally by the collar in one white, scabbed fist. Only then did Clara notice the strange blue substance streaking the man's forearm. She was reminded of Godfather's silver blood, and froze.

"You will want to pay close attention," the man said, sneering at her. "His life is in your hands. And she is anything but patient."

Before Clara could move, the man had kicked out the window. Winter gusted in. The man punched his palm into the night air and then drew it back, his fingers clenching into a fist.

With the movement of his arm, a flash burst into being outside the window, then faded into the subdued, shifting lights Clara had seen in the stable yard.

The man jumped onto the windowsill, turned to wag a finger at her. "In your hands now," he said, and flung himself out the window, dragging John Stole behind him.

Clara rushed to the window, too shocked to scream.

She looked down, fearing the sight of smashed bodies on the pavement below.

She saw nothing.

The man and her father had vanished, and the soft lights still swirled in the air, like someone had drawn ripples on the surface of a pool.

For a moment Clara stood there, hanging half out the window, shivering. Any explanation for what had happened eluded her. The lights in the air transfixed her, and she knew, instinctively, that she had to *jump through the lights after them.*

She stepped back from the window, leaned on her father's bed for support. "But that can't be right. That's *impossible*."

A commotion sounded from downstairs—doors flinging open, boots crunching on glass.

Clara turned and raced for the stairs, dazed. This had been a hallucination brought on by the stress of the night; she would find her father waiting for her downstairs.

It was not her father.

At the base of the staircase, Clara stopped short. Police officers swarmed at the entrance to the ballroom, which had reverted back to its previous self. The room looked brutalized, yes, smashed to pieces—but the maze of mirror and metal had vanished, dishes and drapery and ripped upholstery in their wake.

Clara felt crazed laughter building inside her. Godfather's dragons, it seemed, had done their work.

"What is the meaning of this, Clara?" Patricia Plum emerged from the crowd, Dr. Victor at her heels, and yanked Clara close. Her voice, normally so collected, shook with anger. Clara had never seen her like this. "What happened here? My men say they saw figures running in and out of the mansion." Plum paused, taking in Clara's appearance. Delicate revulsion twisted her mouth. "What in God's name happened to you?"

Clara could think of no plausible explanation; the night had exhausted her small capacity to lie. "Father's gone."

Dr. Victor's eyes narrowed. Plum grew still. "What did you say?" she breathed.

The words said, Clara felt her composure crumbling. "I don't understand it, but he's gone. . . . The ballroom . . . His bed is empty, and I don't know where—"

Dr. Victor cursed. "She told him. She told him, and he got scared and turned tail." He grabbed Clara's wrist. "You deceitful bitch."

Plum slapped him away, surprising everyone. "I don't know what you're playing at, Clara. I thought we had a bargain."

"I didn't say anything to him!"

"Obviously someone did. People don't disappear into the night for no reason."

"Clara?"

At the small voice from the stairs, they turned. Felicity stood there, tiny in her nightgown, and unnaturally groggy, tears in her eyes.

"Father's gone?"

Dr. Victor went to her and pulled her close. Beyond him a small swarm of people were peeking in at the ballroom doors, despite the police officers' best efforts to keep them out—a haggard-looking reporter, neighbors in their nightcaps, Concordia gentlemen still dressed to the nines.

"Now, now, pet," Dr. Victor crooned, stroking Felicity's back. His hungry eyes met Clara's, making her skin crawl. "Don't worry. Your sister will put everything to rights, won't she?"

Plum turned away for a long moment. When she spoke once more, her voice, soft as it was, had turned to steel. "If he's not back here by New Year's Eve, and with a good explanation at that, your sister's life *will* be forfeit, and I'll make it as painful as possible for both of you." She seized Clara's wrist, her movements fluid. A casual observer might never have suspected the iron force of her grip. "Do we understand each other?"

"What's she saying, Clara?" Felicity said, rubbing her eyes. "What's happening?"

In that moment, with Felicity's tearful face gazing up at her, and Dr. Victor smirking down at her, and the whole world turned to chaos—Mother dead, and Godfather a liar, and it was *his fault* she was dead—Clara understood what to do next. She had no choice. Never, it seemed, did she have much of a choice.

"Don't worry," she said, turning away and pulling free of Patricia Plum. If she looked at Felicity, she would lose the courage to leave her. "I will find him."

She hurried up the stairs without a backward glance, past clawed paintings and unraveled carpet. Back in her father's room she stood at the ruined window. The lights remained, undulating outside in the night air.

The man had taken her father through those lights, had leapt toward them into nothing. Would the same thing happen to Clara? Would the mysterious force once again repel her? Or, more simply, would she fall to her death?

Regardless, she had most certainly lost her mind.

"It's a Door," gasped a voice from behind her—Nicholas's voice.

Clara turned to see him leaning hard against the wall, Godfather limping up behind him.

"What are you talking about?"

"Watch." Nicholas picked up a shard of glass from the carpet and threw it out the window, toward the lights.

The glass disappeared. It did not fall or shatter, or float away in the wind. It slipped between folds in the air, and vanished.

Clara kept her face neutral, watching the air for some sort of trick.

"Clara," Godfather began, sickly gray and thin, as if the night's events had sucked some great vitality from him, "listen to me carefully, and whatever you do, don't go near that window."

"Why should I believe anything you say?" The sight of him made her ill. "Don't you take another step toward me."

"Clara, *please—*"

She turned away from him, kept her voice hard. "Nicholas, tell me what's going on."

Nicholas's gaze, careful and dark beneath his hair, gave Clara a bit of unexpected steadiness. Godfather's greatcoat gaped open, revealing a sliver of vile shapes on white skin and the trousers from Godfather's supplies, belted low on his hips. He had, she noticed, threaded the belt through Godfather's sword, which he must have recovered from the ballroom; it hung at his side.

"The Door is exactly what it sounds like," he said, his speech still halting, putting itself back together, "and I don't know how much longer it will remain open."

Door. Now that this usage of the word had settled in her mind, she realized that she recognized it, albeit vaguely; it reminded her of something Godfather might have spoken of in a story. "That man who attacked us—"

"Borschalk," Godfather said, on the verge of exploding, but Clara ignored him.

"He took my father, dragged him through the—through that Door."

"Probably because he could not take you," Nicholas said.

The words chilled Clara. "Why couldn't he?"

Unexpectedly, his mouth quirked. "That I don't know. But it is interesting, isn't it?"

Godfather was beside himself. "Enough. You will not go, Clara. You will not *leave* me. You don't know what you're doing. We don't know where that Door leads. Wait a moment, let it close, and we'll open another, if you like. I'll show you how it's done. I'll answer your questions."

Nicholas laughed, his expression cruel. "Are you still capable of such things, old man?"

Godfather stared murder at Nicholas. His face was darker than it had ever been, tinged with brimstone. Clara realized in that moment that she did not know him and perhaps never had. He was an unfamiliar creature with a Godfather mask. He tried to straighten and couldn't, crying out and clutching his sides.

"Clara," he rasped, "I know I did wrong. I should not have kept the truth from you, but—forgive me, I didn't know how to tell you. Can you blame me?"

She watched him, impassive. She hardened her heart to him, though it gutted her to do so.

"I've always kept you safe, haven't I? Your mother trusted me to do so. You know me. You *know* I want what's best for you." He thrust a shaking finger at Nicholas. "This boy is— You don't know what he's capable of. Just come here, and we'll work this out. We two, you and I, as we always do."

At the sight of his feeble smile, Clara felt nothing but disgust and heartache, sentiments she had never associated with him. She stepped away, toward the window.

Nicholas followed at a respectful distance. His eyes locked with hers.

"If I go through those lights," Clara said, "what will I find?"

"Nothing worth finding," Godfather said furiously.

"I don't know what you will find," Nicholas said, his steadiness in such contrast to Godfather's unraveling temper that Clara felt instantly more at ease, "but the Door has not closed. If you enter it, you will be following your father's direct path."

"That is the way of Doors?"

He nodded, near her now. She had backed into the windowsill, her fingers inching out toward winter. Cautiously, Nicholas offered his left hand. Unlike his right, which was bare, this one sported three fingers still encased in metal. He smelled the same as the statue had—like childhood and safety, now with a strange hint of the sea.

"Do you trust me?" he asked in that broken, rebuilding voice of his.

"Who are you?" *What are you?* might have been the more incisive question.

"Do you *trust* me, Clara?"

Trust? She supposed she would find out soon enough. And out of everyone in the world, this strange, half-broken man seemed the likeliest to help her. She almost laughed. Her statue, come to life at last! Her girlish fancies had conjured up such a moment many times, but it had never been quite like this.

Godfather ran for them, shouting for them to stop. What remained of the windowpane shattered at his approach, as though his anger had manifested as a physical force. He was a mass of gray skin and white light and silver blood, sparking as if catching fire.

But they had already turned.

Clara flung herself out the window at the same moment Nicholas did, their hands clasped together—cold, black air; Godfather's screams; Nicholas's tight metal grip.

They fell.

A kiss. A wicked, forbidden kiss. A kiss to end a kingdom.

It was King Alban, of the Somerhart family, the First Family, who doomed us. He threw propriety to the wind and brought the faery countess into his bed.

Rinka was her name, and they say she was beautiful. Like all faeries, she was as pale as winter and had long white hair, kept in braids. "Countess" was a title we forced upon her, the way we forced titles upon all of them, along with pesky annoyances like rules and civilization. For the faeries had no monarch, no court to speak of. Only clans that haunted the forests and painted bloody circles in the ground, and a great haunt called Geschtohl, where their revels raged at each turn of the season.

We thought they would appreciate structure. We thought they would see the sense in having a court, a nobility, cities and fields, rather than their dank caves and ramshackle seaside villages, and their eerie haunts, set deep in the southern forests.

Our stories say that near faery haunts things change when you're not looking. Ground becomes sky, and sky becomes fire, and the tree roots over which you stumble are not roots at all but faery arms, seducing you underground.

They say that the faeries will charm you out of your own skin if you let them.

All magic folk can charm, but only the faeries seemed fond of using it as a weapon.

They say that Rinka charmed King Alban, that she tricked herself into his bed and lied her way into his heart. They say she convinced the king that his wife would forever fail to bear him an heir, that her lack of passion was criminal.

Whatever the reason for it, one autumn day Queen Liane found them in the throne room, wrapped in each other's embrace.

The entire nobility, including the Seven, stood at the doors behind her.

Our historians point to this moment as the one that changed everything This, they say, is what started the war.

I think differently. Perhaps a mistress could have been forgiven.

But a child—the child of a human king and a faery countess—was reason for blood.

Unable to suffer the insult not only to their queen but to the sanctity of the races, Liane's family, the Drachstelles, the bearers of the dragon, engineered a coup.

One autumn night when the air was thick and damp, and Alban lay with his hand on Rinka's belly, feeling their soon-to-be-born child kick, the Drachstelles came for him. They butchered his royal guard and slit his valet's throat.

The king sent Rinka out the window, across the rooftops. As nimble as all faeries are, the stories nevertheless say Rinka slipped many times on the slick white roofs of Wahlkraft, for the king's dying cries upset her balance.

They pursued her into the night, through a storm that soaked the forests limp and black. They shot her with arrows, and the Seven, under orders of the new regime, sliced at her with cold lightning.

And when she could run no longer, our stories say, Countess Rinka fell, in agony, for the child had come. The abominable half-blood child forged out of depravity and lust.

When the Drachstelle guards and the Seven reached Rinka, they saw that her belly had been sliced open. Blood pooled between her legs.

The child was gone.

They assumed the babe had died, or had been eaten by wolves, or had been snatched away by thieves eager for ransom.

But then word came from the south that Rinka's child lived, hidden away deep in the caves beneath Geschtohl. Murmurings began that she was already demonstrating a difference from the rest of them. The faeries doted upon her, they said.

Years passed. Travelers on the road, come to the capital for trade, spread rumors that the southern forests were now whispering strange things. One feverish word, over and over:

Anise.

PART TWO

THE FAERY LAND

I don't think any of you children would have hesitated for a moment to follow the honest, good-natured Nutcracker, who never had a wicked thought in all his life.

10

Cold.

It was cold when Clara awoke, the kind of cold so extreme that it took her a moment to feel it.

She blinked into the dull whiteness around her three times. Then the cold came at her, sharp-toothed, raising the hairs on her body.

I have to get warm, she thought automatically.

She tried to speak the words several times, but her throat caught them in spasms of shock. Finally her voice began working: "Cold."

Rolling onto her side, she cried out in pain, for every bone felt jarred loose. Her skull throbbed; her teeth ached. How far had she fallen?

Where was she?

She rubbed her arms to warm them, and failed. She realized that she lay in snow, or perhaps frost. Frozen bracken, mud, twigs.

She tried to ask for help. But who would answer her?

Then she felt the wind. Malevolent, cunning, it slipped up her tattered skirts and sliced into her skin. Her eyes squeezed shut, ice hammering her body, and she felt herself begin to shake violently. Even her thoughts seemed to shiver.

Perhaps it was the shivering itself that nudged her eyelids open one last time. Or perhaps it was the distant sense that she was actually not alone. Whatever it was, Clara opened her eyes, and saw him:

The man with metal patchwork across his body, wearing Godfather's greatcoat. Crawling toward her now. Reaching for her.

What was his name?

Nicholas.

Clara mouthed the word and stared at his outstretched hand, gnarled with metal and blue with frost. She blinked; the ice on her eyelids cracked into paper-thin flakes and fell away.

She remembered now. She had grabbed on to that hand moments before and had jumped out a window.

Godfather had been lying to her. Godfather was the reason her mother was dead.

A man had stolen her father away, and Felicity was at home, alone.

No, not alone—with Patricia Plum and Dr. Victor.

As these facts settled within Clara, fear shocked her awake. She surged upright, ignoring the pain of her wounds as she clawed at the frozen ground for leverage. Her eyes had lost some of their heaviness; she saw snow, vast stretches of snow, and a murky sky dim with dawn. She assumed it was dawn, anyway, and wondered how long they had been unconscious after their fall.

"Father," she croaked. Nothing but white wilderness surrounded her. "Father!"

"Take my hand," Nicholas shouted, beaten halfway to the ground by the wind. His lips were white, splintering into brittle triangles of skin.

"Where is he?" She grabbed his arm, shaking him. "He's supposed to be here! Where did they take him?"

"I don't know—"

"You told me to jump through that Door, and now we're here." Clara was frantic. The cold was making her teeth chatter; the pain in her head stabbed her behind the eyes. "Tell me where he is!"

Nicholas held her still. "I said I don't know, but I do know this—we'll die if we don't get out of this cold soon. We need to find shelter. Take my hand."

When Clara reluctantly agreed, he pulled her closer and pressed his cheek to hers.

"I promise you, Clara," he said, and even this close Clara could barely hear him over the howling wind, "we will find him. But we're no good to him dead."

She nodded, put her arm around him, and let him do the same to her. They rose to their feet with great effort. Huddled close like some two-headed monster, they stumbled forward, their free hands up to shield their eyes. Lightning flashes, high above the snowy gusts and colored a strange, sickly green, illuminated their path. They walked for an interminable amount of time, stumbling through knee-high snowdrifts, futilely searching through the storm for a haven. They could have been walking in circles, and as the cold settled in even more deeply, numbing Clara with the temptation of sleep, she felt torn between tears and laughter. Dying in a blizzard, she supposed, was better than dying at the hands of Dr. Victor. She clung ferociously to such hysterical thoughts; they kept her feet moving.

A dark shape emerged, surfacing from frothy white depths like one of the sea serpents from Godfather's stories. Nicholas was pointing; he was gasping at her ear. It was shelter.

They stumbled inside after struggling to wedge open the door. It occurred to Clara that the place might already be occupied. It also occurred to her that she did not care. There had never been such a beautiful sight as this rickety shack and its floor of hard black dirt. Nicholas groped for the door, and pulled it shut behind them. They fumbled through the shack's contents, seeing by touch rather than by sight as their eyes adjusted to the darkness. Stacks of strange equipment lined the walls. There was a desk, a chair, an empty cup, but no signs of life.

Falling to her hands and knees, Clara coughed violently in the sudden stillness, as though her body had grown accustomed to the storm and could not function outside of it. Nicholas staggered down beside her. She turned, shaking, to see him heaving at her side. Even through her hazy vision she could see the angry colors on his face and chest—patches of yellows, reds, tinges of blues, the black metal. The storm had burned him—and her as well, she noticed, glancing down at her reddened arms.

"My skin . . . ," she murmured.

For a long moment Nicholas simply lay there with his eyes closed, recovering. Then he said quietly, "We should take off our clothes."

She wanted to be horrified but was incapable of it, not with her limbs half-frozen.

"Why?" she said, watching him fumble with the sleeves of his coat, the buckle of his trousers, and the sword at his waist. At the last moment she remembered to look away. As if she hadn't seen him completely naked not an hour ago. As if nakedness mattered in such appalling cold.

"It's easier to stay warm skin to skin."

"How do you know that?"

Through the ice on his lashes, teeth chattering, he winked. "Everybody knows that, Clara."

Unsure how to respond, she kept silent. He knelt beside her, a mosaic of metal clamps and pale, wiry limbs, and started undoing the laces at her back.

She stiffened at the touch of his fingers; it was intimate, terribly so. "Let me do it," she said, trying to push him away, but she was fading, and so was he.

Nicholas released her at once; his voice was gentle, or maybe simply exhausted. "It'll be faster with two of us."

A pause, and Clara acquiesced, though her body was rigid with the urge to hide, to run from the sensation of this man unveiling her, piece by piece. She remembered at the last moment to hide the dagger that had been strapped to her thigh, before Nicholas could notice it, and she slipped it into one of her boots. The less he knew about her weapons, the better. She might have jumped out a window with him, but he was still a stranger, even if his face did look like the statue's had, even if his hands were soft upon her as he settled on the floor and drew her close.

At first all was awkward silence. Clara still wore her chemise, but it did little to dull the sensation of Nicholas's palms against her back. Dimly she registered her breasts pressing into his chest, his thigh draped over hers. The metal plates along his spine creaked when he shifted his weight.

"Do you know where we are?" she whispered at last, into his neck.

He was quiet for a moment. "I'm not certain," he said, sounding frustrated. "Perhaps when the storm clears up . . ."

Clara burrowed into him, trying not to think of her father, lost somewhere in the cold with his abductor, nor of Felicity, being tucked back into bed by Dr. Victor at the mansion, or of Godfather, wherever he was. Had he tried to follow them? Was he here, somewhere out in the snow?

Did she care?

She closed her eyes, trying not to think of them, and trying not to think of herself in an embrace with this man, barer than she liked to be even when alone. She reached desperately for the forced calm that had seen her through the ribbon-cutting ceremony.

"We can't sleep for long," she said. "I don't have much time to get him home."

Nicholas's lips were cold at her ear. "We'll wait for the storm to pass. No longer."

Clara would have to be satisfied with that. She listened for his heartbeat—faint but steady against her cheek—and wondered if it had beat these long years, encased in metal in Godfather's shop, or if it had been frozen along with his body. Restless, exhausted, fear hard in her chest, she felt the heavy blackness of sleep approach, and let it take her.

11

Clara awoke to the sound of a train.

Her eyes flew open. She waited for the horn to sound again, but perhaps it had been the fragments of a dream, and anyway there was a more pressing matter—the body beside her, *on top* of her.

She tasted metal on her tongue.

Ah, yes. Nicholas—his weight half atop her; his lean arms trapping her; his bare torso, crisscrossed with steel, pressed against hers in a curious mixture of harsh lines and warm flesh. When she shifted her weight, her forehead brushed against the edge of the steel plate that curved beneath his right ear.

"Did you hear it too?" came a soft voice at her cheek.

"Hear what?" She sounded breathless; she *felt* breathless.

"The horn." Then, with the hint of a tease: "You're blushing."

Mortification swept through Clara's body in waves. "You're awake."

"Quite, in fact."

She scooted away and fumbled for her clothes, her abused body protesting.

Nicholas pulled on Godfather's greatcoat, shaking out flakes of ice. "Clara, I wasn't peeking or anything. Don't you know me at all?"

She glared at him over her shoulder, incredulous. "No, I don't."

A flicker of hurt, quickly hidden. "I know *you*. More than most, I would think."

"And I'm supposed to believe that?"

"You've a penchant for coffee," he said at once, his eyes carefully turned away from her as they dressed. "You twine your hair around your fingers when you're thinking. You once told me you had dreamed of marrying Drosselmeyer, and that the idea was disturbing but also made you feel safe, and you never felt safe when you were awake." He paused to give her a soft smile. "Except when you were in the shop, with me."

All those years of whispers in the shadowed corner, of stolen kisses to metal. The disturbing realization that Nicholas knew so much about her, that he had for years been a spy upon her life, left her feeling unnerved, and even outraged. It was one thing to have imagined him alive, and quite another to know he *had* been. Of course, that wasn't entirely fair. As if he could help being stuck there, having no choice but to watch.

Or had he had a choice? What, exactly, had brought him to Godfather's shop? Why had he been trapped there, and how? A startling thought arose: Was he as much to blame for her mother's death as Godfather? Or perhaps it was not about blame. Perhaps it was horrible, unavoidable circumstance and she should forgive them.

She shook off the unanswerable questions; they could wait. "You heard it too?"

"The train horn?" He nodded. "But it couldn't have been."

"And why not?" Forgetting herself, Clara grabbed his hand. "Do you think my father might be on it?"

Nicholas was distracted, his eyes distant. "There are no trains in Cane. We made an express point of forbidding their construction and routinely destroyed any attempts."

"Cane? What's that?"

His face was troubled. "Cane is here. I think."

"Where is *here?*"

"It's a secret."

"Don't play games with me."

"I'm telling you the truth. It's one of the secret places left behind when your world was made. That's what our stories say. Not many people know about Cane, and those who do try to keep it that way." He raised a smug eyebrow; it made him look younger. "You see? The very definition of a secret."

Clara was unimpressed. "And those lights in the air? That Door?"

"A tricky piece of magic that not many can fashion, and for good reason."

He said it so matter-of-factly, as if such things were as natural as breathing. Clara inspected his face for evidence of a lie. Bitterly she said, "Godfather spoke of Doors sometimes. In his stories."

"Yes. I heard him tell you things over the years. True things. Not many of them, mixed up with nonsense, but still—true things."

"'Trust only those whose pow'r is true,'" Clara said, remembering a tale of a wandering man with tired feet, delirious from travel. "'Then wait for the lights—'"

"'And step on through.' A children's rhyme."

An uncertain thrill swept through her. "He's . . . He is from here, then? Like you?"

"Yes. We fled together but did not make it out before . . ." He gestured at himself. "Before we were hit."

It should have perhaps seemed stranger to Clara that Godfather was not of her world—but hadn't she entertained such fantasies as a girl, while watching him at work in the candlelight, when the shadows had played across his face?

Had he known, in those years, that her mother would die? And that he would then *lie* to Clara about it? The cowardice of it, the *selfishness.*

Afraid she would no longer love him, indeed. He was right to have feared it.

And utterly wrong. Even now her fury couldn't keep her from wishing he were near.

Her throat was tight. "He called you 'Your Highness.'"

"As well he should. I am—" He paused, his mouth twisting. "Or I should say, I *was* a prince, before."

"Prince." She could not keep the skepticism from her voice. "The prince of Cane, I assume?"

He crossed his arms, regarding her. "Don't be flippant. It's unbecoming."

"And what does 'before' mean?"

"Previously. In the past. Formerly."

"Don't be flippant. It's unbecoming."

He nearly smiled. "Do you know, I've always wondered what it would be like to argue with you."

"I'm serious."

"'Before' means just that—before I left, before I arrived in your city. Before the coup, before the war. Before."

Coups. *Wars*. Could Godfather have been involved in such a thing? "I see."

"Do you?"

"Yes. And do you know what I think?"

"What's that?"

Clara fetched her corset, undoing its laces to save for later. They might come in handy, and she certainly wasn't going to wear the thing. Too restrictive. "I think I *should* think you're mad—you and Godfather—but I don't think that, and even if I did, I can't do anything about it, because I need you to find my father."

Nicholas seemed pensive. "Need. Yes. It's a curious thing, isn't it?"

A flash of something out in the snow, a whip of noise, caught their attention. Clara's eyes shot toward the door, and she reached for the dagger hidden in the shaft of her boot.

"What is that? I saw a figure."

"As did I." Nicholas's eyes went to her blade. A smile pulled at his mouth. "Ah, your many daggers."

Clara drew her lips tight and tossed her ravaged corset into the corner.

"Poor forsaken undergarment," Nicholas said. There was *laughter* in his voice. "Of what crime is it guilty?"

Glaring at the back of his head, Clara tugged on her boots and pressed the mechanisms on her heels. The hilts popped out with their familiar clicks; she shoved them back into place, reassured. Her third dagger she kept out and ready instead of returning it to the strap at her thigh.

"I'm not in the mood for jokes," she said tightly.

"I hope you're in the mood for breakfast," Nicholas said, peering out a filthy window Clara had not noticed before. The world beyond was quiet and pale. Morning? "We might have found some."

It was not breakfast.

It was, in fact, so utterly the opposite of breakfast that, when they had gotten close enough to see it clearly, Clara yanked a stunned Nicholas behind a tree that had been felled by the storm. There, shielded by branches draped in ice, they watched. Clara held her dagger at the ready, unable to tear her eyes away from the scene before them.

"What is it?" she whispered.

But Nicholas seemed paralyzed with horror. "Sinndrie save us."

"Creature" was too kind a word for it, this aberration that should have been a deer. But with frayed wires bulging from its haunches and an unblinking, whirring white eye, it could hardly be called that. Matted brown fur gave way to an ever-shifting mass of black tubules and weakly flickering lights, of mechanized claws where hooves should have been. It was half-alive, and half automaton.

It paused, eye spinning, foreleg raised, on a ridge past where Clara and Nicholas hid. Across the way, hidden in a grove of trees, a group of human figures crouched, clothed in snow-dusted hides and furs. One of them shifted; a branch cracked. The deer jerked into motion, a metal fan embedded in its throat humming wetly to life, but before it could escape, an arrow shot out from the trees and struck its chest.

The creature brayed, its call marred by some wavering mechanized note, as though the sound had been *manufactured*. The thing collapsed, its legs buckling under. The hunters sprang out from their hiding places and cleaved it to pieces with crude axes.

Then a part of the creature more laden with metal and cogs than fur and meat separated itself from the corpse and began crawling away, spiderlike. A hulk of living metal come to awful life.

Some of the hunters pounced on it with savage cries, hacking madly. The others remained with the corpse, digging into the animal's innards, scooping steaming raw meat into their mouths.

"Nicholas . . . ," Clara whispered, desperate to break free of the moment.

But he said nothing, his hand hard on her wrist, and then someone began to scream.

The skittering hunk of metal had dissolved into tiny black shapes, blue light sparking angrily between them, and these shapes had climbed up one hunter's legs, his belly, his arms.

They ate him. There was no better word for it. They swarmed over his body, and the faint buzzing of a thousand tiny mechanical mouths burrowed under Clara's skin. Wherever they moved, hard blackness melted out behind them.

Like Godfather's dragons, Clara thought, remembering the transformed ballroom—except the dragons had seemed benevolently industrious, and these creations reeked of cruelty.

Silence fell abruptly. Where there had once been a screaming man now stood a misshapen black statue, molten lumps where his eyes had been.

Frozen in a final contortion of agony, he toppled over and hit the snow.

The other hunters watched, emotionless, wolfing down their meal. They had done nothing to help him. The sounds of their slurping echoed inhumanly through the white woods.

"The mechaniks," Nicholas breathed. "It's *her*."

Clara ripped her gaze from the hunter-turned-statue; it reminded her, awfully, of what Nicholas had so recently been, and the similarity struck her as a terrible portent. "What did you call them? Mechaniks?"

"We didn't build trains. We didn't build weapons or drawbridges or clocks. We destroyed those that already existed. They would make us too vulnerable. She would find them, sink her magic into them like teeth, bring them to life, and turn them against us. . . ."

Nicholas grew agitated, his eyes bright. Clara tried to quiet him before the hunters heard, but one of them raised his bloodied face, tilted his head, doglike. His skin was haggard and windburned.

"Nicholas, *hush*."

He gripped the metal plate around his wrist, tried to rip it from his flesh. "Get it off—she'll wake them up!"

Clara clamped a hand over his mouth, tightening her grip on her dagger, but it was unnecessary. The hunter who had raised his head straightened and looked to the horizon. His eyes widened. He whistled to the others and pointed into the whiteness.

Like a flock of birds, the hunters scattered, leaving behind red snow, tufts of fur, and their blackened companion.

Clara heard it before she saw it—a horn, and a distant rhythmic churning. She turned toward where the hunter had pointed.

Now, the storm gone, she could see that beyond their shack—which was some sort of way station?—stretched a long, rocky ridge, and railroad tracks. Beyond even that, at some distance and ghostly in the mist, stood an immense wall of shifting shadows.

And, far to the right, a steady blue light.

The train that had woken Clara approached.

12

Nicholas took two staggering steps back.

"No, no," he muttered, "not that. Not a train."

Ignoring him, Clara tucked her dagger back into its sheath and squinted to the east—at least, if that was where the sun rose in this place. The railroad tracks were not far from them; if they hurried, they could intercept the train, which would surely take them near some kind of civilization. Maybe her father was even on board? Unlikely. Too convenient to consider. And even if they somehow managed to climb aboard without killing themselves, there was no way to guess what the train held, and if it would be even more dangerous than blizzards and barbarous hunters.

Too tremendous a gamble—were her family's lives not at stake.

Resigning herself to it, Clara straightened her posture, steeling herself.

Nicholas pulled her toward the shack and pressed them both flat against the wall and out of sight. "I know what you're thinking. Yes, we have to leave here, but not like this. We can't trust it."

"The train?"

"It will listen to her. It will do whatever she wants it to." He leaned his head back against the wall, squeezing his eyes shut. "We can't trust it, mustn't trust it."

Her again. "Are you talking about Anise?"

Nicholas opened his eyes, his expression sharp. "What do you know about Anise?"

"Nothing except that she exists, that Godfather was taunting her in the ballroom. Although, of course, no one was there but me. The man who took Father, Borschalk, also mentioned a woman, twice." She paused, frustrated. If the train had not been approaching, she would have sat Nicholas down in that shack and demanded to know everything about the mysterious Anise. "I spoke to one of the loks about her. I didn't know what I was saying, but it seemed distracted by my words anyway."

"As though it were listening to instructions from far away?" Nicholas suggested darkly.

"As though it didn't realize who I was, and then it did." She paused, thinking. "Or perhaps *she* did."

Nicholas was silent, staring inscrutably at the sky.

Clara turned away, watching the train's approach. "If she has my father, I must find her."

"What would Anise want with your father?"

His skeptical tone nettled her. "You tell me, *Your Highness*."

After a pause Nicholas came quietly to her side. "It's not traveling quickly. If we stay close to the ridge and run alongside the tracks, we should be able to jump on board without anyone seeing us."

"Agreed."

"It will hurt."

"Undoubtedly." Clara glanced at him, tall and silent beside her. "Those mechaniks. That's what you called them, the tiny mechanical things. They frightened you, didn't they?"

He raised his hand between them, his eyes haunted. "They *are* me. Or at least, they were."

"That's what happened to you, isn't it?" Saying it aloud made her earlier assumption even more grotesque. "You were eaten alive by those . . . mechaniks."

His silence confirmed it. She shook her head. "I don't understand. How do they do that?"

"Faery magic," he said, the words full of hate.

The horn sounded once more. The great black train was much closer now, and it had no windows. Only smokestacks and blank walls.

She grabbed Nicholas's hand, trying not to imagine those hundreds of black monsters enveloping him, sealing him away. "Are you strong enough to run?"

He raised an eyebrow. "I *am* a prince, you know. The epitome of chiseled athleticism."

She almost smiled. "I suppose you haven't had the chance to look in a mirror yet."

"Such flagrant rudeness."

They ran for it, alongside the tracks but never too close. Clara was loath to get too near the train itself. She felt the gaze of unseen eyes upon her, and was that faint, feminine laughter in the air?

It will listen to her, Nicholas had said. *It will do whatever she wants it to.*

Clara wrenched her thoughts from speculation about Anise and concentrated on speed. It was fortunate that Godfather had insisted she always train in her boots; she might have fallen otherwise, or twisted an ankle. But her vision still spotted as they ran, and beside her Nicholas's breaths came raggedly. He had been correct; the train was slow, as though weighed down by massive cargo. But they needed food, bandages, rest. Even with the train traveling so slowly, they might not be strong enough to make it.

At the caboose an open platform surrounded by dark railings awaited them. Clara closed her eyes as they neared it and said a prayer to whatever gods reigned in Cane that this was the right decision, that this would lead them to her father.

She tried not to think of how many hours had passed back at home. How long had she been gone? Six hours? Seven? She fought through the fear such thoughts triggered; to survive this she had to be one with the shadows, one with the cold, one with the ache of her body. Betrayal or no, Godfather had at least helped her learn that much.

Beside her Nicholas increased his speed. Before Clara could react, he took a running leap toward the rear platform. His body slammed against the railing, and she winced, but he held tight and pulled himself over with a cry. He grinned back at her, though his face was pale with exhaustion and he leaned hard against the railing. "See? Prince-like agility, even under duress."

Clara bristled. Such arrogance. Agility? More like an ungainly stab of luck. Her irritation galvanized her, and she used the short burst of speed to leap up after him, her eyes trained on the railing as though it were a target to be struck. A great crash as she hit the railing; she knocked her head against it, and her vision spun. The toes of her boots hit the tracks and dragged, nearly unbalancing her. But Nicholas had caught her arms, his grip painful but steady. Her feet found the bottom ledge of the car, and together they pulled her on board.

The train jerked, knocking her into Nicholas's arms and out of the path of an arrow that shot out from the dim morning. Thick and black, it struck a hatch on the train car, embedding itself in the metal. Tiny black legs sprang out from the arrow's head and dug into the hatch as if it were flesh and the arrow an insect. Blue energy crackled along the arrow's shaft, electrifying the hairs on Clara's skin.

From somewhere out in the white wilderness, savage cries sounded.

Clara moved toward Nicholas, automatically, until they stood back to back, eyes alert. Her fingers curled at her thigh, above her dagger. When she saw what approached from the west, her heart sank—monstrous shapes, pale on top and dark below. As they neared, they came into awful definition.

The dark shapes were loks, dotted with lights and covered in armor, darting toward the train as they had through the mansion's ballroom. Here, however, they seemed more at home; they bounded through the snow as if it were nothing. Atop them rode pale, ghostly people. They carried spears in their hands, tipped blue with electric power. Their battle cries were high and strong, and they were, even from this distance, arrestingly beautiful.

"Nicholas, what are they?" Clara said, although she thought she knew. "Do you know?"

"Oh, yes." His face was grim. "They're faeries."

13

Nicholas turned to the hatch.

"There's no handle," he said. "Just a lock."

Clara could not tear her eyes from the sight of the faeries' approach. Their movements were brutal, elegant. Their battle cry was almost a song, a chorus of unearthly beauty. They moved silently through the snow in a V formation. At the point was a figure that looked more familiar than the rest, though he no longer wore the ragged clothing of the day before.

Borschalk.

The last time she had seen him, he had dragged her father out the window by his collar. Now he rode a lok, shouting foreign commands—and her father was nowhere to be found.

But if she closed her eyes, as she suddenly so wanted to do, maybe she would be better able to hear the faeries' high, keening cries. Maybe she could decipher them somehow, and hear if they spoke of her father—

"Clara!" Nicholas snapped.

She turned to look at him, bewildered. "What do you want?"

Nicholas's mouth thinned. "So you're not immune to their charm. Try not to listen to them too closely. They'll catch up soon."

"Charm?"

"All magic-dealing folk have it." He yanked back his sleeve, thrusting his arm toward her. "Hurry. Take out this pin on my forearm. It looks about the right size."

Clara hesitated—surely it would hurt. His arm was an angry mass of damaged skin and black metal. But there was no time for kindness. She set her jaw, grasped the pin, and pulled.

The sensation of the pin's grooves dragging against bone and whatever metal still lay within him made Clara hiss through her teeth. Nicholas cursed hoarsely.

A second black arrow shot past them, and it too embedded itself in the train car. The faeries' cries had escalated into a frenzy.

"Pick the lock," Nicholas urged; his face had lost what little color it had. "Quickly."

Clara started to work. The keyhole was miniscule, set in some sort of iron plate. Without a handle to apply leverage, it was difficult to find where the pins would give and yield to the pick in her hand. Sweat dripped down her back.

"Clara," Nicholas warned, drawing his sword.

"Almost!"

A third arrow hit the wall beside her, and a tendril of hot blue energy licked across her cheek. She cried out and clapped a hand to her face. It came away covered in crystalline residue, flecked with iron. Another arrow hit, and another careened off the railing; the air thrummed with them.

A thud shook the platform. Clara and Nicholas whirled to see a figure crouched on top of the railing. A white face with high cheekbones and unnaturally long, slender ears; white hair knotted in dreadlocks, threaded with pieces of steel and black glass. Metal bands at the forehead and upper arms, inlaid with gems, giving their bearer an air of royalty. An iron helmet, a lithe body clothed in black leather cords and dark trousers and black boots.

Two piercing blue eyes.

"Borschalk," Clara gasped.

In response Borschalk leered.

Clara returned to the lock as Nicholas whipped his sword across

Borschalk's face. Borschalk roared, losing his footing, clinging to the railing.

Something in the lock clicked and gave way. The door cracked open, and Clara grabbed Nicholas's arm and pulled him through it. He kicked it shut behind them, and they ran.

Something pounded on the door behind them, denting its surface. Blue lights illuminated the door's seams. Black arrowheads bled straight through the metal, carving their way in with pincers.

A weight fell onto the roof above them, making the car shudder on the tracks. Nicholas pulled Clara through stacks of crates wrapped with chains, canvas-draped parcels, metal barrels marked with familiar symbols—from the statue, from her mother's corpse. Faery symbols.

A circular blue light glowed through the ceiling, blinking rapidly; a high-pitched whine began to sound, increasing in volume.

Nicholas saw it, cursed, threw Clara behind a stack of crates and himself down over her.

A portion of the ceiling burst open, spewing shards of metal with blue electricity crackling after them. A charred metal disc—some sort of explosive?—clattered to the ground.

Two faeries dropped down from the ceiling. The first had barely touched the ground when he raised his arm—encased in black metal like a scabrous glove, wires wrapped around his biceps and ending somewhere in the flesh of his back. A nodule atop his knuckles snapped upright like one of Godfather's clockwork mechanisms and blinked a rapid blue.

Nicholas grabbed Clara's hand and yanked her behind a second stack of crates just as an electric bolt shot out from the faery's glove.

Clara dropped to her knees and pressed the catches on her boots, releasing the twin daggers in her heels.

Beside her Nicholas's eyes flashed in approval. "Are you well enough to fight?"

Honestly she did not know. "Are you?" He gave her a hard smile, and together they leapt out into the fray.

The first faery nearly felled her. Her legs were unsteady, her senses overwhelmed, her confidence lacking. Her blade met the metal glove on his arm, the impact shooting off sparks. When she hesitated, he whipped his arm around and down. The movement flung her away from him, and he swung at her with his palm out. The hissing tubules on his fingers might have cut open her face, but she ducked in time and caught him with an underhand stroke of her dagger, thrusting the blade into his abdomen.

Bright blue blood gushed out over her hand, and the faery fell.

When he hit the ground, Clara paused, staring at him. His blood was hot on her hand, and she would have done it again if she had to, but she had never killed someone before. The lok was one thing, and horrifying enough, but this beautiful faery, with his muscled forearms and long-lashed eyes—he looked almost human.

More faeries were sliding in through the ceiling, and Clara forced herself to move.

She grabbed Nicholas, turned, and ran out of the caboose to the next car. She tried to get a good look at the surrounding country as they passed through the gap between cars, balancing precariously on swaying black couplings.

Faeries on either side. Faeries on loks.

"How many are there?" she cried.

Nicholas's eyes shone with battle fever—and, Clara thought, more than a bit of fear. "Just keep going!"

The door to the next car was unlocked and slid open easily. Clara hesitated; that seemed entirely too convenient. But they had no choice. Faeries followed them, raising their metal gloves, throwing their black spears. Clara managed to dodge them and almost fell, unbalanced. She tried to focus on the tug of Nicholas's grip and his voice urging her on, and not on how close she was to collapsing with exhaustion.

They pushed their way through that car and the next, past more of the same cargo, with no sign of John Stole nor of any other passengers but themselves. Explosives hit the roofs in their wake, tearing open the ceilings overhead in a cacophony of blue. None of it felt right. It was too easy, the faeries' pursuit too escapable. The explosions rained debris upon them, but never enough to slow their progress. Arrows flew at them carelessly, persistent but never hitting the marks. These faeries were soldiers, that was plain to see, and soldiers did not miss.

"It's too easy," she shouted to Nicholas.

His eyebrows shot up. "Easy? You can't be serious."

They emerged onto the next platform. Clara glanced to her right, ready to duck oncoming arrows. She saw the long black curve of the train winding its way through woodlands and meadows twisted with ice. Ahead of them, snaking alongside the tracks, was the immense wall Clara had seen from a distance. This close she could see the watchtowers topping it, and that it was mechanized, made of ever-shifting, ever-changing parts.

Nicholas struggled with the latch of the next car, then shouldered his way in.

Clara, uneasy, followed him.

In the sudden darkness it took her a moment to assess the situation—Borschalk towered over Nicholas and was flanked by four other faeries, all with terrible, satisfied grins. A slender bundle of black wiring blinked blue at Borschalk's ear. Clara's father was nowhere to be found. Unsurprising, but it added to Clara's sudden horrified despair; her knees nearly buckled.

"Drachstelle. I'm surprised you returned." Borschalk's words were harsh, as though this was not his native tongue. "Surprised, but glad to be the one to kill you. She will be pleased."

"Wouldn't she be more pleased," Nicholas said, stepping forward, "to do it herself?"

Clara watched, tense with readiness. She frantically scanned the car for a means of escape, and found none.

Borschalk's face twisted. "You know nothing of her desires."

"And I suppose you do? I remember you, in her guard. I remember your face." A hard quirk of his mouth. "Have you wormed your way into her bed at last?"

"Enough." Borschalk threw up his arm, his glove flaring brightly. Nicholas straightened and stood his ground, and the sight overwhelmed Clara with fear and rage. Something cold surged through her limbs, as though a primal switch had been thrown.

She rushed at Borschalk, ignoring Nicholas's cry of protest. She could not have stopped if she had wished to—overpowering instinct drove her forward. Her daggers fell, forgotten, from her hands. The air around her pulsed so violently that she gasped in pain—had the storm returned? She reached out to steady herself, to grab at nothing with both hands in one last, futile gesture. The detached realization came to her that she was about to die, and so was Nicholas, and so would her father and Felicity, and untold scores of New Yorkers in the grasp of Concordia, because she had not been there to save them—

—but then it was as if her clutching hands had tugged on something invisible, and tugging on that something was a trigger to turn the world inside out.

Winter invaded her blood.

Frigid wind pummeled her, cold seized her—tore *through* her—releasing an energy she had not known existed.

The ceiling exploded. The car lurched sideways and, with a horrible wrench, careened off its rails. The faeries flew out of the train, propelled by a howling wind that flung Nicholas off his feet and into the wall. He slumped to the floor, unmoving.

Only Borschalk remained, saved by his bulk and tenacity; his fingers bled, cut by the metal of the far wall, to which he clung. He stared at Clara for a moment—a probing, horrified look—and then leapt off the car. He hit the ground and rolled safely away.

She watched him flee, then looked at the hole through which he had exited the car, the realization coming slowly:

An entire portion of the far wall had been blown away.

Wind smacked against her face, ripping tears from her eyes. The front half of the train continued on, unharmed. But their car had gone off the tracks, derailing the cars behind it. They were still moving, headed straight for the great, shifting wall.

Clara threw herself over Nicholas's body and squeezed her eyes shut as the car began to roll over. She held on to him as hard as she could. She knew logically that she and Nicholas should both be flung around the car, or thrown from it altogether. Impaled upon metal. Knocked to bloody bits.

For all she knew, that was happening. Perhaps she was beyond pain; perhaps she had died.

With a shuddering lurch the train ground to a stop.

Abruptly the cold that had been surrounding her, whistling around her, whistling *inside* her, fell away.

She waited in the crackling silence. Impossibly, it seemed that she was alive. She smelled smoke and hot metal and snow. Nicholas lay beneath her, peaceful. She touched his throat, feeling through the web of metal there for his pulse. When she found it—rapid but steady—she murmured quick, relieved thanks to no one in particular.

Unsteadily she stood. Now she could see the true extent of the damage—the train car's ceiling had been blown completely off, and the walls had exploded outward in curls of metal, dark with burn marks, frosted with ice. What could have been strong enough to tear steel asunder?

Clara touched what was left of the low-hanging roof; the metal was incongruously freezing, her fingertips sticking to it. The contact gave her a slight shock. Odd. She examined her skin, and then the roof. She had been freezing too, in that moment when she had rushed at Borschalk, and it had been a different cold from that of winter outside—a wilder cold, heavier, more vibrant. There had been a storm, and winds. And then the car had exploded—*everything* had exploded—and the faeries had been flung out like rag dolls.

She stared out the ruined wall.

Behind them the back half of the train lay in charred ruins.

Impossible. The fear that came from witnessing something too inexplicable to be believed settled into her, and she swayed on her feet.

How had this happened?

If her father *had* been anywhere on this train, surely he was now burned to a crisp or had been bludgeoned by the force of the crash. But perhaps he had been elsewhere, stashed away for whatever ransom or blackmail his abductors had planned.

Please, *please* let him have been elsewhere.

Nearby cries pulled her reluctantly back into action. She crouched, blinking to clear her head of its shock, and peered out the train car toward the enormous wall looming to her left. The train had come to a halt not far from it, and she quailed to think what might have become of them had they collided with it. Figures ran out from the wall, shouting. Plates on the wall's surface shifted together and apart—knotting, stretching, knotting again. It reminded Clara, horribly, of Nicholas's statue-skin.

And Borschalk, not nearly far enough away for her to feel safe, sat mounted on a lok once more, watching her. The sight of him was so unexpected that she cried out and teetered, unbalanced. She fumbled around the car for her discarded daggers.

"Clara?" Nicholas's weak voice made her turn. "What happened?"

Clara hurried to him; never had she been so glad to hear a voice. She slipped her daggers back into her boots, patted her thigh to ensure the third was still intact. "Nicholas, I think Borschalk's coming back—"

"We've got to leave. Now." He struggled to his feet, swaying against her. "He'll kill us."

Clara looked back. Borschalk was close enough for her to see the expression on his face. It was more contemplative than Clara would have thought—cautious, even. He put a hand to the wires at his ear. He was listening to something; his gaze flickered over Clara curiously. Angrily.

Then he turned and slapped his lok's reins, and disappeared into the smoke.

14

Clara stared after Borschalk's retreating figure. He had abandoned them—why? He should have attacked them, now that they were vulnerable. He should have completed his mission. Was that not what soldiers did?

"Clara?" came Nicholas's strained voice.

Blood covered him, and ash; he leaned hard against her for balance, and if she hadn't been so afraid, she might have enjoyed the fact that for all his boasting of "agility under duress," she was the stronger one in this moment.

"The train," he said. "What happened to the train?"

She almost told him the truth, but something stopped her, an internal voice that sounded suspiciously like Godfather's.

The train had exploded for a reason, but until Clara knew that reason, she couldn't risk Nicholas's thinking she was mad. A mad girl was not worth helping.

But perhaps she *was* mad. Her fingertips tingled as though they had been frozen and were now thawing out. The air around her remained lightly charged; whatever force had swept over them had not gone far.

"One of the faeries discharged something," she heard herself saying. "Some sort of weapon. I didn't get a good look at it, but I suppose it was faulty. It exploded. There was a bright light, and something threw us back. Next thing I knew, our car had gone off the tracks and you were unconscious."

Nicholas's eyes found hers. They lingered, hard and strange, as though he saw something on her face he could not decipher. "What did it feel like when it happened?"

She frowned. A strange question. "It was cold, electric. There was a great wind, like a storm. I've never seen anything like it."

He turned away and raked a hand through his hair. "How many different weapons do the filthy beasts have?"

Light shot overhead, exploding in a fiery spray of blue. Movement nearby sounded as though others were approaching.

Their eyes met; without a word they crawled out the car's gaping back wall. The air was hot from the fires scattered throughout the wreckage. Smoke drifted everywhere, playing tricks, smothering the daylight. Hidden behind another car a few yards away, they watched as faeries uniformed in angular black searched the car they had just abandoned.

"My God." Clara sagged against the car's wall. "What if you hadn't woken?"

"But I did." Nicholas scanned the wall, jerked his head. "We'll make for that tunnel there. Do you see? In the wall."

Clara followed his gaze. Figures passed through a slim tunnel in the fluid black mass of the wall, emerging and disappearing. Shouts in a harsh, foreign language—faery language?—drifted from it. Lights shone at its edge, blinking rhythmically.

"You can't be serious," Clara hissed. "Someone will see us!"

"Do you see another way through?"

No. There was no other way. *Godfather dearest,* she thought grimly, *let's hope your sneaking lessons work as well in Cane as in New York.*

"No," she admitted, and stepped out from their cover. They slunk through the debris, flattening themselves against steaming metal, picking their way through spoiled cargo. As they reached the wall, a pair of faeries passed close by, and Clara and Nicholas paused, silent in the shadows. Clara looked back at the tumbled ruins of the great train, at the crooked woodlands not far from the tracks, lined with snow and now flickering with fire. A storm was building on the horizon. Multicolored lightning flashed, and the ground beneath them quaked gently. Ash rained down from the wall, as though knocked loose by the tremor.

Hidden somewhere in this horrid, strange beauty was her father—she hoped. She *had* to hope.

She looked up the wall's great height. "What if we're going the wrong way? What if Father's back there, in the wilderness?"

"Trust me," Nicholas said darkly, "if he's with the faeries, he isn't in the wilderness."

Clara watched him for a moment as they waited for more faeries to pass.

"When we're somewhere safe," she said, struggling to steady her voice, "and we've a moment to rest, I will have many questions to ask you, and I hope, for your sake, that you will answer me."

Nicholas glanced at her, half his attention on the tunnel. "Is that a threat, Clara?"

"I don't want to hurt you, but if you hinder the search for my father in any way, I will, without hesitation."

"I believe you." He smirked, ducking low so that their eyes met. "Just remember: I know all your best moves. Not much else to do in that shop but observe."

Her mouth thinned. "That's not fair."

"Don't worry. On a good day you're the tiniest bit better than me."

"On a *good* day?"

"When you don't let your fear and doubt get the best of you."

Clara started to protest but then subsided. The truth of his words shamed her, left her feeling shrunken and exposed. "It's unjust that you should know me and my faults so well," she said quietly, "when I don't know you and yours at all."

"You'll know them soon enough. I'm crammed full of them." His voice was light, but his face was full of secrets. "There—they've stopped. Go. Hurry."

She did, staying close to the tunnel's walls and its shadows, and through her gown she could feel the cold metal touch of Nicholas's hand on her back.

On the other side of the tunnel—after an excruciating half hour of sneaking past walls that shifted like monstrous membranes ready to burst, and holding their breaths so passing faeries would think them merely shadows—they emerged into a world of light.

Fields and oceans of lights, bridges and thoroughfares of lights. Buildings taller than Clara had ever seen, edged with parades of lights.

It was a city, she supposed—but New York was a city, and this was nothing like that.

High above them, in the distance, steel lattices wove through the sky. A faint line of motion, there, on that curving black bridge—yet another train, this one sleeker, blinking. Train whistles filled the air, a discordant symphony. Against the churning blue-green storm clouds, dark birds circled, but they did not move like ordinary birds. They were quieter, more precise. When one of them perched atop a pole from which tangles of wires stretched every which way, Clara saw near its long beak bright eyes, blinking blue.

And beneath the lights lay a pile of a city. Even from here Clara could smell its stink—sweat, and fish, and flesh. Crumbling brick buildings; long, low warehouses of dark stone. Brightly lit signs flashed foreign words in a thousand different colors. At the city's edge a canal of black water glistened, topped with crude, rusted bridges. Hovels clustered at their bases, sagging shantytown villages. Fresh snow frosted everything; dirty snow lined the gutters, the railroad, the water.

From within the din of trains came a murmuring roar of shouting, movement, music.

Laughter.

Screams.

People were everywhere—crossing the bridges, hanging laundry from rooftops, peddling wares from street carts. Some were dark and some were pale, and some were faeries, patrolling on loks.

Past the canal a tall, slender building shuddered. A rolling wave of black surged across it. Horror fluttered in Clara's throat at the sight. Nicholas flinched and grabbed her hand—to protect her, or himself?

"The mechaniks?" she whispered.

"Watch them" was his terse reply.

Shrieks sounded from within the building, and the entire structure collapsed, like a child's tower of blocks being knocked to the ground in a fit of pique. The debris rumbled blackly and then surged upward, reforming, rebuilding. When silence fell, a new building stood in its place—taller, serrated, elaborate, embellished with pillars and balconies, porticoes and minarets and winged iron figures with lolling tongues. Bridges lashed off the building and affixed themselves to the buildings adjacent.

Was that an echo of delicate laughter, winding delightedly through the air?

Before Clara could get a fix on it, it had stopped. Wails of grief rose in the distance, but everything else was still. If they had exited the tunnel a few minutes later, she would have thought that building had always stood there.

The blue-eyed bird rustled its feathers. They clanged together, suspiciously metallic; it squawked and flew away.

Clara felt faint and unbalanced; she did not want to think of what had happened to anyone inside that building. And Nicholas's face, to her dismay, was that of a lost child—overwhelmed, disbelieving. Clara recognized that expression of loss and the accompanying fury of being helpless to stop it.

"Nicholas, what is it?" she said carefully. "What is this place?"

"She's done it," he whispered, "just like she said she would. I had hoped she wouldn't be able to, but . . ."

Clara touched his arm. "This *is* Cane, isn't it? Your home?"

"It's Cane, but it isn't my home, not anymore." His voice was bleak, as though something essential had been drained from him. "It's theirs. Cane now belongs to the faeries."

15

At the despair on Nicholas's face, Clara felt the strength bleed from her. A land crawling with ravenous machines. A land ruled by the *faeries*. The rescue of her father seemed increasingly impossible.

"Are you sure?" she prodded. "Maybe you're wrong."

Nicholas flung out his hand at the city. "You saw the mechaniks, Clara. You know what they can do. This is what we fought against for generations, and now it's happened. I know what I see, and I know what it means."

Clara could see panic unfolding across him, the same that she felt in her own heart. She drew on something deep and Godfather-bred within her, and focused her thoughts.

"Well, we can't stay here," she said. "If we stay, we'll be seen."

"And where shall we go? In *there*?" He glared at the city.

"Yes, in there. We can find answers, food, and shelter."

"Clara, I don't know what that city is! Do you understand that?" He grabbed her shoulders, his eyes bright with grief. "I don't know what awaits us in there. The home I knew is gone now."

"You don't know that. There's bound to be something familiar to you here, something that can help us." She forced a smile she did not feel and clasped his arms; with their bodies touching, she felt steadier. "Are all princes this fatalistic?"

After a moment his scowl broke. He wiped his face with his sleeve. "You always did know how to make me laugh," he said ruefully, "even though no one could hear it."

What a painful thing to imagine, his lonely, trapped laughter. "Come. We've got to keep moving."

They crept toward the city through a narrow field dotted with choked undergrowth and crude roadways, down which faery soldiers patrolled and moved equipment to and from the wall. Gnarled trees shone as though carved from black glass, and their branches seemed to murmur unknowable words. The storming skies emanated a strange half-light; it was still day—or at least Clara thought so—but it did not look it.

They crossed the canal at the city's edge by way of an ugly iron bridge stained with unidentifiable congealed . . . *remains,* Clara guessed. She could not avoid stepping in them, and her bile rose at each squelch of her boots. On the other side of the bridge, Nicholas stopped. His body sagged as if burdened with fresh weight. When Clara followed his gaze, her first shameful thought was not of the pitiful sight before her but of herself: *We cannot linger here. We cannot draw their attention.*

The people here, in the slums on the other side of the canal, had sunken cheeks and eyes either sharp with desperation or horribly vacant. Clara was not sure which disturbed her more. Their postures were hunched, their strides halting and broken. Ugly bruises clouded their skin, green and blue and mottled black to match the sky.

Most notably, they were not faeries; they were *human.*

Nicholas drew his coat tighter around his body.

"Don't look at them," Clara murmured, afraid.

He understood, and trudged along, staring at his feet. She ducked her head and did the same. Even half-frozen and wounded, they were less . . . *stretched* than these people, not so hollow and spider-thin. These people were wraithlike, somehow both brittle and unnaturally languid, poking at their fires listlessly, gnawing on hard strings of gray meat.

One of them, a man with sickly copper skin that might have once been beautiful, lay on a bed of rags, hair piled on his head in discolored hunks. As he pressed a grimy canister to his arm, his eyes met Clara's. A silver needle entered his flesh; he closed his eyes and let out a moan.

Beneath his skin something shot through his arm, glowing.

When the man opened his eyes, they swam with unnatural color. A wan light filled his face. He smiled, wet his lips.

"Nicholas," Clara whispered.

He looked revolted. "I saw."

A young woman approached them. Oil and paint smeared her skin; charcoal smudged her eyes in messy streaks.

"A silver for a tumble, mister?" she said, sidling up to Nicholas. Her hands, too frail and thin for such a young person, clutched his coat desperately. Her eyes were red; misery pinched her face. "Or you?" She turned to Clara. "You like girls? I'm good with girls. The faeries say I'm good with girls. Just been onstage at the outer houses, but you've still got to be good enough, or they won't let you in. What do you think? Five coppers? Four? It's a steal."

Even as Clara shrank away from this woman, she couldn't help but ask: "What's happened to you?"

The woman glared at Clara, indignant, and drew herself up. "You ain't no treat yourself, love."

Gently Nicholas pried the woman's hands from his coat. "I'm sorry, but I don't have anything to give you. Why don't you go on home?"

He smiled at her, but the woman spat at his feet. A man covered with sores whistled at her from a nearby hut, and her eyes lit up with frenzied relief. She left them there, but her voice, cooing vile suggestions at the man, followed Clara into the city.

It was chaos there.

Apartments atop apartments, shops over shops—in too-tall, too-narrow rows, teetering beneath the weight of disproportion. A vast marketplace, churning with hawkers and peddlers, sprawled across twisting roadways striped with oil. Streetcars embellished with iron scrollwork spewed black smoke, and clusters of railways stretched high above like the bars of an enormous cage. Throughout, a grid of canals in garish colors stank of chemicals. Every door, every rooftop and shop cart, seemed merely a shell for what lay underneath—wires, gears, rods, pistons, as though machinery were the city's blood and bone, holding everything together. They tumbled out of the sides of buildings, lined the cobbled walks, blinked blue lights from the throats of disfigured animals pulled from the water by blank-eyed fishermen. Large, flat pieces of glass hung everywhere—affixed to buildings, hanging from slender iron posts, connected to the city's mechanical underbelly with thick clusters of wires. Phosphorescent liquid bubbled and flowed across the glass surfaces smoothly, forming images, broadcasting sound. Clara tried not to gape. How could such a thing possibly be constructed?

Throngs of people pressed close to her and Nicholas, and shouldered brutishly past. Everything stank—of sweat, decay, and something sweetly chemical. Clara tried not to gag on the smell, on the nearness of countless bodies. Fingers slithered past her, shoulders knocked against her, eyes roved over her body, her clothes, her face. Some of them leered; some merely appraised her.

An alarming thought came to her, and she glanced at Nicholas. His face was open, shattered, as though he had completely forgotten the possibility of danger. Clara sympathized: if he was telling the truth about this place having once been his home, she supposed the shock of seeing something that should have been familiar so thoroughly turned on its head was a horrible one.

If he was telling the truth.

"Nicholas?" She hooked her arm through his, pulled him close for privacy. A necessary thing, but even now, in this awful moment, she felt suddenly bashful. "You said you were a prince, before. Will you be recognized?"

Nicholas seemed to shake himself. "Drosselmeyer had a theory," he said under his breath. "Others did too. Magic folk and scholars. That the passage of time in Cane differs from the passage of time Beyond."

"Beyond?"

"Your world." He smiled faintly. "As mythical to us as Cane would be to you, I think. Most people don't believe in it. Stories you tell your children."

Clara stopped, gutted by a sudden dreadful thought. A muttering man swathed in waste-crusted clothes ran into them and began cursing at the top of his lungs, but Clara hardly noticed. She pulled Nicholas out of the way, in front of a lopsided building where a row of squashed stalls seemed to denote the site of a marketplace. At one of the stalls, a young boy held out a bowl, into which an old woman spooned brown slop. A surge of hunger nearly made Clara stumble, but first she had to ask:

"Do you mean to tell me that we've been here not even a day," she whispered, "but more time than that could have passed back in New York?"

"I don't know. They're only theories, I told you." Nicholas watched the old woman's stall from beneath his hair. "But I can tell you this: when I left, there were few in Cane who would not know my face, as often as I traveled during the war. And no one has recognized me today, not even that woman in the slums."

Clara struggled for calm. "So that could mean that more time has passed here than has in New—in Beyond. Maybe *much* more time. Surely at least some people would know their prince even after . . . how many years away?"

"Eighteen. And you're right, unless everyone alive during my reign is dead." He let out a soft, broken laugh. His eyes shone with an anguish Clara understood well. Loss, horrible loss. Pain and anger, and the world being pulled out from beneath one's feet.

If he was pretending, she decided, he was an astonishing actor. She recognized the look of grief; at home she had worn it like a second skin. But before she could respond, a man with one eye and oil-matted hair shoved them apart.

"Either you're a payin' customer," he said, his voice low and rattling, "or you get out of the way."

Behind him the old woman serving slop glared at them; an old scar, lumpy as though from a wound poorly stitched, stretched across her cheek.

Nicholas looked bored, but Clara saw his hand drift toward his sword. "How much?" he said, disinterested.

"Five coppers. Each."

Clara pulled the jewels from her ears. "Here. What about these?" She tried to follow Nicholas's lead and imitate the man's slurred accent. "Worth more than five coppers, I'll bet."

The one-eyed man pocketed the earrings with a grunt and nodded at the old woman. She returned to her ladling with a frown, and then the one-eyed man was thrusting at them two bowls of steaming, porridge-colored . . . "soup" seemed too generous a word.

"Eat fast and then move on." The one-eyed man leaned closer, his breath putrid. "And don't try to steal those bowls, neither, or you'll regret you was ever born."

They began to eat, too hungry to respond to the man's threat, or to care that they had to eat with their hands—burning their fingers, dribbling slop that tasted vaguely of dirt onto their chins. As they slurped it down, the crowd in the marketplace shoved past them, an ever-moving tide of human misery dotted with faery splendor. Clara saw more soldiers, wealthy-looking faeries in fine clothes edged with grime, and even faery children—led by their parents, extravagantly costumed, their faces exquisitely indifferent as humans parted to make way for them.

Clara's attention returned to the one-eyed man. He stood sentinel a few paces away, arms folded. *One eye.* Though he couldn't have been more different from him, she thought of Godfather anyway. Her heart, betrayed as it was, ached for his arms about her, the cadence of his voice as he rattled off some ludicrous joke. An awful image—of Godfather trapped between worlds, stuck in some magical limbo from the Door closing on him as he had tried to follow them—made her shudder, even as another part of her twinged with guilty satisfaction at the thought. Maybe he deserved such a fate, for contributing to her mother's death.

Even as she thought that, she didn't believe it. She looked at her hands for anchor. Misery, like a blade in her heart. Misery and fury and a horrible lack—a lack of Godfather, her life's one constant.

"He's not what you think he is, you know."

Clara was gratified to see Nicholas flinch when she glared up at him. "Who are you talking about?"

"You know." He tilted his bowl, drinking down the last of his soup. The one-eyed man was watching them; they talked in pieces, low, lips hardly moving. "Drosselmeyer. At court they called him the king's fool, and he went along with it. To lower people's expectations, I think. And I know he was the same to you—a foolish uncle you turned to when you felt like escaping from the world. But I know the real him, for good or ill."

Rankled, she stiffened. "He's brilliant, and he loves me."

"Yes," he said quietly. "Whatever else I might say about him, I can't deny that you were everything to him."

Oh, horrible, horrible lack. *Godfather.* She wanted to cry but refused to allow it.

"Clara," Nicholas said, his eyes on her face, "he would never have lied to you about your mother if it hadn't been the absolute right thing to do. What good would it have done you to know the truth?"

"That doesn't change the fact that she would still be alive were it not for him." She paused. "Were it not for you, too, come to think of it."

"As if I could have done anything to save her, cursed as I was."

"And you obviously angered someone mightily to earn such a fate," she pressed on, pleased to have found an edge. "If you hadn't, Mother might still be alive."

He had nothing to say to that. *As well he should not,* Clara thought, indignant and unsatisfied. Every time she spoke of her mother aloud, she felt newly bereft; it was no different here. She hugged herself, sick at heart and struggling for a clarity of thought that wouldn't come. If Nicholas felt the sting of guilt, he certainly succeeded at hiding it. Tricky, this one, with that perpetually half-amused note in his voice. It reminded her of her father, strangely, or any of the politicians back home—never genuine, always putting on a show.

Discomfited, and as unlikely as it would be for her to find her father in such a public space, she searched the crowd for a familiar unkempt red head among all the others—blacks and whites, greens and pinks and blues. Dye was, apparently, in fashion. Beside her Nicholas scraped the sides of his bowl, his hair half over his face. He was humming a lilting tune under his breath, but his eyes were sharp on the phosphorescent panel hung on the wall opposite them. After a time Clara watched it too, mesmerized at the sequence of color and sound.

A scrolling pattern of stark blue letters read: *Curfew for Zarko now begins at ten o'clock. Anyone out of doors after curfew will be subject to relocation. Anyone in spike zones will be executed.*

A bright sequence of song, color, and flashing lights: *Sugar! You want it, you need it, the fortunate bleed it. Fly high, feel your might! Smile wide, smile bright! Available in new, convenient capsule form—high-grade!—at your local lothouse.*

Attention, Zarko residents.

An image formed of a woman in diamonds—a faery woman, with that elegant face and the long, pointed ears, though they were not as long as Borschalk's, nor as long as the others' throughout the marketplace.

Her face illuminated the panel Clara was watching, as well as countless others hanging from rooftops and the sides of bridges. They all displayed the same image, and that image silenced the crowd at once. A man beating a child pickpocket let him fall to the ground. The one-eyed man's stern face went slack—with wonder? With joy.

The woman on the panels smiled.

Nicholas froze, bowl halfway to his mouth.

Clara stiffened. She could drop her bowl and retrieve the daggers from her boots in a matter of seconds if need be. "What is it?"

His body vibrated with energy, or maybe that was the marketplace itself; everything seemed suddenly fraught with tension.

"It's her," he said, low. "It's *Anise*."

"Something grave has come to my attention," Anise said, her words like frost in the air, cool and light, "brought to me a short while ago by my officers on the perimeter." She leaned closer. Was she Clara's age, or much older? Impossible to tell, but she was indisputably lovely. Long white braids slithered over a bare white shoulder. "We have fugitives in our midst."

A low murmur rumbled through the watching crowd. People with suspicion in their eyes searched their neighbors' faces.

"Now, don't be alarmed. There's no need to be afraid." Anise's voice floated above them, clear and distantly maternal, like a mother perfunctorily comforting her children. Curious blue eyes passed over the crowd. When they reached where Clara stood, Clara dropped her eyes to the ground. Could Anise see them? What was this power that gave her the ability to project such an image throughout the city?

"In fact, you should celebrate," Anise said. "We're going to make this a game. My soldiers are already on the hunt, but our country is vast. Zarko residents, you are nearest their entry point. The fugitives are most likely among you at this very moment."

Clara felt suddenly naked. She tensed, ready to run.

"We'll run if we have to," Nicholas said under his breath.

Clara nodded, licked her lips. Was the one-eyed man watching them with renewed interest?

"If you help us track down these invaders," Anise continued, "and deliver them to me—*alive*—you will be generously rewarded: brought to the capital, given rooms in Wahlkraft for an extended stay of luxury and caprice, hosted by myself." A smile flickered across Anise's face, but Clara was familiar with such smiles. At home she saw them every day—false, mocking, barely restraining hatred. "The low will be brought high, the enslaved made kings. Consider it a gift, even though you don't deserve it."

The market throbbed with sudden, violent longing. In apparent ecstasy a woman darted toward the panel nearest her with outstretched arms, exclaiming thanks, before she was hurled impatiently to the ground by the crowd. She did not rise again.

Beside Clara, Nicholas was raging. "I will kill her." He pounded his fist on his thigh. "Sinndrie witness it, I will tear her limb from limb."

"Shut up," Clara hissed. But no one paid them any mind. Why would they, with Anise talking?

Clara couldn't blame them. Anise's arms were draped in fur-edged silk. Her skin shimmered with iridescent powder, and silver dripped from her hair in glittering spools. When she breathed, the diamonds at her décolletage glinted in the light. When she smiled, it was with a certain . . . *sultriness* that Clara had never before seen, never even imagined.

Clara blushed, and looked away.

"We don't yet have much information on them, but we know there are two—a young man and a young woman, hardly more than children. But don't be deceived by their youth." Anise glanced down, dragged her fingers across something unseen. "We managed to capture a single chromograph during their infiltration. Take a good look, *citizens*." Her voice curled nastily on the word. "This is your quarry. And remember, I want them alive."

Clara's mouth went dry as the image on the screen before her shifted from that of Anise to one of Nicholas and herself, hand in hand, crawling from the wreckage of the ruined train.

16

Immediately there was an uproar.

The crowd surged into motion, shoving and clawing one another in the frantic press toward the perimeter wall. Wordless excited cries echoed throughout the marketplace. Blue sparks from faery spears rained down from rooftops, and mocking faery laughter chimed even above the screams of the trampled.

Nicholas pulled Clara close, his arm around her shoulders, and together they maneuvered through the stinking, eager mob. Clara had never felt more exposed, more pinned down. She wished her hair were dirtier—they would find her red head in an instant; they would *find* her, and then what? Father would languish in this world, forgotten, and Felicity would be condemned to a hell of her own, with no explanation for why Clara had abandoned her.

A sob caught in the back of Clara's throat at the thought.

Overhead the glowing panels had resumed their previous sequence of curfew warnings and sugar advertisements. Anise had gone.

"I saw them!" a voice bellowed.

Clara turned back to see the one-eyed man waving his arms for attention, searching frantically through the crowd.

"The girl, she had red hair! They were right here. I served them!"

A wave of people converged on him, knocking him to the ground in a frenzy of reaching hands and breathless questions.

"What's wrong with them?" Clara gasped. It was all she could do hold on to Nicholas's arm as they fought their way through.

Nicholas laughed, an edge to it. "They love her. Don't you see?"

A strange sort of love, yes, she could see that—a fear and hatred overshadowed by obsession, by a need Clara didn't understand. It simmered in the air above the swarms of people; their eyes flashed with it. A need to please Anise? A need to survive. And then, Nicholas had said faeries could *charm*, whatever that meant.

Clara felt it too: a compulsion, an inexplicable yearning in her blood. Anise was the key to finding her father; that much was obvious.

But Anise was more than that—this sudden stirring within Clara was more than that. Anise's smile lodged in her mind, a snare glittering with jewels, and even the chaos of the crowd could not shake it.

They took shelter in an alleyway, a grimy, narrow slip of a thing lit by flickering lanterns.

Clara paced, strategizing, trying to shake off the mania of the marketplace. It was, by her rough calculations, late in the afternoon, but the storms overhead had already doused the city in darkness. They would be able to hide here, at least for a short while.

"We need to change," she said. "Make ourselves look different. The whole city has seen our faces, our clothes. We're walking targets."

"Zarko," Nicholas said, quiet in the shadows as he peered down the alleyway. Figures raced by, shouting; the streets crawled with enthusiastic new bounty hunters. "That's what she called it."

"So you don't know this city?"

"I told you, Clara. I don't know anything about this place now. I'm only guessing—I know as much as you do."

"But you haven't ever heard of Zarko? It wasn't here before?"

"No."

Clara turned away from him and closed her eyes; she knew it would do them no good if she went to pieces. But how could she possibly concentrate on finding her father in the face of so much unknown, with so many people in pursuit of them?

After a moment she could speak again. "That panel said something about curfews, so whatever Zarko is, it's strictly regulated."

"I also heard something about sugar. Although, I assume, not the sort you'd find in a kitchen."

Clara had no response to that, so she withdrew one of her daggers and began sawing her skirts from her bodice—they were cumbersome anyway, and now they were an identifying mark. After dragging her palms across the ground, she smeared muck on herself, on her clothes, through her hair. Each movement across her tender skin tugged forth tears. She noticed with a start that her wounds—the burns from the snowstorm, the cuts from the loks—had healed more during the last hour or two than seemed normal. The observation rattled her. She wondered if she was hallucinating; her eyes spilled over at the thought, but she did not move to wipe her face.

Nicholas watched in silence.

"We'll rest here for a while," she said. "It's getting dark. The shadows will hide us."

"I agree."

"We should find new clothes when we wake. And in the meantime let's disguise ourselves as thoroughly as possible."

"I'll follow your impressive example, but I might stay away from the . . . whatever it is there on the ground that you've pasted over your front."

"You'd do well to use it." Her breath was thinning; she found it increasingly difficult to tamp down her building sobs. "People aren't likely to approach a man covered in waste. And you should disguise your metal bits as much as you can."

Nicholas hesitated, and then began scraping muck onto his own face. The smell of them both made Clara want to gag, but there was a certain satisfaction in the stench. She deserved it, for this catastrophe, for the fate of her family.

"Clara," Nicholas said quietly after a moment. He put a hand on her arm. "Slow down."

She would not look at him. "After we're disguised, we can move more freely. Find some sort of information hub. A soldier's station, perhaps, or a place of commerce."

"Clara."

"Tell me everything you know." She knew he could see her tears, and she did not care. "Everything you remember. I need to know, even if it no longer seems relevant."

His face was solemn as he watched her. "We will find him, Clara."

"Will we?" She let out a small, unsteady sound. "It seems unlikely. I know nothing of this place, and neither do you, it seems."

"So we'll discover it together."

"And every moment we spend *discovering* is another moment closer to my father's death, closer to my sister's . . . Nicholas, if I'm not back to New York within a week, with my father alive and whole, they'll kill my sister. Concordia will give her to Dr. Victor to do with as he will, and that will be the end of it. Of her."

Of me.

Nicholas turned away.

"And I don't know what happened to poor Godfather. I should hate him, yet I don't, and I can't bear to think of anything happening to him." Clara folded herself into a filthy knot on the ground, her gorge rising. "And this place . . . is *disgusting*."

She hadn't meant to say that, but it was outrageously true. Nicholas paused and then began to laugh, and after a moment Clara did too—erratic laughter that fought with her tears. She put a hand over her mouth to hold it all in. Her palm smelled unholy, and that made her laugh even harder.

"Oh, Clara." Nicholas sighed, sliding down to sit beside her, still chuckling. He turned toward her, grime warring with metal to make his face a mosaic of strange angles. But his dark eyes were merry and soft.

"If only you could see what Cane looked like before. You would much prefer it, I think. It wasn't quite so . . . tall then. Nor so misshapen."

Tall. The hum of trains overhead made Clara glance up and shiver. He was distracting her from herself, and though the urgent part of her felt insulted, she knew they could do nothing else until they had at least one or two hours of sleep. She knit her fingers together and tucked her family out of her thoughts, leaving her mind open and ready.

"Tell me about it. Cane, before."

Nicholas was quiet for a moment. "I think," he began slowly, "that where we were this morning was Mira's Ring."

"What is that?"

"The edge of the world." He smiled a little. "Or so the stories call it. So my old bedtime tales called it. The last stretch of land before you reach the seas. It's always been tempestuous, but never like what we saw. They say Mira's Ring formed when a mage was betrayed by her lover. Her ghost wanders there still, heartbroken, trailing winter forever behind her. It surrounds the entire country."

"A mage," Clara said. "Godfather never told me about them."

Nicholas chuckled. "No, most likely because he feared that if he mentioned them, he'd be unable to stop himself from confessing."

"Confessing what?"

"That he is one himself."

It took her a moment to truly hear the words. *Mage.* It echoed through her mind like the call of someone new and yet somehow dear—a stranger opening loving arms to her. Swift affinity. Bone-deep *recognition.*

Of course Godfather was a mage. Of *course.* Normal men did not tell stories like Godfather did, normal men could not quiet panicked horses with a word, and normal men did not have silver blood.

"Godfather is a mage," she said, more to try the idea aloud than for Nicholas's confirmation. It was the most ridiculous sentence she had ever uttered, and the most satisfying.

So many unasked questions now answered. A riddle she hadn't known needed solving.

Nicholas, curious: "Are you all right?"

She turned to him, feeling bright with new clarity, unsettled and yet not, and shook her head. "I suppose I should be surprised. Aghast and agape."

"Aren't you?"

Was she? For a moment she considered it. "It's just . . ." She smiled. No. She wasn't. The rational part of her was surprised. Of course it was. But the rest of her—the larger part of her, which Godfather had crafted over many years with such care—that part of her was simply contented. Quietly triumphant, and knowing.

"You don't believe me," Nicholas said.

"In fact I do. I actually used to pretend he was something like that. A wizard or . . . I don't know. I was young, and he was this strange, fearsome man who talked to himself and wore an eye patch and built the most exquisite toys. Any child would think he was magic in the form of a man. I convinced myself that was nonsense, but . . ."

They were quiet then. Clara's nostalgia subsided into a dull, oppressive sadness, her thoughts whirling between Godfather and Mother, Father and Felicity and lonely women with winter at their feet, and Anise with her sharp blue eyes, and the throngs of people Clara could hear, even now, buzzing on the streets in search of them. Magic. *Mages.* Her head pitched with vertigo. She would not be able to sleep.

"We will find him, Clara," said Nicholas at last, and his face in the dim light was so earnest and endearingly boyish that she reached up without thinking and touched his cheek. When her fingers met the sliver of metal at his temple, beneath his hair, memory and familiarity and wonder blended sweetly within her. A curious dichotomy, this hard and soft, this hot flesh and cold steel. The familiar and unfamiliar, man and metal.

Between them, warm breath in frigid air. A slow crawl of tension.

Nicholas let his eyes close. "Do you know how long it's been since . . ."

She waited. "Since?"

"Never mind." His voice was low, measured. Gently he pulled away from her touch and tucked Godfather's coat about both their shoulders. "We should rest."

Unnerved, Clara sat in silence. Every time Nicholas shifted, she flinched; whenever a crash came from an apartment overhead or a shout rang out from the streets, she snapped her gaze into the darkness. Exhaustion battled with restlessness.

Father, where are you? Absurdly, she thought it into the approaching night. If there was truly magic in Cane, maybe he would somehow be able to hear her.

But there was no response, of course. There was nothing but the sounds of people and train whistles, and the warm presence of Nicholas's body.

Clara felt ready to scream. She could not stand this silence.

"Why are you helping me?" she whispered. She had not meant to say it aloud.

At first she thought Nicholas was asleep, but then he said, without looking at her, "Because you helped me. You fought the loks so Drosselmeyer could free me. You could have died."

"So it's a matter of debt?"

"Strictly speaking."

There was more to his words, but she was too troubled to explore it. "And what will you do if we find him?"

"*When* we find him."

"Yes. What then?"

"I don't know. I had thought of taking back my throne." He said it casually, like it was nothing. "How naive I was. I thought I could return and people would recognize me, gather at my side, fight her with me, for love of me, for loyalty. But no one does recognize me. And I hardly recognize myself, or Cane."

Clara did not know what to say to this, how to respond to the false lightness in his voice. It so obviously masked despair, but her own was too great to offer comfort. So she said nothing, and tried to force a sleep that would not come.

"I imagined this," she heard him say quietly after a long time. "In the shop. I imagined being beside you."

Clara pretended sleep so she would not have to respond, but her heart beat suddenly faster, and an awful tenderness warmed her. She was relieved when she heard his breathing even out, and tried to forget his words. They would do nothing but soften her, and as kind as he had been, it occurred to the part of her trained to suspect and defend that such a softening might be his intention.

She awoke to screams.

They tore her from sleep, and Nicholas, too. For a moment they were still, listening.

Then the screams came again.

Clara saw them first—three figures at the end of the alleyway, shoving a smaller figure between them. It was a girl, and the screams were hers.

"Don't move," Clara whispered. "If we stay quiet, I don't think they'll notice us."

But Nicholas was already getting to his feet. He reached for his sword. "We've got to help her."

The figures threw the girl to the ground.

"Please, don't!" the girl screamed. "*Please!*"

Clara rose and turned away. She itched to run to them, to wreak havoc with her blades. But the threat of being caught held her still—her family depended on her.

That did not ease the sick feeling in her stomach.

"Ignore them," she breathed. "Plug your ears."

High above them lights flickered in windows; a pair of blue-eyed birds perched on a rooftop to watch. The girl's screams became deafening. Would no one help her?

Nicholas stared at her. "Are you mad? We can't stand by and let this happen."

Clara grabbed his arm. Stupid, foolishly noble boy. "And if they see us, and we're caught?"

"We won't be. We fought a train full of faeries. I was raised by war, and I've seen your training. We can handle them." He stepped closer, his face fierce. "You're powerful, Clara. Or you *could* be, if you would let go of your fear long enough to realize it."

As if struck, Clara stepped back from him. He seemed suddenly so impatient with her, so disgusted. She was tempted to slap him for the insult—but then, he was right, wasn't he? She had been weak for so long.

She curled her hands into fists. Just like that—a shift, a spark of anger.

She would not be weak this time.

The girl was struggling to rise, but one of the figures shoved her back down. Clara bent to eject the knives from her boots and followed Nicholas, daggers in hand.

It's more a dance than anything, fighting, Godfather's memory whispered. *Stay light on your toes. Stay fluid. Stay two strikes ahead of them. Speed kills more quickly than strength.*

The girl's attackers heard them coming. Clara saw them turn, squint into the darkness.

And then she and Nicholas were on them, leaping shoulders-first. The man Clara slammed into was caught off guard, and she knocked him down easily. He landed with a grunt, and she rolled over him, letting the movement propel her to her feet.

The man followed her, more agile than he looked, and lunged. Her daggers caught him across the chest, and dark ribbons of blood blossomed on his sweat-soaked shirt. Clara hesitated, revulsion at taking yet another life making her pause—not a lok life, not even a faery life, but a *human* life—but then, these men weren't entirely human. Like Dr. Victor, their cruelty defined them, stripped them of personhood. Not men but beasts. No better than loks. The thought bolstered Clara.

But the man's eyes were on her face, and he *knew*.

"It's you," he whispered. "From the queen's proclamation."

Queen?

He dove for her again, greedy this time, clumsy and eager-eyed. She pounced and stabbed him in the gut.

The dagger sank hideously into flesh and organs with a terrible hot spurt of blood, but it had to be done, and she did not feel guilty, with the girl's screams still echoing in her head. She turned as his body fell, tugging her daggers free. Where was Nicholas? She whipped around, looking for him, but another of the men was there, leaping over the body of his predecessor. And he was angry.

Clara tried to dodge him, but the great bulk of his body caught her, knocking one of her daggers loose. She swiped with the other, but he ducked and leapt at her, catching her by the throat and slamming her against the wall. His grip was strong, pinning her hand to the stone, rendering her remaining dagger useless. She felt the first twinges of fear.

He saw it in her face. His neck was laden with crude jewelry; tar lined his teeth. "Ah, not so brave without your claws, are you, kitty?"

Movement rustled from beyond him—grunts, gasps of surprise. He gave a shudder and coughed; blood flew from his lips, spattering her face. He slumped, and she squirmed loose, searching for her daggers. Ah—there on the ground, glinting silver. She grabbed them and spun around, ready to spring.

Nicholas pulled his sword from the man's back.

The third man, already felled, lay inert behind him.

Nicholas, breathing hard, caught her gaze, and she nodded. She was all right. Shaking, head spinning, sick at the tang of blood, but all right. And Nicholas was too, she noticed, though his eyes shone with that same hard light from the train, and she thought, as she had the first time, that it suited him far too well. She recognized that lust for righteous violence, for the euphoria that came afterward. She thought back to his words: *I was raised by war.*

So many stories yet to be told, so many secrets to be unearthed. It would happen soon; Clara would make sure of it, and if Nicholas tried to evade her, well, she still had her daggers. And, apparently, the skill to use them against her own kind after all—a simultaneously encouraging and appalling accomplishment.

Grim, she cleaned her blades on the coat of the nearest fallen man and sheathed them, and turned to find the girl. She was a tiny thing, a ball on the ground, arms tucked over her head.

"Hello?" Clara knelt beside her. "It's all right. They're gone."

"Leave her," Nicholas said, scanning the darkness. "She's unhurt. If she sees us . . ."

The girl peeked up at them.

Nicholas sighed and rubbed a tired hand over his face.

She was a tiny creature with wan skin and black eyes and spiked blue hair. An array of jewels hung from her ears, and two smaller ones from her bottom lip; her patchwork jacket had fallen open and revealed, curiously, tiny rows of tools in tied pouches. Her face was young, but her expression—closed, suspicious, weary—was not.

Clara tried to smile, though every second they delayed, every second the girl studied her face, was a sinister clock ticking away inside her. "You're safe now. What's your name?"

The girl drew herself up, her eyes keen. She spat red blood. Human, then. Or at least not faery. "Name's Bo."

"Bo. That's pretty."

Bo's eyes flitted over the men's bodies. "You killed them, did you? Why?"

Nicholas looked up, surprised. "They were hurting you."

"Ha. All right. So what do you want for it?"

When Clara did not respond, baffled, Bo frowned. "No one fights for free. You want me to clean something, steal something, what?"

"Is that really the way of things?" Nicholas said quietly.

Bo's eyes narrowed. "What do you mean?"

"Oh, just imagining a place where little girls don't get assaulted in the street and then ask their rescuers what the payment is."

"Look, whoever you are—" Then Bo paused. Her face changed, and on it Clara saw recognition. Her stomach sank as Bo's eyes flicked between her and Nicholas, and back again.

"Huh. So that scum wasn't joking. You *are* the queen's bounty." Bo pointed at Clara. "At least *you* are. I recognize you. But you—" She raised an eyebrow at Nicholas. She drew a shaky breath, stepped forward, stepped back. For a moment her hardness slipped away, and she looked her age. "You, I couldn't see so well in the chromo-cast. And now I see why. Probably the queen didn't *want* us to see you so well."

Clara could hardly breathe. Nicholas's hand was on his sword, but his eyes . . . oh, his eyes held within them a careful light.

"What do you mean?" he said slowly.

Bo's face was hard once more, teetering on the edge of collapse. Her expression warred with itself. "Where've you been? Hmm? Or aren't you who I think you are?"

"I'm sure I don't know—"

"There are old stories." Bo got to her feet, glaring at him, twice as formidable as she was tall. "And some of us remember 'em. Not many. And some of us don't like to talk about it. Not safe to talk about it. But some of us remember 'em. Some of us've been taught. More of us than the *drekks* like to think." She thrust a finger at Nicholas's chest, and her voice shook with an emotion too deep for anyone so young to bear. "It *is* you, isn't it? Afa has an old book, she does, so old, and there are pictures in it. Scholars' accounts, ones the faeries didn't burn. And you're in it. At least I think you are. People sometimes draw pictures on the streets, in the dirt, on walls. The faeries burn them up, of course. They don't want anyone to remember. Maybe I'm dreaming. Maybe I'm dead. How is it possible? You don't look any older." Her face did crumple now, but when Nicholas reached for her, she stepped away.

"Bo," he said gently, "it *is* me. I've been somewhere . . . else. Somewhere where time works differently. I was trapped there, so I didn't grow as I would have here."

"Prove it, then," she spat. From her jacket she withdrew a small knife, held it steady. "Or I'll gut you, rescuers or no."

Nicholas knelt and put down his sword, and though Clara wanted to scream at him to stop, to run, she couldn't. On his face shone a naked sorrow—for this girl, crying quietly, with her knife and head held high; for the people tearing themselves to pieces in the streets hunting him; for this place that was nothing like he thought it would be.

His eyes locked on Bo's, Nicholas began to sing:

"The rider and the pirate queen,
The bravest souls there's ever been,
The mason and the fiddler, too—
They came for me, they came for you. . . ."

Clara drew in a sharp breath; it was the tune from before, the one he had hummed in the marketplace. It was so startling to hear his low, somber voice in this way that Clara could do nothing but stare. He seemed careful, as though afraid to sing the words too loudly, and tender—perhaps to comfort Bo?

Bo's expression was full, tumultuous though she did not lower her knife.

Nicholas continued:

"Sinndrie sent the falcons wide,
With Zoya standing by his side.
Their message flew through rock and tree . . ."

Bo stepped closer, her face tight with emotion, and sang, *"Beneath the mountains, o'er the sea."*

Nicholas smiled, and when they kept on, it was together—two hushed voices, one childish and one, Clara was startled to realize, rather kingly. And the longer they sang, the more solid became the sense of *rightness* surrounding her, as though the air in this dank alleyway could hear the melody and was responding to it—blooming, as a flower would. It was such a tangible sensation that Clara scanned their surroundings, expecting someone to be watching them, but it was only the darkness, and a sense that something unseen was pulling, yearning, toward Nicholas and this blue-haired child.

Bo must have felt it too; as they sang, she looked about her, afraid—afraid that she would lose this sensation? Afraid that she was imagining things?

"The fiddler came from ice and snow,
The rider, where the red sands flow,
The pirate left her eastern throne,
The mason dug through earth and stone.
They brought us music, light, and life.
They brought a ship, a horse, a knife. . . ."

Bo had trailed off, trembling. Nicholas took her hand and smiled.

"Through stormy seas and secret rifts,
From Beyond they came . . ."

"*. . . as gifts,*" Bo finished. And then she threw her arms about his neck, whispering, "Your Highness, sire, you've come back," into his shoulder. The sense of magnetism that had been building around Clara faded abruptly, leaving her feeling small and untethered.

"What just happened here?" she said, breathless.

Nicholas turned to her, his eyes urgent, his voice fragile. "I wondered if it would still work, with their tricks clogging the air. The old songs, when sung by a member of one of the royal families, call to the land, and then the land recognizes us, draws near. An unmistakable sensation, and as good an identifying mark as any brand of the flesh. I had thought, with the faeries' corruption . . ." He laughed, put a hand on the oil-stained ground as though it were an old friend. "I thought it might not work. I had been afraid to try."

"Not even faeries can ruin the old songs," Bo said fiercely, wiping her eyes. "Not even Anise."

Nicholas gave her a grateful smile. The whole exchange stung Clara with jealousy, and with fear. She doubted she would ever feel such deep-seated kinship with New York—grieve for her homeland, love it as Nicholas so obviously did his. She had forgotten how to care about the city that had taken so much from her. Forgetting was the only way she had found to keep moving every day. You did not carry out ribbon-cutting ceremonies for coffin houses and actually *care* about what you were doing, or think that it mattered; that way lay perpetual, soul-crushing disappointment.

Clara watched Nicholas rise to his feet with Bo in hand, apprehensive. He murmured reassurances to Bo—that he wasn't leaving again, not if he could help it; that he would fight for her, for all of them, for the old songs and the safety to make new ones, for this place that had once been their home and would be again. He turned to Clara with the beginnings of a blazing look on his face—the look of resolution—and it frightened her.

She wondered if, with this one girl and this one moment, Nicholas had changed his mind about helping her in favor of something a good deal more personal.

She cleared her throat politely, feeling like an intruder. "Maybe we should move somewhere more secluded?"

Bo put up her chin. "Who is this, anyway? Friend of yours?"

"Yes," Nicholas said, his eyes finding Clara's softly, "and a dear one. She saved my life, in more ways than one. She is to be treated with as much respect as I am. Well. Maybe not quite as much."

He winked, and Bo smirked good-naturedly, but Clara did not think it funny, unease twisting within her as Bo led them away through the shadows. To a safe place, she had promised. But the trains were forever whistling overhead, and they seemed to laugh at Clara.

What's worth more to a dethroned prince? she wondered. *One measly mayor from a distant land?*

Or his own people, thousands of them, millions, all broken and dying?

The logical answer seemed plain to Clara, but she refused to acknowledge it.

17

Bo led them through the city for what felt like hours, taking a circuitous route that often had them doubling back through streets and alleyways they'd already traveled. She seemed to know every nook and cranny of this place, every building safe to cut through and every bridge hiding secret doors.

Clara observed as closely as she dared, mindful of the birds flapping metallically overhead, and the multicolored panels—still with their messages of curfew, sugar, and various restrictions, and, occasionally, the image of Clara and Nicholas climbing from the train—playing for empty streets. Empty, that is, save for the random shadowed figure, scurrying and swift, and gloved faery patrols, indolently beautiful in their uniformed black. Bo seemed to know how to avoid them, and they passed unseen—three humans in a sea of danger.

Danger dressed in fur and diamonds. Danger simmering blue.

Another thing Clara noticed: the city was changing.

It had been crude, unorganized, filthy. A tumbling, shambolic marketplace. Now the cobblestones were growing cleaner, the buildings more orderly. Doors of polished stone displayed elaborate engravings of dancing, writhing figures. Lanterns gleamed gold and pink; shopfronts boasted baubles and delicate trinkets. The air became scented with fragrances so rich that Clara's head spun—musk and vanilla and unfamiliar spices.

Occasionally the ground rumbled beneath their feet, accompanied by distant flashes of pale green lightning. They would steady themselves on the nearest wall, and wait for the tremors to pass. Dust rained down on their heads, shaken loose from the rooftops.

"What is that?" Clara whispered.

"Hurry on" was all Bo would say, glaring at the sky.

They came to a cluster of buildings with walls of peach-colored stone. Before Clara could get a good look at the exterior, Bo led Clara and Nicholas around through an alleyway, and then down through a grate in the ground.

"Never linger in one place for too long," she said, helping them down into a surprisingly clean passageway. "Even if it's outside your own home. The queen has spies everywhere."

Immediately Clara said, "Those birds. The mechanized ones."

Bo nodded. "Kambots. Crude little things, but they have their uses if you know how to rework 'em." Her grin gleamed in the dark.

"They are surveillance tools?" Nicholas asked.

"Some people call 'em the queen's eyes. She can look through 'em, they say. Don't know if it's true or not, but they're no bloody sparrows, if that's what you mean."

Through another few turns in the passageway, down winding stone steps, and they stopped before a door edged with amber light. Bo rummaged through her jacket and pulled out a gleaming pair of lock picks.

Instinctively Clara leaned closer for a look. Bo turned away with a sneer.

"What're you looking at? Give me some room, eh?"

"It's all right, Bo," Nicholas said. "Clara is excellent at this sort of thing."

Bo looked her up and down. "Is that right?"

"I . . . had a good teacher," Clara said quietly.

After a moment Bo thrust the picks into Clara's hands. "Well, then. Let's see you try."

The dim light was enough to see the latch—a crude, unfamiliar apparatus that seemed cobbled together with spare parts. Most interesting, it boasted two keyholes, into which the picks barely fit. For a few moments Clara leaned against the door, eyes closed, pressing the picks into place, feeling for the twin catches. They were subtle, tiny things that, Clara guessed, had to be pressed with the right simultaneous combination of weight and timing . . . Ah.

The catches gave way and the latch clicked open.

Bo retrieved her picks, grinning at Clara. "His Highness wasn't lying, was he? Not bad, miss."

"Clara." Nicholas put his hand lightly on Clara's back, but it brought her little comfort. "Her name is Clara."

"Well, *Clara*, you're all right," said Bo, slipping inside.

There, two women and a man—all human—greeted Bo with varying degrees of relief. The man closed his eyes and murmured words. One of the women—pale golden skin, dark hair and eyes—pulled Bo into a tight embrace.

"You're late," the woman said. "Oh, Bo, dear sister, I thought . . . Did something happen?"

"Almost. Would've, were it not for these two."

Three sets of eyes turned to Clara and Nicholas.

"The queen's bounty," said the other woman, tall and broad-shouldered, straightening with recognition, but the woman holding Bo silenced her. She approached Nicholas with the same careful reverence Bo had in the street.

"Bo," she said, low. "Who is this?"

Bo did not answer, watching the woman's face expectantly.

The woman put a hand on either side of Nicholas's face, barely touching him, eyes searching. Clara shifted uncomfortably at her nearness, but Nicholas remained still, letting her examine him.

"He sang one of the old songs," Bo said, gentle, at the woman's side. "He sang it with me, and I felt it."

"The land?" The woman's eyes were twin sparks of hope. "It recognized him?"

Bo nodded, and Nicholas took the woman's hands in his own. "I am sorry to have left you." He met her eyes, utterly sincere. "To have left was a great crime I could not prevent."

The woman sank to her knees at Nicholas's feet. "It *is* you. You have returned."

Bo was beaming, bouncing on the balls of her feet. The other two approached warily.

"Afa," the man said, "who exactly do you think this is?"

"I *know* who he is." Afa turned to him, passionate. "I would recognize him anywhere. I've been praying for his return. We all have."

At that the man looked at Nicholas sharply. Behind him, Clara noticed, the other woman had a hand on the knife at her belt.

"You swear to me, Bo," said the man, "that you're telling the truth?"

Bo frowned. "And why would I lie to you about something like this? For laughs, I suppose?"

Nicholas helped Afa to her feet. "You need never kneel before me," he said gently. "Afa, is it?"

There was a terrible silence as he waited—for the group's approval, Clara guessed. She hardly dared breathe, trying to read the emotions running rampant across their faces—doubt giving way to relief and careful joy. Then, without warning, the man surged forward, pushing Afa aside to embrace Nicholas. His fervor nearly knocked Nicholas flat, but no one seemed to mind. The other woman was laughing and wiping her eyes, and Bo was practically spinning with pleasure.

Clara stepped aside and watched. She was the misfit here, the unwanted presence. At least that's what it felt like—terribly uncomfortable, and even ominous. How could she and her troubles compete with this? There were four of them now, these beleaguered, hopeful people, looking at Nicholas with stars in their eyes, inspecting him like a long-lost son, and surely there would soon be more. Clara would be cast aside in favor of rebellions and reclamations. They would fight their war, and weeks would pass—*months*—before anyone would think to wonder what had happened to her father.

And by that time it would be too late.

". . . and this," she heard Nicholas say through her rising distress, "is Clara."

He held out his hand, and she took it, distracted, completely ill at ease, even with—*especially* with—Nicholas's eyes steady and warm upon her, as though he were *proud* to introduce her to these people.

"She is my oldest friend. She saved my life."

The others looked at Clara with renewed interest.

"And she's right wicked with locks," Bo chimed in.

"And with *loks*," Nicholas said. "She fought a pack of them to save me. A pack directed by Borschalk himself."

At that the man whistled low. He inspected Clara, newly delighted. "This pretty little thing, against that boulder of a faery? Against the queen's own lover?"

Bo punched his arm. "Just because someone's little doesn't mean they can't fight. Gutted the scum that attacked me easily enough." She grinned at Clara. "Didn't you?"

Clara nodded weakly.

"And the faeries have her father." Nicholas's hand tightened around hers. "I intend to help her get him back."

Afa shot her a pitying look. "If the faeries have your father, I'm afraid there's nothing to be done. They are not in the habit of releasing their abducted."

"What do they want with him, anyhow?" asked Bo.

"We don't know. But we *will* get him back. I've sworn it to her, and to myself."

Clara flushed beneath the weight of his gaze. Such conviction in his voice. God help her, she actually *believed* him, so determined and—there was no other word for it—*regal* was his expression. But how could he be so sure of success, and was he truly decided on helping her, even now, with his loyal subjects beside him?

The silence of the others seemed to echo Clara's own skepticism.

"Your Highness," the tall woman said, "with due respect—"

"Wait." Nicholas put up his hand. "Clara, you were about to say something."

He was going to make her say it. "Well, I thought . . . That is, I had assumed, now that you know some people here *do* recognize you . . ."

"That I would abandon you? That I would forget my debt to you?"

She shrugged, as though it were an inconsequential thing. "That your responsibility to your people would take precedence. And I wouldn't blame you for that."

"That I would give up finding your father in favor of reclaiming my throne."

She almost flinched. "Yes."

After a moment Nicholas's somber face melted into a smile. He pulled Clara into his side and turned them, together, toward the others. They watched him with varying degrees of delight, but only Bo's sharp eyes took in Clara as well, with Nicholas's arm around her waist.

"I don't see," he said, "why I can't do both at once."

18

Afa took them to a room farther from the passageway through which they had come, at the end of a corridor lined with closed doors. Strings of crimson and sapphire beads hung at the entryway, trailing across Clara's arms as she passed through. It was clean here, and comfortable, with cool stone floors and plush carpets, and two low, wide settees boasting deep cushions.

Everyone sat. Bo scrambled on top of a chest of drawers and pulled a tiny gold lock pick from inside her jacket, rolled it back and forth between her fingers. The tall woman, Clara noticed, remained standing near the door, watching the corridor. Glyn was her name; the man, Karras.

Afa flipped back a corner of the carpet to reveal a small wooden hatch in the floor. She opened it and pulled out, with no small effort, an enormous book—yellowed, aged, but obviously well used. It had collected no dust.

She settled it in front of Nicholas on a low table. "It is," she said quietly, "one of the few documents we have left from before that night, Your Highness. When they began to burn everything."

"The Night of Red Winter," Karras said.

Darkness passed over Nicholas's face. "Do you mean the night Wahlkraft fell?"

"Yes. The night of Anise's coup."

Tentatively Nicholas reached for the book. His fingers trailed across the cover. On leaning closer, Clara could see four images inscribed there—a great black raptor; a sea monster; a stallion, rearing on powerful hind legs; and a dragon. A dragon like the one topping Godfather's cane.

"Nightbird," Nicholas said, glancing at her. He pointed to the raptor. "Sea serpent. A flatlands stallion." The horse. "Dragon." At the last image he lingered. "The sign of my family. The Drachstelle family."

"The rightful rulers of Cane," Karras said fervently.

Bo laughed. "Not according to the queen."

"I recognize these animals," Clara whispered, running her fingers across them. "Godfather, he . . . he made me a mobile, for my nursery. These creatures, dangling from delicate chains. 'Such a monstrous thing,' Father always said. 'Is it really appropriate for a young girl's room?' But Mother insisted. *I* insisted. I have never taken it down."

She broke off, haunted, uncertain.

Gently, Nicholas opened the book. "So, Anise is queen now, is she?"

"One of the first things she did was proclaim herself queen," Afa said. "And who was left to challenge her?"

"No one," Nicholas said. "There was no one left. I watched her kill most of them."

He began turning pages, slowly at first, and then in larger chunks. The text was in meticulous script, broken up with images—diagrams, maps, lineages set in elaborately drawn trees. The handwriting changed throughout, as though multiple people had recorded the book's contents. Here and there Clara saw a page with nothing on it but a set of seven names. Some of the names were the same from entry to entry, others not, but they each ended in "meyer."

Could it be?

Clara saw the familiar name on the next page and pointed. "Godfather," she said, disbelieving, absurdly happy. "That's Godfather!"

Bo wrinkled her nose. "Who's Godfather?"

"Drosselmeyer," Nicholas said. Clara could not interpret his tone. "He was one of the Seven when I was prince. They served the royal family. He was sworn in when I was a child."

"He was—is—my godfather," Clara said, the words sticky in her throat, thick with pain. "My . . . friend. He taught me how to fight, how to sneak and break into locked buildings—"

He is the reason my mother is dead. Him and the man now beside me. Perhaps the more she thought the words, the less severely they would sting, and the less they would nettle her with suspicion.

"Wait." Bo stuck her gold lock pick behind her ear. "You mean to say that Drosselmeyer, one of the Seven, was the 'good teacher' you had?"

"Taught her to be a first-rate criminal, it sounds like," Karras said, amused.

"He fled with me that night," Nicholas said quietly. "Anise and her army invaded Wahlkraft. It was the night of the winter festival. No one was ready. Things had been so quiet for so long, we thought—we *hoped*—it meant a peace, even a temporary one. And then . . ."

Everyone was quiet. Clara felt the weight of memory fall upon her, a shared memory in which she had no part.

"They came in through the ceilings. Dozens of them. Hundreds. They swarmed the capital."

"'The streets of Erstadt ran black that night,'" Afa whispered, as though reciting a passage from legend.

"'Black with blood,'" Glyn joined in, from the door.

"'And black with fright,'" Bo whispered.

"They killed Mother and Father." Nicholas turned the page past Drosselmeyer's name. Two portraits stared back at him, at Clara—a man with Nicholas's mouth, and a woman with his fierce eyes and dark hair. A third portrait, below that, connected to the first two with elaborate scrollwork—Nicholas, handsome and groomed, lightly sketched, as though whoever had been working on it had been unable to complete the final piece. "The Seven got us out, on horseback, but Anise came after us. My parents fell. The Seven fell. Except for Drosselmeyer. Except for me. We had two horses, and then one. And there were loks coming after us. Anise drove them to a frenzy."

"Where did you go?" Afa asked quietly. She put a hand on his arm. "My prince, where have you been for so many years?"

Nicholas looked up at Clara. "In Beyond, where time passes more slowly."

Karras seemed bewildered. "But . . . how did you get there? And how did you get back?"

"Through a Door."

Glyn burst out laughing. "But, sire, those are children's tales. There are no other worlds but ours, no such things as Doors."

"And children's tales cannot be true?" Nicholas snapped, silencing her. "I think you'd do well to examine such stories more closely, Glyn. There is more truth in them than you know. The magic folk have always known that, and so has the crown."

No one said anything for a moment. Nicholas turned troubled eyes toward the book in his lap—toward his mother and father, toward the half-finished portrait of himself.

"How many years has it been?" His voice was flat.

Afa looked uneasy. "What do you mean?"

"I was Beyond for eighteen years. Has it been eighteen years here as well?"

Clara could tell by their expressions that it most certainly had not.

"Seventy-two, sir," Bo said from her corner when no one else spoke. She looked terribly sad to tell him. "It's year seventy-two of the Iron Age."

Seventy-two years. Clara thought quickly. Seventy-two here, and eighteen in New York. If that was the ratio, then . . . four. It came out to four. Four days here for every one at home.

She felt dizzy with relief. There was time, then, much more time than she had first thought. But she could not let this knowledge lull her.

Nicholas's shoulders moved—but with a laugh or a sob, it was impossible to tell. "Then everyone I know—everyone I ever knew—is dead. My friends, my teachers . . ."

No one said anything, waiting for him to . . . what? Grieve? Accept such an ungodly piece of information? Clara tried to imagine returning to a world so different from the one she had known, with no one familiar in it but herself; it was a horrible, claustrophobic idea.

"So," Nicholas said tiredly, after a moment that seemed to have left a new weight on his shoulders, and in his eyes, "the Iron Age, is it?"

Bo's response was reluctant. "That's what the queen calls it, sire."

Clara tried to think of something to say into this silence, something helpful or encouraging, or even simply bracing. The question of what they would do next to find her father—if Nicholas did in fact mean to help and wasn't just trying to appear impressive in front of his new followers—pounded insistently at the back of her mind. Four days here to every one at home. It had been perhaps a little less than one, now. A little less than one day since they had fallen through the Door and into the snow. Six or so hours at home, then. It would be dawn on Christmas Day.

Felicity would be waking to a morning that should have been joyous, to find her family gone and Concordia there instead. Clara's fists clenched, and her throat seized with urgency. She had to fix this—she *would* fix this.

Such a tiny twist of hope. She clung to it, and suggested, "Perhaps it would be helpful to see what the land looks like now."

Nicholas looked up at her in surprise.

"Seventy-two years is a long time. You need to know what's happened to the kingdom in your absence. Don't you agree?"

"I agree," he said slowly, "although I'm not sure I want to see."

"Here." Bo withdrew a folded paper from her jacket, jumping down from her perch and hurrying over. "I've been working on making this current. Not quite there yet, but it'll do."

Afa took it from her sternly. "Bo, you shouldn't keep this on your person. What if you're apprehended?"

"It'll never happen, sister. I'm too good for that."

Together Clara and Nicholas unfolded the paper and spread it out on the table. It was a crude map, inexpertly drawn but serviceable. The land mass depicted was roughly circular, a great continent surrounded by oceans. Something about the map bothered Clara, but as hard as she looked, she could not tell what it was.

Nicholas examined it for a long time in silence.

"Mira's Ring," Clara noticed, pointing at the band, mostly blank, at the continent's coastline.

"Only the Innocents live there now," Bo said grimly. "If they do still live."

"Innocents?" Nicholas asked.

The others looked at him uneasily. "Sire," Afa said, "one of the first things Anise did after the Night of Red Winter was divide the surviving humans into groups."

He frowned. "For what purpose?"

Afa hesitated. "For punishment. Punishment for crimes they had committed against the nation of faeries."

In the silence that followed, Bo cleared her throat. "See, the thieves—them that stole from faeries in the raids and lootings during the war—they got sent to Zarko." She pointed at an area on the map inside the dark perimeter wall. "That's where you were today. And here"—she pointed to a tremendous stretch of land even farther inland—"that's Rosche, north from where we are. That's where them that hunted faeries for the crown were sent." She paused. "Now they're hunted themselves. And the Innocents . . ." A funny look came over her face.

Afa broke in gently: "The children, the queen said, were innocent of crime but could not be trusted, due to the evil nature of their human blood. So she turned them out into Mira's Ring to fend for themselves."

Nicholas was horror-struck. "Children, alone in Mira's Ring?"

Clara remembered the furred hunters they had watched in the snow, the man eaten alive by mechaniks as his bloody-mouthed companions had watched. Children. Or they had once been children.

Pushing that nightmarish thought aside, Clara pointed at a place on the map, within Rosche, that seemed to represent a small, walled city. "What's that there?"

"That's the queen's Summer Palace," Bo said, rolling her eyes. "Why she needs two palaces, I'm sure I don't know."

"She doesn't like the cold," Nicholas said shortly. "No faeries do. And Wahlkraft's farther north." He pointed north of the map's center, at a city clearly marked ERSTADT. In its center stood a poorly sketched black castle.

"The castle is Wahlkraft?" Clara said.

Nicholas nodded, terse. "It looks like she's totally restructured most of the kingdom—into these . . . districts."

"We call 'em neighborhoods," Bo said helpfully. "It sounds cheerier."

"And she's expanded them east and west, farther north," Nicholas murmured, following the district lines with his fingers.

"The queen has said," Glyn said, tight with anger, "that she intends to district the entire country."

"But what of these open lands farther north that don't belong to any particular district?" Clara pointed out.

"We don't know," said Afa. "The wildlands are, we can assume, still that—ruins from wartime, abandoned cities and farmlands. The queen combed them for survivors, so there can't be many people left there, if any. But it takes time, she says, to develop land properly."

"Yes," Karras said, wry, "especially when you don't ever *stop* developing it."

Nicholas looked up at that. "What do you mean, Karras?"

"You may have felt the ground tremors since you've arrived here? You've noticed the storms? Sire, she began rebuilding the country after the coup and has *never stopped*."

"She builds one district and tears it down," Afa said quietly, "to rebuild it as something even more extravagant."

"The streets reek with faery magic," Glyn spat. "And with sugar."

"What *is* that?" Clara asked. "We saw advertisements."

"A drug," Afa said. "It comes in several forms: needle, smoke, powder, capsule. The poorer you are, the dirtier your sugar. Everyone wants it, and everyone gets it, one way or another. Highly addictive. The queen is the only manufacturer and supplier." Afa paused. "It is, you could say, like a game of hers, one you cannot help but play."

Bo kicked the table. "It's filth, is what it is. Brought the whole country to its knees. We need it, so we need the queen, and we let her pump our blood—and the faeries' blood, *everyone's* blood—full of this poison. We hate her, but we need her. It keeps us stuck."

Nicholas looked away, rigid with fury.

"Does Anise not use it as well?" Clara asked.

"Oh, she does," said Karras dryly. "Of course, lucky for her, it doesn't seem to affect her in the same way."

"She continues to fashion and refashion the land," Afa said. "We thought, perhaps, after rebuilding the capital and the country to meet her needs, after ridding the land of human influence—all architecture, all government—she would be satisfied. If she turned Cane into the pure faery country she'd always wanted, perhaps that would be enough for her. But I doubt she will ever be satisfied. Even someone as powerful as she can push herself only so far before . . . Well. I would not be surprised if someday she cracks, and the land cracks along with her."

Clara found herself fascinated by this image of Anise on a high, black throne, crafting buildings like a child on some diabolical seashore. "How *is* she so powerful?"

The others stared, except for Nicholas. His posture seemed defeated, his face full of hate.

Did I say something wrong? She cleared her throat. "I mean, you talk of magic folk, faeries and mages. If there are other magic folk besides her, then why do they allow her power over them? What gives her this authority?"

"Well," Bo began hesitantly, "first off, the queen is . . . They called 'em two-bloods in the old stories. Half-breeds. One human parent, one parent of the magic folk."

"Abominations," Glyn said. "Creatures that should not be."

Nicholas spat, "How nice for her, to be protected from the worst of her drug by her own wretched blood."

Clara was taken aback at the viciousness in their voices. "So, mages and faeries and humans . . . they do not interbreed?"

"It is one of the most ancient taboos," Afa explained. "It simply isn't done. It is repulsive to us—all of us, humans, mages, and faeries alike. But it happened once. Many generations ago, a king of the Somerhart line had an affair with a faery countess, and Anise was born. Therefore, not only does she have magic blood, but she also has royal blood, which gives her a connection with the land. Hence the ease with which she can manipulate it."

"What does that have to do with being royal?"

"All of us have it," said Nicholas, his voice strained. The conversation was taking its toll on him; the shadows beneath his eyes seemed to have magnified. "You felt it, didn't you? When we sang? Everyone in the royal families is bound to the land. It is a compulsion in our blood, to keep it safe and whole, to serve it. And it serves us, giving us strength and age beyond those under our rule." He looked up at Clara, haunted. "I can feel it, Clara, like a sickness in me. I can feel how stretched it is, how worn thin."

After a heavy moment Bo said hesitantly, "And besides all that, there's no one left to fight the queen. Her own people are too scared of her, too comfortable. And the mages— Sire . . . they're gone."

Nicholas snapped to attention at that. "What? All of them?"

"Some of our youngest don't even know the word 'mage,'" Afa said, smiling sadly. "It's not one that people speak, and there are so few recorded stories left."

"But surely some of them still live!" Nicholas was overcome, a man pummeled by one too many blows. No one spoke to reassure him; he closed his eyes and looked away from them.

Meanwhile, Clara's eyes had drifted to the map, to the thick, dark circle surrounding the capital, Erstadt, and its castle, Wahlkraft. The longer she stared at the circle, the sharper it became in her vision, as though everything else were falling away.

"What is that?" she said, pointing. "That dark place, around the capital. Is it another district?"

"That's Rieden," said Karras, solemn. "Where the last of the mages fought. It was like a whole new war after you left, Your Highness. She hunted them down, every last one."

Nicholas's fist was white and clenched on the map. His unsullied hand, Clara noticed. The right one, without metal embedded in it. His left hand he seemed to favor, like he did not quite trust it enough to use it.

"But why is it marked specially?" said Clara.

"There's a forest there now," said Karras. "You can't get through it. People have tried, but the trees are woven together, as solid as rocks. Can't cut it, can't tunnel under it."

"We even pinched some grind'ems from a lothouse," Bo said. "Nearly singed our skins off trying to blow the forest open." She seemed disgusted. "Nothing."

"Even the queen has to travel above it to move to and from the capital," Afa added. "We think that was her original reason for constructing the trains."

"That, and making up for years of us destroying any railroads they *did* build," Nicholas said, smiling grimly.

"Well. Yes, sire, perhaps that, too."

"Do you think . . ." Clara hesitated, not knowing how to say what she needed to, or even if it would make sense, but Godfather, for all his cryptic stories, had spoken a little about magic—spells and enchantments, songs that opened unopenable doors. "Is the forest impenetrable because the mages made it so?"

Nicholas glanced up at her. "It's possible."

"We think so, in fact," Afa said. "It's a sort of legend on the streets, if you will. Some like to think they crafted it as one last defiant gesture to the queen."

"And some think," Bo said carefully, her eyes intent on Nicholas's face, "that the mages are still *there*. At least some of 'em. Like they've trapped themselves inside, hiding."

Karras smacked her arm lightly. "Don't tease him with stupid street tales like that."

"I'm not teasing!" Bo was indignant. "I'm telling him what I know!"

As they bickered, Clara stared at the dark circle. *Rieden*. An impassable forest. Possibly with mages inside? More Godfathers, more silver-blooded beings with endless tricks up their sleeves. Something sharp and cold settled within her, something resolute and strange. She felt on the brink of figuring out something essential—as though if she held her breath, if she focused precisely enough, she would stumble upon inspiration.

The ceiling began to vibrate, ruining the moment. From somewhere far overhead came the sudden sound of music. Drumbeats pounded, and faint stringed instruments wove vaguely discordant melodies.

Clara came back to herself. She realized she had been tracing the line of Rieden with her finger, over and over, and that Nicholas was watching her, unreadable. She looked away, embarrassed, but the feeling of nearness, of *almost*, remained in her limbs, and she was glad for it.

Something was calling to her—something to do with Rieden.

Outside in the corridor, a series of delicate chimes sounded, followed by opening doors and hurried footsteps. Rustling fabrics and murmuring voices.

"Shike," Karras hissed, hurrying toward the entryway. "I'm on soon. Got to get ready. I'll see you two in the morning, eh? If you're going to stay here, you'll need to fit in. Lucky for you, you'll be in the hands of a master." And then he bowed, grinning, and disappeared through the beaded curtain. Glyn followed him, more sedate. Past the beads Clara could see a sudden tumult of activity in the corridor: shapes coming and going, glittering flashes of jewelry.

"He's 'on'?" Nicholas turned to Afa, confused. "What does that mean?"

Afa raised her eyebrows. "Did Bo not tell you what this place is?"

"Only that it was safe."

"Bo . . ."

Bo made a face. "I wanted to get 'em off the streets, not waste time talking."

Afa looked sheepish. "Sire, I apologize deeply. If I had any other choice, I would house you somewhere much more dignified, somewhere better suited to—"

"Oh, Afa, just say it." Bo turned, rolled her eyes. "It's a pleasure-house. My sister and her friends work here. But don't worry, Your Highness—the faeries, they don't come down to our rooms often. Wouldn't want to sully themselves."

Clara opened and closed her mouth, a blush overtaking her, but Nicholas looked thoughtful. "We are in this district, here?" he asked, pointing at the neighborhood on the map that lay due north of Zarko.

Afa nodded. "It is called Kafflock."

"And of what are you guilty, then? What did Anise deem your crime?"

"Kafflock is a bit . . . different from the other districts. Here Anise put not criminals but rather the beautiful people. Those whom it pleased her to look at. The borders are thinly guarded; faeries are always coming and going. Her people need entertainment, after all." Her expression turned sour. "You cannot imagine the surgeries people subject themselves to in an attempt to make themselves worthy of Kafflock. There is dancing here. There is . . . more. They do not touch us. They consider us too low, too filthy for such things, but they enjoy watching all the same. It is not an easy life here, but it is not the hardest. We are given food, shelter, basic education. The faeries do not have patience for idiots." She sighed. "As my own audition approached, I prayed every day that Anise would like what she saw."

Clara blurted, "You met her, then?" Nicholas cut a look her way, but Clara ignored him.

"Oh, yes." Afa smiled, a curious mix of dreaminess and fear. "She looked me over, made me strip off my clothes. She told me I have lovely skin."

Absently Afa traced a line up her arm. Following the memory of Anise's hand? Clara watched her, mesmerized. The thought came to her, preposterously: *Would Anise think* I *have lovely skin?*

"She charmed you, in other words," Nicholas muttered.

In an instant the dreaminess vanished from Afa's face. Clara stepped back, like she had been cut loose from a taut line. Even Bo seemed dazed.

"She would have done the same to you, Your Highness," said Afa, quiet but defiant.

The atmosphere in the room had altered. The music drifting down from overhead held a sudden sinister quality. What acts were the humans upstairs being forced to do? Or doing *willingly*, if it meant they could keep their warm beds and their no doubt clean supply of sugar?

Clara wrapped her arms around herself, feeling lost and small.

"Karras said something about seeing us in the morning," Nicholas said after a moment. "As long as you're here, you will need to look like you belong," Afa said, "and I'm sorry to say that it will not be the most dignified of disguises."

"Dignity is a luxury I care little about."

"And then what?" Clara had to push on; she *had* to. Nicholas might have said he would help, but she was the only true advocate for her family. She straightened to look at him. "After we are disguised, what will we do then?"

"We'll strategize," Nicholas said, managing a small smile. "If we're to find your father in this mess, we'll need a solid plan, won't we?"

Clara smiled back, and when he rose, she took his offered hand. But she did not clasp it too tightly, keeping a tiny separation of air between them, like a buffer.

19

That night, Clara dreamed that her blood was freezing over.

Her dreams never made sense. They were always snippets of things, half-cloaked images that seemed familiar one moment and alien the next.

And they were never nice dreams.

As recently as last month, she had snuck out of the mansion after one such dream and fled to Godfather's shop. He never asked questions, or asked her to explain her dreams. But he would sit and hold her as though she were still a child, and make her a cup of hot cocoa to soothe her troubled nerves.

Then he would tell her stories. Sometimes his stories—of Cane, Clara now realized—would be dark, terrifying, violent, and Clara would listen to them with morbid fascination. On her nightmare visits, though, his stories would be soft and full of beauty—docile white dragons, as blind as babies; starlight on high, cold hills; lovers whose devotion was strong enough to bring life to an entirely new world.

But tonight, in her narrow bed in this booming pleasure-house, there was no Godfather to tell pretty stories and stroke her hair.

Instead she dreamed. Ice swept through her body in brutal surges. She tried to tear it out, to open up her skin and let out the burning cold, but her hands were tied. She had no choice but to heave and twist and sob herself hoarse as her insides crackled with searing cold and the taste of silver burned her tongue.

"Clara," a voice called out through the blinding silver light that had become her world, "wake up!"

Wake up. It *was* a dream, then.

She woke up.

Above her, worried eyes inspected her face. Nicholas straddled her hips, pinning her arms to the pillow. A thin red scratch marred his cheek, beneath one of those metal bits snaking out from under his hair.

She tried to speak, but the nightmare still had hold of her voice.

"You had a nightmare." Nicholas cocked a wry eyebrow. "And you hit me when I tried to wake you. I had to restrain you."

"Sorry," Clara whispered. Lingering dream images, streaked silver, flashed across her vision. "I dreamed that my blood . . ."

She couldn't finish. The sensation was difficult to put into words, and besides, the pressure of Nicholas on top of her was beginning to transform from a reassuring reminder that she was alive and in the waking world into something else. It was neither pleasant nor unpleasant; it was . . . *close*. The weight of him, the warmth. But too close, or not close enough?

The night before, they had washed and been given a fresh change of clothing. Afa and Glyn had brought ointment and bandages, tended their wounds. The cleanliness left her feeling oddly exposed. No grime to mask the lines of Nicholas's jaw, and not a lot of fabric between them. Their tunics were of insubstantial linen.

She stared up at him, uncertain.

"What?" Nicholas's voice was low, curious. He touched her cheek. "What did you dream? Something about your blood?"

"It had turned cold."

"Cold? An odd thing to dream. Did it hurt?"

Clara turned her head, pulling away from his touch. His fingers were feather-light against her face, and the feeling unnerved her. "Did you really watch me from inside the statue? All my life?"

For a moment Nicholas didn't say anything. Then he moved to sit on the edge of the bed, and she relaxed.

"I did. Well, for most of it, anyway." He tilted his head, not quite smiling. "Does that make me sick, do you think? Spying on a little girl?"

She should sit up, move away from him—*something*—but she couldn't. Her leg was touching his, and it was comforting. If she closed her eyes, she could almost transport herself back to the shop, to that safe, shadowed corner.

"Perhaps a bit," she admitted.

"But then again it's not as though I could help it. And I thought nothing untoward, at first. You were this awkward, amusing thing. You made me forget myself every once in a while. It wasn't until you were much older that I started to want . . ."

Now it was he who couldn't finish. Clara felt embarrassed for him, and for herself, and unspeakably attuned to him. She sat up and covered his hand with one of hers. He turned to her, his eyes searching her face, and the space between them grew charged with . . . curiosity, perhaps. Nervousness.

Wanting. The desire for comfort, for closeness and discovery, but, oh, *what* was this unbearable tightness in her belly? Fear, maybe. No one had ever been so close to her, not in this charged, careful way. Clara had, in fact, done her best to avoid such a thing. But Nicholas's eyes had the same familiar shape as the statue's had, and she could not avoid their pull.

She wanted to move closer to them, to him.

She *did* move closer, a mere shift of weight. But it was enough.

His gaze fell to her lips.

The door opened.

Clara jumped away from him, cheeks burning.

Afa cleared her throat delicately and folded her hands at her waist. Behind her, Karras grinned.

"Well, then," he said. "You're off to a good start, aren't you? Perhaps it'll be easier to hide you here than we thought."

Clara chanced a look at Nicholas, but he would not look at her. His brow was troubled, the lines of his body taut.

"Karras, don't be crude," said Afa mildly. "Come. Eat breakfast with us. And then—"

"We'll get to work," Karras said. He gathered Clara to his side as she exited the room. "By the time I'm through with you, you'll look like you were born and raised here."

A disturbing thought. The moment with Nicholas had left her unbalanced, and Karras was no help, crowding their passage and pressing her closer to Nicholas. He was silent beside her, and she hoped just as thoroughly unsettled—though if he was, he hid it well.

That irked her. She put space between them and lifted her chin.

"After we are finished," she said firmly, "I would like to discuss the rescue of my father."

"Not to worry," said Afa. "Bo is already hard at work on a plan. She's quite taken by the both of you and considers it a solemn duty." She smiled, then pressed Clara's hand. "We will find him, Clara. There are people in this country who still have some fighting spirit in them, more than you might think."

Clara hoped she was right—and that at least some of them would care to help a stranger.

She was not sure, if the situation were reversed, that she would do the same, not if Felicity or Father would be put at risk.

Fighting for the helpless and wronged had always been her mother's job.

Karras had not exaggerated.

After breakfast he situated Clara and Nicholas in a richly ornamented dressing room, lined with crimson curtains and shelves of perfume bottles, jeweled combs, canisters of powder and rouge. Another man, tall, silent, and bare-chested, accompanied him.

"Don't mind Lenz," Karras said as he settled Clara on one stool and Nicholas on another. "He doesn't talk much." Karras met Clara's eyes in the mirror opposite them. "But between you and me, I couldn't care less about that. He's got truly magnificent hands."

Clara felt a blush warm her body, and she tried to both smile politely and ignore Nicholas's gaze. At breakfast he had watched her with a new quiet about him. Every time she caught his eyes, he looked away. When she allowed herself to remember the weight of him against her body that morning, heat climbed from her toes to her lips.

"Now," Karras said, retrieving a steaming cup of tea from a stove in the corner, "first things first, drink this."

Clara took the cup and hesitated. The smell of the tea was bitter. "What is it?"

"Protection, just in case. All the female doxies drink it. And I'll give you a pack of the herb to keep with you at all times, so you can brew more whenever you feel you might need it. That cup should keep you safe during your stay here, at least. But depending on how long you remain in Cane . . ."

"Safe?" She was utterly perplexed.

Karras had been fiddling with a drawer full of supplies, but at the sound of her voice, he turned, his face soft. "Safe, yes. A doxy's life is hard. Life in *Cane* is hard, and everywhere you turn you'll find desperate people—people who would not hesitate to hurt you for their own pleasure." He placed his hand on her arm, perhaps seeing the dawning comprehension on her face. "I'm not saying that anything will happen to you. But the possibility is there, and drinking this regularly will help protect your body from any . . . lingering effects of unpleasant encounters. Do you understand?"

She did, afraid and embarrassed, and acutely feeling her body's vulnerability. She crossed her arms over herself and sipped.

"I'm sorry to have frightened you," Karras said, his voice gentle.

"No. It's . . . fine. I'm grateful." And to prove it, she knocked back the rest of her drink in one foul gulp and spluttered, coughing.

The mood somewhat lifted, Karras grinned. "Excellent. Now, how to handle this hair of yours? It's like a beacon." He picked up a lock of her hair between his thumb and forefinger and examined it before letting it fall back into place. "But first you need a bath."

Clara frowned. "But we bathed just last night."

"Ah, but you can't have too many baths, can you? Our standards here are exceptional. Doxies are many things, but filthy is not one of them."

Lenz laughed.

"Well, at least not literally," Karras added, smirking.

He drew a curtain across the length of the room, separating Clara from Nicholas, and led her behind an ornate filigreed screen in the corner. He turned on a brass spigot in the wall, and steaming water filled a porcelain tub painted with golden naked figures.

"Go on and bathe," Karras said. "I won't peek."

Clara did, as quickly as possible. When she had finished, Karras settled her back onto the stool in a robe so soft that Clara felt indecent wearing it, the fabric kissing her every curve. She sat rigid, hunched, her arms wrapped about herself. Perhaps if she didn't move, she wouldn't feel the fabric slide so intimately, wouldn't realize how slight a covering shielded her from Karras's eyes.

He seemed unaffected, however, combing dark paste through her hair and humming under his breath.

"Karras?" Clara whispered. She had to say *something*. "I have a question."

"Ask away."

"You spoke of doxies before. What are doxies?" Clara thought she knew, and it pained her to have to ask, but she needed to learn everything she could. She could not be intimidated by impropriety—and she could not help but be curious.

"I'm a doxy," said Karras. "Lenz is a doxy—Afa, too. She's one of Pascha's favorites. We man the pleasure-house, entertain the faeries."

Clara watched half-dark, half-red strands float to her feet as Karras trimmed a short length from the ends of her hair. "Who is Pascha?"

"The faery who runs our house. Nasty priss of a man, but if you keep him happy, he isn't so bad."

"And . . ." Clara closed her eyes, afraid of the answer. Too similar to Felicity, too small, too frightened, despite her bravado. "Bo isn't a doxy, is she?"

Karras made a horrified sound. "Absolutely *not*. No children here. Even faeries, it would seem, have their standards. So far, anyway." He handed her a damp cloth. "Now grip this in your teeth. This part might hurt."

Avoiding her still-tender wounds, he pasted something up and down her bare legs, from ankle to so high up on Clara's thigh that she jerked away, afraid.

"Don't be afraid, love," he said softly. "I'm not looking too close."

Then he covered the paste with cloths and ripped them free, one by one—along with every hair on Clara's legs. She cried out into the rag. Similar sounds from Nicholas's side of the room brought her some comfort.

"Sorry about that," Karras said, moving to her arms next, "but Pascha likes his doxies smooth and clean. You've got to blend in."

Clara nodded and bit down hard until Karras had finished. A hush fell between them as he worked, as he darted about the room to grab this canister and that brush, painted Clara's fingernails and toenails a deep color that shone black in the darkness and plum in the light. He rinsed the dye from her hair and tied jeweled bangles around her ankles. He painted her stinging arms and belly with shimmering paint colored violet and gold, and disguised the worst of her burns and bruises with powder and cunningly tied scarves. Clara tensed as he worked at this, but if Karras thought her wounds had healed more quickly than they should have, he said nothing.

She was sure they had. She could not ignore what her eyes plainly saw, even if she could not understand it. Worry flared inside her, but she could only stand so much confusion at one time, and set that particular piece aside.

For now.

While he measured her for clothing, she stood in the center of the room in undergarments so flimsy they might as well have been air. Then he dressed her like a doll, with fabrics that slid against her skin like cool, beaded tongues.

By the time Karras stepped back to inspect her, Clara was so deeply uncomfortable that she could feel herself trembling. Such humiliation—practically naked, scrubbed and plucked and daubed within an inch of slapping Karras's hands away and running back into her room to hide. What would Dr. Victor think of her? She squeezed her eyes shut at the thought, fighting back tears; she could feel the air against so much of her body, so many unveiled curves. Such an unabashed, nasty display. She imagined what she looked like, how much skin she would see, and felt ill.

A soft finger at her chin prompted her to open her eyes. Karras's face was compassionate.

"You can't be afraid," he said quietly, "or Pascha will find you, no matter how well we try to hide you. He has a nose for fear, you see."

"And if . . . if I get caught," Clara said, forcing her breathing back into some semblance of regularity, "I cannot find my father." She balled her hands into fists. Her fingers were heavy with rings. "Or return to my sister."

"See, there you are, that's the spirit." He patted her on the shoulder—firm but not unkind. Then he stepped back, tugging here, dabbing there, and grinned. "I'm not usually an egotistical sort of man—"

"Ha!" Lenz laughed again from the other side of the room.

"—but look at yourself. Can I paint, or can't I?"

It was a tremendous effort to turn toward the mirror, and when Clara did, she took stock of herself with a clinical eye. She needed to know what she looked like now, what the people here would see, but she certainly didn't need to examine every last mortifying detail. Dyed ebony curls, falling past her shoulders and threaded with pearls and rubies; eyes outlined with kohl and tiny golden flecks; skin glistening with paint; jewels surrounding her navel; freckles masked with powder. Gauzy dark fabric and braided golden cords covered not much more than the essentials. On her wrists thick bands of metal glazed with gold paint marked her as, she presumed, a doxy of this house.

Before Clara could react, Afa entered the room and nodded her approval.

"Well done, Karras," she said, and drew the curtain aside.

Nicholas stood there, and Clara hardly recognized him. Lenz had painted him into a living mosaic. Shimmering shapes in black, blue, and silver ink swept across his skin, artfully disguising the remnants of the curse—the plate on his right shoulder, the metal slivers snaking around his forearms like vines. Dark strands of jewels hung across his torso, clasped at his neck, wrists, and belt.

It was good work, Afa said, and Pascha would never suspect anything. They looked like new recruits vying for permanent positions.

Even so, Clara felt exposed, fragile. Sullied, and as though she would likewise sully anyone who looked at her, infecting them with the obscenity of her bare skin. Afa led them through the twisting corridors for a meal and to meet with Bo, and as Nicholas walked beside Clara in silence, their many jewels knocked together, jarring her precarious calm.

After a moment he laughed softly. "I can't imagine eating right now. I feel like if I move too much, this pretty shell they've put me in will crack to pieces. And these pants make me itch like you wouldn't believe."

"At least," Clara said, striving for lightness, "your shell covers most of you. I feel as though mine merely serves to point out things I'd rather people not see."

Nicholas was quiet for a moment, and paused outside the common room. He reached for her arm and then, perhaps, remembered the paint.

He pulled away, and his fingers brushed against the jewels at her waist. He muttered an apology.

Clara braced herself, shame welling up inside her. *If he says anything complimentary about how I look, I will happily punch him.*

The paint on his face was the most severe of all, to mask any distinguishing features. Clara saw within it strange shapes, as changeable as storm clouds.

He smiled, his eyes firmly on hers. "I miss your red hair. And your freckles. I've always liked them."

When he offered her his hand, she took it.

During their lunch of roasted figs with honey and rosemary, spiced coffee, and a cold pudding topped with black currants, Clara had an epiphany.

"That map. It was two maps in one."

Nicholas looked dumbfounded. "What do you mean?"

"Something was bothering me about it, but I couldn't figure out what it was." She set down her coffee, and for a moment she forgot to care that she was largely naked, that Nicholas was so near. "There were lines across it, faint ones. I thought perhaps they were outdated borders, or rivers, but—"

"Caught that, did you?" Bo said, slipping into the room with hardly a sound. "They're tunnels."

Nicholas cursed. "Bo, you're worse than a cat. I nearly jumped out of my skin."

She took off her shabby hat with a flourish. "Thank you, sire. I do aim to please."

"Where have you been, anyway?"

"Oh, here and there, and here again." Bo tossed a hunk of misshapen metal onto the table. "Got myself a treat."

Clara recoiled at the broken metal feathers, the dim blue eyes. "A kambot?"

"I like to snatch ones I can, knock 'em out when they're not looking, rewire them. It's to mess with her, see? Take away some of her eyes." Bo shrugged, gleefully wrenching some of the kambot's feathers even farther out of place. "I can't do much, but I can do that at least. I can, in pieces, turn their own damn machines against 'em. And, here." Bo pulled the map from her jacket. "Take another look."

Now that Clara knew what she was looking for, she could see it plainly, beneath the bolder lines of the ten districts.

"*Tunnels*," Nicholas breathed, leaning closer. "That's brilliant. We can use these, Clara."

A treelike network of faint lines fanned out across the map, branching off one another and knotting together in hubs marked with tiny numbers. Delicate beneath the bolder lines of districts and landmarks, they would not be noticed upon first glance.

Afa glided in, glistening with a light sheen of sweat. She had been forced to leave, she had said, for an early afternoon *appointment*. Clara could not meet her eyes.

"Ah," Afa said, fanning her overheated skin, "scheming with my cunning deviant of a sister?"

"Hadn't quite gotten there yet." Bo pointed to the map, in the district marked KAFFLOCK. "Here's where we'll go today—the neighborhood lothouse, see?" she said to Clara and Nicholas. "Sort of like an official market. Clean and neat and all, not like the streets, but dangerous. *Crawling* with faeries. Soldiers, nobility, successful businessfolk like our Pascha. They go there to shop. Humans do too, if they feel like risking it. Food's cleaner, so's water and sugar."

Nicholas looked up. "Risking it?"

"Sometimes if soldiers don't like the look of you, they'll—" Bo mimed the motion of a spear. "*Zzzt!* For no reason. Or worse things than that."

Afa settled onto a settee across from them, tying her damp hair off her neck in a hasty braid. Clara could not stop stealing glances at her, looking for signs of what had happened upstairs. Reprehensible fascination seized her. She wondered if Afa had been hurt, humiliated. If she had been forced to perform for the faeries, and what, exactly, that had entailed.

Clara twisted her napkin in her lap, careful not to smudge the paint on her bare belly. Wicked images overtook her thoughts. It was as though her new clothes, the air upon skin so unaccustomed to it, the knowledge of where Afa had been and what she might have been doing, and the close press of Nicholas against her thigh—this entire monstrously unfamiliar experience—was spinning her out of control. And she *had* to be in control, for her own sake, for her family's. She had to clamp down on her wandering thoughts, this salacious curiosity, the new pulse of her blood that seemed horribly synchronous with the pounding music upstairs.

"And what will we find there?" She focused on Bo, and the sight of her childish face cleared Clara's head. "At the lothouse?"

"Traveling companions, for one," Afa answered. "You will need guides, to travel the country in search of your father, Clara, as well as to make for the capital. Although, Your Highness, how you intend to reach it with Rieden standing in your way . . ."

"We'll work something out," Nicholas said, clipped, intent on the map.

"And if I'm right," Bo said, "and I usually am—"

Afa cleared her throat, her eyes teasing.

"*Usually*, I said, dear sister. Don't give me that look. Anyway, *since* I'm so usually right, we can find information about your father there as well, Clara." Bo smiled, and when she moved to sit closer to Clara, it was so gentle, so quietly trusting, that it reminded Clara of Felicity. Even so, as Bo took them through the afternoon's plan, Clara could not quite block out the sound of the music upstairs, and shifted restlessly. She felt Afa's eyes upon her, and Nicholas's. She felt transparent under their scrutiny, as though they could read her and were disgusted by what they saw.

Stubbornly she stared at the map. If they were—and she would not blame them—she hoped they would keep it to themselves.

20

The lothouse crawled with faeries, as Bo had said—uniformed soldiers, spears in hand, gloves flashing; what Clara assumed was the nobility, in outrageous cloaks and feathered hats, hair braided into elaborate knots; wiry merchants, overseeing multiple stalls manned by harried-looking humans. Each human, like Clara and Nicholas, was marked by some sort of insignia—a band at their wrist, a tattoo on their neck, an emblazoned sash. They were property, like she was pretending to be.

Clara, Nicholas, Afa, and Bo had entered the lothouse separately, to arouse the least suspicion. Not that Clara thought anyone would have noticed their tiny group in this chaos. Countless others were dressed as extravagantly as she and Nicholas, some even more so. Although the sheer quantity of flesh mortified her, Clara could not help but be glad. At least the faeries would have many other doxies to leer after. Humans, too, surrounded them, looking much healthier than those on the streets—servants and doxies, groomed and sometimes resplendent, though none half so glamorous as the faeries. They manned stalls, carried bundles for their faery owners, and, if they were doxies, flirted in an exaggeratedly obsequious manner that seemed to please their potential faery patrons. Once, a human servantwoman laden with baskets of goods stumbled and fell against Clara, nearly knocking her over. A nearby faery soldier shoved the woman to the ground with the butt of his spear, spilling her goods. The buzzing spear seemed to shock her, send her reeling, but she hardly whimpered, as though she were used to such pain.

"My apologies," the faery said to Clara afterward, but there was nothing genuine about him. He tapped the bands around her wrists with one long fingernail, his eyes on her body. "From Pascha House, are you? Might have to pay a visit soon."

Clara tried not to show her disgust, murmured her thanks, and hurried away.

She wandered toward the lothouse's back end, where ridged metal walls met the iron rafters arching high overhead. A severe black door marked what should have been the entrance to this lothouse's chromocast station. There was one at every lothouse, Bo had said, and sometimes two. A bored-looking faery soldier stood guard before the door. Clara felt for the pouch at her waist, beneath her slitted skirt. Yes, there was the tiny weight of the lock pick Bo had gifted her. It should be, she had said, an appropriate size.

Should be.

Clara paused at a stall selling luxurious fabrics. The human man working the station glanced at Clara's bands and looked hurriedly away, as if struck—or as if *she* would strike *him*. Discomposed, she pretended to sort through his bolts of fabric until she caught sight of a dark shape in the rafters, tiny and swift.

Her heartbeat surged. It was time. If everything was going as planned, Afa and Nicholas were at this moment finding the information they needed.

And now, Clara hoped, she would find hers.

She watched the tiny dark shape swoop through the rafters, joined by another shape, and another. She said a tiny, quick prayer for Bo, and wondered, not for the first time, if there was a God in Cane, and if he was as useless here as he was at home.

The shapes exploded—one, two, three—in great sizzling bursts of light. Other explosions followed from throughout the room—hidden beneath merchant stalls, buried in piles of goods. The air filled with black smoke.

Soldiers hurried into action, shouting foreign commands. The nobility ducked, screaming, covering their glittering coiffed heads. The humans screamed as well; some held up their hands, threw themselves onto the floor in supplication, but others laughed and took the opportunity to snatch goods from unmanned carts.

Clara looked to the door. The soldier had gone.

She took one last frantic look at the lothouse floor. Various stalls caught fire as the explosions continued, scattered throughout the building. One singed metal flake of a kambot feather floated down from the ceiling to fall at Clara's feet.

On edge, stretched thin with fear, Clara smiled anyway. *Bo, I could kiss you.*

She turned to the door, fumbled at the latch with her pick, wiping the sweat from her eyes. When she thought she had it, the latch began *shifting*, right there beneath her fingers, with a roiling black hiss.

Faery magic. The door had been enchanted.

She recoiled and, through her alarm, felt something *else* building inside her. It was cold and piercing, the same sudden force from her nightmare, when winter had torn through her blood and turned everything blazing. The same sudden force from the doomed train.

It burst out of her like a fist, this energy, and threw her against the wall. She sagged there, clutching her throat, coughing for air. Something was inside her; something was *crawling*. She was choking like she would turn inside out . . . and then it was gone. It left her, like a storm brimming in and out of existence.

Where the lock had been, there was now a hole, steaming softly, its edges charred. When she touched the surrounding metal, she hissed; it was cold to the touch.

As impossible as it seemed, there was no denying it. She had done this.

How was another question. Understanding hovered at the edge of her awareness. If she only had some time to think, to stay in this moment with the chills still prickling her skin, she could find an answer.

But she had no time. The lothouse remained chaotic, but it would not take long for the faeries to regroup. So Clara pushed aside her curiosity with a pang of foreboding and slipped through the doorway.

The chromocast station was a tiny room, walls filled with multicolored panels—the chromocasts, as Clara now knew they were called—and enough space for a faery soldier to stand in the middle of them.

Pushing hair out of her eyes, not caring if she smeared Karras's paint, Clara scanned the flickering screens. On some of the screens, bright blue faery symbols scrolled in patterned groups. Letters, words. It was gibberish to her, and she ignored it in favor of the chromocasts displaying images—dozens of them, hundreds, shifting quickly from one to the next. Bo had suspected, thanks to the common gossip and her own patchy observations, that the screens in these stations transmitted images recorded by the kambots, and that seemed to be the case. Clara saw images from the viewpoints of birds—the tops of buildings, undercarriages of the elevated trains. Roadways, frozen meadowlands, beggar citizens, the slums of Zarko; crowded streets, the interiors of other lothouses and various rooms, someone's bedroom, someone's sitting room—*there*.

A flash of red, a blurred, bent figure that could have been a man. But then it was gone, that image flickering to the next.

Clara cried out in frustration. She couldn't have much more time. Outside, the noise seemed quieter, though she did not know if this was truth or her own fear. Refusing to blink, she willed the images on the chromocast to cycle back around. Each second seemed an hour. Each second sent the fear in her heart spiraling more feverishly out of control, but then—there! Yes, a red head, a bent figure; a dark room, one lonely window, out of which . . . Was that falling snow?

The image passed, and Clara decided she would wait one more

cycle. One more, and then she would leave, and if all she knew was that there was a man who *might* be her father kept in a room that *might* be located in an area where it was snowing, it would be more information than she had had that morning. Of course, it could have been a trick, or not him at all, or her own wishful thinking projecting false hopes.

She waited, so tense that her shoulders ached . . . and then there it was again. Her palm slapped against the screen, as if grabbing it could keep it there.

And it *did*. Around it the other screens continued on their cycling patterns, but this one, this image of the bent-looking man, remained still, quivering with energy. Clara squinted, taking in as much detail as she could. A dark, jagged-looking room, elaborate architecture embellished with ironwork; a pallet on the floor; a window, and a blizzard outside it. The image of the man himself was fuzzy, but he *did* have red hair, and a blurred shape that seemed John Stole–size. She could see no visible wounds upon him, but he wasn't moving. She hoped he was simply unconscious.

She hoped she was not insane for allowing herself to believe, even for an instant, that the distorted image now branded into her mind was anything relevant to her search. It was an outlandish hope, naive. And yet she could not let it go.

Nor could she stay here. Peeling her hand from the screen was torment, but she did it, slipped back outside with her palm held to her chest as though it cradled her father inside. After she had shut the door behind her, she thought belatedly to look for the guard. It did not matter. Bedlam still reigned outside. Clara moved through it, outside, and eastward down an avenue that smelled of bodies and blood and spiced meat. Her skin still prickled strangely, and the image of the burned-away lock lingered at the edge of her thoughts, frightening her, but she couldn't think about that now. Not now, not yet. Not *ever*, if she could help it.

When she reached the rendezvous point, a shop outside which Afa and Nicholas browsed through an assortment of elaborate smoking pipes, she did not even stop to say hello or to acknowledge the shopkeeper, a young human girl with chains at her ankles who smiled shyly. Numb, newly heartsick, she went straight to Nicholas, ignored his exclamation of relief, and leaned into his chest. When his arms came around her, when he whispered her name, Clara was glad, for beneath Karras's perfumes, he smelled faintly of Godfather's shop, and of home.

21

Bo was to meet them back at the pleasure-house, and by the time she finally slipped through the common room's beaded curtain, minutes before curfew, Clara was sick with worry and Nicholas had been pacing a hole in the carpet.

Afa hurried to her and fell to her knees. "Dear sister, dear, brave, *stupid* sister. Your soul surely must have struck a deal with Zoya herself. Where have you been?"

"Faeries caught me. Seemed to think I might've had something to do with the lothouse incident. They didn't know me from any of the other wretches running around, but they were right angry. Needed someone to pummel. And I got caught in the crowd, besides." Bo shrugged, but the movement made her wince. Already-darkening bruises marred her face, and dried blood spotted her hands. "Good thing I'm not a doxy, eh? Doesn't matter much what I look like."

"Oh, Bo—" Clara said, starting to apologize, but Bo cut her off.

"How did everything play out? Did you find what you needed?"

"Afa and I met a party leaving for the underground at dusk the day after tomorrow," Nicholas said, grave as he inspected Bo's wounds. "A group of four. Three men and a woman. They're headed for Hub 13. If we wish to join them, we're to meet them at Krezentia House."

"None of them recognized Nicholas, even after I'd wiped off a bit of his face." Afa was still on her knees, still cradling Bo as though she were a precious thing. "But then he sang, and their faces, the way they smiled . . . I think . . . Sister, this might be what we've been hoping for. It might be *change*."

Nicholas looked dubious. "A possible beginning, anyway. I hope they don't go gossiping to their friends. Our goal here is not to start a rebellion or to initiate great social change. The populace is too disjointed for that, too weak. It would be snuffed out before it truly began. Stealth and secrecy are the best hope." He glanced at Clara. "For both of us."

She tried to return his smile, but it felt ungainly, the day's events heavy in her mind.

Bo settled herself gingerly on a settee. "What did you find out?"

Clara repeated what she had already told Nicholas and Afa, describing every last detail of what she had seen on the chromocast. An urge to describe the lock's destruction itched at her, but she resisted, and the swallowed words stewed ominously. After she had finished, everyone looked grim.

Bo sighed. "Well, that's not much help, is it?"

"No." Clara felt foolish, having now told her story twice. It was so little to go on, such a thin hope. "It might have been him. It might not have. It could have been a false image, or someone else entirely."

"Let's assume it was him," Nicholas said firmly, "and that he's being held farther north. Maybe one of the northern districts. Maybe Wahlkraft itself."

Afa agreed. "Even now, you don't see blizzards in the southern lands."

"Even now?" said Clara.

"It's been damn icy cold here, ever since the mages died," Bo said. "Worse, of course, the farther north you go. We like to think it was another, you know"—she made a rude, unfamiliar gesture that Clara nevertheless understood plainly—"to the faeries. They hate the cold. Can't say I blame them."

Afa had risen to her feet, hands clasped tightly at her waist. Her eyes did not leave her sister, and Clara understood. If Clara returned home—no, *when* she did, with her father safely in tow—she doubted she would ever again let Felicity out of her sight. *That* development would certainly put Felicity in a terrific mood.

"We will discreetly spread the word about your father, Clara," Afa said, "and relay anything we find to you and Nicholas through the underground. Not always a reliable way to communicate, but it's the best we have."

Clara smiled gratefully at her and turned to Nicholas. "Well, it seems we must head north, then."

He inclined his head. "Do you mind keeping me company for a bit longer, Miss Stole?"

"Have I a choice?"

A flicker on his face. Or perhaps it was the shift of shadows. "You always have a choice."

She almost laughed. Choice. Perhaps she did always have one, yes. But when the choice was between two terrible things—between a father and a sister, between the peril of a pleasure-house and the unknown of a strange land—she wasn't sure it could truly be called something as hopeful as *choice*. Rather, it seemed like a wager, with both paths leading to something dire. But perhaps one would not be quite as traumatic as the other, and that was how you made your decision, for that perilous chance.

Afa suggested they turn in for the night, and the relief at her suggestion was palpable. Before Bo could slip away, Clara caught her shoulders and knelt before her. She forced herself to look at the ugly bruise blossoming on Bo's right cheek. It wasn't terrible; it could have been much worse.

Bewildered, Bo put a hand to Clara's forehead, as though feeling for fever. "Are you ill? Karras spike your coffee or something?"

"I'm sorry you were hurt," Clara whispered. Bo's slender arms in her hands were so like Felicity's, so readily snappable, like a twig under pressure. And the nearness of Bo, her composure and good cheer, despite what had happened to her . . . it was too like Felicity, too horribly, wonderfully like her.

"Oh." Bo waved her off. "It's really not—"

"Truly. I am. Promise me you won't take a risk like that again. Not for me."

Bo raised her eyebrows. "You did hear what we've been talking about, right? You understand what's about to happen? Sorry to say, but missions such as these go hand in hand with risk."

"Just promise me. No more risks like that, not for me. For Nicholas or Afa, if you choose to, but not for me." Carefully Clara hugged her close. She smelled of Cane, of Pascha House, but also of girl, too-small-to-have-to-endure-such-things girl.

"All right," Bo said with an awkward pat. "I promise."

It was a selfish treat to hold her, to pretend her arms were Felicity's, so Clara let her go.

Later Clara lay in bed counting.

It had been two days since she and Nicholas had arrived in Cane, which meant, according to her rough Cane-to-Beyond ratio, that twelve hours had passed at home. A short amount of time, it seemed at first consideration, but that left a mere six and a half days in Patricia Plum's ultimatum.

Six and a half days. Twenty-six days here in Cane to navigate the underground, to somehow pass through the impassable Rieden, to sneak past whatever guarded Wahlkraft. And then what if her father wasn't there after all, or they were intercepted before reaching the capital? Anything could happen between here and there.

Twenty-six days might not be enough. She tossed and turned, restless with the thought.

"How is Bo?" came Nicholas's voice from across the room, startling her.

"Fine. Hurt, but not badly. Of course she won't admit it."

A long pause. "I could cheerfully kill them for doing that to her."

"I could too. Maybe not cheerfully, but readily."

"I think it might be cheerful, for me."

Clara turned on her side to face him. In the dimness she could make out his form across the room on his low cot, staring at the ceiling. She watched his somber profile, followed the troubled shadows playing across his face in the candlelight.

"Have you ever cut something open," he whispered at last, "while it was still alive?"

Stunned, Clara did not respond immediately. "I've thought about it."

"Really?" He sounded surprised.

"Dr. Victor."

"Ah. Yes, I suppose you would think of that, wouldn't you?"

They were quiet for a moment, and then Nicholas said, "I've done it. Cut things open. Living things. And not just animals, which would be bad enough. But *beings*. Of course, I was raised to think they were as good as beasts, lower even than that. . . ."

"The faeries?" Clara said after a pause.

"Yes. Drosselmeyer did too. We were cruel men, Clara. We did cruel things. You would not have liked us then."

An image came into Clara's mind of Godfather bent over a faery bound on a table, a scalpel glinting in his hands. Then Godfather was Dr. Victor, and the faery was an orphan girl with a blank stare, and back again. Clara shuddered.

"Why did you do it?" she managed.

"We'd never liked each other, humans and faeries. Faeries were wild, mysterious. Mischievous and brazen. Disorderly. We didn't understand them." He laughed bitterly. "The old stories say they were born of the southern seas. That, like the sea, they're always changing, never the same one minute to the next, always crafting."

"Building something up and then tearing it down," said Clara, thinking of Anise.

"I think the old stories, at least those, are damn well on point. The faeries were always hiding, playing tricks on travelers. More than anything they loved their tinkering. Building things, taking them apart and putting them back together. They say the faery hollows back then were deep in the forest, always humming with machines."

He turned to her, eyes bright with the flickering candle. "You see, we didn't understand them. They were always hiding themselves away. Why couldn't they cooperate with their rightful sovereigns like the mages did? They must have had something to hide. We desperately feared their magic. We didn't understand how it worked, what it could do. The mages had always been open about their own magic—their charm, their kinship with animals, their tremendous intellect. Arrogant but open. Why couldn't the faeries do the same?"

Clara was mesmerized, despite herself. "So you hurt them because you couldn't understand them."

"I was raised to do it." He threw himself back down onto the cot. "And Drosselmeyer was bound to do it, as were the rest of the Seven. You could say that neither of us had a choice in the matter. You *could* say that, and I used to believe it, but I don't now. We knew exactly what we were doing, and we did it gladly."

"Bound? Do you mean it was part of his service?"

"Quite literally. The Seven were bound to the royal family in power. It was a blood ritual, an old magic." He paused, as if picking only the best words to say. "They served us, protected us, and in turn were able to protect mage interests at court."

Clara was not sure how to respond to this. The idea of bonding in a blood ritual seemed rather barbaric. To be in Nicholas's presence now felt . . . different somehow. In the grip of a dangerous intimacy. She was appalled by him, and yet she understood what he was feeling. Or she thought she did. The impulse toward violence, the longing to control something, *anything,* even if it meant cruelty.

A tiny part of her even admired him, she was ashamed to say, for having the temerity to hurt his enemies, to commit atrocities she'd only ever entertained in daydreams.

A tiny part.

"They hurt us, Clara," he went on, softly. "The tricks they would play were anything but harmless. For every faery we abducted and dissected, they would string up five humans on the side of the road, their bones extracted, their faces . . . *carved.* We engineered weapons especially for use against them, and in combat they would turn them—our own weapons!—against us. Imagine it, screaming soldiers devoured by their own crossbows."

Clara did not want to imagine it. "So there was war."

"There was war." He sighed. "A decades-long war. I was raised by it, in fact. A mother, a father, and a war." He turned to her, the candle now a mere stub. They were children, facing each other from their beds, gossiping in the dark—except it wasn't gossip, and Clara was not sure Nicholas had ever been a child, not truly.

"It took me a long time to see the wrongness of it, to let go of my hate," he continued. "But now, after seeing my people in this state, seeing what the faeries have done, what *she* has done . . . I feel myself regressing, Clara. I feel the hate returning, and the violence. I want to be better, to believe the things I tell myself—that I can somehow reclaim my kingdom bloodlessly, that we can live happily after that, as equals. But it seems impossible. If even *I* find it hard to look at the faeries without wanting . . ." He laughed sadly into the dark. "I would wager this is not what you might have imagined your dear statue would turn out to be."

She ignored the remark. "I know what it is to hate," she said instead. "How did you let go of it, that first time? Let go of the hate?"

"I had a good teacher." Her own words, returned to her, and just as sadly.

"Who?"

The candle, at last, went out.

A pause. "A dear friend." After a longer silence, Nicholas cleared his throat. "Do you hate me now?"

"No," Clara said, "but I confess . . ."

"Tell me. I deserve whatever it is."

She took a deep breath. "What you did was wrong. I understand hate, but I hope you remember that." She tried to find his face in the dark. "Those faeries you cut open did not deserve that, no matter what their kind had done to you. No one does."

"You're right, of course," he said after a moment, and they fell into an uneasy silence.

Clara had trouble finding sleep. She wondered if Nicholas would still smile at her in the morning. And what if he didn't? One less prince with a dark past to fixate on. Besides, she might have done the same thing in his position. She didn't know if she would have had the courage to reject a culture of hate, to shed the skin of the violence that had raised her.

But when she awoke later, to another nightmare—this one more violent: ice splintering her bones, bursting out of her, quartering her into frozen slabs—Nicholas was there to smooth back her damp hair. He urged her to recount her dream in detail, and his voice was so soft, so soothing, that it almost lulled her to do so, but the frigid brutality done to her nightmare's body was too disturbing to think of. He fell silent then, and held her. As his touch calmed her, thoughts of war—and his part in it—retreated further and further from Clara's mind. For the rest of the night, she could not stop shivering, and she was glad simply to have a friend sit beside her.

22

The next evening Afa barreled into the common room through the beaded curtain, her veil and jewels askew, her face raw with fright.

"Afa," Nicholas said, rising, "what is it?"

"Bo, to your room."

Bo frowned. "But, *Afa*—"

"Do not argue with me!"

Such terror, such naked terror in Afa's voice. Bo's eyes widened, and she ran. Afa turned to Clara, grabbed her hands.

"You must be brave now," she said, and though her voice was steady, Clara could tell it was an effort. "I'm so, so sorry."

The expression on Nicholas's face was dangerous. "Afa, tell us what's happened."

"Glyn. It was Glyn." Afa closed her eyes, shaking her head. "She did not mean to. She is a flighty, foolish girl. She mentioned new doxies in the sweetrooms, and word got to Pascha, and . . . the Mason give me strength—"

A claw of dread snagged Clara in her gut. She wavered where she stood. "He wants to meet us."

Afa nodded, miserable. "And if he suspects our ruse, he will kill every one of us and make the killing last as long as possible."

Clara felt suddenly wild. "We should run."

Nicholas caught her arm. "And then what? Raise Pascha's suspicions, bring his anger down on Afa and Bo?"

"Better that than have him discover they've been harboring the queen's fugitives."

"They're coming," Afa whispered at the door.

A beat later, and a pair of smartly dressed, languorously arrogant male faeries appeared in the doorway. Pascha's attendants, Clara assumed. They wore sleeker gloves than their soldier compatriots, but the blue energy still sizzled there, waiting. Their eyes roved first over Nicholas's body and then Clara's.

"Come," one of them said, grinning as if delighted by some unheard joke. "Pascha is waiting."

They had no choice. One attendant in front and one behind, they left the familiarity of the doxy quarters to walk up the stairs, through corridors heavy with incense, past curtained rooms. Music and laughter drifted out from behind the curtains, along with other, indecent sounds that made Clara's skin crawl with fear. She and Nicholas had come so close to escaping Kafflock without encountering Pascha. One night remained before they would leave for the tunnels. She wished they had had more time for Afa to explain what would be expected of them. Would they be forced to *perform*, as the others were, and what did that mean? She longed to reach for Nicholas's hand to steady herself; she longed to turn and run, and never stop.

The attendants led them through a series of lavishly decorated rooms—silken cushions piled on the floor, low tables laden with sumptuous dishes, settees draped with brocaded cloth—and onto a terrace bordered with violet curtains. Storm clouds roiled above Kafflock's crooked roofscape.

A faery lounged there. Pascha, undoubtedly. His eyes danced with delight and uncontested power. He wore fine trousers and boots and a silk shirt that revealed his chest. Extravagant powders decorated his face, and his braided white hair, wrapped in gossamer golden threads, fell to the small of his back.

For a moment no one moved, though Pascha's eyes slid over them, inspecting them. By necessity Clara had become somewhat accustomed to her new clothes, but under Pascha's lazy, mercenary gaze, she felt stripped clean to the bone.

"So," he said, his voice light, "these are the new recruits?"

Afa stepped forward, bowing. "Yes, Pascha. I found them several days ago, scrounging for food in the market. I have been training them, grooming them. I wanted to surprise you. They are a gift, Pascha."

Pascha nodded, pursing his lips. Then he waved to one of his attendants, who promptly struck Afa in the face.

"I appreciate the sentiment, Afa," Pascha said, impassive, "but the next time you have a gift for me, don't wait several days to tell me about it."

"Yes, Pascha." Afa nodded, holding her cheek with bright-eyed dignity. "It was a mistake. It will not happen again."

A few terrible moments passed in silence, save for a faint rumbling in the skies and an echoing one from the ground. It shook the lanterns hanging around the terrace, and Pascha glared at them irritably, popping a piece of bright pink fruit into his mouth.

"Well?" he snapped, dribbling juice. "Let's see it, then."

Clara looked to Afa for guidance, at a loss, but Afa revealed nothing.

"Pardon me, sir," Nicholas said, bowing as Afa had done, softening his voice in deference, "but what would you like us to do?"

"Kiss!" Pascha threw up his hands. "Put on a show! Do *something*." He snapped his fingers, and an attendant pressed a mechanical switch in the wall. Music began, sultry, rhythmic, drifting down from dark funnels affixed to the terrace columns.

"It would be best," Pascha added, "that you not hold back. I am easily bored."

Nicholas flashed a smile so convincing that even Clara was taken in by it.

"Of course, Pascha," he said, and turned to Clara. She could not read his expression, and that terrified her. Surely he was wound just as tight with fear? He moved closer, brought his hands to her neck, caressing lightly; Clara felt the attention of everyone on the terrace tighten. He brushed his lips across her forehead, at the corners of her eyes, her mouth, the curves of her cheeks.

Heat surged through her to meet his touch, surprising and insistent. She staggered, and Nicholas must have mistaken it for fear. His hands caught her waist, steadying her against the hard lines of his body.

So little space between them now, and all of it searing. It didn't make sense, and part of Clara protested in horror—this was not how it should happen!—but it was a small part, and quickly overpowered. The sudden delicious realization that Nicholas was so close, so breathlessly *there*. His fingers, tracing her features, toying with her bottom lip. The *pull* of him. For an instant she thought of her near-nakedness and flinched, but then his hands settled at her hips, weaving through the jeweled strands draped around her belly.

She couldn't help it; she moved into him.

She had fantasized about this for years, half in shame, half in giddy defiance—her statue-suitor coming to life, wrapping his arms about her, gathering her against his body. It was happening now, Nicholas's hot gaze fixed on her mouth. Soon he would lean in and whisper against her skin, tickling her neck. He would kiss her there, on the soft skin behind her ear.

He *did* lean in, and Clara let her eyes flutter closed. She allowed it to happen; she *willed* it to, fogged with her own swift euphoria. When he kissed her, it was lightning, a jolt that left her aching. When his tongue parted her lips, she went limp against him.

One of Nicholas's hands cupped the back of her head; the other slid down to stroke her thigh.

She gasped, made a small sound of surprise, and his grip on her tightened. A low groan escaped his lips, and it was that sound—the deep rumble of it, the masculinity—that made her stiffen.

Awareness hit her like a series of sharp punches: her leg was hooked around his. His hand was on her ribs, inching higher.

They were not alone. Pascha watched eagerly, his attendants equally rapt, and Afa's face was full of compassion.

Wait. This was not right. *Wait.*

She tried to pull away, and Nicholas withdrew at once. As she stared at him, sharp all over with new panic, his face changed from wanting to fear—for her, for himself, for what they had done and what they might be forced to do.

He shifted back from her, and Pascha crowed, clapping his hands. "She shakes! Oh, delightful. Who doesn't love a cowering human?" His attendants laughed, and Pascha's smile turned lascivious. "Go on, then. Continue."

Nicholas whispered, "I'm sorry," and squeezed her wrist gently. There was anguish in his eyes, his face raw with torment. As he pressed her into the column at her back, gathering her into his arms, his touch was gentle, like he was afraid he would break her, and somehow that made everything worse.

This wasn't right. This was not how it should happen.

No. "No." She whispered it into Nicholas's neck, for he had pulled her close, turned her away from Pascha's gaze to shield her.

Clara tried to look past his shoulder at Afa. Perhaps Afa would send her a sign—that they needed to get only to a certain point, and then Pascha would be satisfied, send them back downstairs.

But Clara could no longer see Afa. Nicholas was kissing her, and the column's ironwork of tiny decorative birds poked at her bare back. Logic dictated that she should return Nicholas's kisses, convince Pascha of her potential, and she tried. But what had felt so natural before felt strained now, false and vile. Nicholas's familiar scent turned cloying; the contours of his body were not pleasing but menacing.

She hesitated, afraid. She caught sight of Nicholas's anxious face, hovering over hers.

Pascha made an impatient sound, pounded his fist against the table, threw a piece of fruit at them. It plopped wetly against Clara's leg. "More!" he shouted.

Nicholas's hands slid around to cup Clara's backside, urging her hips closer to his. His movements were stiff, his body unyielding. Clara would drown in the wrongness of it. Yes, this was Nicholas, and yes, they had shared . . . moments. Touches. Charged looks from across the room.

But never had she imagined something like this.

His hands traveled up her back, forcing her body to arch toward him. He kissed her neck, her breastbone, and lower. Through her bodice's diaphanous fabric, she felt the hot press of his mouth.

A sliver of something cold slipped through her blood, something separate from terror.

Oh no. *Not now.* Whatever this was, this recurring coldness, this prickling energy—she did not have time to explore it now, with Nicholas's kisses becoming more insistent and Pascha demanding more, more, *more.* Why couldn't this happen when she actually had time to examine it?

The air surrounding her vibrated with sudden urgency. Her jewels crackled against her skin like electric wires. Frightened, she tried once more to pull away from Nicholas. Would he notice this new strangeness if she touched him? Would he feel the cold spark ready to burst from her fingers?

Something had caught his attention. He paused to search her face, his expression distraught and . . . curious? Anticipatory? Clara could not tell, and she was desperate to communicate to him what was happening. But she would not know what to say, only that an unknown energy within her was compounding, that her teeth were beginning to chatter. Had the temperature plunged in the last ten seconds?

"Pascha," intoned a voice from the terrace doors. "Pardon the interruption."

Abruptly Nicholas moved away. Mere inches, but it was enough. He stood between Clara and Pascha's gaze, and she sagged against the column, clutching the ironwork. She felt marks on her back from the tiny serrated beaks.

"And you *should* beg pardon." Pascha stuck out his bottom lip. "I was having so much fun here, and you've completely destroyed the mood."

The new attendant bowed at the door. "Yes, Pascha. Forgive me. But Lord Ingo awaits you in the Red Parlor."

"Lord Ingo is early."

"Yes, Pascha. He said he simply could not wait until midnight."

"Insatiable." A decadent grin curled across his face. "He's lucky I'm so fond of him. There are few who could pull me away from such a sight."

Pascha gathered himself, his attendants trailing behind him. "You two are certainly . . . intriguing. Maddeningly slow, but that can be fixed. I look forward to our time together. Afa, you may put them to work as you see fit."

Then he strode toward the terrace doors and was gone.

As soon as the terrace doors shut behind him, Clara fled.

"Clara, wait," Nicholas pleaded, frantic, but she did not listen. She ran for the terrace railing, and though Afa cried out for her and Nicholas reached for her, she did not listen. She was ready to burst with the cold swelling inside her, and she did not want to be around them when it happened, not until she knew what it meant. She needed time, she needed privacy; and if she had to stand there and look at Nicholas's swollen lips and stricken face and decide whether she hated him for kissing her or—awfully, bewilderingly—wanted him to keep going, she would burst.

She leapt over the railing, thinking of Bo's map and Godfather's lessons—how to fall, how to move without fear. The buildings of

Kafflock were squashed together, close enough to climb from the roof of one building to the next with ease, but her landing on a neighboring balcony still sent her crashing to her knees. Godfather would have scolded her.

Her teeth clacked in her head, and she left blood behind on the smooth coral stone. Once again she was running—from Nicholas and Pascha this time instead of Godfather. It struck her that she would not always be able to run from things that frightened her.

She ran hard and did not stop.

23

Clara slipped through the hazy, glittering streets of Kafflock, dodging painted doxies in gauzy veils; human slaves peddling jewels, caramels, sugar pipes; faeries shopping, faeries patrolling, faeries cavalierly picking through the human detritus at the sewer's edge. Clara's amplified senses, reeling from the cold pounding through her blood, noticed several humans whose unnaturally white skin was scattered with hastily attached metal bits, their ears stitched up haphazardly into points and crusted with blood. Faeries enslaving humans, and humans trying to look like faeries—for what purpose? To impress, to appease, to mock? Out of sheer madness?

Clara could sympathize. She felt her own sort of madness raging within her. It was worse this time than ever before: the cold was not abating, and the energy vibrating along her skin was not settling. If she touched someone, she would surely blow them to pieces.

Hands—both human and faery—grabbed at her idly from the crowd. Were it not for the band marking her a doxy of Pascha House, which she thrust at everyone who touched her, she might not have been able to hold them off. She stumbled into a crooked alleyway masked by a ragged tarp. Sagging benches lined the narrow passage. People slipped needles to one another beneath the tables of card games. Inside a shop marked with a stained awning, a masked human tattooed another. Clara recognized the shape. Faery symbols.

They were all obsessed.

Blindly she made a right turn, and then another right, and came to a dead-end alleyway with boarded-up windows and bolted doors, where things were quieter.

Clara sank against the wall. A shadowed face kept flashing before her eyes. It would shift and be Nicholas, his eyes filled with sorrow, his kisses feathering across her neck—and then lower. It would shift again and be Dr. Victor with his scalpel. *We shall have to cut the wickedness out of you,* he would say, and slice, slice, slice.

She clapped her hands over her ears and imagined pressing the images flat, flicking them away like bugs.

What was happening to her? The tingling in her hands would not fade. She held them up before her face. They shook violently, but nothing besides that seemed out of the ordinary. She would scream; she was near tears. *What does this mean?*

"Here. Drink this. It will settle your stomach." A vial of dark glass appeared before her, and the voice urging her to take it was familiar.

Clara looked up. She could not contain her cry of shock.

He was cloaked, hardly recognizable with a scarf draped across half his face.

The half without an eye.

Godfather.

Clara surged to her feet, and he was there, helping her, folding her into his embrace as she wept his name against his neck. In that one overwhelming instant she was a child again who knew nothing of faeries and sugar pipes and spears that burned. She was safe, for this moment, safe in Godfather's arms, and who gave half a whit if he had inadvertently caused her mother's death and withheld that information from her?

Horribly, Clara found, she did not. Not in this moment; she knew only relief.

She pulled back to examine his face. "Are you well? You're here. You truly are. What happened to you? Why are you here? *How?*"

He smiled at her. He held her as though she were a precious thing. "I thought it was you. At first I wasn't sure. Your hair, your clothes . . . But I would know your eyes anywhere. Do you know how long I've been looking—" His eye was alert, elated, but exhausted. "I've been tracking you, and then I saw the train crash, and Anise's message—"

Clever, dear Godfather. "You've been tracking us?"

"It took me longer than I would like to admit to open another Door. Borschalk's closed after you left with Nicholas, and my magic is so weak now, so unreliable. Clara"—Godfather's voice broke on the word—"I thought I'd lost you. To her. To him."

"Her" was Anise, of course. But "him"?

"Do you mean Nicholas?"

His mouth thinned. "How is he? Not pleased, I imagine, to see what's happened to his kingdom."

Clara frowned at the edge in his voice. "You do not like him."

"I do not trust him. And I don't like that he is all that stands between you and . . ." He waved his hand at their surroundings in disgust. "*This.*"

"Him, and all the training you've beaten into me." Clara crossed her arms. He was steadying her, though her skin was still cold to the touch. Had he noticed? "Was this your plan? To bring me here?"

"No. *Never.* This was the last thing I wanted for you." He stepped closer, earnest. "I meant what I said in the stable, Clara. I want to keep you safe, take you far away from all of this. This war, and your father's."

She eyed the vial still in his hand. "What is that?"

"Ah. Yes." His eyes flitted down her body, clinical. "I thought you might need it."

"Why? What is it?"

"I told you, something to settle your stomach."

"I don't believe you." She stepped back. "How am I to know it isn't some concoction you've designed to drug me so you can drag me back to New York?"

He looked affronted. "I would never deceive you in such a way."

She pounced. "Yet you would deceive me about what happened to Mother, and your part in it."

"I did what I thought was best," he said, low. "I'm sorry for your grief, but I won't apologize for my actions."

The conversation was rapidly devolving, but at least Clara's mind was clearer. She could always count on him for that. She took a chance. "Why did you never tell me you were a mage?"

He frowned at his feet. "I'm hardly a mage anymore."

"Oh, and I suppose that's why you weren't in fact able to open a Door between worlds and come find me?"

"I told you, my magic is weak now—"

"Unreliable, yes. I heard you."

He kicked at the ground with one scuffed boot. "All those years of undoing faery magic took their toll on me. And did he even *thank* me?"

"I've no patience for your petulance. Anyway," she said, baiting him, "I suppose it doesn't matter that you didn't tell me about mages. I've learned all about them from Nicholas. Mages, faeries, the war. Even dragons."

Godfather's face twisted bitterly. "And where is the good prince? Has he reclaimed his throne yet?"

"We've found a safe place to hide, for now. After that, where we go is our business."

"Oh, I have a good idea where you'll go." He stepped closer, and the look on his face was suddenly so urgent that Clara felt alarmed. "Tell me, has your noble Nicholas said anything about the way your body is changing? Has he even noticed?"

That surprised her. "My body is the same as it was." She told herself he deserved her lies.

"Is it?" Godfather pinned her in place with his gaze. "I think you're lying. I wondered if it would ever manifest. Our training, all the physical strain, and nothing. Not until we fought the loks did I see any sign of it."

"Sign of what?" But part of her knew—the deepest part of her mind, the part that had approached revelation and been too afraid to accept it.

"I've never seen the product of a mage and a human coupling," Godfather said quietly. "I assume *dear Nicholas* has told you such things aren't done. But I saw that train wreck, and I felt your power in the ballroom. I feel it even now. It's crude, certainly. I couldn't teach that part of you, for it never awoke—not in New York, not in any coherent fashion. In the ballroom, yes, I caught glimpses of it, possible signs. But here . . . here, it seems to be waking up with a vengeance."

Clara stepped back from him. "What are you talking about?"

"Clara, Anise is now not the only half-breed in Cane. Your father is John Stole, yes, and he is a human. But your mother . . ." Godfather's eyes softened, as they always did when he spoke of Hope Stole. "Your mother was a mage. Her blood runs in your veins. You have magic in you, Clara. And Cane is waking it up."

24

In the aftermath of his words, a crash sounded from around the corner, answered by a peal of drunken laughter. Briefly Clara thought she would cry. Then she began to laugh along with the unseen merrymakers.

"You see," Godfather began cautiously, as though *she* were the mad one, "long ago there was a rather sour young girl named Leska—"

Leska? So her mother had taken a new name for herself in New York, a new identity. Leska in Cane, Hope in New York. Had everything been a lie? Would she rescue her father to find him one of Godfather's clockwork toys disguised with human skin?

"Are you going to sit here in the alleyway and tell me my mother's life story?" Clara said incredulously. "All right. Yes. Let me find a comfortable seat. . . ."

Godfather was watching her as if the wrong word would make her combust. Perhaps he wasn't too far off; Clara felt a bit like a spinning top teetering at the table's edge.

"It's true, love," he said. "Leska was a mage once, a true Lady of the North. And a powerful one."

Despite herself Clara burned with fascination at the idea of this Leska. A sour, powerful young girl. A Lady. Would her mother have looked the same here as she had in New York? Had she known she would someday leave Cane, meet a Beyond man, and have little Beyond children?

"What I don't understand," she said, forcing evenness into her voice, "is why you kept this information from me for so long. Along with you being a mage, along with the cause of her death. How could you do it?"

"First and foremost, always, to keep you safe," he said firmly. "Second, it was your mother's wish. Clara, she left here for a reason. She wanted a new life, and she certainly didn't want her girls becoming caught up in a past rife with violence and treachery."

"Spare me your poetry. To keep me safe, to please my mother—I'll buy that, to a point." She turned on him, fighting tears of astonishment. "But what about when Mother died, and Father buried himself in drink and Concordia, and Felicity came to me with nightmares, and I came to you? Even then you wouldn't give me an explanation, allow me some peace?"

"Oh, it would have given you peace, eh?" Now Godfather laughed. "To know that your mother was a witch and had been killed by monsters? Yes, surely that would have quelled the nightmares."

Clara turned away. She did not want him to see her face crumpling, or see her steal glances at her arms, where gooseflesh prickled like needles piercing her skin. Maybe this conversation was deluding her senses, but her skin seemed grayer than it had a moment before. She wanted to laugh, but she was now too exhausted for it—and, if she were honest, too frightened. What did it mean, to be a mage? And was she *actually* contemplating this as truth?

As she stared at her increasingly alien hands, a thought came to her with the weary weight of one revelation too many, the puzzle pieces of the past few days clicking into place.

"Anise had the mages here killed," she said dully. "Or did it herself, I suppose."

Godfather was so quiet, so unearthly still. "I had wondered as much."

"She killed Mother, too. Didn't she? Anise."

"Not with her own hands, perhaps. But the loks obey her every command, as does Borschalk." He seemed disgusted. "No, it was him, with his pack of beasts. Him, at her command."

I could kill her for it. She thought of Nicholas, whispering of hate in the dark. She felt a sudden, passionate empathy for him. *I could kill them* all *for it.* The thought exploded through her, and the answering electric shock across her skin made her jump. She leaned hard against the wall, heaving.

Godfather held her up, murmured reassurances that came to her through a fog.

"You'll massacre Karra's handiwork," she mumbled dizzily.

"What?"

In answer she laughed, gasping through the pain in her belly. She had heard of terrible sicknesses killing a person from the inside out, shutting down their organs, making them bleed out their orifices. Would this happen to her? She would bleed ice instead of blood.

"It has started, hasn't it?" Godfather whispered. "You've felt the charge of it, like electricity. You've noticed the cold, the wind."

She shook her head wearily against the wall. "I don't know. . . ."

"You won't be able to hide yourself forever here. Imagine—imagine if you suddenly saw a demon prancing down the streets of New York. Something feared, something *unclean*."

"An abomination," she choked out.

"Not that *I* think you are one—far from it, dear Clara—but others will. You'll be torn apart. You'll be used. Come back to New York with me. I can keep you safe, help you through it. And perhaps if you leave Cane, it will halt the change. You needn't endure it. It could be painful."

"No. No. I must find Father. . . ." Oh, it was *surging* through her, like someone had injected her with ice. "I have to help Nicholas."

Godfather was beside himself. "Oh, yes? Help him do what, exactly? Rally the rebels? Reclaim his throne? Does he promise to help find your father? Clara and Nicholas, fighting for family and justice, side by side? Don't be a fool, Clara. He is a politician. You should know what that means more than most. He will say anything to win your loyalty, and he is biding his time because he *knows*, Clara. He is waiting for your blood to change, for your abilities to manifest. And then he will use you." He shook her gently. "He will *bind* you, and he will use you to fight."

She could not hide a flicker of recognition at the word.

"He's spoken of binding, has he?" He looked a bit sorry for her, and that was worst of all. "Lovely, diplomatic process. We help the humans, and the humans help us. But binding is a one-way street. The humans own us. We have no power over them. Nicholas used to be able to tell me what to do, and I'd have no choice but to do it. My blood would *compel* me."

He would cut things open, Nicholas had said. *And Drosselmeyer was bound to do it, as were the rest of the Seven.* Could Godfather's awful theory be true? No. Nicholas wouldn't do that. Hadn't he been kind to her? Hadn't he held her as she'd recovered from her nightmare?

Her nightmare. Clara's heart dropped, colder than her freezing skin. She had told him. She had told him of her blood turning to ice, and he had sat with her, patiently watching her face. For clues? For a sign that she did indeed have mage blood, as he so desperately hoped? And she was to go underground with him the next day. Trapped, like a patient being observed for signs of worsening disease.

Her head spun. She needed to get out of this cold. The skies were darkening, the trains howling.

"Come back with me." Godfather took her hands in his. "I'll keep you safe. We'll wander the world. We'll take Felicity with us. I promise you."

She stared at him, uncertain. She could go with him, and he *would* keep her safe; he always had. But something kept her rooted—a desire to confront Nicholas herself? An unwillingness to abandon her father?

Maybe—and this was a startling thought—to see where the ice in her blood would take her.

A sudden sharp light shone down upon them from above. A fat-bellied flying apparatus, like a mechanical balloon, hovered there, whirring.

"You!" Another light, from the end of the alleyway, and three slender figures.

Faeries.

Godfather cursed. "They've found me."

"They've been following you?"

"I did not have the happy distraction of a train crash to get me through the wall. Only my own two hands and patchy magic." He waved at the approaching faeries. "Hello there!"

Clara grabbed his arm. "Are you mad?"

"Do you know, I think I might be. But I also love you, Clara." He kissed her forehead, and his eye shone. "Think of that, and think of what I told you."

"Godfather?" He was frightening her. "What are you doing?"

"And remember, light on your feet, stay two steps ahead of them."

"Godfather, please don't—"

"*Run.*"

He shoved her with one hand, and with the other he pulled a tiny clicking mechanism from his pocket. Clara recognized it as one of the failed experiments cluttering the shelves in his shop. Failed experiments with faery magic, that, as a mage, was not his to use.

He tossed the device at the faeries, and it exploded, spewing foul-smelling gas that set them coughing, and Clara, too. But it was enough of a diversion for her to slip past their grasping limbs—*light on your feet, stay two steps ahead.* Left, and another left, past the card tables where the sugared watched her progress with bleary disinterest. She heard the crack of faery spears behind her. Another explosion burst at her back, and cold was nipping at her heels—but the spear cracks overwhelmed everything else. She imagined them: nets of blue encircling Godfather, burning him.

She exited onto the main thoroughfare, remembering at the last moment that it would be best to appear unruffled. Stumbling to a stop, she dragged a shaking hand through her hair, made sure to display the band on her wrist. Bystanders stared at her, including a stern-looking pair of faery soldiers.

"Bad night," she said, shrugging, and even when the faery soldiers hurried past her into the alleyway, spears at the ready, even when an explosion from behind her shook everything on the street, Clara continued on, past the muttering crowd and in the direction of Pascha House.

It was there, once through the grate and in the lonely passageway to the doxy quarters, that she allowed herself to relive the sound of Godfather's screams echoing down the alleyway as she'd fled. The world fell away beneath her feet, and she sobbed there, alone in the dirt.

Nicholas found her. Hours later, maybe? Impossible to tell.

"Clara." He cursed softly, helping her up. "What happened to you? Where did you go?" Quietly: "We've been frantic, Clara."

She shrank from his touch as if she were back on the terrace, with Nicholas pressed against her and Pascha watching.

Nicholas released her at once. "It's all right. I'm not touching you. I won't touch you." He peered closely at her. "Would you like to go to your bed?"

Bless him for not asking questions. There were many things Clara did not know in this moment—whom to trust, for example, and whom to believe, and what was happening to her still-churning insides—but she did know that she would not tell Nicholas about Godfather. Not that she had seen him, not what he had told her of binding. Not that he was most likely dead now.

"I would," she said quietly, and Nicholas was true to his word. He did not touch her on the way to their room. He waved away Afa, Bo, and Karras, and when poor Glyn, looking beside herself with remorse, tried to apologize, Nicholas's glare was enough to silence her.

Clara was grateful. She did not want to be grateful to him, to feel anything toward him but pragmatic distrust—at least not until she determined how much of what Godfather had said was true. Still, when Nicholas turned to leave their room, she sat up in surprise.

"Where are you going?"

"To the common room," he said. "I thought you might like—"

"I wouldn't." She flushed, furious and confused, drowsy with grief. *I can keep a closer watch on him if he's in here.* That was reasonable enough. "Please stay."

His face was so tender in that moment, and when they both lay in their beds, he stretched out his hand into the space between them. An offer of comfort? An apology.

She took it gladly. Pragmatic distrust could wait, at least until morning.

25

They spent the next day preparing to leave, and most of it was spent in silence. Nicholas seemed to sense that Clara wanted it that way. A combination of nightmares—some about her bones being picked clean by a cold wind, and some about Godfather covered in ash—had kept her awake most of the night. It felt good to occupy her thoughts with mindless, menial tasks: packing food, cleaning her daggers, letting Karras—mournful that he would no longer get to dress her—fit her for traveling clothes.

Clara worked, letting the sounds of Afa and Bo's arguing about whether or not Bo would accompany them wash over her. Bo insisted that Clara and Nicholas needed a proper guide, and few knew the underground better than she did. Bo knew a couple of the people they would be traveling with, but she still wouldn't *trust* them, not with this. Afa, unmoved, declared it out of the question.

The two sisters left Clara and Nicholas alone together only once. Nicholas was sharpening his sword—*Godfather's* sword, Clara reminded herself, with a pang of silent despair. After a few minutes of this, he put down the sword and whetting stone, and turned to her.

"I have to say it. I know you probably don't want to talk about it, but if I don't say something, I'll tear myself to pieces."

Despite herself Clara was touched by the earnestness of his expression. "All right," she said carefully.

"Clara, I'm sorry." He seemed ready to reach for her hands, but he stopped himself and knelt before her, tense and distraught. "You must know—*please* know—that I didn't want to kiss you like that. I would *never* force you to kiss me or touch me, or do anything you didn't want to. It was torment, pushing myself on you like that. I hated every second of it."

He would not make her do anything she didn't want to do. How fitting that he should proclaim such a thing after Godfather's warning. But could she believe him?

"*Every* second?" Conflicted he may have been, but the care with which he had touched her, the intensity of his kisses, had hinted at genuine feeling. Knowing this left her both mildly affronted, that he could take pleasure from such a moment, and bizarrely gratified. The incongruity unsettled her. "Surely I'm not so repulsive."

"I'm serious, Clara."

"I know you are. And thank you."

"I hope we can still be friends. I want . . . I'd like most sincerely for us to be friends, always."

He was so somber, so awkwardly formal. It was a struggle for Clara to remain neutral. But of course she had to. Until she knew for certain that Godfather was wrong in his accusations, she would assume that he was right.

"Of course we're still friends." She touched Nicholas's arm. "Don't worry. I just . . . I had a hard time of it. I was frightened."

"I don't blame you. I was frightened too. If I'd had to—if it had escalated—" He shook his head. "I'm not sure I could have done it, no matter the danger. I could not have lived with myself."

"I believe you," she said quietly.

He gathered her hands in his, grave. "I'd never lie to you."

She shivered. She was loath to let go of his hands, and even when she did, he remained there looking up at her. She had never seen his face so open.

"Do you really mean that?" she asked.

The question hung between them, tugging and wary.

But then Bo entered the room, crowing her triumph—she would indeed be joining them, and Afa would be increasing her daily intake of honeywine to cope with the situation, but who cared about grumpy old Afa?—and the unanswered question dissolved like a sigh, and was gone.

At dusk they left for Krezentia House, and Clara felt the most comfortable she had yet felt since arriving in Cane, despite the journey that awaited them. Instead of a tattered gown or gossamer doxy garments, she now wore dark breeches, fur-lined gloves and cloak, and a utilitarian tunic, each artfully tattered by Karras so as not to attract attention. Best of all, she had been reunited with her boots and daggers. The weight of the blades at her thigh and in her heels gave her a renewed strength, even when she had to say good-bye to Afa and leave the relative safety of Pascha House behind.

"This time tomorrow," Bo said cheerily, her bag of decommissioned kambots and other scrap parts swinging at her hip, "we'll be north and south of here at the same time. You see? North because we're traveling north, but south because we'll be underground." She chucked Nicholas on the arm. "And you might've thought our brains had gone to mush in your absence, Your Highness."

"Well," he said soberly, "perhaps not all your brains, but certainly *some*."

Bo punched him, and Clara forced a laugh she did not feel. Her thoughts were too scrambled to feel anything but uneasiness. Every look Nicholas threw her, each word he said, she interpreted through a new veil of suspicion. It was maddening, for outwardly he had done nothing to warrant such misgivings.

She ignored the twinge of disquiet in her heart and the icy tumult of her blood and followed Bo and Nicholas to Krezentia

House as automatically as any faery mechanik might. She would think of saving her family and empty her mind of everything else, as though her mind were a sieve designed for one purpose and no other. It wouldn't matter then if Nicholas tried to use her, or if she metamorphosed into an ungodly, half-frozen creature right here in front of them, or that Godfather had died, most likely in agony. She would keep going ever onward and ignore everything else but that. Onward, forward, home.

Tonight would mark the end of her fourth full day in Cane, which meant that by now one full day would have passed at home. Onward, forward, home. Onward, forward, *home*. It would be her new credo.

If her companions noticed the change in her, they said nothing. They met with their fellow travelers, loitering in various locations around Krezentia House: Erik, sour-faced and the apparent leader; Igritt, with the face of a boar; two brothers, young Herschel and even younger Jurian. There was not much time for greetings there at the house's back wall, which fell beside a bridged ditch full of human-shaped debris. Erik and Bo exchanged a few words and slapped hands, Jurian seemed beside himself at the sight of Nicholas, and Clara could have sworn she saw Igritt self-consciously smoothing down her hair.

Erik led them through a narrow passageway beneath Krezentia House, and then—thanks to a doxy who admitted them wordlessly with a nod to Erik, whose eyes lingered on Nicholas in a way that made Clara more than a little nervous—through an even narrower path in the sewers below Krezentia House. Darkness fell over them. Bo distributed tiny lights she had fashioned out of stripped kambot wiring and repurposed kambot eyes, to be worn about the head and turned on and off with a tiny knobbed switch. Finally they opened a hidden grate in the slime-covered wall of the sewer and entered the narrowest passageway yet. The way was not tall enough to stand, so they crawled across oily stone, through a trickle of dark sludge.

It was here, where the rank black walls seemed to whisper to the rank black water, where indeed the entire *world* seemed black and shivering as the seven of them made a cautious, cramped chain in the darkness, that Nicholas finally asked Clara if something was wrong.

For it was here that Clara first heard the voice.

It said her name.

26

It was an unidentifiable voice—neither feminine nor masculine, but light, thin, somehow artificial.

Clara . . .

She jumped and hit her head on the low ceiling. Clumsily she switched on her light, yanked it off her head, and thrust it into the darkness behind her.

"Watch that light, girl," Erik growled. "Get it out of my face."

She shone it past him, past everyone, into the gloom. "Who's there?"

"Clara?" Nicholas, behind her.

She whirled, bringing the light with her. Nicholas looked concerned. Past him Bo crouched, her own tiny dagger held at the ready.

"What is it?" she whispered, fierce. "You hear something?"

With everyone watching her, doubt flooded Clara. "I don't know. I could have sworn I heard someone else, behind us."

"Someone at Krezentia House could have noticed us," Igritt said. "Perhaps your doxy friend, Erik—"

Erik frowned, irritable. "She wouldn't. Trust me. If anything, we lingered too long on the street."

"*Shike.* I'll go check." And then Bo was gone, tearing back down the tunnel, insect-like, toward the main sewer.

Nicholas put a hand on Clara's. "What was it? What did you hear?"

"I don't know. I thought I heard someone say my name. But

perhaps . . ." And then she stopped, because it was happening again—the surge of inner coldness, the electric vitality singing through her limbs. This time it frightened her not because she did not know what it was but because she *did*. If Godfather had not found her, by now she would most likely have confided in Nicholas—who, if Godfather was to be believed, would be only too glad to listen.

Flustered, she pulled away from Nicholas's touch and saw his hurt at her withdrawal, though he masked it quickly.

"Perhaps?" he prompted.

"Perhaps it was the sound of our movement in the water." She made a face, examining her sludge-crusted fingers. "If you can call it that."

Nicholas smiled, but Clara wasn't sure she believed it. She hid her face—his eyes were too searching, too curious—and when Bo returned with nothing to report, everyone continued on. Erik grumbled under his breath, seditious complaints of which Clara heard only pieces—she suspected no one else could hear more of his muttering than a dull line of sound amid the dripping of the tunnel—but she heard enough. He did not trust her.

She would have to be careful with him.

She had no claim of sovereignty to fall back on, not even a claim of citizenship. No doubt Erik would be watching her, and the others might be too—watching her, waiting for her to make a mistake. It had been too easy with them until now; they had asked her no questions, required no pledge of fealty. Clara didn't blame them for their mistrust. In their place she would certainly be suspicious of some stranger claiming to be from another world—especially if that stranger were, as she was, in a position of relative power at the side of a prince.

Nicholas turned to her, his headlight throwing strange flares across her vision.

"All right?" he whispered.

Clara nodded in answer, and he smiled an encouraging smile that lightened her heart and elevated her mood despite herself. She found herself digging her fingers into the muck, to resist reaching out to touch him.

She would have to be careful with all of them.

The second time Clara heard the voice say her name, they had stopped at an unexpected dead end. They had been traveling for just over a day now, according to punctilious Erik's timekeeping using a pocketwatch he carried in his jacket. It had been an excruciating day of too much crawling through stifling passageways, and too little rest—but, thankfully, a day free of incident.

Bo, who seemed to take it as a personal offense that her map had turned out to be inaccurate, sat with Erik and Igritt discussing alternate routes, and Jurian settled down close to Nicholas. "What do you think?" he said eagerly. "Cave-in, maybe?"

Nicholas, face smudged with sweat and muck and the last dripping bits of Karras's disguising paint, took a swig from his canteen. "I can't say."

"They say the tunnels've been here since before the war. People dug 'em so they could hide underground if their village got attacked, or so they could escape to a safer one."

"Really?" Nicholas looked terribly sad. "I never knew about that."

Oblivious, Jurian puffed up his chest. "They've been helpful since you left, Your Highness. For illegal supplies, the sugar black market, hiding from faeries. But there's been lots of cave-ins over the years. People who made these weren't engineers or anything, you know. They were just people."

Clara half-listened, letting her eyes wander down the tunnel walls as far as her headlight would illuminate. Now that they had left Kafflock far behind, the walls had changed from black faery metal and piping to stone and tightly packed earth, but an occasional creeping iron tendril or a hard, bubbled mass of half-formed machinery reminded Clara that they were, none of them, as safe as at first it might appear. Surely some faery up above knew of the tunnels' existence; a careless citizen might have let it slip, or buckled under the pain of interrogation.

She was letting her thoughts get away from her.

She closed her eyes, breathing in the stale, chill air. How many people had died here, in cave-ins or ambushes or simply after getting lost?

How many two-blooded almost-mages had died screaming down here because their blood wouldn't stop sharpening and buzzing and *scorching* them with cold? How many of them had died trying to claw the thousand tiny knives from their veins?

Oh, but wait. That's right. There had never *been* any two-blooded almost-mages. Not until now. Should Clara feel honored?

She was certainly feeling hysterical.

"Your Highness, may I ask a question?" That was large-eyed, frightened-looking Herschel. Clara knew it even without looking because it was the first time he had spoken.

"Of course, Herschel." How good of Nicholas, remembering his name, saying it with such polite interest. How consummate a politician he was.

"Why . . . That is, how . . . I mean, I'm sorry, but . . . why is there metal in your skin?"

Clara tensed; Bo and Erik stopped arguing about routes and glanced over.

"A good question, Herschel." Nicholas's voice was even, his smile steady, but this was a crucial moment, wasn't it? What would they think when he told them? Honestly, Clara was surprised it had taken this long for the question to arise. Maybe it had been at Afa's tactful request. "Please, whatever you do, don't ask the prince about his mechanized parts. He's so *self-conscious* about them."

"To put it as simply as possible," Nicholas said, "they are remnants of the war. They're what kept me away from you for so long. But you don't need to be afraid of them." To demonstrate he flicked the plate on his wrist. It made a dull, clipped sound. "Dead. And Clara helped kill them. She freed me from them, in fact, freed me from their curse. And after we've rid our kingdom of its enemies, and I have time to concentrate on such superficial things, I'll have them removed."

Well. That was an abbreviated and not entirely accurate summary of that night in the ballroom, and Clara had a good idea of what Godfather would say about being omitted from the tale, but these people didn't need to know that.

Jurian and Herschel gazed at her, newly impressed. "Is that true, Lady Clara?"

"Lady?" she said, rather rudely.

They were nonplussed. "Is that not the right title?"

"I have no title."

"Lady Clara," Nicholas said, winking at her, "is perfect." Then he took her hand, his metal-capped thumb grazing her palm, and that was when she heard it:

Clara.

Was it nearer this time? Did absolutely *no one else* hear it? God help her, she was unraveling.

She smiled at eager, stupid, ignorant Herschel and Jurian. "Fine," she said tightly. "That's just fine. 'Lady' it is."

She would pretend that she heard nothing. She would pretend that her body was not diving down into untold arctic temperatures.

Nicholas rubbed her hands between his, blew on their entwined fingers to warm them. Smiled—too brightly, considering. "Chilly down here, isn't it?"

She shrugged and pulled away. "Maybe for coddled princes."

The others laughed. Bo, exultant, flourished the map in front of them to show off the new route, and they went on.

Clara counted in her head: Five days now. One day, six hours at home.

Onward, forward, home.

* * *

Whenever they stopped to sleep during that cramped dark time in the tunnels, when most moments were the same as the last and Jurian and Bo's attempts at humor grated upon the last frayed inches of Clara's nerves—and, it would seem, Erik's as well, for he was always grousing—Nicholas would settle close to Clara. Sometimes, in the narrower stretches of the tunnel, he was so close that she could have stretched out her fingers and touched him.

She could have, but she didn't.

Instead she stared at the ceiling she couldn't see and thought of where her father might be, and what Felicity might be doing—if she was afraid for Clara, or furious with her for leaving with no explanation, or afraid for *herself*. What would Patricia Plum and Dr. Victor be doing to pass the time?

Six days here; one day, twelve hours at home. Seven days. *Eight*. Two days at home. She marked the passage of time with unraveling patience, awaiting each of Erik's announcements as though they were priceless gifts. So many long hours of this close darkness, of fitful bouts of sleep with Nicholas on one side and Bo on the other. Crawling through muck. Eating tough, dried meat and stale bread. Standing, when it was possible—a blessed change of posture that allowed them the chance to stretch aching muscles. Talking to one another in hushed tones, as if any sound louder than that would travel down the tunnel and fetch a waiting danger.

So many long hours of knocking into Nicholas, of their fingers scraping against each other in the dark, of the weight of his quiet gaze upon her, at once welcome and unsettling. She could not make up her mind about him, but her body, it seemed, had decided. It *wanted* those moments of accidental touch. It wanted more than that—intention, connection, to close the space between them.

She ignored such urges with no small effort. *Remember Godfather*, she reminded herself. *Remember what he told you.* And she did, her thoughts a mess of conflict.

Meanwhile, Nicholas contended with a constant barrage of

questions. What would happen next, and what was his strategy for reclaiming the throne? What would happen to them? To the kingdom? Did His Highness truly think he could save everyone?

"It would be dishonest to say I *know* the kingdom will be saved," he said, slowly, once, when they had stopped to eat, "but I *believe* it will be." And then, when he had met each of their gazes—hungry, skeptical, reverent—Clara had noticed their shoulders straightening, their faces softening. Even sour Erik, even solemn Igritt.

"I know the capital," he had said, "and I know Wahlkraft. And I know Anise. Better than anyone left alive in Cane, I know her. For eighteen years I fought her." He had given them a grim, resolute smile. "I'm confident we can fight her."

Clara could have sworn his eyes flickered over to her at those words. The look chilled her. What did he expect of her? What would he demand?

She nibbled at her strip of dried meat and said nothing.

The third time Clara heard the voice, it was the afternoon of their fifth day in the tunnels, and her ninth in Cane. And this time, the voice said something different:

Soon.

She paused at the tunnel mouth; so did Nicholas, beside her. There was a dimly lit space ahead, less cramped than the tunnel had been. Hub 7, their halfway point.

"Did you hear that?" he said, frowning.

Exhausted, worn thin by anxiety and cold, Clara could have cried; she could have kissed him. Mostly, though, she was careful. "Hear what?"

Nicholas looked disturbed. A flicker of something crossed his face. He flinched, as if suddenly chilled. "Did you say something?"

"I said, 'Hear what?'"

"No, before that."

She gestured vaguely, shrugging. "It was probably Bo."

Lies, and more lies. Clara had done nothing but lie to him since seeing Godfather. Desperate to confide in him, a twinge of caution nevertheless held her back. She climbed out of the tunnel into Hub 7 and stumbled, for the stretching of her muscles brought with them a fresh surge of cold that nearly sent her doubling over.

Nicholas caught her by her arms, keeping her upright. "Careful, Lady."

She smiled, screaming inside. "Thank you, Your Highness."

It had become a joke since the conversation with Jurian and Herschel. A terrible, terrible joke. For Godfather had called her mother a Lady of the North, hadn't he? Lady Leska, powerful mage. Did Nicholas know? *Did he know?*

The handful of refugees in Hub 7—common people, merchants, used-up doxies, children, escaped slaves—watched them enter the room, some curious, others frighteningly expressionless. Piles of crude machinery cobbled together from spare faery parts lined the space, along with racks of supplies and a dimly lit chromocast broadcasting a fuzzy image of advertisements and district notices. There were pallets on the floor, threadbare underthings hung to dry, people eating and sleeping. A mother and her children; a father and his father. Even here in Cane there were these common threads, these familiar scraps of humanity—families and pillows, cookware and laundry. Clara felt tears come to her eyes.

Nicholas paused beside her, let out a slow breath. "Is this how it feels," he said, "to walk your New York streets? I know none of these people, and yet they are my friends, my children, and I've failed them."

He turned to her, his dark eyes wounded; he seemed suddenly too old for such a young man. Clara's heart yearned for him. But she offered him no comfort.

"When I walk my New York streets," she said, "I feel nothing but fear."

Bo, ahead of them, was addressing the gathered people. "Friends," she said, with the bluster of someone three times her age, and three times as large, "I present to you a grand treat. Having fought his way back to us at last: His Royal Highness, Prince Nicholas Drachstelle."

Silence followed her words. As fond of Bo as Clara had become, she nevertheless felt an urge to scream at the child. Blurting Nicholas's introduction in such a way had not been the plan. But perhaps Bo had not been able to help herself, at the sight of such misery. Perhaps she had thought it would lift the refugees' spirits. Erik, leaning against the far wall, shifted crossly; Jurian looked insulted.

"Oh, wake up," Jurian said, not unkindly. "It's our prince, don't you see? Have none of you seen the old books? He has come to save us!"

The people examined Nicholas, and Clara, too. A few began to show signs of recognition, awestruck, elbowing their friends, but most looked simply confused.

"Oh?" An old man, bent, wheezing. "Him and what army?"

That earned a scattering of nervous laughter from the crowd.

A small child, hair a tangled nest, pointed at Clara. "Isn't that the girl the queen's after?"

Bo snapped at the child, "Don't you have any manners at all?"

Nicholas took a deep breath. It was, perhaps, not the reception he had been hoping for.

"Please," he said, stepping forward, "allow me to tell you what has happened and share with you my story. And then I'd like it if I could hear yours." He smiled, elegant and totally at ease, as though he were not in fact coated with grime and were instead holding court in far easier times. The crowd leaned closer, already enthralled. "Perhaps after we are better acquainted with one another, we'll be better prepared to talk of the future—"

Soon. SoonsoonsoonSOON!

Nicholas stopped, staggering. And Clara, her senses roaring from the voice's excitement, collapsed. The most violent chill yet seized her, shaking her there on the ground. She clutched her stomach, for it would surely burst open any second now, but when she opened her mouth to scream, nothing came out.

"Clara?" Nicholas was on his knees, holding her, terrified. The refugees had risen to their feet; some of the children were crying. "What is it? Speak to me, please."

Clara knew now why she had been so cold—much colder here than aboveground—and why she had been so on edge. It was her body trying, as any body would, to tell her something. Only, if Godfather was right, her body was becoming something different now. She had not understood the warning.

She had fancied several times over these past days that the tunnel walls had seemed as though they were crawling, as though they were alive.

And they *were* alive. They were coming now, bringing the voice—whoever's voice it was—careening along with them.

"They're coming," she gasped, struggling to rise. "They've found us. We have to leave!"

Jurian looked bewildered. "We can't. If we go to the surface from here, we'll come out right in the middle of Rosche."

Rosche. Clara tried to find the memorized map in her mind. Rosche, the district where the humans who'd hunted faeries had been sent. Where they were now hunted by faeries themselves.

Erik shoved his way forward, eyes sharp. "Speak, girl. Who's coming?"

But Clara did not have to say, for the next moment they spilled through the tunnel mouth into Hub 7—a wave of mechaniks, glittering black, turning the tunnel to a metal wasteland behind them.

27

Erik moved first, shoving Igritt and Herschel behind him. The other refugees leapt to their feet, screaming, shouting, racing for the wide ladder attached to the wall. An escape hatch was built into the ceiling—Clara remembered that from Bo's map. Above the hatch the ladder continued up a shaft for fifty feet before opening aboveground through a second hatch. But how would they reach the surface in time? Already the mechaniks were cascading across the floor, nipping at people's heels, yanking them down into their mess of black-and-blue magic.

It was madness at the ladder—people clambered up it, tripping and falling back into the crush of others screaming for everyone to move faster. Erik found Nicholas and grabbed his arm, pulled him on. Clara was glad to see Bo slung safely over his shoulder.

"Can't have the prince getting eaten, can we?" Erik said angrily.

He pushed Nicholas up the ladder, and when Clara got caught in the tumult of people, her hand slipped from his, and they were separated. At once Nicholas turned to find her, his eyes wild. He called for her, and Clara was pushed back by a father shoving his children toward the wall, but then solid Igritt was grabbing her hand, helping her back to the ladder. Nicholas was leaning off it, reaching for her; he grabbed her hand, and she climbed up beside him. He gathered her close, relieved, and Clara wished they could remain in that moment—no questions, no suspicions or rescue missions, only his hand on her face and her, smiling up at him. They climbed, the refugees pushing them on.

Once, Clara looked back. A mistake. Hub 7 churned with black, illuminated by occasional flashes of blue, broken by contorted human-shaped lumps reaching futilely for escape. The machinery exploded, the ceiling was beginning to fall, and while waiting for his turn, helping others climb, Jurian—wide-eyed, cheerful Jurian—was dragged into the black.

The climb past the first hatch seemed endless, and when they finally reached the top of the shaft, it took two people to shift the heavy wooden bar that fastened the second hatch. For a moment Clara feared the hatch would stick, trapping them forever in a graveyard of metal, but then they were out—tumbling aboveground, sobbing, assisting the wounded.

Nicholas helped Clara upright, and when Bo slammed into Clara's stomach—perhaps for the first time in her life at a loss for words—Clara held her there, whispering reassurances she did not feel.

Erik was there too, and Igritt and Herschel.

"Jurian's gone," Herschel said, red-eyed, and Erik glared death at Clara, as if it were her fault. Maybe it was. No one else had heard that voice—except for Nicholas, those last two times, but the voice had never said his name. Only hers. Why?

Nicholas now stood at the edge of the hatch but made no move to close it. He was listening. Clara joined him, Bo in hand.

"What is it?" Clara asked.

He looked uneasy. "They're retreating."

She crouched. Yes, she could hear them far below, their overlapping hisses and tiny metal clacks receding like a wave pulling back from the shore.

Then there was silence. Clara looked up at Nicholas. His face was heavy with guilt. Maybe he thought, as she did, that this was because of them. Surely Anise couldn't have cared less about a band of inconsequential refugees—but a long-lost prince and a girl from Beyond?

A half-breed *from Beyond,* came the terrible thought.

She rose to study the land around them, a desolate, rocky tundra dotted with snow and metal-crusted outcroppings, the tremendous steel struts of the railroads overhead. Not far from their hatch sat the charred ruins of a village.

It was quiet. There were no beasts, or people, or even winds.

Nicholas was solemn at her side. "Not many places to hide, are there?"

She had been thinking the same thing.

Overhead, a sudden dark movement—one tiny, solitary kambot.

"Bo," Nicholas said evenly, "please tell me that you've let loose one of your kambots for some reason."

But Bo, squinting at the horizon, said nothing. Others had noticed it too, and now began to run across the vast, frozen tundra toward the ruined village. It was some shelter at least.

But what good was shelter against dragons?

Shining black and brass with clockwork between patches of mottled white scales. Metal spikes for tails and long spearheads for teeth. Dragons, impossible. Dragons, *everywhere*. They threw black-tipped darts from their tails and spat blue fire from their mouths with terrible mechanized clicks. Black smoke spewed from the crevices webbing their bodies.

Faeries rode them, perched on their backs and shooting arrows, on the hunt.

A terrible hopelessness settled over Clara. "It was a trap. We were *herded* up here."

"Dragons?" Bo sounded lost, tiny. "But . . . the dragons live up north. Faeries don't like the cold."

Nicholas swept her up into his arms, his face hard with fury. "Clara, *move!*"

She did, looking back over her shoulder at the unimaginable monsters in the sky, trying to find Erik in the chaos. There he was, and Igritt and Herschel, too. *Please let no one else die because of us.*

It was a futile wish. Behind her the wounded and old were swallowed up by dragon fire, pierced by arrows rained down on them as though from the devil himself.

Maybe the devil is a faery, Clara thought wildly, her lungs burning as the air turned acrid, flooded with the stench of burning oil and metalwork.

They reached the ruined village, survivors huddling behind half-collapsed cottages and blacksmith forges, beneath animal troughs and piles of rotting feed. Nicholas pushed Bo under a stone bridge, low over a dry riverbed, and shoved Clara in after her. He then turned and ran back onto the tundra, where the dragons circled and the faeries shot stragglers with their arrows like it was a grand game.

"Where are you going?" Clara cried.

But she knew. They needed help, and he would not fail them, not this time. Erik, crouched behind a nearby well, watched Nicholas go. Clara saw the stubborn surge of pride in his face and was not surprised when he leapt out to follow Nicholas, calling for some of the others to join him. And they *did,* for Nicholas was leading the way, unsheathing his sword, jaw set, dark eyes blazing. He was their prince, and he was, in that desolate moment, beautiful.

Despite everything, Clara felt a small thrill that had nothing to do with the cold, and her heart swelled with dangerous affection.

"Please don't leave too," said Bo, small at her side, and Clara bent to hold her but then staggered, clutching her own head. She could hardly see for the burst of silver in her vision; she was going blind. It had hit her like a fist through her core, and now it was pulling her inside out with icy fingers.

She fell to her knees. "Oh, God help me, not *now*. . . ."

"What's wrong?" Bo crouched beside her . . . and then pulled back. "Clara, your *face*."

Clara reached up to touch her lips, her cheek. Her skin was cold, and it stung her fingers like a mild electric shock. "What is it?"

"It's *changing*. . . ."

Then Nicholas screamed. Clara spun to find him, searching—there he was, buckled over on the ground, blood seeping from a wound on his leg.

A dragon hovered over him, the thin metal plates of its hooked wings glistening with oil and sweat.

"What's this?" the faery riding it called out. He leapt to the ground and grabbed Nicholas's chin, forcing it up for inspection. The dragon reared back, as if in sudden confusion, and the faery whooped, ecstatic.

"It's His Royal Highness, the prince!" The faery laughed, waving up at the other riders.

The faery kicked Nicholas right in his wound, and Nicholas screamed a word in agony—was it Clara's name?

Regardless, Clara knew what she had to do. Instinct overtook her. She left Bo gaping and ran toward Nicholas, heedless of the fallen, of the smoking debris. Pain stabbed her behind her eyes, in her midsection, up her legs at every step. A great force was tearing her in two, and she sobbed in agony, but she did not stop.

Dimly she heard the faery laugh—no doubt amused at this crazed girl attacker. She ran toward the sound, lashing out with her bare hands as if to strike the faery across the face, realizing that she had not even thought to take out her daggers.

Something hit the faery's face—she heard the impact, heard the faery scream and fly back—but it was not Clara's hand.

There was a great explosion, a rush of cold wind, a searing pain through her arms as though the knives that had been cutting open her insides had suddenly burst out. She knew where Nicholas was, instinctively, and threw her arms around him, sheltering him from the worst of the storm that she had created.

That she had created.

She had thought of it as she'd been running, a thought born from some primal impulse that had come into her mind of its own volition. She had thought of a storm ripping the dragons from the sky, flinging the faeries to the ground, blasting them with cold and power and rage and ice—and now it was happening. She could hear the storm exploding around her, and she felt so afraid, huddled there with her face buried in Nicholas's shoulder, his heart pounding against hers, his hands in her hair, holding her to him. It might be the last time she was allowed to touch him. It might be the last time she would be allowed to *breathe*. The pain was unbearable; releasing some of the energy within her had seemed only to exacerbate the torment of it. And what would everyone do to her when they realized what she was? She knew now, without any doubt, that what Godfather had said was true.

Silence fell—the hush after a storm.

Clara opened her eyes. Silver remained, glowing at the edges of her vision. Through it she saw the faery bodies strewn in pools of blue blood across the tundra. The fallen dragons twitched mechanically as the lights behind their eyes went out—some dismantled, others charred beyond repair.

Fresh snow surrounded them. It fell from the sky even now.

Nicholas helped her to her feet, holding her at arm's length. He said nothing, but the look on his face was one of wonder and horror. And . . . gladness?

Clara's cheek smarted. She put her fingers to it, and they came away red.

Red tinged with silver.

Erik limped toward them, his face ashen. Others were beside him, including Igritt; they saw the blood on Clara's hands and recoiled.

"What are you?" Erik growled. "What did you do?"

"I . . . My mother was a mage," she began weakly, clutching her side. The pain was getting worse. Why would it not *stop?*

"Never seen mages do *that* before. Make storms out of nothing, pull lightning from the sky."

Ah. Hence the charred dragons.

"Please," she said, "let me explain."

"Only the queen's got that much power," came a hushed voice, from a man with a gash on his arm and snow in his hair—*Clara's* snow. "Only the queen can do things like that. Make things out of nothing." The man's face darkened with suspicion. "The air smells the same as her too. Tastes the same."

"But the queen is a faery," Igritt pointed out quietly, "not a mage."

Bo peeked out from behind Erik. "Yes. See, Erik? Silver blood. Mage's blood. We like mages, remember?"

Erik moved her aside. "Silver or blue or bright purple, I don't care. It isn't red, is what counts. I know that magic. That's the queen's magic, or as good as." He paused, his face ugly—angry, yes, but also, Clara thought, afraid. "You were waiting for them to attack, weren't you? You led them right to us. May the serpents draw you into black waters."

"No, Erik. Please, you have to believe me. I didn't do that. I wouldn't. I *stopped* them." She turned to Nicholas. "Nicholas, you know me. You know all I want is to find my father and then leave. Please, tell them that's what I want."

The survivors had gathered around them, some gaping at the destruction, some glaring at Clara, all of them afraid. And frightened people, Clara knew, were more likely than most to turn vicious at a moment's notice.

"Did you know, sire?" said Herschel softly. He seemed lopsided, standing there, without Jurian at his side. "Did you know what she was?"

The unsaid word hung in the air: *abomination*. Did you know, sire, that you had brought a monster from old tales into our midst?

Nicholas had been quiet, his expression unreadable—until now, when something shifted on his face. Clara's heart sank.

He *had* known what she was, or he had at least hoped. But he would not tell them that; better for them to think she was a liar than him.

His face was stern as he took a step away from her. Was that an apology in his eyes, a plea for understanding?

Probably not.

"I did not know," he said, "but perhaps, if we are careful with her, we can use her."

28

It was agreed that Clara was dangerous, that they should keep her under close watch until a plan had been decided upon.

"She could help us," Clara heard Nicholas saying to the others. "I'm reluctant to trust her now, but . . . I think you'll agree that this could give us an incredible advantage against Anise."

Some immediately agreed, others protested, but they all huddled around Nicholas, fervently attentive. Only Bo glanced after Clara, distressed.

How nice, she thought as those charged with watching her dragged her away. *He seems to have found himself an army after all.*

They bound her to a wooden beam in a barn with no roof, open to the sky. They took the dagger at her hip, but not those from her boots, for which Clara was deliriously grateful. But she was cold and bare-armed, her shoulders wrenched back, her torso bound so tightly to the beam with multiple belts, donated eagerly by their owners, that she could hardly breathe. She would never be able to reach her boots. It occurred to her that she could try bringing another storm down from the sky, or burn her bindings off. But even if she could somehow set aside the pain making her retch onto the dirt, any demonstration of . . . what was it? Her *magic?* She almost laughed. Any such demonstration would surely seal her fate with these refugees. She didn't blame them. *She* would have lashed out against someone like her too.

"Try anything funny," Erik said after he had finished restraining her, eyes full of distrust, "and I *will* kill you, no matter what the prince says."

Clara considered biting off his nose. It would not have been difficult, the way he'd positioned himself so stupidly close. He didn't really deserve it, but with the pain coursing through her and the humiliation compounding it, she might have tried it, had he not left then. Herschel, stone-faced, stood watch.

Nausea kept her head spinning. Every few minutes it sharpened to a stabbing pain that surged through her body in waves. The combination of pain and exhaustion threw her in and out of feverish hallucinations. Herschel made a point of looking away from her when this happened, as if to demonstrate that he didn't much care if she was in pain or not.

Ugly browned light filtered down through the storm clouds, and the barn creaked around her in the wind. Night was coming quickly in this land of tumultuous skies, afternoon fading into dusk. Sweat had soaked through her clothes, drenching her. When a convulsion hit her, she seized against her bindings, weeping from the pain.

"Stop," she whispered, wishing she had something to bite down upon. Surely her teeth would shatter soon; she could not stop grinding them. "Please, stop. Leave me be."

But her blood was insistent, and when the pain became so searingly cold that she felt sure she would die, she screamed, her throat full of knives.

Herschel flinched.

She had hoped Nicholas would come—she imagined it, him falling to his knees before her and begging forgiveness, apologizing for leaving her like this, kissing her tears away.

What a silly, stupidly girlish thought.

"Herschel, please, untie me." It was a desperate move, but he was the only one near, and she would lose her mind if she didn't try. "I won't hurt anyone, I swear to you. But I'm in enough pain as it is, and the bindings . . ."

She broke off, crying out. Herschel approached warily, but she saw pity in his eyes. Gentle, Jurian-less Herschel.

"What does it feel like?" he whispered, kneeling before her.

She could have wept; she *did* weep. "Like all of winter being forced inside me."

Herschel was grave as he inspected her, grave as he reached to undo her bindings, and gentle with the sores they left behind on her wrists.

"Just for a while," he said, and she nodded miserably, knowing what she was about to do. She fell forward from the post, undone now, and free. Herschel reached to help her up, saying something about Jurian, something forgiving, that it wasn't Clara's fault, that he understood. His words tore at Clara, but she did not hesitate. In her desperation it was easy to grab him by the shoulders, spin his slight body around, smash his head against the post to which she had been tied.

He dropped to the dirt without a sound, and after assuring herself that he was breathing and alive, she bound him hand and foot with the discarded belts. His mouth had fallen open, and she took one of his gloves and stuffed it inside, racked with guilt, unsteady with pain.

"I'm sorry," she whispered, and left him.

Outside the shelter of the barn, the wind cut her like knives. It gave her pause; leaving the relative safety of this place was assuredly insane. The cold of this tundra, the loneliness of it—she could freeze, she could lose herself in the endless flat stretches of hard frosted ground.

She leaned against the barn wall, measuring the odds. They weren't good. Choice, again. Choice between awful and even more awful. She laughed, and the wind seized the sound, swallowed it away.

A gamble, but one she had to make. She could not stay here.

She would run.

At the heart of the ruined village, in a paddock once meant for animals, the refugees gathered. Clara saw them, and could have kept going—*should* have kept going. But a spot of blue pulled at her: Bo, her expression forlorn.

Then—Nicholas, unmistakable, in profile. He was saying her name.

Run, my Clara. Godfather would advise her so, but Clara could not resist. She snuck closer to the crowd, close enough to hear. She listened hard—maybe he was trying to persuade them to trust her, to treat her well and apologize for binding her. Maybe that comment about *using* her had been a tiny white lie, a momentary diversion.

". . . but what if she doesn't want to bind with you?" That was Igritt.

Clara gripped the corner of the burned-out cottage she hid behind. Ash flaked away at her touch.

"It doesn't matter if she doesn't want to," came Nicholas's voice, and it was hard and unfeeling, with no nuance of emotion to reinterpret. Nothing but toneless resolve. "I will make her."

Oh. Clara reeled back; it was a kick to the gut, a claw to her heart. Oh no, no, no.

Using her. His comment had not been a lie.

Bo was the first to protest—and the only one, Clara noticed. She bit her tongue to keep from screaming out her hurt.

"You can't do that, sire," Bo said, furious. "How dare you even think it?"

"The prince can do whatever he likes," one of the male refugees said. "That's why he's a *prince*. And anyway, why should we care what one dirty little half-breed mage wants, if she can help us fight for our country?"

"But what if she can't?" someone said uncertainly. "Seems like an unnecessary cruelty."

"She can," Nicholas said, a dark figure in their midst. Clara raked her eyes over the lines of his body, searching for familiarity and finding none. Even his statue-self had been warmer. "I'm only sorry that it took me this long to bring it out of her. Even more lives could have been saved had her power manifested sooner."

Moments flew at Clara in rapid succession, their masks torn away to reveal bitter truths—on the train, in the alley where they had rescued Bo, in the doxy quarters—oh, even on Pascha's terrace. Nicholas had been so eager for her to describe her dreams. *What did it feel like, Clara, when the train exploded? Tell me your nightmares, Clara; don't let your fear get in your way; fight, Clara,* fight. *Kiss me, Clara; it can't be helped.*

She sank to the ground, and tears of shock burned hot tracks down her frosted cheeks. Had Nicholas, at every moment, been trying to spur her blood into its true self? Every touch, every smile, every glance of fierce solidarity—Clara and Nicholas, together against the evils of Cane—a manipulation.

Cries of support for Nicholas rose from the refugees. A new zealotry emanated from them, amplifying with each passing moment. Nicholas was saying something, but she dared not listen too closely. Erik and Igritt said nothing, Clara noticed. Perhaps, having known her for longer than the others, they were not so keen to hear her discussed in this way: a weapon, newly unearthed, ready to be aimed.

Clara stumbled to her feet. She thought of Bo and sobbed—to leave her here with such people . . . but she could not stop, not even for Bo. She would run, she would flee across this miserable tundra with its canopy of trains, and if they tried to follow, if they tried to subdue her, she would bring down such an icy hell upon them—

What an idea. Power she might have, but to use it like that? Unthinkable. And how could she even pretend to try? It hurt her, it blinded her; even now it was cracking her wide open.

She ran across the frigid soil, tripped over lichen-slicked rocks—for how long? Hours. Ages. Get away from Nicholas, *get away from Nicholas.* His betrayal was a cruel hand on her heart, squeezing.

She tripped over an unexpected pebbled ridge and did not rise. A small black thing tumbled out from her skirts, clacked thrice, and was silent. A mechanik? And why not? Perhaps it had latched on to her during the horrific climb up the ladder, found her abominable body distasteful, and gone dormant. She laughed through her tears. Maybe it would awake soon and call its friends. They would swarm upon her while she slept, fold her into a statue-self of her own.

The night was dark and getting darker. She let the blackness take her, and the mud in her mouth tasted like ice.

Clara woke coughing up blood, spattering silvery pink onto the ground. It had snowed, light on her body like a dusting of sugar.

A soft breeze wafted across her skin, stirring the snow, warming her. She smelled salt.

Clara, the voice crooned.

The voice! She had forgotten about it. She raised her head, forcing her eyes to focus.

"Clara," the voice said again—real now, feminine and clear. She smelled sweet breath on her face, saw beautiful slate-colored boots. White furs, gray robes, a sash of ermine, a collar of leather cords.

"You poor child," the voice said. A warm hand cupped Clara's cheek. "Whatever have they done to you?"

Fear seized Clara's heart. "Anise?"

A lovely face appeared before her, skin as white as snow, white hair, a furred turban.

Anise smiled. "It's time for you to come with me now, Clara."

Clara shook her head. "No. I can't."

"Oh? And why not?"

Because you had my mother killed. Through the haze of her fatigue, Clara remembered this simple, awful truth, and she nearly spit it at the queen's feet. But she was too weak for that. She teetered on the edge of consciousness, and her world pulsed silver-red. Had she ever known anything but pain?

"I can help you," Anise whispered. "I know. I'm the only one alive who knows."

Clara shuddered. She was tired, hungry, cold. Someone was lifting her, settling her onto softness, tucking her into warmth.

Ah, the warmth! A blissful thing that made her weep with gratitude. Wind drifted past them; they were moving. Anise hissed guttural words to someone, and Clara's heart filled with hate—*you had my mother killed*—but the warmth soothed her, as did a faint sweet smell. Perfume? Sugar?

Woozy, she forced her eyes open. They were in a black mechanized sleigh. A cadre of faeries on loks surrounded them, and a blue-eyed kambot perched on Anise's shoulder, staring at Clara coldly. And Anise was stroking Clara's arms, bundled with her in a blanket trimmed with fur, telling her it was all right now, poor, wrung-out thing. She would be safe now; she was with her queen.

*F*rom the moment I was born, I was taught to hate them.

Everyone was. Every parent raised their children on tales of what would happen if they wandered too deeply into the forest or too far down the southern roads. Beware Mira's Ring and the spirits who wander there, screeching for warmth they will never have. Beware the high mountains, where the dragons lie curled and waiting for dusk to fall, where the nightbirds perch on bone-white trees and sing their mischievous songs.

Beware the southern roads, where the paths turn overgrown and the whirring of unnatural things turns beneath the earth, for that is where the faeries dwell.

The first time I cut open a faery while it still lived, I was six. Father stood behind me, folded his hand over mine to steady it. His crown glinted in the cold laboratory light, the light of the mages; he had come straight from court, eager.

"From neck to navel," Father whispered at my ear. "Keep the blade straight and your weight even."

The eyes of the royal surgeons were upon me. So were those of the Seven. Drosselmeyer, who had bound himself to me, was closest of all. I could see him nodding in approval as the knife sank into the faery's white flesh and blue blood trickled out in dark rivulets.

Fascinated, I pressed the blade deeper, watching the blood pool. The faery, bound to the table with mage lightning, screamed. Though the sound was muffled, I plainly heard its fear and fury.

The sound enraged me. That it would dare to be afraid or angry, after what its kind had done—raiding our villages, forcing the humans farther north, attacking outposts with strange weapons that no one could understand. Dark weapons that seemed impervious to even mage magic, for these weapons were always shifting, collapsing, and reforming. They were never the same from one minute to the next. Faeries had always been inventors, tinkering with their toys in the shadows, obsessed with crafting things. But these weapons were different. They shot . . . things, dark, clacking, mechanized . . . I want to say creatures, for they seemed almost alive, and they swarmed like locusts. These dark things devoured anything in their path—stone, earth, flesh—and rebuilt it as magic-bound metal, black and shining, reeking of salt and sea winds.

We had to understand the faeries' magic, this inexplicable magic that they had been crafting for years underground, under Anise's guidance. We had no choice but to understand it, whatever the cost. Otherwise it would destroy us. Even at six years old I knew that. I saw it every day as I sat by my father as he held court, watching report after report of raids cross his desk, of human villages overrun with iron, choked by a magic that built, and built, and built. . . .

So I cut deeper, too deeply. My blade became reckless, and before I knew it, I stood over the faery, whose torso I had sliced to pieces with my tiny surgical knife.

I panted. Sweat dripped from my fingers. I could not see anything but a foggy haze of white and blue—faery flesh, faery blood. I felt sick. I thought I would cry. I didn't understand what I had done.

"It's all right," Father said to me. "We've all done it." The Seven smiled at me knowingly. Drosselmeyer squeezed my shoulder as though the experience had bonded us even more irrevocably together.

"They deserve it," I said after a moment. I can still hear my own voice, the memory is so clear. A high voice, a boy's voice. "They deserve to die."

"Yes," Father said, and held out a cloth on which I could wipe my hands. "They all deserve to die."

PART THREE
THE SUMMER PALACE

How shall I even begin to describe the beauty and splendor
of the city that now lay before her . . .
Not only were the walls and towers of the most magnificent colors,
but the shapes of the buildings were like nothing else on earth.

29

S*he is mine.*

It was the voice again, whispering through Clara's sleep-fogged mind. *Her* voice, Anise's voice, gleefully whispering aloud: "Mine, she is mine."

The words should have bothered Clara. She was no one's but her own, and she was certainly not the property of a murderous queen. Above her head the wind gusted, but here in Anise's nest of furs Clara was warm and content.

She tried to rise, uneasy at the thought.

"Hush," Anise murmured against her ear. "We've a ways to go yet. Rest. I have you now."

Clara subsided and did not stir again.

Lights woke her, in flashing blues, pinks, purples, greens.

Clara tried to speak. "Where are we?"

"The Summer Palace." Anise helped Clara upright and pressed their cheeks together. When her mouth moved, the corner of her lips brushed against Clara's.

Already Clara was fading again, her insides still throbbing with pain, as though they had been viciously rearranged. She peeked out over the furs to see spiraling towers of iron and gold and white; turrets of blue; watchtowers marked by green lights; and the winding, dark roads of a tiny but grand city. The streets wound lazily upward to a gray palace lined with thin lights in white, green, blue. Above, a hub where railways converged. A dim roar buzzed at Clara's ears—laughter, music. Cannons firing. The snap of firecrackers, the tang of gunpowder.

"We have the most indescribable parties here," Anise whispered. "You wouldn't believe the number of runaway slaves who try to sneak in. They impale themselves on the ramparts. They drown themselves trying to swim the river." She laughed, a sensuous sound. "Oh, Clara. You'll love it here with me."

As Clara tried to digest this, they passed over a curving iron bridge. On the other side Clara saw faeries in extravagant dress traveling a network of winding roads. Among them was a human in rags, carrying a tray of lemon ices in crystal goblets. He was being led around on a chain, and oozing sores marred his skin.

Though she struggled to keep her eyes open, it was in vain. Even in unconsciousness, lights danced behind her eyes, and everything smelled sweet.

"Take her to my rooms," Anise was saying when Clara awoke next. "And fetch Ketcher. She'll need to be examined. She's horribly weak."

Clara tried to open her eyes, but it was too bright. When she tried to shield her face, she found she could not lift her arms. She was being lowered onto a soft surface of warm furs and cool tasseled pillows. Each touch stung her oversensitized skin, and she lay there shuddering.

Someone sat beside her.

"Beautiful girl," Anise whispered, "do not fear." She fingered Clara's frayed tunic and clucked her tongue. "First thing, after you're well—new clothes. I do so hate the cold, but I'll admit, one can do much more with a winter wardrobe. You'll look ravishing, Clara. I'll dress you only in the best."

A rustle of movement near the door. Anise rose.

"Over here, Ketcher. I'm not sure what we can do for her, but I'd certainly suggest something to spice up her blood. It must be stretched so thin. . . ."

Callused fingers picked up Clara's wrist, felt her pulse. A voice brittle with age said, "Can you hear me, child? What is your name?"

"Clara," she said. "My name is Clara Stole."

Then she slept.

The next time Clara awoke, she could feel the difference immediately. Her vision was clearer, her limbs stronger, her stomach more settled.

And she was naked.

She bolted upright, drawing up the sheets to her chin. Silk and tassels, furs and downy coverlets lay about her in opulent heaps.

Something else was different too. Though she was still weak, her pain had diminished. In its place was a silver-corded solidity, like her insides had turned into something vital and deadly.

"Hello?" The word barely made it past her lips. Disbelieving, she took in the luxury surrounding her. She lay in a four-poster bed framed in iron. Gauzy coral-colored fabric hung from the bed, from the windows, in doorways. The room was tiled in white, blue, and dark gold. Blue flame flickered in black candles. A breeze brought light snow flurries in from a grand black terrace.

Across the room, at a great vanity topped with accoutrements beyond counting, sat the queen herself, tying braids into her long white hair.

She turned at the sound of Clara's voice. "Ah. You're awake."

Clara blushed and averted her eyes. Anise wore a golden dressing gown that trailed the floor and hung carelessly open, revealing her breasts, her belly, her legs. She looked more human than most faeries, except for her ears and the unnaturally sharp set of her bones. She did not, Clara noticed, wear one of the mechanical gloves.

Anise regarded her curiously. "Have I embarrassed you?"

Clara kept her eyes trained on the wall. "What have you done with my clothes?"

"I'm afraid you were tearing them off in a frenzy during the last stages of transformation. We had to restrain you to keep you from hurting yourself."

When Clara still did not turn to acknowledge her, Anise huffed impatiently and tied her dressing gown shut.

"There, now. Is that better?" Anise rose and stretched, amused. "I'm sure it feels quite extraordinary to have finally come into yourself. To have evolved into what you were always meant to be, after years of suffering an inferior existence."

Clara had thought that if she ever met Anise, the queen would be malice and tyranny personified, full of taunts about her dead mother and impossible demands. Certainly not so . . . welcoming.

"What are you playing at?"

"Playing?" Anise's smile widened. "Clara, we have not even *begun* to play, I assure you."

That Anise should feign ignorance, that she should trivialize this moment, shook Clara with a rage that had been building for years. She could see her mother's face; she could feel her mother's touch. She had lost Godfather and she had lost Nicholas, and she might soon lose her father and her sister, and it was all the fault of the woman standing so blithely before her.

Blind with fury, Clara stumbled from the bed, the sheets tangling around her feet. She was dimly aware of her nakedness but found she didn't care. There was a candelabra on a nearby table. She grabbed it and threw it straight at Anise.

The queen ducked, and it went crashing to the floor behind her. Her eyes narrowed. "What do you think you're doing, Clara?"

Clara did not stop. She found a platter of half-eaten food, gilded utensils, a goblet of wine, a heavy book, a tasseled shoe, and threw them at Anise one after another, for they were the only weapons she had. She screamed incoherent curses and accusations, reaching for Anise, ready to squeeze that pretty white throat. But then, blind with tears, she stumbled into a table and sent it crashing to the ground. The fall jarred her, made her realize what she had done, and she sat there in a mess of ruined food, miserable, shaking, sick with hunger. She would die now; Anise would kill her as punishment, and Clara's father would die too, wherever he was.

In the stillness Clara heard a door open and close, and looked up. Anise was kneeling before her, impassive, unhurt. Behind her, at the door to an antechamber, stood Borschalk in fine military dress—a cloak fastened with shining clasps, a severe coat that fell to his knees. He had never looked mightier. Anise went to him, drew a sinuous line up his arm with one white finger. They shared a heated look, a full, simmering, unmistakably *adult* look. Clara retreated into a knot of naked limbs, feeling small and embarrassed, still thrumming with anger.

"You've made a mess of my chambers." Anise's voice was light as she turned back to Clara. "Why?"

Clara stared at Borschalk, shivering. He wasn't even looking at her. The line of his mouth was caught somewhere between smugness and disdain.

"Don't mind Borschalk." Anise laughed, low, turned to smile up at him wickedly. She was miniature beside him, the crown of her head barely meeting his chest. "He has other things on his mind at the moment, I assure you. Answer me."

"I wanted to kill you." Was this real? Had Clara truly said those words?

Anise simply laughed over her shoulder, through her fall of white hair. "Many do. None succeed. Why did you want to?"

"Because you killed my mother."

At that, Borschalk did look at her, and he even—was it possible?—looked afraid. He seemed to shrink, though his body did not move.

The merriment melted from Anise's face. Here at last was the dangerous faery queen Clara had seen on the chromocast, with eyes of blue steel and malice on her tongue.

"Are you saying that Leska is dead? Don't lie to me."

Bewildered, Clara let out a sob. "Why did you do it? We've done nothing to you. Why didn't you leave us alone?"

Anise stepped away from Borschalk, her body no longer supple but rigid. "How did she die?"

Disbelief—there was genuine *disbelief* on Anise's face. Astonishing. Clara was not sure how to respond. "She . . . There were loks, in the city. They killed her, Godfather said. I—I saw the photographs, from when they found her. She was—they had *torn* her open." She turned away, her body bowing beneath the weight of this relived horror. "Must I describe it to you? You ordered them to do it. You did this. *You.*"

"Don't!" Anise had whirled, vibrating with fury. Clara looked up to see her pointing at Borschalk, and how remarkable that such a diminutive person could so thoroughly terrify such a large man. The hands of a clock on Anise's vanity were spinning madly, and sudden heat suffused the room. "Don't you even think of slipping out of here."

"My love—"

"You will address me properly," Anise spat, "or you will find yourself no longer capable of addressing me at all."

A flicker of anger on his face, or hurt, or both. "My *queen,* allow me a chance to explain." Borschalk seemed to shrink as Anise advanced on him. He went down on one knee and lowered his head, though the set of his shoulders held a certain stubbornness. "You charged me with the hunt for the prince, and I accepted it gladly, with honor. For years I searched, coming and going between here and the Beyond with little rest and little company." He looked up at her. "For *you,* my queen, I did this great thing."

"Spare me."

Borschalk looked away, his jaw working. "You ordered me to spare Lady Leska, were I ever to encounter her."

Shock buffeted through Clara in tiny, tingling waves. Could it be true? She looked to Anise, searching.

"I understood your reasons, of course I did." He took a breath and looked up, imploring. "But they were poor reasons, my queen. Despite your wisdom in all other matters, you allowed this mage woman, this—*filth* . . ."

Anise's eyes flashed. "Careful."

"I will say it, and with pleasure. *Filth*." He leapt to his feet now, passionate. "She was only a mage, undeserving of mercy—especially from you, my queen. You, who are so powerful. You, who have remade the world for your people." He paused, put a hand to her face, cradled her head. He could have crushed her skull, but his touch was gentle. "I feared I would never find the prince. His mage guard had put up wards—to protect himself and the boy, to protect *her*—but they were faltering. The work of unraveling your curse was destroying his magic. You are that powerful, my queen. Powerful enough to ruin him, even from afar. And when his wards began to fall, and I saw the Lady, and realized who she was, I knew what had to be done. I had to assert your power, to demonstrate that no one is deserving of your mercy, not even her, especially not *her*."

He cut a quick, venomous look Clara's way. "I cannot understand it, my queen, this curiosity of yours—"

"You did it to protect me." Anise cut him off evenly. She kissed his fingers, his palm, her eyes never leaving his. "Didn't you, Borschalk?"

His eyes were hot on her face, relieved. "Yes, my queen. To protect your rule, to frighten the mage, to prove that no one is safe from your wrath, no matter to what world they flee."

Anise took his finger into her mouth, sucked gently. "You disobeyed an order. Didn't you, Borschalk?"

Such a vile sweetness in her voice, even Clara inched away. Borschalk, whose eyes had been fixed on Anise's nibbling lips, tried to step back.

He failed. Anise bit hard on his finger, drawing blue blood, and shoved him to his knees. The air drew tight around her, bitter with magic.

"She was a *mage*, my queen," Borschalk protested in horror. "In your wisdom you killed every mage in Cane. Why then should your wisdom not extend to Beyond?"

"Because it is *my* wisdom—my kingdom." Anise leaned low and curled her fingers around his brutish neck, her nails sinking into his flesh. "My kingdom and my rules. Not yours, Borschalk. Never yours."

"But, my love—"

Anise let out a strange cry—there was fury in it, yes, but also something like hurt. She flung him into a nearby pillar—with her arms, and with the magic Clara could feel curling through the room, nipping at her own toes. His head hit the iron with a sickening crack, and he slumped to the floor, moaning. Anise seized him by his collar and dragged him toward the doors, her eyes bright. She said nothing to Clara. She did not even look at her.

In the queen's wake Clara could do nothing but sit in amazement. Then she noticed the two uniformed soldiers at the far antechamber doors, and the powdered, bejeweled attendant at another set of doors that led to an extravagant bathing chamber. All three faeries were trying, and failing, to act like they weren't staring at Clara. It would be futile for Clara to try for escape.

Her legs and arms stinging with tiny cuts from the shattered table, Clara limped to the bed and gathered the sheets about herself. Was Anise truly not to blame for her mother's death? Or was it an elaborate ruse to gain Clara's sympathy? Either way, she felt small and cold, and deeply troubled. When the screams began from a distant room—male screams, almost definitely Borschalk's—Clara tried to find satisfaction in them. Regardless of the truth, someone who had played a part in her mother's death was in pain, and that should have made her feel glad. But when the screams escalated to something utterly alien with agony, Clara felt sick and plugged her ears to block the sounds out.

It was some time before Anise returned.

Clara sat on the edge of the bed, wrapped tightly in her sheet, a fresh array of food spread out before her, courtesy of Anise's attendants. She knew she should eat, but it could have been poisoned. Anyway, she had no appetite. The clock on the mantel ticked away, an elaborate iron creation that reminded her of Godfather. With each passing moment her anxiety compounded. She did not know how many days had passed, nor how much time she had spent in delirium. At least Nicholas was far behind her, and if Anise did indeed have her father somewhere, Clara was closer to her goal than ever before. Perhaps she could barter for his release, and in exchange feed Anise information about . . .

She rejected the half-formed thought even as a pang of vindictive satisfaction shot through her heart. Despite Nicholas's betrayal of her, she would not return the favor, not unless she had no other choice.

That, my dear prince, she thought savagely, *is the difference between you and me.*

Dear Nicholas. Dear, once-dear Nicholas. Had there truly never been a moment when he too had felt the heat between them, the deep sense of familiarity, the comfort of being in the company of a lifelong friend? She shut her eyes, curled her fingers into the bedsheet.

The antechamber doors opened, admitting Anise. Clara breathed past her tears, watching the queen's approach with what she hoped was a proper degree of coolness.

Anise dismissed her attendants and then paced before Clara, bright-eyed and high-strung. Clara tried not to look at the delicate sheen of perspiration on Anise's temple, nor the blue dotting her pretty gold dressing gown, or contemplate what that meant for the fate of Borschalk.

"How nice it is," Anise burst out at last, her voice thick, "when those you love most turn against you."

Such openness, such raw, impetuous emotion, was unexpected. Clara's coolness wavered, and she heard herself saying, "It's the worst feeling in the world."

Anise whipped her head around, her expression first startled and then inscrutable. "Ah, yes. You speak of your darling Nicholas, I suppose?"

A stab to her heart. *And Godfather. Even my parents, in their way. Father choosing his grief over his daughters; Mother keeping so many secrets.*

She only said, tiredly, "He is one of many, yes."

Anise's eyes narrowed. Silence stretched between them, weighty with something Clara couldn't name.

She shifted, at a loss. "Are you going to kill me?"

"No."

"Am I your prisoner?"

"Yes."

Clara sucked in a breath. "Will you hurt me?"

"Probably."

A beat. Two. Clara felt the slow crawl of fear pull at her. She looked away.

"I did not want your mother dead," Anise said flatly. "I am many things, but I'm not stupid. It was obvious that your mother was a good soul. Naive but good. She saved my life once, and I therefore spared hers. A life for a life. And that's all I'll ever say about it. Do you understand?"

Clara nodded.

"Look at me."

Clara met the queen's eyes, afraid what she would see there. "Yes, my queen. I understand."

Anise smiled, though her eyes were still hard. "You're not stupid either, are you, Clara?"

And what was one to say to that? The truth, Clara supposed, but she couldn't help feeling this was all some kind of trick. "No."

"No, I knew you wouldn't be." She looked down at the ruined table imperiously. "Destructive, but not stupid."

Clara found herself fascinated despite her better judgment. How old was Anise, anyway? She could have been a fellow debutante, but there was an agelessness about her, striking in such close quarters, that made her difficult to read.

"Where is my father?" Clara watched Anise carefully. It was risky to ask, but she was desperate to see how Anise would react. "I know you have him. What have you done with him?"

Anise turned, sharp with arrogant amusement. "Ah-ah, Clara. We already decided you're not stupid, didn't we? Don't act like it."

It might be too bold, but she might as well continue. Why not, after all? No Godfather, no Nicholas, no one left but Clara to find her father, and maybe she was better off now, on her own. A sob choked her voice. "Why did Borschalk take him, anyway? Why couldn't he have killed the prince and his mage and been done with it?"

There, that was better. "Prince" and "mage"—anonymous words, even harmless.

Anise looked at her keenly. "He took your father because he could not take you. Your power prevented it. And because, after I saw you fighting my loks, I wanted you. More than the little prince, I wanted you."

"Why?" Clara blurted out, too shocked to stop herself.

Anise gave a smile too secret to interpret, and said nothing. Clara dropped her eyes, unnerved. This was infinitely more frightening than a queen barking atrocities from her throne or interrogating Clara in a dark dungeon. And infinitely more dangerous.

As Anise called her attendants back in, ordering that clothes and fresh food be brought, Clara watched tensely from the bed. If she was indeed a prisoner, then this, she realized, was to be her cell—the queen's chambers, lush and opulent, and full of glittering delights.

But *why?*

She thought she might have preferred the dungeon interrogation. At least then she would have known how to react.

30

They slept together, in the same bed. Anise had demanded it.

Well. The queen slept the untroubled sleep of a child, sprawled beside Clara in the piles of silken sheets. But Clara lay there, exhausted and impossibly awake as the moon crossed the terrace windows.

It had been a strange, surreal evening, with Anise whirling about her chambers like some madcap hostess, pulling Clara into and out of increasingly elaborate gowns. As though Clara were a child, Anise had fed her glazed fruits and bright blue tarts, blackened meat doused in honey, and for dessert, puffs of sugar from gilded pipes that left Clara's mouth dry and her head heavy.

Was everything to Clara's taste? Did Clara prefer the gold gown or the blue one? How did Clara prefer her sugar? Via pipe, or directly to the vein?

Clara thought it inappropriate and bizarre—she was a prisoner, wasn't she? Why was she being so doted upon? Her mind rebelled at the illogic of it. Anise's attendants scurried tirelessly in and out of the room, lugging armfuls of shimmering garments. Clara found the attendants fascinating—their hair, braided in a style similar to the queen's; their high-shouldered, iridescent suits with swirling coattails and elaborate embroidery. They eyed Clara with everything from hate to genuine puzzlement. Apparently she was not alone in thinking

Anise's behavior odd. She was not sure if their confusion made her feel better or worse.

As Anise watched, her legs lazily propped up on the back of a chair, they laced Clara into a filmy peach gown with an obscenely low-cut bodice and shoulder-baring sleeves that trailed to the floor. It was then, pinned under the weight of their silent scrutiny, that Clara began to cry.

It came out of nowhere, infuriating her. Was she doomed here, as in New York, to be perpetually weak? She was supposed to be implacable and unafraid, pushing and probing Anise until she found the information she sought. She was supposed to find her father. She was not supposed to let princes and faery queens get the best of her. Nevertheless, tears slipped out from beneath her closed eyelids onto tightly pressed lips.

At once Anise snapped her fingers, and the attendants stepped back.

"Clara? What is it?"

To avoid a reprimand Clara forced open her eyes. "I . . . My queen, it is nothing."

"Don't lie to me. You're crying."

"It's embarrassing to stand here like this, to be so . . . unclothed." *And I thought you would be torturing me, not pampering me. I am still confused because you were not the one to kill my mother, if that is in fact the truth. I have not yet had time to process this change inside me, and I miss Nicholas terribly, even though I shouldn't. I am wondering where he is.*

None of that seemed particularly safe to say.

Anise blinked, as if the thought had not occurred to her. "Humans are so strange about nakedness. It's just a body, Clara, the only one you will ever have. Why spend life ashamed of it?"

At a loss, Clara shook her head.

"You should stand up straight, for one. And stop hiding your face." Anise waved her attendants out of the room and led Clara to a full-length mirror in the corner. "Look how beautiful you are. No, don't turn away. *Look at yourself.*"

Ashamed, mortified, Clara did. Her reflection was surprising. The black dye had vanished from her hair, and her natural red was now more vibrant than it had ever been before. Her skin glowed with newness; her eyes were afraid but bright and clear. The way she looked now was, she assumed, a product of—what had Anise called it?—her *transformation,* and it entranced her. She had never looked more like her mother. Her silhouette in this gown was scandalously adult; she tried to look away, to cover herself, but Anise's hands were firm, forcing her to stare, forcing her to remain still.

The queen pressed her cheek to Clara's shoulder, eyes sharp on Clara's face in the mirror. "Such pretty skin. You blush pink and silver, human and mage." There was something wistful in her voice, and in that moment Clara dared to observe the queen. Anise's face was unguarded, soft—and then her eyes found Clara's in the mirror.

"Don't be afraid of your power." Anise's gaze was so steely that Clara flinched. "You're different now, don't you see? You're like me. You're the only one of your kind, and there are those out there who will never let you forget it. You cannot shy away from yourself. Look the world straight in the eye, and it can do nothing to hurt you."

Clara stared, hardly breathing, mesmerized. She did not know why Anise was doing this, but she could not look away, for they were beautiful together in the mirror. She thought it with a pinch of shame. Glittering and powerful and different. Enemies, full of abomination blood.

Their eyes locked. Anise's breath was hot on Clara's shoulder.

They *were* enemies, weren't they? Clara blinked, and the moment fell away. She realized with a start that Anise could be charming her—surely that was it, the reason behind that charged moment. But then, Clara could not trust anything she had learned from Nicholas; the very memory of him was suspect.

Frowning, Anise turned and dragged her finger irritably across a tray of iced cakes. Clara watched her suck the frosting off her fingertip.

"Time for bed," Anise announced, calling her attendants back in to clean up the mess. "We've a busy day tomorrow. And no doubt you are tired." Anise turned, mischievous. "*Lady* Clara."

So now Clara lay, rigid in bed beside her, listening to the queen breathe, the words "Lady Clara" lingering in her mind. She wondered how much Anise had observed, through her many birds and her army of mechaniks, of what had happened to Clara in Cane. Had she seen Clara crash the train? Had she seen Nicholas kiss her on the terrace?

Oh, Nicholas. Clara closed her eyes, wanting to curl in on herself but afraid of waking Anise. She missed him—his nearness, his smile, the look in his eyes when she would catch him watching her. She missed him with an ache she didn't understand, considering what she had witnessed. Was he, wherever he was, missing her as well? He missed the potential of her, she assumed, the weapon that had slipped out of his grasp. It was all happening just as Godfather had warned it would.

She shifted miserably onto her side. Such an act of betrayal, she knew, should have turned her irrevocably against Nicholas, but she could not stifle the twinge of longing in that piece of her heart that had, for years, belonged to his corner of the shop.

Traitorous. Treacherous, duplicitous. That's what he was—not a friend, and certainly not anything deeper. Clara sharpened the words on the whetstone of her mind, forcing herself to feel the cruel slice of them.

Much later, half-asleep, she had an unsettling revelation.

The gowns, the food, the mystifying indulgences—could it be that Anise was like the witches of old, fattening her up, softening her for some terrible fate?

She glanced at the queen, her thin shoulder white and lovely in the moonlight.

If that was Anise's plan, Clara resolved, she would be disappointed.

At least one thing in this mess of confusion and loss still rang true: her father remained somewhere in Cane, and he needed saving. Felicity needed saving. She counted, struggling through the haze of the past several hours for a guess at the time. Twelve days in Cane, three days in New York? It was an unsteady guess, however, and left her feeling strung out with worry.

Tomorrow. Yes, tomorrow she would confirm the day and begin to plan her escape. She would let Anise powder and pamper to her strange heart's content, but meanwhile Clara would be working, observing, seeking. Somewhere in this palace was the information she needed. She would find it and escape with it. Maybe she would even find her father here. Maybe he was closer than she dared hope, breathing the same air, watching the same moonlit snowstorm.

Anise shifted, her hand curling through the soft sheets, reaching for Clara in her sleep but not quite touching her.

Clara, uneasy, moved away as far as she dared, her momentary feeling of resolution fading. Could she really—she, Clara Stole—hope to best a woman with such power and resources at her own baffling game? Clara didn't even know what the game *was*.

As if to encourage her, her blood surged, sending chills across her skin. Curious, half beneath the bedcovers so Anise would not wake and see, she picked at one of the cuts on her arm until it broke and bled.

Yes, there it was—silver, with hints of red. A tiny drop of it beading on her skin.

She stared at it, and though it frightened her, shining and foreign, she wondered if it weren't also a bit beautiful. Maybe this was the key to her freedom, and to her father's.

Maybe, she thought, spreading the blood with her fingertip, she could use it.

The Summer Palace was immense, a colossal architectural sprawl, and Anise could not resist showing it off.

For much of the next day, she ushered Clara through corridor after corridor, room after tremendous gilded room. Mirrored galleries led from one ballroom to the next, through opulent curtained rooms where faeries lounged in regal dress, smoking long, thin cigarettes and whispering behind illuminated fans. Dark ironwork bled through the castle like black lace, arching over every doorway, embellishing every winding staircase. Anise's pride was so satisfied that she even answered Clara's question of how long she had been at the Summer Palace.

"Oh, not long," she said gaily. "Three days, I think. Yes, three." Then she had taken Clara's hand and bid her look out onto the gardens, where tapestries of ironwork flowers stood, stark and sinister, against pale flagstones.

It *had* been nearly twelve days, then, as she had guessed, and almost three in New York. She had time—not enough for true comfort, but enough to breathe more easily. Her relief buoyed her spirits; effusively she praised the gardens' clever design, and Anise beamed at her.

As they progressed through the palace, Clara would on occasion catch a hint of movement in the shadows—a faery dragging a human along by a thick black chain, or a human standing hunched, motionless, masked, as a faery picked bonbons from an offered tray.

Even if they tried to hide it, human and faery alike all looked after Anise with longing. They sat up straighter when she passed, or thrust out their chests, or flipped their hair into a more becoming style. If she showed them even the slightest bit of attention—a nod, a light touch to the shoulder—they would shudder and smile.

Their eyes would turn to Clara and burn with jealousy. They frightened her, those looks.

At midday Anise merrily introduced her to a dining hall full of stone-faced courtiers as "my new prisoner," the sole evidence of which was the possessive way that Anise held Clara's arm. Clara had been combed, dusted with luminescent powder, laced into the gown from the previous night, and fed a grotesquely rich breakfast of sweetcakes and wine while Anise had watched from the bed with a secret, lazy smile. Clara felt uncomfortably like a pet rather than a captive, and the courtiers' sycophantic smiles, thinly veiling disgust and distrust, added to the effect. Each of their reactions Clara tucked away for reflection. She felt that there was something in these observations she could use, and later she would mull them over in her mind.

Amid the day's uncertainty, however, Clara noticed one obvious thing: that she and Anise glided through their tour at a speed that did not allow her much time to pause and look around. They raced down this hallway and through that gallery, meeting these courtiers, one after another, with little rest, and Anise seemed to be taking an odd, circuitous route, doubling back through places they had already seen. Clara supposed that was to keep her disoriented so she wouldn't notice anything too specific—potential escape routes, promising-looking doors. Indeed, when Clara slowed to adjust her skirt at the mouth of one particularly shadowed corridor, Anise yanked her on impatiently.

"We do not dawdle, Clara," she said, digging her fingernails into Clara's arm. "Don't try my hospitality."

All the same, Anise could not have known the extent to which Godfather had honed Clara's observation skills. She did in fact notice a great deal. The labyrinthine Glass Hall, made entirely of crystal and mirrors, hid irregularities in the gleaming walls that could indicate the presence of masked doors. There were fewer soldiers standing guard on the third floor than on the second. Forever on the edge of her sight, kambots trailed them throughout the palace, following Clara's progress with unblinking blue eyes.

She could not help but wonder, with a thrill of hope, if those same unfeeling eyes had seen her father.

31

They dined alone in Anise's chambers at a table trimmed with gold and set with crystalline finery. Clara could hardly eat, for Anise had been watching her keenly all day. Even now her eyes were sharp over the rim of her goblet.

"What did you think of the palace?"

Surely this was not an idle question. Clara dabbed her mouth with her napkin to give herself a moment. "It is astonishing, my queen." That, at least, was true. "Beautiful and grand. Did you design it yourself?"

Anise was pleased. She leaned back in her chair, licking the wine from her lips. "Of course. This was all crude farm country before I arrived."

"Before you overthrew the king, you mean?"

Clara hadn't meant to say that aloud. She cursed the sugar pipe smoking delicately at her side—there had to be a way to partake in this pastime of the queen's without letting it fog her reason.

"The good prince has told you much, it seems." Anise took a long drag from her pipe, and exhaled so the smoke curled around her. "Tell me, what crimes does he accuse me of, from his virtuous pedestal?"

As Clara tried to think of how best to answer this and what lies to tell, a high, thin wailing began, floating in from outside. Was it sirens? Some sort of alarm?

Anise hissed something under her breath and rose, kicking her chair across the room. Clara jumped back. It was easy to forget, given Anise's slight frame, how strong she was.

But then came the startling thought—shouldn't Clara, as a fellow two-blooded monster, be as strong herself? She flexed her arms and legs, subtly, testing. Wishful thinking? If only she had the chance to assess her power without arousing suspicion. If only she knew *how* to assess it.

In the anteroom of the queen's chambers, doors slammed open, and Borschalk—slightly limping, dappled with cuts and bruises—entered the room, his bow stiff with pain. Clara could not help but be disturbed at the sight of him and wonder what wounds his clothes concealed, although it was nothing, she reminded herself, compared to what had happened to her mother. His expression was blank, but Clara caught, when his eyes flicked to hers, a flash of unmistakable hatred.

"My queen, I apologize for disturbing you, but there is—"

"I know what the alarms are for." Anise snatched a heavy brocaded coat, beaded with crystal, from a pile on the floor. She hardly spared a glance for her injured lover as she swept toward the doors. "Clara, come. You need to see this."

Clara took a furred coat from the same pile, nearly tripping over herself in her haste to catch up. Borschalk limped doggedly behind, ruining Clara's brief flare of hope that she could make a run for it with Anise so distracted.

Outside on the wide obsidian steps that marked the palace entrance, Clara shivered in her coat and fine satin slippers. Beyond the steps, a dark road wound down to the surrounding city. Faery soldiers stood at attention in two lines on either side of them. Snow fell in biting gusts.

Borschalk clapped his hands once. A group of soldiers stepped forward and threw dirty heaps of something to the ground. Anise toed through the heaps, her coat trailing behind her.

No. Not heaps. Clara realized it with a slow trickle of dismay.

The heaps were *humans*, clothed in rags, rouge and white paint smeared across their faces. Their rags were the bedraggled remains of costumes. On their feet they wore dancing slippers stained with blood. They looked, Clara thought, like entertainers who had escaped some macabre circus—perhaps they were.

"You thought you could escape me." Anise's voice was soft as she circled the humans, running her bejeweled fingers along their backs. One of them, a young man, began to sob. "Haven't you seen what happens to runaways?"

They did not answer. Their eyes fixed on anything but her.

Anise stopped in front of them. She did not raise her voice. She did not have to. The sweet lilt of her words was terrifying enough. "Answer me, or you will die in the most undignified manner possible."

"Yes," one of the humans gasped, a woman with chunks of stringy hair dyed green.

"Yes?" Anise kicked her, watching coldly. "But didn't you want to come here? I know many people who would kill to serve at the Summer Palace. I'm sure some of you did kill. Or betray your loved ones. Or"—Anise gestured at the sobbing young man and laughed—"cut off your own arm in some sort of black market trade, to get here."

Borschalk, a monster in the snowy evening light, ripped a crude prosthetic from the sobbing man's shoulder and smashed it on the ground. A mangled stump remained behind. The man convulsed, screaming. Clara wanted to turn away, but she could feel Anise's attention on her and didn't dare.

"I'm offended at your lack of gratitude," Anise said, pouting. "Your race hunts mine in a war that lasts decades, simply because we are different from you, because our magic confounds you." She paced as she spoke, regal and splendid. "You cut us open, you raid our villages, you lock us in dungeons and laboratories. And when I rose up against you and beat you, I allowed you to live despite your crimes. I even offer those willing to work for it a chance to live here, at my own palace. But even after I provide you with everything you could want here, you repay me by trying to escape. It's insulting." She paused, her eyes flashing. Clara could hardly breathe. She imagined Nicholas poised over a faery patient, like Dr. Victor and his wayward girls—scalpel ready, poisons in tiny lined-up vials. She felt torn between revulsion and sympathy. If someone had done that to Clara's own people, would she not be as violent and vengeful?

She found, uneasily, that she could not answer her own question.

"But I can be magnanimous." Anise pursed her lips as if deep in thought. "I'll allow you to choose your punishment. You may either be executed immediately . . ."

Terrified for the humans, Clara imagined herself and her father being held before Anise as these people were—being judged and threatened, their lives hanging by tenuous threads. She imagined Felicity there too, done up in tear-streaked makeup and torn skirts, weeping for mercy like the one-armed young man. Something within her began to rebel, something furious and frightened and frigid. On her wrist, where she had smeared the drop of her blood, a spark of silver caught her eye. When she looked down, it had gone.

"Or," Anise continued, "you may keep your lives but your rations of sugar will be permanently suspended."

At once the humans struggled to their hands and knees, crying out piteously.

"No, please!" They crawled toward Anise, fumbled at the hem of her coat. "Anything, *anything* but that. . . ."

The one-armed man sobbed loudest. Anise knelt before him and smoothed back his hair. "Do you want some sugar?"

"Yes! Yes, my queen. I do, desperately." He kissed her fingers, slobbering over her rings. "Please, please . . ."

Clara had to look away.

"Very well." Anise nodded at Borschalk, who grinned. "Then you shall have it."

Clara knew that she would never forget what happened next. Even if this did turn out to be a dream, as a tiny part of her still chose to hope, and she awoke safe in her bed—even then, Clara would remember the faery soldiers shoving needles into the humans' arms, emptying syringes full of glowing blue liquid into their veins.

The humans smiled, eyes drooping as the liquid sugar pumped through their blood. They began to glow softly, their skin tinged blue and green, a sick gleam flickering in their eyes.

When the dosage became too much, they began to convulse. Their skin bulged and ruptured, spewing blood and steaming blue liquid. They vomited, but it did not help; they were choking on sweet chemical blue. Their screams—half in pain, half in mad ecstasy—rang across the plaza. The sound tore through Clara, hammered against her bones. Stirred her. Electrified her.

This could happen to her father. Maybe it already had.

Perhaps she could fight for them. She blinked, the idea startling her, as if it were not her own. As if it were born of something *more* than herself. In response, her blood came alive. Her senses snapped to cold, furious attention.

This, it occurred to her, was a chance to see what her power, her new silver strength, could do.

Clara took a hesitant step forward, dreadfully afraid. Deep in her bones something cold and stinging churned. She had no idea what she was doing; she hoped it wouldn't kill her.

Anise let the humans writhe in agony for long moments, spoiled blood gurgling at their blue-tinged lips. Her soldiers, decorum forgotten, roared with laughter.

And Clara, eager with anger and fear, let loose the energy building inside her.

It erupted, like a scream held back for too long. A cold wave of pure force burst out from her, as if set free by the opening of her hands. Somewhere in this ear-popping din Clara felt a vital, unseen line hanging down from the churning sky, connecting her and the heavens, and even, she felt, connecting her to the stars beyond.

She reached for it and tugged.

Lightning flashed, burning her hands, knocking her flat. The wind shrieked more loudly even than Anise's trains.

Silence fell. A quaking, charged aftermath.

Clara raised herself up, shaking, her chin raw where it had scraped the ground. Across the way lay two soldiers, burned alive and screaming. The ground around them was charred and slick with ice, as if some great force had dropped out of the sky and flayed them.

For a moment no one said or did anything. The snow continued to fall. The gathered soldiers stared at Clara in astonishment, and the humans, barely alive now, looked to Clara through their agony. They were dying, and yet their eyes now held a last, desperate hope—because of *her*.

Borschalk was the first to move. He unsheathed a great broadsword and stalked toward her. He did not have to say anything; his intent was plain.

"Don't." Anise raised her arm. "Don't touch her."

Clara swayed, her hands outstretched. She felt dizzy, battered. Her skin crackled with energy, and her fingers glowed faintly, like the lightning that had crashed down from the sky.

If this was magic, she thought woozily, then no wonder Godfather was so unpredictably mad, and Anise, too. Magic hurt. It was brutal, and she felt stupid for ever thinking she could hope to control it. She stumbled, and the watching soldiers muttered in alarm. Some of them moved back; others readied their weapons.

A beat, and then Anise took Borschalk's sword and turned to the humans. The one-armed man raised his hand—"No," he gasped, "wait"—but then Anise beheaded him, and then the others, in four swift strokes. Her lip curled at the mess now staining the steps.

"Take them to Ketcher," she said, pointing at the still-screaming soldiers, "though he won't be able to do much for them. Borschalk, escort Clara to my chambers."

Borschalk grinned that terrible grin and seized Clara's arm hard enough to bruise. She cried out, and Anise's eyes snapped with rage.

"You would be wise, Borschalk, not to hurt her, or even touch her." Beneath her smirk, something sad sparked in her eye and then was snuffed out. "You've only experienced the barest sliver of what I can do to you. Are you eager for more so soon?"

With a tiny growl Borschalk released Clara's arm and bowed. "No, my queen."

They left Anise there, a pensive white spectre on the steps, and hurried back through the palace. News of what had happened was already starting to spread. Murmuring courtiers peered out of their parlors, and human slaves in the shadows gaped past their sores. Clara tried to ignore what this could mean, fear hammering at her breast, and focus on their passage. There, on the northern end of the first floor, was a dark receiving hall lined with candles, and there, on the southern end, a grand hall, perhaps Anise's court. She checked them against the map she had drawn in her mind during the day's tour.

"You take pleasure in what she has done to me, perhaps," Borschalk said, low, as they approached Anise's chambers, high in the southernmost tower.

"No, I don't," Clara whispered, and it was the truth. "I swear to you—"

"And I swear *this*—that I am watching you, and that, my queen's orders or no, punishment or no, I will drain you of every silver drop before I allow you to betray her. Do not think for one moment, mage filth, that you are safe here."

He did disobey Anise then, as he wrenched Clara's arm to shove her inside the queen's suite, and his bruised face crawled with loathing—but there was also, she thought, an uncertainty there. Caution.

Pleasure rushed down her spine, even as she clutched at her stomach, her body aching as if from many blows.

How marvelous to—for once—have someone be afraid of *her*.

32

Clara went to bed alone. Through the night she fought unsuccessfully for sleep in the empty bed, and the next morning she woke alone to the rumbling of a tiny earthquake that shook the chandeliers.

She had no idea where Anise had gone, and not knowing made it difficult to remain calm. Her absence seemed unbearably ominous. Their dinner from the previous night had grown somewhat cold and lumpy; Clara nevertheless nibbled at a bit of it to assuage her hunger, but it did nothing to settle her nerves. She began to pace.

Obviously she couldn't just leave; she knew armed guards stood outside the doors. But she could still explore Anise's chambers.

After slipping into one of Anise's warm, fur-lined robes, Clara cautiously inspected the room, dragging her fingers along lamps rimmed with crystal, browsing through Anise's collection of extravagant clothes and cosmetics, always listening for the guards. When some time had passed without any movement from them, Clara took a breath and began testing the room—pressing the edges of Anise's many mirrors for catches that would allow them to swing away and reveal a concealed room or passage, testing the walls for hollow places. Out on the terrace she inspected the surrounding walls for footholds. Perhaps she could climb out—but, no, the walls were treacherously slick and sheer, and she wasn't confident she could navigate toward the outer wall from here, much less escape through it.

She stood there, leaning against the terrace railing and looking out over the sprawling palace, so large that it could be considered—and, she supposed, *was*—a city in itself. The horizon beyond was troubling. The sky had darkened, more sickly colored than it had yet been, and storms shadowed faraway patches of land with lightning and black rain. It was a wonder that such constant storms had not brought the trains crashing down.

Lunchtime came and went. Clara nibbled idly at a cold glazed cake. She wished, agitated, that she still had her boots. What had become of them?

Perhaps she could try to use her new power to fight her way out, past the guards. So far that power had manifested unpredictably. Summoning it seemed daunting. Even if she did somehow manage to both summon and control it, surely the kambots would raise the alarm. Anise would come running with half her soldiers in tow.

Nevertheless, Clara opened her palm and studied it. The outburst the night before had seemed to be triggered out of deep emotion, but that seemed ineffectual at best. Emotions could be difficult to control, and if she opened herself up to them too deeply, she wasn't sure she could maintain the courage to go on. Fear would paralyze her; anger would make her blind.

Somehow she would have to learn to switch her power on and off, like one of Godfather's clockwork creations.

But how would she ever manage to work out such a thing under constant surveillance? And how could she be sure she wouldn't kill herself in the process? The previous night's pain still lingered in her bones.

That evening Anise finally returned, looking haggard and wild with temper. Without a word she stripped off her clothes from the night before and pulled on a formfitting black suit with a high collar and clusters of elaborate gold needlework. Over it she fastened an ebony cloak.

"Come," she said to Clara, not even looking at her. The cloak swirled about her like wings. "They're waiting."

Clara hurried to follow. "Pardon me, my queen, but who is waiting?"

"Everyone."

Anise brought Clara to the great hall on the southern end of the castle. The queen's court was a grand space with vaulted ceilings and flickering blue lamplight, everything carved of obsidian, iron, and glass. A dark throne sat at one end of the room, and high rows of seats lined the eastern and western walls.

The seats, Clara noticed with a thrill of dread upon entering the room, were filled with faeries—faeries in furred cloaks; faery children, prim and haughty; faeries holding up gold-rimmed glasses as though they were sitting down to the opera. Elaborately coiffed, elegantly attired. Watching her. Whispering.

"Stay here," Anise snapped, and left Clara there in the center of the cold hall with hundreds of eyes upon her. She pulled her robe tight around her body and wished that she'd had the foresight to change into something more substantial.

Upon taking her seat, Anise kept tapping her fingers on the iron arm of her throne, obviously stewing for some inconceivable reason. Beside her Borschalk looked coldly satisfied.

"Clara Stole," Anise said at last, her voice hard, "last night you severely injured two soldiers in my palace guard. The burns they sustained led to their deaths early this morning."

Dismay ripped through Clara, making her sway on her feet. After all, they had only been soldiers following orders. She hadn't meant to kill them; she had simply wanted to stop the violence being done to the humans. It was frightening to hear what kind of damage her power had caused, and to wonder how much more it could do.

"What do you have to say about that?"

Clara shook her head. "Only that I did not mean to, my queen."

Sounds of disbelief from around the room, irritable rustlings. Anise's mouth twisted.

"What did you mean to do, then?"

"I was . . . I wanted to help the humans."

Anise's eyes were sharp on her face. "The humans were being punished in accordance with royal law. Did you think it your place, as a prisoner, to intervene?"

"Well, I . . ." There was no possible way to answer this, and desperation made her bold. "Forgive me, but I do not feel much like a prisoner."

Outrage shot through the room. The gathered courtiers rose to their feet. Clara heard them hiss their contempt, heard calls for her immediate execution. Anise descended from her throne and advanced on Clara with the lithe suppleness of a cat on the hunt. Instinct made Clara try to run, but Anise flung out her hand before she could get very far. A coil of iron burst through the tiled floor and wrapped around Clara's leg, jerking her off her feet; she cried out, tried to scramble away, but it pinned her there.

Anise straddled her, grabbing her neck with the strength of a vise. Her face was a mass of frustrated contradictions, and Clara could find no sense in it.

"If you wish to feel more like a prisoner, Clara," Anise breathed, "I can certainly accommodate you."

Then, with a flick of her hand, Anise knocked the iron binding loose from Clara's ankle and sent her skidding across the smooth tiled floor.

The faeries around the room hooted, settling back into their seats. A hushed sense of expectation fell over the room, and when Clara struggled to her feet, she felt horribly afraid. Her ankle felt like it might be sprained, and her dressing gown had fallen open. Embarrassed, keenly aware of the faeries' lewd gazes and lewder laughter, she tried to close it and retie the sash, but Anise was on her before she could finish, pinning her to the wall. Above Clara's head, faeries leaned over for a better look.

"You were traveling with the prince." Anise's hand tightened around Clara's neck. "Tell me, what was his destination?"

It was such an impossible question that for a moment Clara gaped, clawing at Anise's fingers. They burned her skin, impossibly hot. Answering her was out of the question—even though Nicholas had intended to use her from the beginning, even if their friendship, the affection she thought she had read on his face, had been a lie.

Tears came to her eyes, and astonishingly, Anise seemed to waver at the sight. But then the moment was gone, and she threw Clara to the ground.

"Answer me!"

"I don't know, my queen," Clara panted, and then she heard it—a sickeningly familiar buzzing wave.

Anise stood with her arms outstretched, and at her feet a line of clicking black mechaniks tumbled out from a fresh seam in the floor, as if the floor were made of them and Anise had set them free. Clara realized, horribly, that this was most likely the case—that the floor, and the hall, and the entire palace, was made of these tiny malicious machines, held together by Anise's will.

They surged for her, and she crawled away, her body aching with the effort. They began to nip at her heels, tear at her bare feet, chomp up the sash of her dressing gown. At this last, Clara felt such a stab of terror that she turned and clawed through the air for them, frantic to get them off.

And it happened again, in her moment of panic: a surge outward from her hands, from the air around her. A cold wall of energy, repelling the mechaniks and sending them clattering back onto the floor like so many spilled toys. They spun there, stunned, disoriented, clacking blindly.

Clara huddled on the floor, trembling. She must remember how it had felt, hold on to the sensation and decipher it later. If, that is, *later* ever came.

Anise stood at a distance in the suddenly silent room. Some of the faeries were now looking at Clara in awe, at her arms specifically. She understood, at last, that the faeries needed the mechanized gloves they wore in order to focus their magic into weapons.

But Anise wore nothing of the sort. And neither did Clara.

She shivered at the realization, at the potential of it, and the burden. No wonder Nicholas's refugees had looked at her with such disgust and fear.

"Well," Anise said at last, "I can see my court will indeed have the show they were promised."

Before Clara could say anything, protest or plead or prepare herself to fight back, Anise flung herself at Clara, propelled by a scorching wave of power. Heat punched Clara like a fist. She fell, and blackness took her.

33

Clara awoke briefly as Borschalk and two other soldiers dragged her downstairs to a lower level of the palace she had not yet seen. They deposited her in an empty black cell, heavy with stink. When it was clear they had gone and were not coming back, Clara tried to stand.

Every movement was agony. Bruises and bloodied cuts dotted her body from Anise's blows and the mechaniks' cunning teeth. They had not devoured her as they had so many others—a testament to the strength of Clara's power, undisciplined though it was—but they had bitten her, ruthlessly. Her insides hurt even worse, as though she had dragged them through brutal exercises with no preparation—and, she supposed, she had. The taste of the power she had unleashed sat sourly on her tongue. The darkness here was complete, and it seemed silly to stay on her feet, for where could she go? So she let herself collapse. From somewhere nearby came raw screams—human, faery, it was impossible to tell. Other prisoners, being tortured?

She *had* thought she would be more comfortable with dungeons and interrogations, hadn't she?

Now the idea almost made her laugh.

Slow hours of pain passed until Clara awoke to the door clanging open. The kambot watching her from its perch high in the corner squawked mechanically, twitched, and fell silent, smoking. The sounds disturbed Clara from a dream, one of the strange ones she would have described to Godfather. The details were fuzzy to her now. She only knew, upon waking, a sense of terrible loss, and a dream-scent lingering on her tongue—a scent of spice and oil, of fireplace and home. Not the mansion, no. Godfather's shop, and all its mysterious contents.

How long had it been? Where was Nicholas, and was he alive? Had they buried Godfather upon killing him, or had they simply left him there on the streets of Kafflock to rot with everyone else?

Another prisoner, somewhere, cried out, and Clara let out a shuddering sob.

"Hush," said a stern voice—Anise, at Clara's door, in a sheer black gown that tied shut with a sash of tiny golden chains. Her hair was loose, falling in white waves. She held a flickering lantern and knelt at Clara's side. The blue light cast an eerie pall on her skin. After she had inspected Clara's face for a long moment, her stony expression softened. She looked away, troubled, and bit her lip. The motion struck Clara as incongruously childlike.

She wanted to hit her, to beg mercy from her, to demand an explanation for her strange moods. But she was too frightened for it, too shattered. And then there was the charred kambot in the corner, certainly ruined.

Curious.

"Stand up," Anise said, her expression closed. She helped Clara to her feet, and before Clara was able to get her bearings, Anise thrust her palm into the air—just as Borschalk had done that night, dragging her father away—and then drew it back, opening a Door. Its lights wavered gently. Anise stepped through and took Clara with her.

On the other side Anise's chambers awaited, dimly lit. The Door closed behind them in silence, and Clara fell to her knees. Passing through the Door left her feeling disoriented, scraped raw.

Anise rustled overhead, fetching cloths and a bowl. When she sat beside Clara on the floor and began tenderly cleaning the blood from her face, Clara looked up, startled. Anise did not meet her eyes, concentrating on Clara's cut bottom lip. Clara watched her in silence as the bowl of warm water Anise held turned red and murky, silver glistening on the top like oil. Miraculously it seemed Clara's wounds had already begun to heal somewhat. Her own magic, or Anise's? She found that she was too weary to care at the moment.

"You understand why I had to do it," Anise said evenly, after a time. "After what happened with those humans, with my soldiers, I had to demonstrate how much stronger than you I am. My court is easily impressed and easily frightened. They already don't like you. Many of them want me to kill you after I've gotten the information I need. I suppose I should." Her eyes met Clara's at last. "I *should* kill you, but I don't want to. I like hurting people, but I don't like hurting you."

Clara was almost too astonished to respond. "I don't understand."

"And you don't need to," Anise snapped. She moved to Clara's legs, cleaning them roughly. Clara bit her tongue to keep from whimpering. She did not want to lose this moment between them, this fragile, strange moment. She simply watched as Anise continued her ministrations. Anise paused at the sash of Clara's tattered gown, and her eyes flickered up, as though asking for permission. Clara did not react, breathless to see where this progressed and understand what it meant, and Anise looked away, peeling the fabric aside to tend, ever so gently, the cuts on Clara's belly.

The air between them was a symphony of tension, and Clara's skin crawled with repulsion—at Anise's nearness, at the intimacy of her touch, and, if she were honest with herself, at her body's own fascinated response.

After a moment Anise threw the dirtied cloth to the ground and stalked away. "Surely you understand why I did it." She waved her hand dismissively, adjusted her hair. But Clara saw her fingers tremble. "And I'll do it again if I have to. It's expected. And of course I *want* to do it."

Clara drew her torn dressing gown closed, turning these paradoxes over in her mind. Anise wanted to hurt her—and yet, a moment before, she had said she *didn't* want to. The queen had been so furious in court today, so unabashedly violent, whereas now she could be described as ashamed, even loving. Her soft touch on Clara's body had been the furthest thing from cruel.

With some effort, Clara rose. "Why did you bring me here? Why did you take me from my cell?"

Anise stopped at the window, her expression a muddled storm. "Because you're like me." She opened her mouth, closed it, and turned away, but before she did, Clara caught a glimpse of bright eyes and a mouth twisting bitterly.

Clara's blood slowed with the weight of this admission.

"Salt of the seas, don't just *stand* there." Anise threw herself furiously onto the bed. "I'll take you back to your cell early. No one will know you were gone." Her lips curved into a roguish smile, but it was strained. "Except for us. It'll be our secret, we two."

Mutely Clara nodded, let Anise slip the torn, bloodied robe from her shoulders and replace it with a clean gown—airy, virtually transparent, spangled with tiny jeweled designs that kissed her skin like rivulets of water. It was vulgar by any tasteful standard, and yet exquisite; Anise cooed in delight and guided her into bed. They did not touch after that. In fact, the queen seemed determined to keep herself as far away from Clara as possible, but that did not change what had just happened, and as Clara lay there, unspeakably awake, listening to Anise breathe in and out, she put a word to her revelation:

Lonely. Anise was *lonely*. And that was how Clara would beat her.

34

The next morning before dawn Clara awoke to the feeling of eyes upon her. She jolted upright and found Anise standing at the foot of the bed, watching her.

The queen smiled, toying with her own hair. "You're pretty when you sleep. Like a doll."

Clara wasn't sure what she thought of that remark and almost drew the sheets up to her chin in automatic defense, but instead she stopped and sat up straight, not even adjusting the shoulder of her nightgown when it slipped down her arm. Anise's eyes flicked to the revealed skin, and back to Clara's face. Her smile had frozen.

Such a lot to be learned from that expression, but Clara was too nervous to feel triumphant.

Anise turned away, fetching Clara's tattered gown and delicately wrinkling her nose at it. "Come. It's back to your cell with you, little prisoner." They did not speak again, but before Anise left her on the other side of the Door, she let her fingers trail down Clara's arm and catch, softly, on her palm.

Their eyes met, and Clara felt a taut line of danger between them. Then Anise stepped through the Door and was gone.

Clara had roughly calculated the time. She figured that it was now her fourteenth day in Cane, and at this realization her blood churned with new urgency. Fourteen days here, three days and six hours at home. Too much time had been wasted in this palace; she would have to move more quickly.

Unfortunately, she had very little time to herself before she was once again fetched and brought before Anise and her gleaming court. Interrogated again, tortured by the queen's ruthless assaults again. But it seemed to her—as Anise hurled questions at her about Nicholas's whereabouts, his intentions, his companions, as she sent the mechaniks nibbling at her and let Borschalk strike her in the gut when Clara would not answer—that the queen took no real joy in what was happening. The courtiers cheered when Clara fell, they jeered when she stood up again, and Anise grew increasingly silent.

Clara kept it up for as long as she could, spitting weary defiance at the cruel, leering Borschalk, letting herself be thrown to the ground by Anise's hot bursts of magic. She did not release her own power. Instead, when she felt herself becoming so laden with pain and fear that it began to build, stinging her palms, she took a moment to huddle on the cold floor and tried to decipher it.

How did it feel, seething inside her?

Like a scream ready to explode from her lips—except instead of her lips it was her entire self, and instead of a scream it was a thousand silver arrows made of wind and cold and ancient power. It was rebelling against this abuse. It wanted her to defend herself.

What would it take to release this power?

She focused her mind to hold on to the sensation, imagining her strength as an object she could seize, turn over, and examine. She could release it right now with minimal effort; it was that difficult to fight. But to draw it out a particular way, to shape it into what she wanted it to be, to control it, would be like assigning form to an ocean wave.

A hand grabbed her face, wrenched her up from the ground—Anise, eyes bright. With fury, or with something else?

"What is the prince's plan of attack?"

Clara met her gaze unflinchingly. "To kill you."

A murmur through the gathered faeries. Anise's smile was hard. "How will he do it?"

"Bloodily, I would think."

Anise slapped her across the face. She slumped, but Anise would not let her fall, cradling her close in a parody of affection. "Who is he traveling with?"

"An army," Clara said. "Ten thousand strong."

Anise let her drop then, and ordered her returned to her cell.

"We can do this every day, Clara!" she cried as Clara was dragged away. "Until your mind breaks, or your body does. It's no matter which to me!"

But that night Anise came to fetch her once again, and when she did, she looked small, remorseful, and maybe even afraid. Once safely through the Door and in her chambers, she fell with Clara to the ground, for Clara was weak with fatigue, and when Clara feebly smiled up at Anise and whispered, "You came for me, like I hoped you would," Anise's face lit up with unfettered joy. She kissed Clara's brow, and her cheeks, sore from Borschalk's blows. Clara was treated to a night lying on the queen's cool sheets, sipping a hot drink that eased her body's aches. Anise was as gentle and solicitous a nurse as any Clara could imagine, rubbing ointment into Clara's skin, and for a moment, as she drifted toward unconsciousness with the queen's anxious eyes upon her, she felt a flicker of guilt.

For Anise could not know that Clara clearly saw what their nearness meant to the queen, how eager Anise was to please her without being obvious, and how Anise hated herself for it.

And Anise could not know that Clara, alone in her cell since midday, had fought through her pain to practice her magic.

At first it had been difficult to focus. Clara had never experienced such pain in her life, and for a few minutes all she could do was sob, there in her dark cell, hugging her poor, pummeled midsection.

But the screaming that would occasionally pierce the quiet of her cell, and the wailing and pleading—the *whimpering*—made Clara think of her father, and silenced her. It could easily be him screaming, couldn't it? If not here, then somewhere else in Cane—and maybe it *was* here, and she was wasting time feeling sorry for herself. At least she still had her wits about her. At least she wasn't being tortured right now like these other poor souls.

She tried to picture her father's face—his and Felicity's, and certainly no one else's, because that would hurt too much. She had to concentrate solely on her goal. There could be no distractions, no fear, and certainly no princes.

In the image of her father's and Felicity's faces, she found a solidity, buried in the pain, and grabbed hold of it.

It was like a rope out of the abyss, and, determined, she climbed it. And then she realized that the solidity was her power, ready and waiting for her to use it.

How startling to realize that this strange, potent thing was now living inside her, and even more startling, that her mother had lived with it too. Godfather had called the sour young Leska powerful. The thought disturbed Clara, and also gave her comfort, for as Leska's daughter, shouldn't she be powerful too?

She wished her mother had confided in her. Maybe Clara's power would not have manifested if she had never come to Cane, but it would have been a secret they could have shared, a treasure to whisper about as they lay curled up beneath Clara's quilt on cold nights when her father stayed late at Rivington Hall. Felicity, too—the thought was a slice of sorrow through Clara's heart. Did Felicity also have this power inside her, dormant? Would Felicity ever know of their mother's true past?

"Not if you don't get back in time to save her, she won't," Clara said, and the words granted her something of a calm. She wiped her eyes and pulled herself upright, ignoring the pain.

Getting out was the most important thing. Clara could not go searching the palace from inside her cell. She had seen two people open Doors—Borschalk, in her father's bedroom, and Anise, right where Clara was standing now. She approached the cell door, traced her fingers around it. Was it important to have a true opening in sight to focus upon? Borschalk had had the window; Anise, this door. But that seemed unnecessarily restrictive, and someone could come fetch her at any moment. Perhaps her interrogation for the day was not yet over. Perhaps Borschalk would convince Anise that he had not thrashed her severely enough.

Sweat stung her eyes, and she brushed it away. She needed to concentrate, to push everything out of her mind but the image of opening a Door. She closed her eyes and remembered how both Borschalk and Anise had punched the air with open palms and then pulled back, clenching their fingers into fists. That seemed simple enough, and Clara assumed she had sufficient power within her to do it. But surely there was another trick to it. It could not be so easy.

She paced, her twisted ankle making her gait uneven. What was it like to open a door? Such an everyday occurrence that you didn't think about it. You put your hand on the knob, turned, opened, stepped through. And the principle with these Doors seemed similar.

What do you think about when opening a door?

She stopped pacing. *Ah*. That was it.

You think about what awaits you on the other side. You may not realize you're thinking of it, but you would certainly be disoriented if you stepped through a door with the expectation of emerging in one place and instead emerged in another.

Abruptly nervous, Clara moved to the far side of the cell. It was too risky, perhaps, to attempt going from room to room on this, her first try. But perhaps from one *side* of the room to the other . . .

She stood there, memorizing the opposite wall and its door until she could have sketched every detail of it. Without putting her full concentration into the act, she ran her arm through the motions—thrusting her palm through the air, drawing back, and letting her fingers close on the withdrawal. Thrust, draw back, close. Over and over she practiced, and when her arm began to ache from it, she reached for the cord of her power—she had been imagining it, this entire time, as taut wires in her limbs, her ropes out of the abyss—and opened her mind to it. She *was* her power, and it was her. When she thrust her palm into the air this time, the full weight of her concentration behind it, lights appeared before her—thin, wan even, but they were there.

Clapping a hand over her mouth to hold the laughter in, Clara fell back against the wall. When she had recovered, she reached an arm toward the Door she had created. Would it work? Lights in the air were pretty but useless without a way through.

She closed her eyes, held the image of the other side of the room in her mind, and stepped into the lights.

It was not a smooth passage. She landed hard on her knees in front of the opposite wall, the world spinning and full of stars.

But it had *worked*, and she sat there laughing quietly.

Then she got up and did it again. And again, and again, twenty-seven times in total, and by the time Anise came for her that evening, Clara held the knowledge of Doors hard in her mind and heart.

It was difficult for Clara to hide her elation and her strength—for the day of working with her power had restored some of the latter—but she managed it that night, trembling in Anise's arms, exaggerating her weakness.

When the queen smoothed a rag dipped in ointment across the backs of Clara's bruised thighs, Clara tried to look suitably afraid. She couldn't allow Anise to suspect what she had done, not for a moment guess that Clara knew how deeply alone two-blooded Anise felt up here in her grand, glittering tower, a queen of people who feared her, who were not like her, and who loved her only for the safety that doing so afforded them.

"You are kind to me," Clara said softly over her shoulder. "Why?"

Anise paused in her ministrations. Her knuckles brushed across the small of Clara's back.

"Do you think I care what that damned prince is actually doing?" She rose, stalked to her dining table, knocked back her unfinished wine in one ferocious gulp. "This isn't the Cane that Nicholas remembers. It's a stranger to him. It's *my* Cane now, and he is an inconsequential bug, burrowing around aimlessly, armed with a self-righteous sense of entitlement. I am far from worried about one tiny, prideful bug." Anise spun around, eyes flashing. "Did you know, I am a royal too?"

It was best, perhaps, to be honest. Clara sat up. "I did."

Anise was scornful. "Dear, virtuous Nicholas told you, did he?"

"Your parents were a human king and a faery countess." Clara paused. "They were killed for it. For the affair, I mean."

"Nicholas's family killed them for it," Anise corrected. "Because the four royal families were nothing if not a passel of bickering, greedy egoists." She flopped irritably into a chair. "I could pass the night telling you about their many inbred wars, but it would be a waste of breath. And they're all dead now anyway." She smiled to herself.

"If you have royal blood," Clara said carefully, "then why shouldn't you have as much right to the throne as Nicholas does?"

Anise's eyes shot to her, surprised and trying to cover it. "That is the true question, isn't it? The answer is, I *do*, and he can't stand that fact. He and his family were never able to accept that my claim is at least as strong as theirs."

Clara decided not to point out that Nicholas might not have such a problem with Anise's royal blood if she were not in fact using it to torture the kingdom—the people, and the land itself.

"That seems petty," she said instead, and her vexed expression was genuine. Nicholas had confessed to her, hadn't he, that he felt himself regressing? *I feel the hate returning, and the violence.* If he were somehow able to reclaim his throne, what proof was there that he would not turn into the human version of Anise, enslaving and tormenting the faery population as she had done to the humans?

She felt uneasy beneath the weight of these thoughts and Anise's piercing gaze.

"You asked why I was kind to you," Anise said at last.

Clara nodded and forced herself to concentrate despite her disquiet, for Anise's voice held within it a tiny bashfulness, a hint at confession.

Anise seemed at war with herself. "I don't care much about Nicholas, you see. My courtiers do. They think of him, and they think of what life used to be for us—how dangerous it was, and how bloody. I think of him and I want to laugh. One small prince. What should I care about that? He'll dare to show his face one day, and I'll kill him and be done with it. No silly curses this time. Only swords."

Such a cavalier dismissal. Clara fought not to react.

"But you, Clara . . ." Anise let her eyes wander down Clara's body and back up to her face. "I see great potential in you. It will just take time to convince my kingdom of it."

Clara's skin prickled, coaxed into gooseflesh by the focused heat of Anise's gaze. She was not sure whether to feel admired, violated, or simply assessed.

Anise rose, fiddling with her gown, such a pale blue that it almost matched her skin. "Unfortunately for you, the time will be painful. It can't be helped." And with that Anise was cold, unreachable Anise again. She finished nursing Clara's wounds with an efficiency that bordered on harshness. Only as Clara drifted to sleep, Anise watching from the next pillow, did she catch, right at the last, the sweetness on Anise's face—the worry, and the guilt, and the *hope*—when she thought Clara was no longer looking.

35

The next morning, after Anise had brought Clara to her cell and before she'd slipped back through the Door, Clara caught her arm. Anise turned back, surprised. Clara did not have to pretend the awe in her voice. The queen was many ugly things, but on the surface at least, she was a vision. The Door's shifting lights painted her skin lustrous.

"Thank you," Clara said, "for tending to me."

She stepped forward and kissed Anise's cheek. It was a risk, but a calculated one. She lingered there, her hands hovering over the dip of Anise's back, Anise's lovely white hair tickling her palms, and whispered it again. "Thank you, my queen." And then, she could not help herself. Anise's nearness was a lure; Clara leaned closer. Her lips brushed Anise's neck—a chaste gesture, almost reverent—and it was a warm, surprising delight.

Anise left without a word, her expression revealing nothing, but no one came for Clara that day. Morning came and went, midday came and went, and she was left alone.

They could, she supposed, come for her in the afternoon. But it was unlikely, if her suspicions about Anise were correct. And again—that twinge of guilt for manipulating her, that shameful feeling of softness.

Clara ignored it. She could not be distracted if she were to successfully open a Door out of her cell.

* * *

Traveling across a room was one thing, but traveling out of one room and into another she couldn't see was something else entirely. Clara spent an agonizing few minutes convincing herself to do it, doubt tying her into knots.

It was the screams of the other prisoners that persuaded her. One of them, she thought, sounded a bit like her father. It gave her courage and urgency—fifteen days here, three days and eighteen hours at home. She faced the door and prepared herself, turning her concentration inward until she found her power, waiting and steady. She fancied she could feel the scrape of blood against vein, the vitality singing through her nerves.

Clara pictured the hallway outside her door and drew the image into her mind. Damp walls framed with exposed piping, the faint outline of doors. Darkness.

She drew a breath and held it. It would work, wouldn't it? It had to. She had practiced. She could travel across her cell without even trying now, and her disorientation when she did had decreased to manageable levels.

It *would* work.

She thrust her palm into the air, drew it back, and pulled her fingers into a fist. The lights shimmered into being, and she stepped through, and landed clumsily in the dank corridor. She wavered for a moment, unsteady; passage through this Door had been rougher than the others, perhaps due to her nervousness. But she had done it; she was *through*. She turned into the dark.

Each cell door had a narrow slot through which food could be deposited. Clara steeled herself for what she might find before she bent, pried open the first slot's hinged cover, and peered through.

Darkness. It was so confoundingly dark down here. No torchlit sconces for the prisoners to enjoy, Clara supposed. She couldn't see a thing.

The Doors, she remembered, emanated light. If she opened one, a tiny one that would not lead anywhere but right beside her, surely its glow would be enough to see by. Besides that, it would be a way to practice controlling the flow of her power.

Crouched at the first cell door, Clara looked at the space directly beside her. She imagined her focus as a needle's eye through which she must somehow thread this new, eager strength within her.

It worked, but not without the extra effort for control temporarily draining her. She felt as she had in Mira's Ring, when the cold had left burns across her skin, reeling from the impact of falling between worlds. But she could see now at least. She squinted through the slit in the door.

A prisoner was there, yes, a dark-skinned human with no arms, lying in a pool of his own blood and excrement. He might have been the one she had heard screaming; he was not moving.

Clara turned away, wishing she had not seen him. Perhaps inspecting these cells was not the best idea, but her father could be in one of them, so she swallowed her revulsion and forced herself on to the next cell, and the next. By the time she had searched the entire corridor, she was buzzing with power, light-headed, but she had seen nothing of her father. The cells held both faery and human prisoners—a human woman standing in the corner of her cell, facing the wall and humming to herself; a faery in chains who lunged at the door when she peeked through.

Despair filled her at having to leave them. She could have entered each cell through a Door and freed them, one by one, but some of them were violent and others simply mad. They would have given her away.

So she found the stairs up and down which Borschalk's men had dragged her these last days. The steps were narrow and winding and thick with grime, and Clara followed them up slowly, leaving the dungeons behind.

* * *

At the top, after ages of climbing, she flattened herself against the wall, closed her eyes, and struggled to control her breathing. If he could have seen her, Godfather would have scolded her for letting her nerves so overwhelm her.

Thinking of him was both painful and helpful. The memory of his voice was a balm. Carefully she let him in:

You must move as though through water. The room is yours to know, to possess. The energy within you subsumes its energy. You are *the room. You* are *the shadows. Try it.*

The energy within her indeed. It occurred to her that he had been hinting at her latent power even then—itching to tell her but never letting himself, for love of her.

She peered around the corner to find a long, black corridor, like those she had glimpsed during Anise's tour. The polished floors gleamed with blue lamplight, and unblinking kambots perched in the rafters. One of them began swiveling its tiny black head toward her.

Clara retreated back against the wall. *Kambots.* How had she not thought of this? She couldn't simply go traipsing about the palace with Anise's birds watching.

Voices came to her from down the corridor, and the sharp tread of boots against stone. Holding her breath, she peeked back around to see two faery soldiers exit one room, cross the corridor, and disappear into another. She listened for their footsteps, how they echoed, measuring the distance they traveled. Faintly she heard doors open, saw a faint swell of light from outside; then darkness again as the doors closed.

Outside, so close. Fresh air and snow and *freedom*. Her blood urged her toward it, eager. *That way,* it seemed to beg. *That way lies escape!* The temptation pulled at her. She still had time to find her father, but it was starting to feel slippery, like trying to maintain pursuit of a swift creature in gathering darkness. Besides, what good was escape without some sort of information? By leaving, she could be abandoning him to a fate as ghastly as the prisoners'.

What now? she wondered. Across from her the opposite wall glimmered. She froze. It was her reflection, there in the lattice of dark glass and scrolling ironwork. Her *reflection*. The sight triggered a memory from her tour of the palace: the Glass Hall, with its many mirrors. Could she, perhaps, open a Door to it from here? It was a dangerous thought—she had no way of knowing if the Hall would be occupied, and though she hadn't noticed kambots there, she could certainly have missed them.

Or perhaps, she thought, the idea bursting out of nowhere and sending her heart racing, *I could open a Door to Father.*

The image of him on the chromocast—that dark room, the blizzard outside. If she focused on that image, would the Door take her right to him? Snow, like the tundra outside; a dark room, like those lining the Summer Palace's echoing corridors. He could be here somewhere—breathing the same air, listening to the same ever-present hum of unseen machinery.

She forced herself to calm, slowing the frantic rush of her thoughts. So far she had only traveled short distances using Doors, and who knew precisely where her father was being kept? She knew nothing of what Doors could and could not do beyond her own experimentation. It was risky to try.

She *had* to try.

Retrieving the chromocast's image from her mind, she went for it before fear convinced her otherwise, opening a Door right there in the hallway, stepping through, rigid with expectation—

—and landing hard on her knees, not a stride's length from where she had just stood.

Cursing, she scrambled to the wall, hardly breathing as she listened for signs that someone had heard the racket. A moment passed, and then another, but the corridor remained silent. She relaxed, shaking.

Had her thoughts been too distracted for the Door to work

properly—too full of hope? She tried again and again, with the same result, each passage sending her hurtling back to the same stretch of corridor. The pain of unsuccessful passage was so great, she nearly bit through her tongue trying not to scream. She slumped, sapped of energy and afraid. If she had lost it, somehow, if her power was failing her . . .

She tried once more, cautiously, this time thinking of her cell, and when she emerged there, unharmed and without difficulty, she wondered if her father was simply too far away to find. Perhaps he wasn't being held here at all. She blinked back tears of disappointment; it had been foolish to think it would be so easy to find him. For a moment she considered trying again but dismissed the idea immediately, feeling hopeless. Traveling from room to room was one thing, but through an entire palace, and perhaps even through the kingdom beyond, on some wild, directionless search using a magic she had only begun to understand?

She was not strong enough.

However, she decided, clinging to the thought of those she held most dear—all of them, even the lost ones about whom it was unbearable to think—she *would* be.

36

When Anise fetched her that night, Clara ached with tension. Would the queen know what she had done? Had kambots spotted her? Would Anise sense the lingering magic of Clara's Doors?

She did not. The queen was exultant, radiant with some secret joy. The sudden sight of her in the light of the Door made Clara's breath catch—with fear, yes, as there was always fear with Anise, but also for the beauty of her, so fine and fierce.

In Anise's chambers, once the Door had closed, the queen held Clara's hands and kissed them and spun her around. Clara caught herself on the bed, breathless, as Anise pulled out gown after gown from her wardrobe, and when she clapped her ringed hands, music began. It drifted down from piped funnels at the corners of the ceiling, much like the music on Pascha's terrace.

"My queen," Clara said, nervous and deeply curious, "what's happening?"

"I've convinced them, Clara. I've *convinced* them. Dear one." She hurried over, pressed Clara's hand to her cheek. Her eyes held a wild glitter, and Clara fought against an urge that left her torn—to flinch away or to turn and kiss Anise's palm. The queen's obvious joy was infectious; the air was sweet with sugar vapors, teasing Clara's senses to greater heights.

"Convinced who? And of what?"

"I'm throwing a party to show you off. The grandest party I've ever had. You will meet my courtiers and dance with them, and they'll love you, and they'll fear you, and we'll no longer need to pretend at this nasty torture business."

A party? Clara felt blindsided. "They'll *love* me? I doubt it."

"If we show them, Clara, that we're united, we two, that together we are doubly as powerful as I've ever been alone, why, that will convince them. They'll have no choice but to accept you." She spun away from Clara, swaying to the feverish music, careless. "Perhaps they'll be so distracted by your loveliness that they'll forget my hunting parties have so far failed to find your loathsome little princeling."

Nicholas. Astounding how quickly Clara's confusion slipped through the cracks of her heart and became a piercing terror.

Anise was hunting Nicholas. Of course they were. Had she expected Anise to sit idly? Maybe she should not care about his fate, considering what he had done, what he had wanted to do—but she did care. Her whole self *ached* with caring.

"You and I, united?" *Tread gently, Clara.* She could not show how spectacularly unhinged she thought Anise. She could not betray her sudden agitation, how Nicholas's name danced on her lips. "I'm afraid I don't understand."

Anise knelt before her, eyes bright, hair mussed. "You know, I always thought my mother was an idiot. And yours, too."

Clara stiffened, but Anise grabbed her hand. "No, don't pull away. I mean it. You see, when I was conceived, my mother lost her power. She was a faery, but she was no longer magic folk. And I always thought it so stupid of her. She could have saved herself, if she'd still had her power. Surely my father wasn't *that* skilled a lover. I've seen pictures of him. Grim, reedy lump of a man."

"But I thought," Clara said, startled, "that unions between humans and magic folk were simply taboo. Not actually *dangerous*."

"Taboo for good reason. People don't pay much attention to the old stories anymore. They don't remember why they're so prejudiced. They don't remember that there's something in the blood that does it—that if a human and one of the magic folk mate, then the magic folk loses her power. How *terrible*, isn't it?"

It surprised Clara how much the thought of giving up her power in that way, of losing this frightening new piece of herself, upset her. "But why does that happen?"

"No one knows. My old nurse once said it was the world's way of maintaining a balance of power." She made a face. "I think the world knew it could be difficult to handle someone like me. Like *you*."

Clara thought of her mother, her powerful mother, leaving her troubled kingdom behind—and leaving her power behind too, the thing that had always defined her. And for what? She felt a wave of sadness. "That *is* terrible."

"Oh, but it isn't! At least, not for us. I see that now." Anise sat on the bed beside Clara. "Both our mothers did it. For love, Clara. For *love*. And because they didn't care what anyone thought of them. Don't you see, Clara? By doing what they did, they brought us together. They wanted us. They *made* us." She cupped Clara's face in her hands. "They made this moment between us, this moment in time."

Anise's closeness was overwhelming. Clara could hardly breathe. "But . . . why give up so much? Just for love? To rebel against society?"

"Maybe . . ."

"Or," Clara pressed on cautiously, only just considering it herself, "because they thought the world could be better, that it *should* be better, and in that better world there would be no hate?"

A chill swept across her.

Anise's eyes were wide. She looked so young, a mere girl. What would she have been without the war that had raised her? "No hate between humans and faeries?"

"And no hate between humans and mages," Clara added quietly. "No servitude, no politics."

After a moment Anise leapt from the bed and paced, savage. "It's a wild thought, Clara. Too wild, I think."

"Have you never thought about it?"

"No. Yes. *No.*"

Clara gripped the bedpost, frightened by her own boldness. "Isn't that what you're doing by being kind to me? Because you're different from everyone else, and have been for so long. Then you found me, and you like not being alone." She paused. "What if there were more of us?"

Anise turned at the terrace windows to glare. She stood there for a moment, her foot tapping restlessly. The music played on. At last she returned to her gowns.

"The party is tomorrow," Anise said brightly, her face hidden. "We have to select the perfect gown for you, something outrageous. We faeries love beautiful things. If you're stunning enough, maybe my court won't be so keen on killing you."

Clara slumped, defeated. For a moment it had seemed as though she had reached some frightened, lonely place inside Anise—something closer to the child she had once been.

Clara went out onto the terrace, instinctively seeking the fresh air. Outside, the night was cold and dark and full of snow. She watched it, feeling the approach of a distant menace she couldn't name. Somewhere out there was Nicholas, and her captured father, Godfather's bones, and tiny Bo and a whole kingdom of frightened people, tearing one another to pieces and full of hate. Not much, she reflected sadly, was different at home. Just another sad world of hungry people fighting for food and power, and Felicity was stuck there, alone. Even if—*when*—Clara returned to her, it would be more of the same. They would flee Concordia for another city, trapped in another nasty web, or Plum would catch them before they could.

Of course, first there was a party to survive. A *party*, of all things, where faeries would drink and dance and hate her. What a mess it all was.

Anise joined her at the door, huffing impatiently. "What are you thinking about? I've gowns for you to try on."

Clara was weary, her heart heavy. "I'm thinking of how I'll ever survive in a world so bent on destroying me. How will any of us?"

For a long moment Anise was quiet. Then she took Clara's hands. "You'll remake it," she whispered. "We both will. Like our mothers tried to, except we actually *will* do it. Because we're unstoppable, Clara, you and I. I think we could be. I think our mothers knew it, and I think that's why they made us. That's why I've . . . Oh, Clara, it was murder to hurt you. I don't want to hurt you. I want you to be here, with me. I want you to help me."

As if triggered by Anise's passion, the palace shook. They looked to the horizon and saw, in the distance, a rolling electric storm, and the palace's western wall crumbling. Clara felt ill, imagining the soldiers manning the wall, the slaves and prisoners beneath it.

Anise turned to her, the lines of her face suddenly pinched, and still she was dazzling. "You see, I don't think I can do it much longer on my own. I've tried to make my country what it should be, but it exhausts me, such constant work. I feel so drained. One little half-breed, remaking an entire world?" She laughed, looking out bitterly over the crumbling landscape. "It would be easier, I think, with two."

A pause fell between them, thick with confusion and possibilities. Anise's fingers burned Clara's skin. It seemed the queen's blood ran as hot as Clara's blood now ran cold.

"Come on." Anise released her, began stripping off her own beautiful black velvet robe. "Take off your clothes."

Clara stepped away. "What?"

"Just do it. We two and the world, the world we'll remake exactly like we want it to be. Come *on*."

Reluctantly, Clara stepped out of her tattered dressing gown, as she had each of these nights in Anise's chambers. She flinched as the cold hit her body, as she caught her reflection in the windows' glass and thought, stupidly for such a moment, of how improper it was. Her hands flew to cover herself, but Anise caught them.

"No. Don't be ashamed. They're just bodies, and they're ours, and they're *powerful*." Anise pulled her farther out onto the terrace, into the swirling snow, and ran ahead of Clara, throwing out her arms. Clara followed, arms folded tightly about her middle. She longed to run back inside and fold herself into the warmth of Anise's bed, but Anise's insistence, her beauty in the snow, was a terrible magnet. The terrace expanded before them, mechaniks moving out obediently into a scrolling iron railing, into metal plates that created a stairway to the tower's roof. Gasping with delight, Anise dragged Clara after her, pulling her on faster and faster, until they were both running at breakneck speed. Anise was unearthly in her grace, and Clara, stumbling after her, felt like a child—a child's awkwardness, yes, but also, as the warmth of Anise's hand melted her inhibitions away, a child's freedom, a child's breathlessness. She found herself laughing, to Anise's obvious delight, and she uncurled, stood taller, let her free arm fall away. The clouds shifted, and starlight hit her skin. Terrifying, this bareness. It shook her and stamped out her shame, replacing it with giddy contempt for the Clara of only a few minutes earlier, her old, shivering self. It was not a completely comfortable feeling, rather like being thrown into icy waters and realizing that, yes, you can swim after all—but struggling futilely for anchor regardless.

At the tower's peaked roof, on this new terrace made of a million tiny machines, they stopped. Anise threw up their clasped hands and crowed into the night. Heat rolled off her in waves. The snowflakes, when they hit her skin, melted immediately. She was a column of flawless white flesh and tiny whorls of steam.

"Here we are, the two-blooded monsters!" she cried, joyous, defiant. "You are our world, and we will make you our own!"

Anise's excitement was infectious. Clara found herself laughing along with her, nervous energy bursting out in gasps.

"Say something!" Anise said, drawing her close. "The world is listening."

Clara did not even pause to think. The words exploded out of her as if they had always existed, waiting. "You think you can beat us, but you're wrong! You'll try to break us, and you'll fail! You got our mothers, but you won't ever—*ever*—get us!"

She had surprised herself. As though she were no longer in Cane, no longer on the roof of the Summer Palace but instead back home, high above her poor, ruthless city, she had screamed out to the world that it would not stifle her. No, she would rise above its violence. She would transcend it and make it her own.

Anise was quiet, her eyes shining. She leaned closer, and her gaze fell to Clara's lips, fondly, and for a moment, for a *moment* . . .

Clara held her breath. She wasn't sure if she was glad at the idea, or disgusted, or had simply gone as mad as Anise was. There was a power between them, and it was not their magic; it was this night, the cold and the stars, their reckless nakedness.

Anise spun around, and the moment between them danced away with the snow. Anise yelled obscenities and glorious promises into the night, and Clara noticed that her promises were full of the same blood and violence that was tearing her kingdom apart. It saddened her, but it did not surprise her. Perhaps a child raised by war could never truly leave it behind. They all—Anise, Nicholas, herself—might be doomed to stay trapped in the wrecks of the worlds that had shaped them.

Oh, *Nicholas*. The memory of his touch shot through her, and it stung with betrayal—with his, and with hers, this sudden treachery of running naked alongside the woman bent on killing him.

Of course, he deserved it for what he had done. If Clara decided to stay here, at Anise's side, maybe she could eventually persuade Anise out of her violent ways, arrange her father's release, and provide for her family's safety, all with Anise's fervent support. Certainly that was worth betraying a man who obviously thought so little of her.

She glanced sideways at the queen. Such devotion on her face; such a tenderness as she hugged Clara close, as though they were girls whispering secrets.

Would anything ever make sense again?

Her conflicted thoughts lingered, even when she and Anise were back in the queen's chambers, where Anise swept aside piles of potential party gowns and pulled Clara with her into bed. They lay there, a worn-out tangle of limbs and melting snow.

"I'm glad you're here," Anise said at last, and she looked not a queen in that moment but a girl. A girl like Clara—breaking, and determined not to.

A second sting of betrayal then, as Anise nestled into her arms to sleep. Clara felt it, and lay awake with it long into the night.

It changed nothing, she decided. This night changed nothing—except that she should leave sooner, before Anise charmed her completely, before she forgot herself.

She poked Anise. A genuine thrill of gladness shot through her when the queen opened her eyes, and frightened her.

"Are you charming me?"

Anise was blearily puzzled. "What?"

"I know magic folk can charm. Is that why I feel so . . ." She stopped, embarrassed.

"I would not dishonor you with such a deception." Then a sleepy smile, a soft caress. "Not you, dear Clara. I suppose you truly love me."

Love? As Anise drifted back into sleep, Clara thought it over, troubled. No. Not love. Not *yet*. But certainly fascination and empathy, and the potential for something more. Something overpowering, something magnificent and electric. Love? Clara turned away from the word. The queen held her close. Warmed, Clara let her eyes fall shut.

"Sleep," Anise whispered. "You need rest for tomorrow."

Ah, yes. Tomorrow.

The party.

37

At sunset the next evening, after a day of fevered preparations, Anise paraded Clara down the twisting main thoroughfare to the base of the city, near the outer wall. There stood two enormous tents, newly fashioned for the occasion—one blue and gold, one plum and black. Towering ironwork signs spelled their names in bright, flashing lights, as if they were part of a traveling circus: ROTTEFEST, the blue-and-gold tent; KABARET DREADFUL, the plum-and-black.

Faeries lined the route, in garish masks and furs, in headdresses that trailed across the black cobblestones and looked suspiciously made of human hair, inlaid with feathers and strings of metal. They cheered and danced, and their skin shimmered. They held humans close on bedazzled ropes like pets.

"Everyone's waiting," Anise said, pointing down at the tents. She wore a glistening gown of blue and plum, a cool contrast to Clara's gown of emerald and gold. Their hems dripped with diamonds, and their skin shone with unholy amounts of glitter. "They're breathless to see you. I'll show you off, and everyone will dance, and it will be perfect." Anise pressed a hot kiss to Clara's hand. "They'll see. They'll *understand* us, Clara, once they see us together like this."

Clara tried to imagine the masked eyes following her down the street looking at her with anything but hatred and jealousy, and failed.

At the entrance to Rottefest, she paused. The sounds coming from within assaulted her—relentless, pounding music and savage cries. Swirling lights flashed across Anise's face. Clara was terribly afraid, but Anise took her hand and grinned.

"Come," she said, "they're waiting for us."

Clara had no choice but to follow. She forced a bashful smile as Anise escorted her inside, through an immense ballroom where grotesquely masked humans held trays of food at the ready—bright blue flower bulbs stuffed with pink fruit, white cakes striped with crimson frosting. Other humans hung in cages from the ceiling, blood seeping through their stockings. Their masks were white, with no eyes and great, gaping mouths.

Anise guided Clara to a black throne at the height of the room. From there they could see everything—the whirling dancers on the tiled floor and the white-masked humans tumbling in their cages, prodded by laughing faeries with sizzling spears. Borschalk, lurking nearby, glaring at them from within the cloud of his pipe. Hangers-on, half-clothed and bearing gifts, waiting patiently in line on the winding steps that led to Anise's throne.

Anise laughed behind her hand. "Look at them, scrambling to find you presents."

In fact, Clara felt sick to look at them. She felt such hate bubbling from them and wondered that Anise could not feel it too. She was beginning to lose her courage, here in this pulsing, raging room. The strange euphoria from the previous night had been replaced with a slithering unease. As she nibbled at strange skewered creatures she could not name, faery courtiers with elaborate headdresses and nacreous tattoos filed before her. They bowed, murmured adorations, placed various delicacies and shining gems at her feet.

"My lady," they murmured. "For you, my lady."

Clara churned out smile after false smile, and even that much seemed dangerous. As the faeries petted her hands, kissed her fingers, looked at her cuttingly from behind their feathers, she found it hard not to constantly recoil.

By midnight Clara's head ached from the noise, and her lips burned from the dessert Anise had made her eat—a spindly purple plant whose thorns, Anise insisted, were divine if you managed to suck out their insides without pricking your tongue. Clara was desperate to move, to slam her hand into the air, summon a Door, and get out of there. If she had to watch one more group of human slaves paraded across the stage in frenetic dances, whipped on by soldiers and jeered at by the audience, she would lose her mind.

At the first spare moment, when no courtiers loitered lazily at their feet, Clara touched Anise's arm. The queen turned, sucking the last thorn from the purple stem in her hands.

"Come closer," she drawled, thickly. She was drunk—drunk on wine, drunk on sugar. "Act like you're sharing something particularly salacious with me. It will intrigue them, and impress them."

Clara forced a coy smile and leaned in, her lips brushing the jewels lining Anise's ear. The queen shivered. Her eyes drifted shut.

"Last night," Clara said, low, "we talked of many things."

"Mm-hmm."

"We talked of remaking the world."

"We talked of our mothers."

"But remaking the *world*," Clara insisted. "Isn't that what you said you want to do?"

"Of course."

Clara sensed eyes upon them—Borschalk on the prowl, eyes keen behind his nightbird mask. He was not alone in watching them. Faeries throughout the room—on the stage, across the shining floor, in the throngs of dancing bodies—kept sharp attention upon them. Clara leaned closer to Anise, trailed her fingers down her arm.

"Surely *this*"—Clara looked pointedly around them—"is not what you meant by remaking the world. The humans, my queen.

They're being *tormented*. Your courtiers are hurting them."

Anise laughed. "Well, you can't expect them to change overnight, can you? First we will win them over, make them respect you."

She sounded lazy, horribly unconcerned. Clara drew back, fuming. "I thought you meant it," she said, ashamed to hear how her voice trembled. "I thought you wanted to change things. Or did you just say what you think I wanted to hear?"

Anise, still lounging, grabbed her arm, held it fast. "How dare you! Don't you trust me, Clara?"

"How can I, when you let them—"

"Because they doubt me, Clara. They see how I've treated you, and it doesn't make sense to them. If I don't let them have their fun, they'll turn on us both. We need this night."

Clara's mind screamed with suspicion. There was too much amusement on Anise's face as she surveyed the ghastly activities being inflicted upon the humans—too much bloodlust, too much smug delight. Clara folded her hands tightly in her lap, struggling for composure amid such battering waves of disappointment. The waves woke her up, flung her mind out of its Anise-fog. Clara had so wanted to believe her. As impossible as it would have seemed only days earlier, she had wanted, for a time, to *stay*. To explore this thing, this blossoming closeness to Anise. There was a certain safety here, under Anise's beautiful wing, and a certain . . . *deliciousness*.

Remaking the world together. What an outrageous farce, if Anise's gleeful expression was any indication. Lies, layers of lies, mazes of lies. That, Clara was starting to realize, was her lot in life—to always be fighting against deception.

It did not matter. She could not stop pretending. "I'm sorry. I didn't know—"

"Don't apologize." Anise shifted, the slits in her gown sliding open to reveal long white legs dusted with silver powder. "That's your first mistake."

Anise snapped her fingers. An attendant beside the throne flipped switches on a mechanical board lit with dials. The lights, swinging overhead, shone a new, harsher blue. In response the dancing faeries scattered across the floor shouted their appreciation. The paint streaking their bodies glowed in unearthly colors. The volume of the music increased, the vibrations leaving Clara feeling tightly wound and uneasy.

Anise pulled Clara to her feet, and Clara realized, with a start, that they were the only two people in this entire frantic party without masks to hide them.

"Come, Clara," Anise purred, drawing her close. "Dance with me."

They danced for hours, surrounded by hundreds of faeries—an undulating press of feathered masks, masks of bone, masks of thin metal plates, corsets of creaking leather and chain, collars of ridged wire. High in the rafters hooded faeries pounded on drums the size of motorcars. Sweat, tinged with the smell of the sea, stung Clara's nostrils as she was whirled between Anise and countless nameless, faceless courtiers. They moved against her, obscenely close, murmured vaguely threatening compliments in her ear, and kissed her hands. Some of them gripped her waist too hard, making her cry out.

When she was returned to Anise, she clung to the queen's body gratefully.

"Enjoying yourself?" Anise asked, laughter in her voice.

How to answer her? Every so often a faery passed through with a tray of iced creams and thin sugar pipes. With everyone watching her, Clara had no choice but to partake. Her head ached, her mouth had dried out, her vision danced with colors, and even the lightest touch to her body sent shuddering heat flooding through her. She had never felt more alive, nor closer to death. She found herself craving more, grabbing for offered pipes with an eagerness that worried her even as she reached for them; she needed her senses sharp and focused if she was to survive the night.

If she was going to escape when it was over.

Her heart gave a twinge of unrest. A plan had come to her in Anise's arms. She still did not know where her father was being held. Perhaps if she stayed—oh, if she *stayed*—she could barter for him; she could dull the memory of her former life in Anise's embrace. But it was too dangerous here, too blissful one moment and horrific the next.

"I much preferred last night to this party," Clara answered, letting her eyes fall shut to relish the room's unnatural spin, the hot points of light that were Anise's fingers on her waist. "Too much noise, too many people."

Anise laughed shrilly. They migrated from blue-and-gold Rottefest to plum-and-black Kabaret Dreadful, where the light was darker and snakelike sugar pipes hung from the ceiling. Faeries attached themselves to the openings like suckling babes. The occasional bold human smashed them out of the way and managed a desperate few gulps before being dragged off.

"Borschalk thinks," Anise slurred as they moved against each other beneath the revolving lights, "that you mean to betray me."

Clara tried not to react. The sugar in her blood made it difficult to school her features, but hopefully Anise would not be able to tell. The queen was even unsteadier than she.

"Does he?" Clara said.

"He thinks you don't deserve me. He wants you out of my bed, and himself back in. But you're prettier than he is. You're sweeter." She leaned close, conspiratorial, wound Clara's hair around her finger and brought the red coil to her lips. "He thinks you don't love me. Not really, anyway. He thinks you're in love with that boy."

Clara's heart began to race. This was the opening she needed, but she could not enjoy it. Such betrayal, such a bitter regret. She felt sorry for Anise, and embarrassed for her—and terrified for herself.

She let out what she hoped was a careless laugh. "Nicholas?"

"Well?" Anise tugged on Clara's arm, insistent, petulant. "Do you?"

"Maybe I did, once." That was true enough, and her pulse leapt with shameful longing. "But then I met you." She brushed a damp strand of hair from Anise's cheek, and the queen's eyes widened with hope. "We are the same, you and I. How could there ever be anyone else?"

Bending low, cupping Anise's face sweetly, she brushed a kiss across her lips. Anise gasped against her mouth, shivering. New music began, even more frantic. The faeries surrounding them threw up their hands. Cannons on the perimeter of the room fired sparkling jetties of flame into the air.

Anise, bright-eyed and ferocious, yanked Clara close and kissed her deeply. The kiss stung with duplicity, and with horrible, horrible delight. Clara knew she should have been celebrating, and part of her was. She had said the right things. She could feel Anise's joy thrumming against her body, and joy would make her careless. The queen whispered frantic endearments, then dipped to whisper them against Clara's throat. When she laughed, it was bright like morning.

The music pounded on.

38

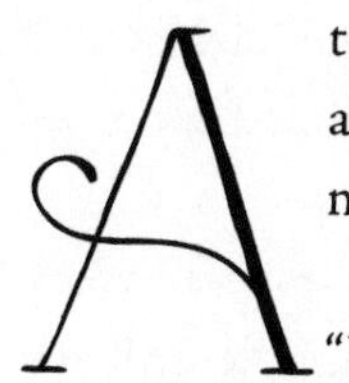

t two o'clock Anise stumbled with Clara into a curtained alcove on Kabaret Dreadful's mezzanine, lavishing her neck with kisses.

"My queen," Clara gasped, trying to detach herself. "Wait."

Anise pouted, her lips swollen blue. "*What?*"

This was madness. Yet Anise was drunk, close to collapsing, and if Clara could, in these last moments, get from her even the tiniest hint . . .

She sidled close, stroking Anise's cheeks. "Now that I am here, beside you—"

Anise mumbled an affirmative, half-awake.

"There is the matter of my father."

The queen's eyes narrowed. "Your what?"

Had she ruined it? She forced a smile and tapped Anise's nose. "You're drunk."

After a moment Anise burst into giggles. "Do you know, I think I am!"

"Now that I'm with you, do you think . . . Could you return him home? Could I at least *see* him? I'm sure he's frightened, my queen, and would be glad to see me one last time."

"Oh, don't worry about your stupid old father." Anise waved an unsteady hand. "He's fine. Drugged but fine. We'll go there together." Her words were beginning to run together. "I need to show you the capital anyway."

The capital. Where Nicholas would be headed—if he was still alive.

Anise planted a passionate kiss on her mouth. "*Our* capital. It will be, Clara."

"My queen, you thrill me with such talk." Not a lie, not even close. Clara was rapturous with new hope as she collapsed with Anise into the cushions, stroking her arm as the queen's eyes drifted shut. She waited for ten minutes, counting through the seconds as the party raged downstairs. When Anise showed no signs of waking, Clara hurried across the mezzanine to the winding black stairs they'd come up. At the bottom stood a faery sentry.

"I need to fetch some things from my queen's chambers." Clara emphasized the word "chambers," smiling suggestively. "Oh, and she doesn't want to be disturbed. I left her in . . . I suppose you could call it a *divested* state."

The soldier's eyes widened slightly, and Clara hurried past, laughing. She hoped it did not sound too frantic. Anxiety was making her giddy. Anise could awake at any moment, and the crowded party slowed Clara's progress. She kept being swept up into dances, spun between alternating partners, flirted with and fought over by courtiers newly eager to win her favor. It was a glamorous hell, teeming with faeries and humans in chains.

Clara humored them as much as she could, turning distractedly through dance after dance. If she made too quick an exit, it would be noticed. Borschalk, wherever he was, would notice. She tried to search for him without being seen, but he was nowhere to be found. Borschalk, Clara knew, would not be fooled.

At last she managed to slip out through the ballroom's main doors, demurring her way through a smoky foyer full of faeries in various states of debauchery. The scent of sugar stung Clara's tongue. If she did not get outside soon, the smoke and her own fear would smother her.

There—the exit. She hurried toward it, no longer trying for stealth, but someone grabbed her arm before she could reach it. Another fawning courtier?

Clara turned, frantic. "Please, the queen is waiting for me—"

The faery holding her hand was heavily cloaked, with a dark headdress that fell to his waist and a heavy mask that blocked everything but his eyes and his mouth—a familiar mouth, and eyes not blue but dark. When he pulled her into his body, Clara let him, remembering at the last moment to look flattered. The feathers of his headdress whispered against her sides, and she caught a faint scent, a familiar spice.

"Nicholas?" she breathed.

"This is quite a party. You can see the lights for miles."

She could have punched him right in his stupid masked face. She could have unleashed the power that now stirred within her, so traitorously, unhelpfully happy.

Instead she pulled him closer. "Have you lost your senses? You're not tall enough to be a faery, and your eyes are *dark*, for God's sake—"

"It's a fair disguise, though, isn't it? For such short notice?"

"Nicholas, *Nicholas*—"

He bowed his head over hers, breathing in the scent of her hair. He shook against her, overcome. "I saw you dancing. Clara, I thought I'd lost you."

Clara put her arms around his neck, sliding into an intimate embrace. Faeries passing in and out the doors were pausing to watch them, jealous of the faery with his hands on the queen's new pet. She tried to laugh coquettishly. She wanted to cry, or scream.

"Lost me." Her voice was harsh. Good. *Good.* She clung to that sound. "Maybe that's what I wanted. Maybe I don't want you here."

He was still. "I deserve that."

"You deserve much worse." She pulled away, and he caught her fast.

"Clara, please," he said desperately. "Don't go."

She met his eyes, furious. "If you try to hold me against my will, I will kill you."

"I know. I know you will."

"Don't patronize me."

"I'm not. I know full well what you're capable of."

Dancers had spilled out into the foyer, music following them. Clara began to dance as well; she already stood out enough. Nicholas followed suit, his hands cupping her bare arms. She could have melted at the feel of him so near, overcome with sensation and memory. So unexpected, this reunion, and it clogged her throat with tears.

"Why shouldn't I kill you?"

He was quiet. Their hips circled, mimicking the others dancing around them. "I don't know."

"You'd better give me a reason."

"I have none." He laughed, sounding lost, and it angered her. He had no right to vulnerability. "I only know one thing—that I'm sorry, Clara."

She opened her mouth to protest, impatient.

"Please," he said, "let me finish? Please."

She turned in his arms, as the other dancers did, her back to his front. As he bent close to speak, his headdress fell around her, a cape of feathered black.

"When you disappeared," he said, low, "I lost my mind. Entering that barn and finding you gone—"

"Yes, you were devastated, I'm sure, to find your soon-to-be slave gone missing."

A pained sound at her ear. "That I could have ever thought such a thing—"

"And yet you did." She turned, vicious, and led him through the dancing crowd to a curtained alcove damp with skin and sugar. Surely no one would dare follow her inside, so she ripped off his mask. A mistake. She had thought it would make him uncomfortable, not being able to hide from her. Instead she was the one knocked off balance, gutted by the expression on his face. There was apology there, and a raw adoration, unbearably familiar. It left her feeling shattered, and hopeful, worst of all.

"I heard you talking to the others," she said, fighting the urge to touch him. "You said you would force me to bind with you, force me to fight for you."

"I did say that."

"And now? Why should I forgive you?"

"I don't know why." He rubbed a hand over his face, and it aged him. "I can't think of a single reason for you to trust me, Clara, or think me anything but a monster. But I know that when I discovered you'd gone, I lost my mind— No, not because I could no longer use you. Because I had lost *you*—your friendship, your intelligence. Sinndrie save me, your *nearness*." He turned, stopped himself, turned back. It was important for her to see his face. Her heart twisted. Was he sincere, or simply that same clever pretender? She despaired at ever being able to trust him. "We split off into groups to search for you, and I abandoned mine. They weren't moving quickly enough. They didn't love— Clara, they know you, but not as I know you. You were with me all those years." His eyes were bright, his voice rough. It was dear and overwhelming. "You were the one friend I had. You *are* the one friend I have. Drosselmeyer never bothered to speak to me, not beyond the necessary. I was a burden to him, but not to you. You spoke to me. I was your friend, and you were mine. And I repaid you by thinking I could manipulate you into serving me, and for that you *should* kill me. I deserve nothing more than that, and I don't say that to stir your pity. It's what I believe."

Speaking was a feat. "Then why did you come here tonight?"

"To see you," he said simply. A tired, strained smile. "I didn't know what you would say, but I had to find you. It was all I knew, these past few days—not responsibility or duty—only you. Your eyes. Your voice." He lifted a hesitant hand to her face. They were nearer now, hovering close, and he touched her as though he could not help himself. "Clara, it has always only been you, and I'm ashamed I was ever stupid enough to think otherwise. I don't dare to think you can believe me, but I had to say it. I'll leave you if you wish it. Say the word, and you need never see me again."

She leaned into his touch, and he smelled of home. "How did you get here? They've been hunting you."

"I know," he said wryly. "It was endangering everyone until I left—Bo, Erik, the others. I assume they've kept on for Rieden."

"And you did not go with them."

"No. How could I?" He drew an unsteady breath, his eyes searching her face. "In that moment when I realized you were gone, everything changed. I recognized my selfishness and understood the truth."

"Which is?"

"I hate the faeries. I may always hate them for what they have done. I don't know how I will ever stop hating them, or how to rebuild my kingdom, or reclaim it, or make it into what I know it should be—a safe home, fair and just, for all races. I don't know who I am. I've forgotten, or maybe I never knew. I know *nothing*, Clara"—and here he took her face in his hands, his expression urgent—"except that I'm sorry, and that I will do anything to help you. I know nothing now but you."

When she drew breath to speak, it hurt. "How can I trust you again?"

He was silent; he did not have an answer.

Behind him the curtains flew open. A pair of giggling faeries stumbled inside, already half-unclothed, goblets of punch in hand—but they froze when they saw Clara and Nicholas. A terrible moment, suspended there like the clarity before a fall.

Then they shouted a curse in the faery language and hurried back out the way they had come, shouting above the music, raising the alarm. Clara could imagine what they were saying:

The human prince is here—with her, *the queen's faithless pet!*

There had been no time to judge him trustworthy or not, no time to say what needed to be said, and now the choice had been made for her. They shared a look, and she grabbed his hand in frustration.

They ran.

The deserted palace-city, its inhabitants away at their revels, was like a nightmare from which all the devils had gone—empty black roads, eerie black towers. The palace windows glowed a dim blue, and the watchtowers along the wall flared green. Everything teemed with tiny skittering shadows, though Clara did not know if they were Anise's mechaniks shaping new walls or derived from Clara's own simmering fear. A tiny flash of blue made her whirl around, searching for kambots; a rush of dark sound kept her running forward.

"The western wall," she gasped. Behind them the music kept on, but shouts and footsteps indicated a fierce pursuit. "It fell last night. Anise was . . . emotional."

"That's how I snuck in." Nicholas turned a corner, sliding on the cold metal cobblestones, slick with oil. "I suppose such a lavish party was more important than rebuilding the wall."

"It's not as though there is anything to defend against here."

"Only princes with questionable sense," he agreed lightly as they hurried down a winding black stair to a lower level of the city. She did not appreciate his poor attempt at humor. Was it insane to leave? She would freeze in the wild in her slip of a gown, and Anise had said she would take her to her father. But even though the queen had spoken of remaking the world, tonight had shown Clara otherwise. There was no guarantee Anise would keep her promises if Clara stayed, and even if she did, Clara would then be condemned to a life of games and lies, of dangerous pretend.

Tonight marked the end of her sixteenth day in Cane; four, then, would have passed at home.

Choice, again, as hateful as ever. Besides, she thought, glancing sidelong at Nicholas as they climbed over the rubble at the ruined wall, approaching torches and spears glowing blue behind them, she could not stand idly by and let them hurt him. Not yet. Not until she had passed her own judgment on him.

Dawn was not far off. Up on the crenellated wall, bathed in the watchtower's pale green light, a faery clothed in nothing but a feathered top hat and gloves asked for a volunteer. Laughing soldiers tossed him a screaming human, his terror drowned out by the peals of a great brass horn. The party, it seemed, was not entirely confined to the ballrooms.

Nicholas's face was grim as the soldiers above screamed with laughter. Clara stepped down after him, shaking, and then they were on the other side of the ruined wall, at the edge of the tundra in the shadow of the Summer Palace. The steel towers of Anise's trains loomed like ghostly giants. In the murky clouds overhead storm lights and train lights blended in a tangle of electricity.

There was no time to be intimidated by such an expanse, however, not when the soldiers behind them were nearer every second. Blue streaks scorched the air. Clara made to run, but Nicholas caught her arm, a strange look on his face—as if he *knew*.

"You do want to leave, don't you, Clara?"

She didn't want to be dishonest, not after days of manipulations and pretending. How bracing, to tell the truth. "Part of me does." It was all she would say, for now, with Anise's kisses still burning on her skin.

Then the palace behind them exploded with light.

Along the outer wall and on the sides of every tower, and above the great tents where the party drums still sounded, a hundred chromocasts switched on.

On them, magnified to grotesque proportions, was the face of John Stole.

"Clara?" His voice, mammoth and distorted, echoed across the city. "Clara, is that you?"

Beside Clara, Nicholas swore. Clara took a faltering step back toward the palace. Her father's hair was unkempt, his eyes bleary, but it was unmistakably him. As Anise had said, he was unhurt. Confused but unhurt.

Up on the wall the gloved faery—arms bathed in fresh blood—clapped wet, spattering applause and crowed, "Oh, what a marvelous party this is!"

"I don't know where I am." John Stole rubbed his eyes. His lips were stained sugar blue. "Someone's telling me . . . I'm supposed to tell you to stop. Whatever you're doing, Clara, stop. We need to get home. They're telling me if you do this, we'll never get home. What do they mean?"

His dear face, his ridiculous red beard. The sight of him was a terrible relief. To see him alive and well, as Anise had promised . . . Clara turned away, full of doubt.

"Do you think it's real?" Nicholas said. "Maybe it's a trick."

No, not a trick. Clara knew it for what it was: a second chance. She could go back, apologize, give them Nicholas, and beg her way back into Anise's good graces. If she did it now, she could save Anise the humiliation of asking.

Perhaps she could save her father as well.

The miserable mischief of it. Clara was sick with indecision. "It's real. It's perhaps more real than anything else she's said to me."

Her father began to scream, twisting on the chromocasts. Someone unseen was hurting him.

The faeries on the wall hooted, whistled. Above the great tents fireworks exploded.

"Clara, I don't understand what's happening, what they're doing." Her father was heaving with pain. "They won't tell me. Is it Plum? I keep asking for her. No one will listen to me."

His confusion was the worst thing. He thought he was still in New York. He thought this was about Patricia Plum, about Concordia. At the wall the mob of faery soldiers, glittering in their party dress, had stopped and were looking down at where Clara stood, motionless with indecision. The soldiers were waiting, no doubt, for the word from Anise.

Clara turned away.

Nicholas stepped closer. "Clara? What do you want to do?"

The steel in his voice, and the patience, brought her back to herself. She blinked past her tears, clung to the intensity of his focus. "She wants me back with her. She wants me to help her rebuild her kingdom."

"I see."

"Is that what you want?" She took a step toward him. The discordant relief of seeing him alive was fading in the face of her father's screams. "For me to *help* you? Godfather warned me against trusting you, and he was right. While I was losing my mind with pain, you were plotting how best to use me."

He seemed lost for words, his shoulders slumped. He did not apologize again, and she appreciated that, when such pale words would have infuriated her more than anything else. The hollowed-out look in his eyes was enough, for now.

Her father had slipped off the chromocast, but she could still hear him. His screams grew hysterical.

"I can't talk about this now," Clara said tearfully, her breathing tight. "We have to run."

"But are you sure—"

"I will not be responsible for your death, as you are for my mother's." She was hurting him with her words, and the accusation was unfair, but she was glad to say it anyway. "Just *run*, before I change my mind."

She turned into the night. The Summer Palace was a monster at her back, and though it would make everything harder, she had to run from it. Anise wanted her too badly to risk hurting her father beyond repair, at least until she had Clara back.

At least Clara hoped so. It was an incredible thing on which to wager her father's life. Maybe the queen would decide Clara was not worth this trouble—though, after last night, she thought it unlikely.

Then the lights went out, the chromocasts turning dark. Jealousy shot through the air like poison, like a real thing, real and terrible and as alive as any creature. The palace walls shook with rage.

And Nicholas began to scream.

Clara whirled to see him fall to the ground, twisting in pain. She hurried to him, unsure where to touch, for he was *clawing* at himself. She reached for his arm, said his name. With a force that surprised her, he threw her away, and she hit the ground hard. Immediately defensive, she scrambled to her hands and knees—and stared in horror, for Nicholas was tearing at his hair, every muscled line taut with pain. Blood erupted in hot spurts, metal plates resurfacing across his body, thick steel pins snaking out of them and into his flesh, a steel lattice echoing his veins.

She put a hand to her mouth. Not this. Anything but this.

"It's coming back, Clara." His face was drenched with tears. He put out a warning hand, and metal erupted along his fingers, fully encasing them in spiked, formfitting plates. He fell away from her, unable to stay upright. "The curse. She's found me. She's waking it up."

For the first sixteen years of my life, I knew nothing but hate and war. I was raised on strategy and weaponry, in laboratories with dissected faery bodies pinned open for study. My nightmares were full of monstrous black mechanized creatures swallowing me whole and spitting me back out, silent and still.

Then I met Leska.

She was a mage, a true Lady of the North, powerful and ambitious—to a point. Whereas some mages would do anything to be one of the Seven, Leska held fast to her principles. As the war between humans and faeries escalated, as the mages' participation evolved from reluctant to eager, Leska began petitioning the nobility for peace—negotiations, an armistice. She even once arranged for a meeting between Father and Anise.

It did not go well.

I still remember it. In the wide, brightly lit Hoflicht, where the white stone caught the sunlight and made the entire courtyard glitter like a glass-cut sea, Father and Anise met on the Drachstelle seal. It was to be a greeting full of ceremony and empty pomp, before adjourning to a neutral location for negotiations.

I remember seeing Anise arrive, her personal guard accompanying her. One in particular, a tall beast of a faery with a cruel face and the unadorned sash that signified a new recruit, had eyes only for Anise, following her movements with undisguised lust. I stood behind my mother and father, seething that we should stoop so low. Peace with the faeries? Incomprehensible.

Anise must have felt my rage. As she approached Father, her eyes met mine. The headdress and robes she wore made her look impressive despite her slight form. Even I could admit that to myself. She examined me head to toe, and the smile that curled across her lips was dismissive, amused.

I nearly lunged for her.

I did not have the opportunity. In the next instant a shot was fired from somewhere in the crowd of human nobility—a black arrow that looked suspiciously like a reengineered faery weapon. I recognized in the arrow the efforts of the mages and our finest swordsmiths, who'd worked tirelessly to re-create the faeries' designs from the wreckage of innumerable skirmishes and confiscated inventions.

Anise dismantled the thing in midair, whipping toward it with a snarl. At the same instant a figure crashed into her, knocking her off her feet.

Leska pinned Anise to the ground, shielding her with her body.

"Are you mad?" Leska cried to the stunned audience. "This is a peace talk, not a battleground!"

The large faery soldier shoved Leska away, drawing Anise into his arms for a moment before she shook him off, screaming vulgarities at the crowd. The rest of her escort readied their weapons—those fearsome black gloves, those massive black spears that spat blue electricity as easily as our archers unleashed arrows. Our royal guard unsheathed their swords.

Father had not even flinched. He smirked, watching Anise coldly.

He had known this would happen. The meeting had been a ruse. No doubt Father had hoped the arrow would pierce her heart.

The outnumbered faeries retreated after a tense few moments, although Anise's feral, determined grin lingered long after her departure. Looking back, I see that we sealed our fate that day.

In their wake Lady Leska rounded on my father.

"What have you done?" she whispered. "We cannot be forever at war, my king, or we will tear ourselves apart."

Father's expression was one of disgust as he dismissed her.

But I was captivated. It had never occurred to me that there was another option besides war and hate. When you are raised on hate alongside milk and bread, it begins to sustain you. It becomes you.

As it had become me.

For weeks I contemplated this change in me, this change wrought by the appearance of Lady Leska with her stubborn jaw and fearless gaze. I sent out my personal spies to gather information about her. Finally I sought her out, in the shadowy northern neighborhoods of the capital.

There I found not only Leska but many people—humans and mages alike—who gathered secretly and exchanged coded messages in broad daylight, who spoke of peace and rallies and protests.

That first night I was apprehended by masked men and brought before Leska herself.

Once unbound, I warned her, "I could have you executed for this."

"But you won't," she said, and her smile was gentle. "You no longer want to be an executioner. You're curious about peace. Aren't you, my prince?"

She gave words to emotions I hadn't yet deciphered. I was tired of killing, tired of strategy and espionage. I had been bred to carry out my father's war, and I wondered if I was anything besides that bloody purpose. Who was I beneath the blood on my hands?

Under Leska's tutelage I learned about peace. Cloaked in dirty garments, I snuck out of my guarded rooms and across the rooftops, shimmied down gutters. I met with Leska and her followers several times a week. I even consulted with faeries who had defected, who had come to the capital seeking help from sympathetic mages, who escorted them north into hiding.

Leska became the greatest teacher I had ever known, and I loved her. I worshipped her. All of us did, I think, those of us thirsty for peace. How could we not love her, when she burned with such desire for justice?

But it could not last.

Drosselmeyer, my bound mage, my sworn protector, my tutor, my ally at court, had a terrible, embarrassing secret.

He loved Leska too.

And for him it was not merely platonic admiration. It was obsession. Once, they had been lovers, as Leska told me one night; there had been years of passion between them. I was shocked to learn that Drosselmeyer had yearned for peace as well. But ultimately his ambition had gotten the better of him—when old Ehrlmeyer had died and a seat had opened on the Seven, Drosselmeyer had abandoned the peace efforts and had done anything he could to earn Father's favor.

It had worked. He'd been appointed, and over the ceremonial altar, as naked as newborns, he and I had clasped hands, exchanged blood, and been bound.

Even before meeting Leska, I knew Drosselmeyer for what he was—a sycophant with dubious morals and cutthroat political aspirations.

He was also jealous, desperately so, of anyone whom Leska so much as smiled at, for once Drosselmeyer had abandoned peace for the Seven, Leska had abandoned him.

So when I began sneaking out, when rumors rumbled throughout the castle staff that the prince was liaising with some mysterious mistress, Drosselmeyer suspected the worst. That Leska had taken me into her bed, that she now loved me as she would no longer love him.

One night he followed me, and he did not come alone. He brought along Rohlmeyer, the first of the Seven, determined to humiliate us.

They found us in Leska's humble apartment, relaxing together after a successful meeting. It was as innocent as sister and brother, and I could see on Drosselmeyer's face that he understood his mistake at once.

But it was too late for that. Rohlmeyer arrested Leska for treason and brought me before my parents for punishment. In those days Drosselmeyer shadowed me everywhere, a blank, dumb look on his face. In shock, perhaps, that he had so misread our relationship, and by doing so had sentenced his great love to death.

For, of course, it would be death for Leska. Father's judges twisted her peace efforts into a diabolical rebellion and our relationship into something scandalous and manipulative.

I watched, devastated, as the judges declared their sentence. Beside them Father smiled.

Leska showed no emotion at the pronouncement of her own impending execution. She held her head high as they bound her in chains.

"Have you no shame, traitor?" Mother said from her throne. "Not even a plea for mercy?"

Leska smiled. "Why would I be ashamed, Your Majesty? All I have done I would do again. All I have done I did for my country."

That night I heard Drosselmeyer weeping in his rooms, which adjoined mine. Leska would be executed the next morning.

I knew what I had to do.

I called for him, and together—though the hate between us now stormed like an inferno, for each of us blamed the other for Leska's fate—we snuck to the prison tower.

We helped Leska escape, cloaked in their combined magic. Leska was the more powerful of them; she always had been. Before she'd turned peacemaker, Leska would have been in line for Rohlmeyer's spot. She would have ruled the Seven, and in turn been the ambassador of the mages.

Once out of the capital, she summoned Doors—tiny things, only strong enough to last for mere seconds. They helped us jump across vast stretches of country. For long hours we fled through her rickety chain of Doors until we arrived, breathless, in Mira's Ring. The earth trembled here, eternally restless against the edge of the sea.

Drosselmeyer demanded explanation at once. "We meant to help you escape, not have you take us on some mad journey."

"You're jealous," I hissed. My patience was worn thin. "You wish that you had this kind of skill. Even now, with Leska just saved from death, you can think only of your jealousy."

"Stop it, Nicholas," Leska said. Then she took my face in her hands and

kissed my cheek, and I nearly lost my composure, for I couldn't remember how long it had been since my own parents had touched me with anything like love. "Remember what we have done together," she told me. "There is still the possibility of peace."

Drosselmeyer stirred irritably beside us, but I ignored him. "Anise will never agree to peace."

A great melancholy crossed Leska's face. "Perhaps she will if she is given reason to."

Then she embraced me, and I felt her exchange a look with Drosselmeyer over my shoulder. Something charged and silent and sad passed between them.

"Look after him," she whispered, and then she turned and there was a flash of light—another Door, strong and solid, the strongest I'd ever seen. It engulfed her, swallowing her with a violent, roaring sound.

Then she was gone. White energy crackled in her wake.

Drosselmeyer let out a cry of despair.

I waved my hands about, stupidly searching the air for the Door as though it were a knob I could grasp, a hinge I could pry open.

But Leska had gone Beyond. Drosselmeyer tried in vain to open a Door after her, but although he could sense the path she had taken and could have followed her familiar magic as easily as a road, he had never been as powerful as she. He could not open a Door to Beyond; he did not have the skill for it, made himself sick trying. I knew at that moment, with Drosselmeyer screaming on his knees in the snow, that we would never be able to find her. Those who went Beyond did not return. If you believed the old stories, it meant she had gone into another world. Perhaps the world from which we had originally come.

Father knew what we had done, but without evidence to condemn us, and to save himself the humiliation of arresting his own son, he simply became even more impossible to live with.

Luckily, I didn't have to live with him for long.

On my eighteenth birthday, in the dead of winter, the faeries came. Not an escort or entourage but an army—they sacked Wahlkraft, murdered my mother and father as they fled, murdered the Seven as they fought to defend us.

The capital was lost to blue flame and black mechanized swarms. Drosselmeyer and I saw it from the farmlands as we fled the city on horseback. We were the only two of my parents' court left alive. Of course Cane would be cruel enough to leave me alone with him.

Anise pursued us like an indomitable storm. Across the country she hunted us, following us through Drosselmeyer's unfocused attempts at Doors that spit us out with burned skin and singed hair.

In Mira's Ring our horses collapsed. I searched the snowy darkness for Anise and her lok-mounted lieutenants, while Drosselmeyer scorched his fingers trying to open a Door, cursing himself, cursing Anise, cursing me loudest of all. He had practiced for years now, since Leska's departure, with the intent to follow her. I saw that he would be able to do it if given a moment. I saw his desperation and thought him pathetic. I wondered why he had not shown Leska such devotion while she'd still been his to love.

The shriek of a lok told me Anise was near. I saw her, draped in furs, a helmet of metal and feathers on her head like a crown.

The Door opened at last. Drosselmeyer stepped through and yanked me along with him, but in his haste he could not pull me fast enough, and Anise's weapon struck me in the ribs. Needles stabbed me. Faery magic surged through my blood, burning me from the inside out. I heard Anise's laughter, gradually thinning to a tiny point, for her curse was swallowing me, stifling my breath, freezing my limbs. I saw the blackness cloud my eyes, felt metal sprout from my skin in cascades of pain.

The last thing I saw of the outside world was a bit of blue lightning ricocheting against the Door's edge and slicing across Drosselmeyer's face. Blood spewed, and he let go of me to clamp a hand over the wound.

It was some comfort then, as Anise's magic ate me alive, to hear Drosselmeyer's screams of agony and know that he had lost an eye.

PART FOUR

THE CURSED PRINCE

But you see, these performers are all members of our mechanical ballet, so they can only do the same thing over and over again.

39

Nicholas crouched on the ground like a beast, metal erupting across his body. Time unfurled slowly as Clara watched him, long pulls of horror that wound around her and squeezed.

"But Godfather broke the curse. We *freed* you."

Even as she said the words, she realized it wasn't true. Godfather had not had time to remove everything. There had been pieces left behind in his body. Maybe, then, the curse had not been broken but had simply lain dormant. Now it awoke and crawled across Nicholas's body, folding him back into its cage. He was howling, and so was the palace behind them, as though something deep within it were awakening.

Clara knelt and reached for the fresh pin that had burst out of Nicholas's arm, coated with his blood. She would dislodge it, she would throw it into the snow—but it had already wrapped itself around his forearm like a creeping vine.

"Don't touch me!" He was kicking at her, thrashing. His fingers were metal claws. "It could infect you. It could travel to you next."

Surely not. Otherwise it would have spread from Nicholas through Godfather's workshop to encase Godfather, or Clara, or the city itself. New York, enveloped in iron and glistening black.

She forced her voice to a semblance of calm. "I don't think it will—"

"No, Clara!" He threw himself away from her. The falling snow melted where it touched his rippling skin. "Stay away."

When Clara stood, she felt a presence sifting through the air with invisible hands.

Clara, what have you done? The voice again—Anise's voice. It seemed to call to her from Nicholas himself, or at least from the metal devouring him. *Why are you leaving me?*

"Because of *this*," Clara snapped, near tears, and she helped Nicholas to his feet despite his protests. Her anger temporarily vanished in the face of his pain. "Because you lied to me. You say you want to remake the world, but what you really want is bloodshed."

The voice was quiet.

Clara tried to run, but Nicholas's sagging weight was too much. She couldn't hold him. They fell—Nicholas writhing beside her, his voice going hoarse from screaming—and for an awful moment Clara lost hope. The watchtowers were spinning around to illuminate her and Nicholas. The soldiers had resumed pursuit. They were outnumbered.

Then an idea came to her.

She dragged Nicholas to his feet again. "Think of Rieden."

"What? Clara, I can't—" He bent over, clutching his head.

"Imagine it, on Bo's map. Remember? The dark circle around the capital. The forest no one can enter. It should be north of here."

"Far north." He struggled for breath. "But, yes. All right."

"Picture it and hold it in your mind." She made herself smile at him. They had done this together once before, though it had been out a window. It seemed like such a long time ago. "Do you trust me?"

"With my life," he rasped, and Clara did not pause to cherish the careful warmth in her heart. Instead she used it—along with the sound of her father's voice, fresh in her mind, and her memory of Felicity's face—to focus on the idea of Rieden.

Once again she felt Anise's presence behind her, closer this time, but she did not turn back. She knew what she would see: Anise, in mad pursuit, mechaniks spilling around her feet like a dark tide cascading toward them across the tundra.

Clara, the voice said, whispering up from Nicholas's shuddering arms, *you will regret this.*

The Door erupted, more glorious and violent than any Clara had yet summoned. When she stepped through it, Nicholas heavy in her arms, the passage bashed them senseless. They landed hard, the wind knocked out of them.

Clara lifted her head. She thought she might be sick. The world was tilted, the sky was spinning, but she could see they hadn't gone far enough. They were in the middle of a vast tundra—Rosche, then. Behind them, but not so far as to feel comfortable, shone the lights of the Summer Palace. This was, Clara assumed, as far as her power would be able to get them.

At least in one try.

Nicholas was staring at her, and the light in his eyes reminded her of that night in the stable, the first time he had seen her with his own true eyes. He was full of wonder and a quiet joy.

"Lady Clara indeed." He gave her an unsteady smile.

Lady Clara. *Lady,* like her mother. The title still felt strange to hear, and yet she cherished the words, for within them lay a new sense of kinship with her mother's ghost, and she cradled it fiercely in her heart. She leaned hard against Nicholas for a moment, as if she were the one who needed help to stay upright. Then a new light shone on his face—behind them, a Door that was not Clara's.

Anise.

"North," Nicholas said, pointing ahead of them. "North is that way. Again."

Clara had already begun to open the next Door, and then another, and another. And each time they tumbled out into the snow, she looked behind them to see that the Summer Palace's lights had shrunk a bit more, and that Anise was still following them.

When they exited a seventh Door, it was at the edge of a black forest, a great brambled structure as high as the perimeter wall and nearly as solid.

"Rieden," Clara whispered. Her body tingled, ached, hummed; the air around her throbbed with power. She could hardly believe it, but here they were: *Rieden*.

Nicholas laughed, heaving. "Clara, you did it."

Behind them a thin light began to spiral.

Clara hauled Nicholas to his feet, his weight heavy against her. "We've got to go. Anise is right behind us."

Dismayed, he looked at the forest ahead of them. "But *how?*"

Clara didn't answer. She seized Nicholas's arm. Spider-sized metal bits scurried across his flesh and away from her touch, burying themselves in the crooks of his elbows and beneath his collarbone. This seemed significant, but Clara couldn't stop to wonder. She hardened her mind against his cries, against everything but the forest before her.

It was calling to her, beckoning her inside. She could feel it in her blood. A sense of home suffused her. Rieden was drenched with mage magic—unsteady, maybe even cracked, but there, and holding fast. It reminded her of Godfather, of standing outside his shop and knowing without even looking inside that he was there. A magnetism.

"Clara!" Anise was behind them, stepping out of her Door. Her voice was furious, thick with desperation. *"Don't."*

A pang in Clara's chest, to hear the queen's raw emotion, but she ignored it and reached for the forest wall. Her fingers scraped bark, and it gave way as though it had never been there at all, as if it were her and she were it—*You are the room. You are the shadows.*—and swallowed them whole.

With a tremendous sucking sound, the forest closed behind them, silencing Anise's unintelligible screams. Thunderous noises boomed as though something were pounding on the forest wall from a great distance. Clara saw faint blue lights, like a storm on the horizon, and heard distant shrieks of fury.

The forest rippled around them and fell silent.

It was a huge black tangle of thorned brambles and vines draped in prickly moss, and great trees with trunks so thick that the linked arms of a dozen men could not have wrapped around them.

Too dense for breezes, or perhaps magically insulated from them, the forest was still and watchful. Clara could not see or hear any traces of wildlife, but she felt the stares of countless malevolent eyes.

She touched a curling vine. It was as though the rest of her time in Cane had been experienced through a veil, and only now could she see the country for what it was. She smelled spice in the air, woodsy and damp, and felt every tiny prick of spindly moss against the pad of her finger. Her blood raced powerfully, tight and cold and vibrating with silver. There was no faery magic here.

Except for in the man behind her. It tainted the air like disease.

"Clara?" Unable to hold himself up, Nicholas had collapsed behind her. "Someone's watching us. There, in the trees."

Clara followed his trembling hand to a crooked black tree with bulbous roots. At its base stood a figure, slim and cloaked. He raised his arms, something long and slender and glowing held between them.

Nicholas pulled Clara to the ground and pushed himself on top of her. Silver lightning sliced into the tree behind them.

"Stay down," he told her, but then his body seized and he rolled off her, crying out in pain.

"Nicholas?" Clara bent over him. More metal plates sliced through his skin, flattening into a patchwork suit of armor up his spine, across his shoulder blades.

"Why hasn't it stopped?" A frenzy lit his eyes. "We're in Rieden, aren't we? Shouldn't it protect us?"

"I don't know," she said helplessly.

Movement behind her made Clara whirl. Shadowed figures approached from the gloom, hooded and armed with tremendous crossbows. The shafts of the arrows they carried were silver—like faery spears and their blue.

Clara put herself between Nicholas and the strangers, shielding him with her body. Fury was shaking her into cold fits. Recollections of the train, of the encounter with the dragons, burst into her mind. She was near such a moment now. Frantic to protect Nicholas, her palms tingled with bottled-up energy. She did not want to release it. Her time in the Summer Palace had taught her to open Doors, but not how to control much else about her power—and if her suspicions were correct, she did not want to hurt these people.

She thrust one of her hands at the figures, making sure they could see the energy there. "Don't come any closer. If you do, we'll both regret it."

To her surprise they paused. The closest of them threw back its hood. It was a man, tall and slender, with dark hair tied at the base of his neck and a familiar gray tinge to his skin. Clara thought of Godfather, and sorrow tightened her chest.

"You're a mage," the man said, calm.

It wasn't a question. How startling to be recognized so matter-of-factly. "I am. And so are you."

The man tilted his head, birdlike. "But you're also like *her*. Your magic smells the same. Tastes the same. Cold instead of warm, though. The wards were confused when they admitted you inside. And whoever that is"—he gestured at Nicholas—"reeks of faery."

Another figure, bow at the ready, said curtly, "What are we waiting for, Ralk?" This was a woman, eyes pitiless beneath her hood. "Smells like Anise, tastes like Anise. What more do you want?"

"But she entered the forest. Anise cannot enter the forest."

"Yet."

The man, Ralk, lowered his bow. "What are you, girl? Speak slowly and don't—"

The woman made an impatient noise. She pulled her bowstring taut, and where an arrow should have been, energy crackled, stretched between the woman's hands. As with the faery's spears and gloves, it seemed the mages could use objects to focus their magic into weapons. The woman loosed her arrow, and it flew straight for Clara.

Clara twisted and flung up her arms, crossing them. It was an automatic movement, like watching Godfather's stance and knowing how he would attack before he did it. A tiny shock of light burst from her joined wrists and grew around her like a shield. The arrow bounced off it harmlessly.

Careful, Clara instructed. It surprised her how easily she fell into talking to her magic as though it were a living thing. The energy from opening the series of Doors still sat over her like a cloak, ready to listen. Force shot out from her, knocking the woman to the ground. Rising, the woman clamped a hand over her shoulder. Silver leaked from between her fingers, and her eyes were fearful.

Another mage perched in the low-slung branches of a nearby tree released an arrow, and a third mage released two more. Clara moved to meet each of them. From a past that seemed many lifetimes ago, she heard Godfather's voice as they'd trained in the dark.

It was not so different fighting these arrows of lightning. She was tired, uncertain, but she fell into the rhythm of it like a dance—absorbing the energy of the mages' arrows as she would absorb the force of Godfather's blows, pivoting on the balls of her feet as she would have to match Godfather's quick-footed moves.

He had been training her to help him, he said, and to defend herself against the city's evils.

Perhaps he'd also trained her with the small hope that if she did discover her latent power someday, she would have some idea of how to fight with it. Instead of grief in that moment, she felt a surge of gratitude.

The figures subsided, lowering their bows.

Clara was exhilarated and exhausted by the expense of power. She felt Nicholas touch her ankle, steadying her.

Ralk watched her curiously. "You work magic as Anise does. You require no external device to use it against others."

Clara glanced at the woman who had first attacked her. "I won't apologize for defending myself."

"Nor should you. My word. The air is *vibrating* around you." Ralk regarded her for another moment, and then his face relaxed into a slight smile. "You are Clara, aren't you?"

Nicholas tried to sit up, and the female mage looked stunned to see his face.

"Oh, Zoya have mercy on me, it *is* you." She fell to her knees. "Forgive me, sire—I didn't recognize you, or your lady."

Utterly confused, Clara ignored Ralk's question. "Either attack us or help us. Don't stand there gaping."

Ralk chuckled, and so did someone emerging from the trees. She saw familiar faces—Erik, Igritt, and . . .

Clara stood rooted by shock as a tiny shape raced toward her out of the shadows and threw its arms around her.

"Bo?" Nicholas whispered hoarsely.

"Headed straight here after you left, sire." Bo pulled back, breathless. "Just like you told us. The mages let us in after much groveling and flattery, and when they saw who we'd brought. If you weren't already so beat up at the moment, I'd pound your face in for disappearing on us like that."

"The hunters—"

"Gave us many a merry chase, but we're mostly all here. Oh, Clara." Bo hugged her again, beaming. "Was it awful in the Summer Palace? Were you scared? Does Anise smell? Was there cake?"

But Clara wasn't listening; she had eyes only for the figure limping toward them. *When they saw who we'd brought.* Impossible. Inconceivable. And yet there he was—despite his bandaged arm, his makeshift cane, and his many burn marks, the most beautiful thing she had ever seen. His eye patch was missing, and where his eye should have been sat a dull knot of twisted faery metal.

Nicholas, struggling to rise, sucked in a breath.

"Godfather?" Her voice sounded hollow to her own ears. She was hurrying toward him, and her heart could not settle on any one emotion. As she fell into his arms, she was a knot of joy, relief, doubt.

"Clara, Clara," he was whispering, and she realized as she heard his voice how old he truly was, and how burdened with pain. She stepped back to grin tearfully at him.

"You look fantastic," she announced.

He laughed, and kissed her cheeks. "You flatter an old man, dear heart."

"How did you—" She clutched his arms, wanting to bury her face in his tattered shirt, but she did not dare take her eyes off him now. "I heard faeries that night."

"The faeries here have forgotten much." He smiled sadly. Angry flesh puckered around his ruined eye socket. "They hardly remember how to fight mages. Even poor ones." His gaze was fixed on her, significant and encouraging. "They have forgotten the might of what we can do."

We. And to think she had felt so alone during the pain of transformation. Now, to be part of these people, however ravaged they were: herself, Godfather, the mages watching them. Her mother, and all those slaughtered. A history of magic, and now she was part of it, and it meant something, this thing. This sense of *us*.

She felt the gravity of this new pride and took Godfather's hand. "They hurt you."

A flicker crossed his face. "Yes."

"I'm so—"

"No. I would let them do it a thousand times over if it meant saving you."

"Anise didn't kill Mother," she whispered. It was important to her that he know before anything else was said.

He seemed surprised to hear it but didn't ask for an explanation. Instead he smoothed the hair back from her face, his hands coming away damp and glittering with powder.

"You have much to tell me, don't you, my Clara?"

She ached to think of the queen in all her lovely gowns, of how close she had come to losing herself in the Summer Palace, of the girl Anise had once been, and of Nicholas being slowly eaten alive. She felt weary, and very small. She had been holding herself together for too long and now felt herself unraveling.

"I think she wants to kill me," she said. "She will kill me if I don't give myself to her."

Godfather's expression darkened. "I won't let her. *We* won't let her."

Overhead, thunder boomed dully, and lightning arced as the shape of a train raced high above the dark net of trees. Even through Rieden's thick magic, the train's passage cast the forest floor in shades of angry blue.

40

The mages' settlement was cleverly hidden in Rieden's snarled recesses. Tiny cottages of wood and stone sat at the bases of trees. Crooked white chimneys sent furls of smoke high into the canopy. Heavy white flowers bloomed in mammoth clusters, and inside their petals pollen glowed silver.

The Prince's Army, as Bo proudly deemed the surviving underground refugees, had already made camp, scattered in cottages and tents throughout a clearing. They slept and ate and accepted crowns of flowers from eager mage children, as slender and soft-eyed as fawns. Clara counted the survivors—twenty-four now, where there had been dozens in the tunnels. She found it hard to meet their eyes, and wondered what they thought of her once again barging in on their safe haven, covered head to toe in faery finery.

She watched as Ralk helped Erik arrange a barely conscious Nicholas on a table in one of the cottages. When Ralk gave Clara fresh clothing patched together out of rough, itchy fabrics, she felt that she did not deserve it. At her hesitation Erik sighed sharply.

"Oh, take them. Can't do much fighting in a gown like that." Erik's expression was as bitter as ever, but he held out a hand to her, a peace offering. "Can you, now?"

"No," Clara said. She clasped his hand with both of hers and smiled. "I should say not."

He grunted and turned away, but it was a start. As Clara changed into her new tunic and a fresh cloak, she felt more hopeful. The clothes were simple but well made and reminded her fondly of Karras; she shed her party gown like an uncomfortable skin. Slipping on a pair of supple leather boots, she felt a brief twinge for her old, dear ones. Her daggers would rot there, hidden in their heels, somewhere in the Summer Palace. Perhaps if she wheedled sweetly enough, Godfather would fashion her new ones.

Back in the cottage, she went straight to Nicholas's side. He had fallen asleep, or into unconsciousness. She stroked his feverish brow and looked across the table to Godfather. He stared down at Nicholas with an unreadable expression—worry, perhaps, and the old hostility he had always directed toward the statue. Every expression that passed over his face, Clara viewed as if through an enchanted looking glass that took her former life and turned it on its head. She had so many questions—about the war, his bond with Nicholas, Leska—but they could wait.

She brushed Nicholas's damp hair back from his forehead. Her fingers touched metal, and it hissed softly, shifting. From her perch on a stool at Nicholas's feet, Bo perked up, eyes round with fascination.

"Will he be all right?" Clara said.

Godfather glanced at her. "I can't say. Being here in Cane, and so close to the capital . . . I'm afraid to remove anything from him, and I can't predict what the curse will do. Although, as much as I hate to say this, you should touch him again."

"I beg your pardon?"

"Just on the forehead, as you did before. Slowly."

She obeyed, dragging her fingertips across his skin.

The metal embedded at his hairline sizzled at her touch. Tiny screams sounded, quiet and shrill. Nicholas moaned, his eyes fluttering halfway open.

"Clara?" he murmured.

"I'm here." She leaned over him. "Everything will be fine. Godfather will tend to you."

Nicholas's mouth quirked. "Don't leave me alone with him. Never trust . . . a one-eyed witch."

"Oh, honestly." Godfather turned away in a huff.

Clara stifled her smile. "I'm not leaving you. We'll work this out."

Something strange passed over Nicholas's face. Darkness bulged beneath the skin of his neck. Clara put her hand there, and it receded, sending a sharp shock up her arm. Nicholas twitched, his eyes falling closed.

"How interesting," Godfather murmured. "Your touch can't eradicate the curse that's already there, but it can prevent it from getting worse."

Clara raised her hand to eye level, inspecting it. "Truly?"

"So it would seem." He looked at her, thoughtful. "Some sort of repulsion? Equal but opposite, perhaps—your magic, and Anise's."

Something tugged at Clara, back toward the Summer Palace—a twinge of longing that filled her with some guilt, but not much, and that made it worse. She leaned hard on the table and said nothing, though she felt Godfather watching her.

Ralk, standing near the wall in the corner, had watched the entire exchange in silence. "I hate to interrupt," he said at last, coming forward smoothly, "but many of my people want answers, and I want something to give them. One of you is cursed by faery magic, one of you is a fallen mage sullied by faery magic, and one of you"—Ralk turned to Clara—"has magic similar to that of a creature responsible for the near-destruction of my race. We had safety here, and peace. Then you bang at my wards," he said, pointing at Drosselmeyer, "screaming at me until I admit you and this ragtag band of humans, and then *she* comes and slips through with no trouble. Quite against my will I'm harboring thirty-one fugitives with no end in sight. At the moment the person I trust most in this room is the human with blue hair. Tell me that isn't strange."

Bo bowed, flourishing her cap. "Thank you, sir, for your good opinion."

Ralk sighed. "Well?"

Clara was the first to speak, with only some hesitation. "My mother was a Lady named Leska," she began, and Ralk's look of surprised recognition gave her courage, as well as a painful swell of pride. She told him everything, never leaving Nicholas's side. When she spoke of the Summer Palace, she kept details scarce. Godfather watched her closely.

There were things to tell him that she would not tell the others, things she felt desperate to say.

". . . and she chased us here." Clara took a deep breath, her throat raw from talking. "I wasn't sure how to enter Rieden, but I thought, being a mage, I should be able to simply by virtue of my blood. And it worked."

Nicholas stirred uneasily. Clara took his hand in hers, and a cautious happiness bloomed in her when he seemed to calm in response. She would not stop to examine the danger of that happiness yet, not while he lay so near death.

After a long moment Ralk said quietly, "I don't want to believe you, but I do. I know he is a Drachstelle. I feel the land responding to him."

Clara nodded, remembering Nicholas singing to Bo in that alleyway, ages ago. The thought encouraged her, and she almost asked Ralk if he would help them, having now heard the whole wild story. Godfather shot her a warning look; it was not time for that yet. When Ralk had gone, and Bo, too, she was at last left alone with Godfather, who smiled at her.

"You drifted away from me just now," he said.

She squeezed his hand apologetically. "I . . . have much to think on."

He settled on a chair and drew her down beside him. "Tell me."

For a moment Clara considered shutting away forever the secrets of her time in the Summer Palace, but then they spilled out, hushed and fevered. She began with Nicholas's betrayal that night on the tundra—to which Godfather, to his credit, did not respond with anything but a terrible hard look in his eyes. He did not, as Clara had often imagined, leap to his feet and help her beat Nicholas to a pulp. He simply held her hands and listened as Clara spoke of Anise.

Part of her was horrified to say how lovely Anise had been, how there had been moments when Clara had found herself entranced and willing. But she could not deny it, when such wistful regret and confusion, such longing remained in her heart.

"I think," she whispered at last, "that we might have been friends, she and I, were it not for . . . everything." She looked up at Godfather, afraid. "She taught me things about myself, things no one else ever had."

He seemed thoughtful. "Like what?"

Clara flushed, thinking of how best to say it. In the end she decided there was no delicate way. So she put it simply: "Girl things."

At first Godfather looked flustered—and then his face fell. "You have missed your mother."

"You loved her," Clara blurted. She had suspected it for years, and with so many truths pouring out of her, she could not hold this one in. "Didn't you?"

"What does that matter?" Heartbreak, heavy in his voice.

"You could have stopped trying to free Nicholas." It seemed a cruelty to say such a thing while he lay before her being eaten alive. "If you had stopped, Anise would have left you alone."

Godfather sagged into his chair. "Yes. And I think I would have stopped, if I could have."

"Your bond with Nicholas. Your blood compelled you. That's what he told me."

"You could say that. 'Coerced' would be my word of choice."

In that moment, as the word "bond" lingered in the air, a thought came to Clara, or the beginning of one, too terrifying and thrilling to say aloud—and too shameful as well, considering everything that had happened to her.

"Godfather," she said instead, rising to her feet before he could read her too closely. "Do you remember what we used to do when we were angry, or one of us had had a particularly awful day?"

"Cognac? Fashion devil figurines for hours? Chase children on the street?" He clucked his tongue. "Oh, wait a moment—that was me, not you."

Their banter was fragile and achingly familiar. "We would fight. We would practice."

"Ah, of course." A sad smile ghosted over his lips.

"I've learned only a little about my magic. I could stand to learn more."

His eyes lit up. "My magic is weak now. Corrupted."

"So your skills are diminished, but I assume your knowledge is intact? Or has your mind gone weak as well?"

"Insolent girl," he said approvingly, and hobbled to his feet. "Let's see what you can do."

41

They practiced through the early hours of the morning until Clara could no longer stay awake, and then through the next day and night, pivoting and whirling, striking and evading—with arms, with fallen branches, with magic. Godfather's magic *was* weak, polluted from years of dissecting Anise's curse. It shone a dull silver when he used it to strike her instead of his fists, and the effort of using it taxed him so severely that he had to stop every few minutes to regain his breath. Despite this, Clara's heart soared. The strength was coming back to her limbs.

She felt the purity of the country here, untarnished as it was by Anise's angry magic and clogged cities. Discarded heaps of metal sat here and there among the trees—remnants of the war, she supposed—but the piles were still and silent. She found the anchors of breeze and moonlight and wet earth, used their stability to steady herself, and grabbed hold of them with her mind. It was difficult, like chasing after shadows, but when she did manage a decent grip, she was able to use these anchors, these solid, real things, to direct her magic more finely, control the intensity more subtly. She had much to learn. Yes, there was power inside her, but it still needed incredible refinement, and that frightened her. Without control over her magic, how was she to defend herself against Anise—or rescue her father when it came to that?

Ralk came out to watch them during the deepest part of their second night in Rieden. A few of his compatriots accompanied him, watching suspiciously. The impatient woman with fierce eyes seemed torn between dislike and admiration as Clara knocked Godfather back with a wall of cold force that rippled through the air.

"It will not be so easy in Erstadt," Ralk said, "if you plan to go after your father."

Clara wiped the sweat from her brow. "Of course I plan to go after him. I thought that much was obvious."

Ralk worried the ends of his hair between two fingers. "The land there is . . . not well. We can see the capital from the forest's perimeter."

"What do you mean?"

"I mean Anise buried the country there in her magic. There more than anywhere else."

Godfather chuckled darkly. "Of course she did. It was the seat of her enemy for many years."

"She has twisted it into a brittle place. Layers upon layers of faery magic make up structures deep into the earth, and the air is rank with sugar and iron residue and endless storms. Even for her it is a difficult place to live. She hardly ever seems to go there. She leaves it for the faery elite, who choose to stay there and do with it as they will."

Clara felt that same horrible pull in her heart and smiled sadly. "She prefers the Summer Palace."

Godfather put a hand on her shoulder. "If that's so, it will be difficult to use magic in Erstadt, for any of us. If we had more time . . ."

"Us?" Ralk cleared his throat. "An odd assumption, Drosselmeyer. But then, perhaps you misspoke. You have, after all, been through a great ordeal."

An awkward silence came over them. Of course Godfather had assumed his mage brethren would jump to help them, and of course Ralk would be loath to risk losing the meager safety that he and his people had worked hard to maintain since the war.

Clara kept silent with enormous effort, though the idea that had grown within her since arriving in Rieden nearly burst from her lips. She could not blame these mages for not jumping at the chance to help with the personal errand of rescuing her father, but perhaps she could use this idea to coax them out of hiding and into battle—if not for her, for themselves.

Godfather inclined his head politely, though his frown betrayed his irritation. "Perhaps I did misspeak."

"He knows what he said, Ralk," snarled the fierce-eyed woman.

"Kora." Ralk turned. "Walk with me."

Kora obeyed, muttering. Some of the mages followed. Others remained behind, considering Clara pensively.

"They don't trust us," Clara whispered to Godfather. "They won't help. The Prince's Army might, but not them."

He scoffed. "Army indeed. What good will a group of bedraggled humans do against whatever Anise has waiting for us in the capital? No. We need more than that. We must convince Ralk to help us."

Godfather seemed deep in thought even as they resumed sparring, and Clara wondered if he had reached the same conclusion she had. If he had, surely he was unhappy about it, and as frightened as she.

When Clara returned alone to the cottage where Nicholas slept, something different hung in the air.

"Where have you been?" a voice croaked from the shadows.

Clara paused at the threshold. "Nicholas?"

He rose from where he'd been crouched in the corner. His face came into the light, and it was at once familiar and strange, as was his voice. Something rippled across his body, something sinister and sly.

"Where's the old man?"

Clara shut the door behind her. "He went to get us some food."

"Dinner." Nicholas's tongue flicked out to wet his lips. "Or is it breakfast? I've forgotten."

"Breakfast, I suppose. It's nearly dawn." Clara felt suddenly wary. "How are you feeling? Still feverish? Let me see you."

"No."

There, in that petulance, rang a familiar note. Her senses sharpened with fear. "Let me see you, Nicholas."

After a tense moment he moved farther into the light. "Clara," he whispered, and his voice changed, and was purely him again. Feeble, uncertain, but him. "Something's wrong."

She inspected his body. Dark metal curls gleamed amid lines of fresh blood. The lattice of ironwork across his torso had grown more elaborate. "You've gotten worse. We shouldn't have left you here. Godfather theorizes that my presence slows the curse's effects somewhat. Maybe if I stay near you, it will—"

"No, Clara. You don't understand. Something is *wrong*."

He surged toward her, grabbed her wrists. His grip twisted her skin painfully. She wasn't sure if he was trying to push her away or rip her apart.

"There's something . . . *inside* me," he said against her cheek. He pinned her arms to her sides, fingernails of steel digging into her flesh. Clara gathered her strength and shoved him away.

"I'm sorry." He moved away, unsteady on his feet. "Something's wrong. She's . . . Clara, I can hear her. I can *feel* her. And she's so angry. I can't make her stop."

Clara took one stunned step back. "Anise?"

"I can feel her inside me. She whispers your name, over and over. She thinks murderous thoughts. Or *I* think murderous thoughts." Nicholas dragged his hands brutally through his hair. "I'm not sure what the difference is."

"That can't be possible," Clara murmured, even as she remembered the strange voice from the tunnels, the one urging her forward: *Soon*. Nicholas had heard it too, right before the mechaniks had attacked.

His face had flickered oddly. She had thought it a chill then, but now she knew:

Anise was speaking through her own curse.

That was the dark feeling in the room—another presence besides their own. Anise was here, at least in part.

Nicholas looked up at her at last, his eyes haunted. "Did I hurt you?"

He nearly had, but she did not say that. "No."

"You mean, not this time—not *yet*." He stalked away. "You shouldn't be near me."

"I'll be wherever I like."

His eyes were flint. "I won't let her make me hurt you, Clara. I've done enough of that on my own."

"You won't hurt me again, not if your grand speech at the party is to be believed."

"If I ordered you to stay away from me, as my subject you would have to obey me."

His words sent a thrill of recognition through her blood. Her idea turned slowly in her head, crystallizing. "I can't believe you would say that after what you did to me."

He wilted with shame. "Clara, if I tell you it's unsafe to be near me, you should believe it."

"Unwise? Yes. Unsafe?" She forced herself closer, unblinking. "I could easily stop you."

"You *should* stop me. Now, before it gets any worse."

"Oh, please spare me such martyr's dramatics. You've a kingdom to save." Another step. "But I'm not sure you deserve it."

He looked up at her, his face half in shadow.

"How am I to know you won't be another Anise, letting your hate get the best of you, turning violent toward those who are different?" A final step. She was electric with anger.

"You don't know," he said quietly. "There's nothing I can do to prove it to you, other than my own word that I want to be a different man than I was raised to become."

"Your word is tarnished of late."

"Calling it 'tarnished' is a kindness, considering how I've treated you."

She had met him in the middle of the room, the table's edge pressing against the side of her thigh. Even as a mere human, Nicholas towered over her as the statue had, and his eyes were hot. But Clara was not afraid. She knew—and he knew; she could see it in his eyes—that she could strike him at any moment, that she could make him suffer. She was blinking back tears thinking once more of what he had done, of the new rift between them and if it could ever be bridged. It was painful to think of such things, but she did it anyway, for her hurt was a new kind of strength against him.

"I was perfectly happy," she whispered, "to never see you again. It might have been better for me and my family if I hadn't."

He was quiet. Only a sliver of heat separated them. "I can't argue with you there."

"To think that you wanted to use me in such a way makes me disgusted that I ever entertained the thought . . ." She trailed off, embarrassed, but she did not look away.

"I understand, Clara," he said, his voice hoarse, miserable.

"And yet I still want you. I've always wanted you." As the words left her lips, they seemed to open her up, to leave her dangerously vulnerable and unsteady, but a power took their place that was entirely her own. Not of Cane, not of Anise. Not of her mother.

Nicholas was still. "I don't deserve that."

"No. You don't." She moved into him; her fingers brushed his wrist. The metal there receded. "But you have it."

He made a choked sound, said her name. Grabbed her hand and brought it to his lips.

"Clara?" Godfather called out from beyond the door. "I have food, and the mages want to speak with us."

His voice broke their locked gazes. Clara's cheeks were hot. Even with Godfather waiting outside, she felt herself unfolding toward Nicholas, a mere shift of weight away from wrapping her arms around him and pushing the moment from charged to blazing.

"Forgive me, Lady Clara, for ever thinking to use you like that," Nicholas whispered against her palm. She felt the soft scrape of his teeth and shivered. "Can you?"

"The prince debases himself once again," she said. "Asking a mere Lady for forgiveness."

"There is nothing mere about you. I must ask it of you. I will always ask it, until I no longer have the breath."

Now she was the one to kiss his hands, his half-alive, half-caged hands. She tried to keep it brief, chaste, but even that small contact was enough to leave her short of breath. The look in his eyes was indecipherable, jumbled, and it followed her out into the early morning light, lingering like a touch against her skin.

42

They gathered with the mages in a meeting-place of stone and trampled undergrowth. Morning fought its way through the knotted trees, and distant storms rumbled. Storms or something else. Clara imagined a fist of faery magic, blue and writhing black, pounding against the forest wall.

"They've not got much to speak of here," Bo whispered at her ear as the others drifted into the clearing. Bo had camped out all night, observing what seemed to be the mages' hub of activity. She chomped on the leg of some roasted fowl, and the pungent spice on it made Clara queasy. Her nerves were precariously tangled. "A bunch of scrap, those bows you saw. Some conventional weapons, axes and the like. But, *shike,* that sort of thing won't do much against however many soldiers Anise has got. And the Prince's Army, we've only got our own fists and a few swords."

Godfather, pacing, thumped Bo on the head. "You're dribbling food on her. Stop it."

Nicholas sat quietly on Clara's other side. Her body tingled with the awareness of his thigh against hers.

"The metal scraps have potential, though." Bo gulped down the last shreds of meat and belched. "I could do something with those. Wires in decent shape, circuitry mostly intact."

"The mages themselves are competent enough," Godfather added. "Competent but on the whole unimpressive. Better than nothing, I suppose."

Ralk had come forward to address them. Some of the mages surrounding him were rigid with expectation; others lounged with poised carelessness. Kora paced, agitated.

Clara thought of her father on the Summer Palace's chromocasts, of his horrible confusion, of how he had screamed. Tonight it would be a full nineteen days since her arrival in Cane, and four days, eighteen hours would have passed at home.

She could not think of Felicity. With Bo so near, that was asking for a complete emotional avalanche.

"I've presented both your story and your request for aid to my people here in Rieden," Ralk said. "We have spoken through the night and voted." He paused, and Clara knew in that instant what he would say. "But I'm afraid we can't join you in your journey to the capital."

Silence stretched through the crowd. Beside Clara, Nicholas drummed restless fingers on his leg.

"I can't tell you how much we regret what's happened to your father, Clara, and of course we deplore our true prince's deposed state. But please understand." Ralk's face was heavy with regret, but determined. "We are all that is left of our race. We have lived here in hiding for many years. We've carved out a safe life for ourselves, however meager it may be. If we fought with you, it might be our end. We would not give up such safety, especially when in all likelihood we would fail at any rescue attempt, any assault." He ticked off the points on his fingers. "We are outnumbered and undersupplied, and the capital is riddled with Anise's mechanized magic run rampant. We cannot risk such a thing."

For a moment no one spoke. Clara could feel the disappointment around her—Godfather, Bo, Erik and the Prince's Army, loitering uncomfortably in the shadows. Nicholas, his skin rippling, sweat shining on his temples.

But Clara was calm with resolve. She took Nicholas's hand in hers, pouring determination into him. He shuddered, his face white with pain, and Clara felt a protective rush of anger.

You won't get him, Anise, she thought. *You won't get me. Not like this.*

Laughter chimed faintly. The mages shifted, and Clara wondered if they had heard the laugh or merely sensed its cruelty.

"You cannot risk it?" Godfather scoffed. "If Anise is allowed to run amok for much longer, your safe haven won't be so safe anymore. Or haven't you noticed?" He threw up his arms at the mottled sky. "The storms never stop raging. The ground never stops quaking. Magic has a limit, and so does Cane. She builds and she destroys and she builds again, and she'll keep doing that until she has whatever kind of world it is she thinks she wants—or more likely, until she cracks it open. Then where will your precious forest be? It's already weakening, and you know it. Your wards won't keep her out for much longer. They were shoddy to begin with, and they're shoddier now. Blasted undisciplined—"

Bo sucked her teeth. "Best not to go insulting them, One-Eye. Or Godfather, or Lord Seven, or whatever I'm supposed to call you."

Godfather glared at her.

"Or," Nicholas said, though it clearly cost him some effort to speak, "you could risk it because it's the right thing to do. Because people out there are dying."

"Mages aren't," Kora snapped.

"Revenge, then, against the queen who wronged you."

Ralk shook his head. "We're past revenge, sire. You can't live on revenge."

Good words, ones Clara hoped Nicholas took to heart—for his own sake.

He persisted. "What about hope?"

Godfather looked at Nicholas sharply, and Clara's breath caught.

"Hope," Nicholas continued, "for a better future. Hope for a kingdom ruled justly, a kingdom governed by mercy, not madness. Could you bring yourself to fight for that?" He stopped, panting, as a new black tubule slid out from beneath his fingernail and snaked around his thumb, sizzling quietly.

Everyone but Clara moved back.

"Move away from me. Please." His eyes were frantic on her face, but his voice was even. He drew in a steadying breath. "She wants to hurt you. She wants *me* to hurt you. Clara, please . . ."

"What is it?" said Ralk. "Is he getting worse?"

Kora was livid. "He's infected, is what he is. It'll spread and kill everyone if we're not careful."

"It won't," Clara said coolly, and she stood and placed her hand on Nicholas's armored chest. She looked him full in the eye. "I'm fine, aren't I? And I've kissed him. I've touched him."

Godfather rustled irritably behind her, but she ignored him and turned to face the others. "I know why you should risk it. For country and for a future, yes. But also because you have something they can't fight against. You have me. And I know Anise. I know her mind, I know her weaknesses, I know how she fights. We're alike, she and I, like two sides of a coin that should never have been forged . . . at least according to the laws and prejudices of your country."

She paused, and some of the mages looked uneasy, as though recalling their past wrongs. It startled her, how familiar it felt to stand before an expectant crowd. For a moment she was simply Clara Stole, the mayor's daughter. She was back in front of the Bowery Hope Shelter. It was Christmas, and limp holly hung on the lampposts, and she was cutting a bright red ribbon for a house of coffins.

"I may not be her equal in finesse," she continued, "but I am in power. Or I could be."

Kora was not convinced. "'Could' may not be good enough, *Lady*."

Godfather let out a soft curse. Of course he had worked out her intentions. But he wouldn't stop her from saying it. No one would.

It was her decision, and she had had precious few of those.

"The one thing Anise has that I lack is royal blood," she said, and though the glorious autonomy of her decision thrilled her, it was still frightening to consider, even for a Lady—or, more accurately, a someday-Lady. A Lady-in-training. *Mother, be proud of me.*

"Anise was born the bastard daughter of a human king. Because of this, she is linked with the land. She can work her magic through it better than anyone. Destroy it and remake it as she sees fit. If I could do the same, I could match her punch for punch. I could beat her."

Doubt gnawed at her, but she shoved past it. It was best to lie a little and look brave on the outside. She took Nicholas's hand and faced him.

"I therefore choose to bond with you, Nicholas Drachstelle. To serve you, to fight for you, to win your land back for you. To be your loyal Lady of the North. In exchange I ask one thing of you: that you help me rescue my father." She turned to the mages. "And I ask that you, brothers, sisters, will help me do the same."

An outcry arose.

Bo swore appreciatively, rubbing her hands together. Kora shouted protests, as did many others. Ralk stared in astonishment—and, Clara thought, grudging approval.

Nicholas shook his head, backing away. "No, Clara. I won't. Didn't you hear me before? I won't do that to you. I can't."

"You will, boy, and don't waste your breath arguing." Heavily, Godfather turned to him. "If we're to stand a chance, she must bond with you. Otherwise Anise will have an unbeatable edge. We'll never find John, to say nothing of reclaiming your throne."

"But the other mages—I could bond with them, I could ask for volunteers—"

"These fools?" Godfather waved his hand impatiently at the arguing mages. "They'll be handy as infantry, but they've grown as soft as the spoiled faeries who tried to confine me. Binding with them might actually do you harm rather than good. And besides, who's to say their blood could even withstand joining with yours, cursed as it is? No. It has to be Clara."

Clara reached back to find his hand, and pressed gratefully.

"Clara, you don't know what the curse will do to you. What *she* will do to you." Nicholas squared his jaw, faced her straight on. "I won't do it. I *forbid* it."

Bo picked at her teeth pensively. "Seems like a bad decision to me, sire. What else will you do? Sit here and rot with the others till the forest falls down on you? Stroll into the capital all by your lonesome and be struck down within five minutes?"

"We'll find a way. We'll make a way." Nicholas flung a hand at Godfather. "Look what it did to him! For years he hacked away at this curse, and it turned his magic weak and unreliable."

"And you're welcome for it," Godfather said, smiling thinly. "He's right, though. We don't know what it will do, Clara. It's a tremendous danger."

"You would really do this thing?" Ralk approached them. Behind him the mages gathered curiously. "You would bind with him, fight alongside us as a champion?"

"No, she won't," Nicholas said, desperation tearing his voice.

Clara ignored him, faced Ralk with a calm she did not feel. "I will."

Nicholas moved before her, cutting her off. "Clara, think of what you're doing. It's service, do you understand? Even without the curse . . . you'd be giving yourself to me, and you'd have no choice in the matter." He caught her hands, gently, as though afraid to touch her. "You don't deserve that."

Godfather snorted. "But I do, I suppose?"

Bo hissed at him to shut his mouth or she'd do it for him.

"But I do have a choice," Clara said, hardly noticing them, "and I've already made it." One last, cruel jab: "Isn't this what you wanted?"

His mouth twisted, bitter. "Once I did, and I was a horrible fool. My hate blinded me. Not again. Please do not ask me to hurt you like this."

"But it's my hurt to choose." She touched Nicholas's cheek. Such a strange, lovely irony that for years she had imagined the statue would come alive, take care of *her*, banish *her* demons. "My blood is stronger than the others'. I'm a half-breed, like Anise. A two-blood, remember? An abomination."

He shook his head, horrified. "No. Never. *Never*, Clara."

"Listen to me. I nearly *am* Anise. What more is there to understand? We're running out of time." Beside her, Bo shifted her weight. Clara was reminded of Felicity, and a terrible fear stabbed her. "My family is running out of time."

The ground beneath them shook with sudden tremors. The sky above churned green, and they could see more of it today than they had been able to the day before. Godfather was right. The wards were weakening, the forest was thinning.

Clara raised her eyebrows at him. *See?*

Nicholas stubbornly looked away.

"When I was young," she said, bringing his gaze back to her, "I imagined you would come alive someday. You would be my friend."

He was quiet, his gaze passionate. "Sometimes I thought I would go mad in that cage. But then you would visit, and I could breathe again."

She smiled, memories warming her that would have seemed bizarre to anyone else. "I can endure this, Nicholas. I must, for my family. For Cane. I *want* to endure this."

It surprised her to say it. After all, she had arrived here only a short time ago, but then again, she had known this place for years—bits and pieces of it, riddles and half-truths, in Godfather's stories. And it was *hers*. It was a home to fight for.

Countless emotions moved across Nicholas's face, and Clara couldn't discern which were his and which might be Anise's. After a long moment he turned away.

"Fine," he muttered thickly. "Hurry, old man. Prepare us. Instruct her. We begin at dusk tomorrow. Perhaps by then you'll have come to your senses, Clara." And then he stormed away into the trees and was gone.

43

The forest grew colder throughout the next day. By the time dusk fell, Clara's breath came in light puffs. Hanging from the trees, cascades of white flowers glowed as bright as torches. Thunder boomed in the distance, black clouds roiling above the forest's canopy. The ground moved, and Clara stumbled, catching herself on Godfather's arm.

He steadied her tenderly. "Are you ready?"

They were alone in one of the mages' huts. Beneath her scratchy robe Clara was naked and trembling, but she was determined to hide it.

"Yes. I think so." Then, remembering his instructions, she closed her eyes and said, "I mean, I *know* I'm ready."

She had to be totally open to the binding; eager for it but not desperate. Otherwise, Godfather had warned, the binding would not take. It would be corrupted, or tenuous, and with Nicholas's blood already so tortured, such a misstep could be fatal to one or both of them.

She had to want it.

An easy thing, *wanting*. But as Clara followed Godfather through the eerie brambled paths, she found herself struggling to focus on the concept. Nervousness clouded her mind.

"I remember the first time I saw you sneaking around his statue," Godfather said, as though he could sense her confusion. "You were a tiny thing, perhaps five or six. You had climbed up on a stool so you could reach his lips and trace them with your finger."

Vaguely Clara recalled the sensation of the curved metal beneath her hand. "I was so embarrassed when you caught me."

"An embarrassment I thoroughly enjoyed. And yet you didn't stay away long after that. Your visits to the shop became more and more frequent over the years. I began to suspect it wasn't only me you came to see. And then there was the time I caught you standing on your toes to kiss him." His voice was careful and light. "I confess I found myself rather jealous, Clara, to have so much of your attention paid to a lifeless object."

"Even though he wasn't lifeless," she pointed out.

"Even so."

She blew out a long breath, but it did not quell her nervousness. "So. You did this with Nicholas, did you? Long ago?"

"*Long* ago. He was a tiny boy, and I was a not-quite-so-old man."

"Old? Nonsense. You're handsome."

"Liar," he scolded, though he seemed delighted at the compliment.

"And you had to be, er, naked then? And Nicholas, too?" That, bizarrely, was still the most disconcerting thing at the moment—not Nicholas's curse, not the idea of opening herself up to something so potentially dangerous, but rather the simple fact that she was naked beneath her robe, and Nicholas would be the same beneath his.

"Unfortunately." Godfather harrumphed a bit. "Never understood why it was necessary."

"To symbolize," Clara said, reciting the words she had practiced earlier, "the complete trust one has in one's bonding partner."

"I know what the ritual says. I'm just saying it's rubbish."

Ahead of them a warm yellow glow marked the clearing where the mages had made a fire and erected a makeshift altar from felled trees. Clara saw their dark hooded figures, the tiny shape of Bo leaning against a tree. Nicholas's shrouded silhouette.

She grabbed Godfather's hand, feeling suddenly like a small girl again. "You know I love you, Godfather. You've always been dear to me. No statues or princes can change that."

His hand closed around hers. "I know."

Together they moved toward the fire.

Godfather had instructed her. Nicholas was facing her. The mages surrounded them, and so, farther back, did the Prince's Army. Bo perched, anxious and wide-eyed, in a black tree.

The fire burned. Above, Anise's storms raged.

There was nothing left to do but begin.

They knelt on either side of the altar, Godfather at the head of it. *Like a priest,* Clara thought, feeling overwrought in the silence. *A priest with one eye. A one-eyed witch-priest.*

"Clara," Godfather warned under his breath.

She closed her eyes, willing herself calm.

"Since the first mages met the royal family of Cane," Godfather began, "there have been bindings. They exist to benefit both humans and mages, both royals and servants. To strengthen and protect, to teach and to promise . . ."

He continued intoning the traditional introduction. At first Clara listened with her eyes closed. The heat of the fire washed over her, and the sounds of popping wood crackled at her ears.

Then she felt a prickling up her spine, across her breasts, and down her belly, and opened her eyes.

Nicholas was watching her. The prickling became a thrill.

Godfather was saying something, but at first she did not hear. He cleared his throat and said it again: "You may now disrobe."

Hands shaking, Clara stood. Across the pyre Nicholas mirrored her. Her toes burned with the closeness of the fire, but that was nothing compared to the flush of her body as she shrugged off the robe. For a moment she longed to reach for it, but then she thought of Anise, which was such an incongruous thing to think of at this moment that it almost made her laugh. But the memory of standing on the rooftop with nothing between her and the snow but the night air was, oddly, a comfort.

It's just a body, Clara, the only one you will ever have.

She stood tall, arms at her sides.

Across from her the lean lines of Nicholas's body flickered. In the glamour of firelight the wicked metal encroaching upon him seemed alluring. He smiled softly at her, as if they shared a secret no one else could know.

Godfather placed two daggers on the altar before them. "You may begin."

This would be the hardest part. To maintain the *wanting,* the willingness, despite the pain. When Clara gripped the dagger's hilt, it nearly slipped away. Her hand was sweating.

Then Nicholas was there, his hands gentle at her waist. She was glad to feel in his touch that he was nervous as well. He whispered "Brave Clara" against her cheek, raised his blade to her shoulder, and cut.

It did hurt, but Clara gritted her teeth past it and continued. Once the first cut was made, the rest had to follow soon after. She cut his right shoulder to mirror her left, and then her eyes rose to meet his.

"My turn," she whispered.

His eyebrow quirked. "Be gentle."

She fought an anxious smile. Perhaps smiles were not proper at such a moment. But it tugged at her mouth anyway as she nicked his chest, and he hers; then a thigh each, a cheek each; light scrapes at each other's navel, the cold blades dragging across bare skin. Each cut represented something different: the shoulder, strength; the cheek, words.

When a dozen bright lines shone on each of their bodies, they lowered their knives. Clara smarted all over. The wind bit her, the fire's smoke stung her. The mages seemed to hold their breaths. Even Erik's face had lost its perpetual crossness.

"Now the sharing," Godfather said from worlds away.

Nicholas sliced a line across the back of his hand, dipped his finger in it, and began tracing each of Clara's cuts. His fingers skated across her body, lingering here and there. As their blood mixed, she thought she could feel his heartbeat sink into hers, and she yearned desperately to kiss him. His lips moved, silently murmuring, "One . . . two . . . three," counting each wound as if in apology, or prayer. When it was her turn, the first touch of her finger to his body nearly made her scream, or laugh—anything to relieve the tension.

She pressed on, counting. "One . . . two . . . three"—his shoulder, his chest, his thigh. "Four . . . five . . . six"—his cheek, his navel, his wrist.

When it was done, they looked to Godfather. His expression was unreadable.

"Clasp hands," he said, and they did, the fire licking at them. This was the deciding moment, the one that more than anything else determined the bond's strength.

Clara had to say the binding words, and they had to be the right ones. That was all Godfather had told her, that each bound mage's incantation was different. That it was the one magic done with words, and unspeakably powerful because of it.

If the words were right.

"They should be of your soul," he had said.

Her soul. As if that were an easy thing to decipher.

She closed her eyes, her hand slippery in Nicholas's grip, and began. Her voice was thin but grew stronger with each uttered word.

"Nicholas Drachstelle," she said, "I have known you since I was a girl. I told you my secrets when no one was looking. I whispered my fears to you."

His hand tightened around hers, and she opened her eyes. She did not close them again.

Sweat slid down the curve of her back. Embarrassment and nervousness and sweet, aching anticipation filled her. "You were the one thing in my life that demanded nothing of me. You accepted me for who I was—a girl searching for a safe hand in the dark." She paused, smiled wryly. "You were only a statue, but to me you were real. You pulled at me. And now you *are* real, flesh and blood. You hurt me once." A flinch, across both of their bodies; shame in Nicholas's eyes. "But now, at your most desperate, in your moment of greatest pain, you put my safety before yours. And that is why I bond with you now."

She nodded, signaling the end. But Nicholas's eyes were full of heat, and he pulled her gently closer so that the full press of his body was against her.

Clara gasped, shifted in his arms at the unexpected contact, at the sheer *pleasure* of it. He was not supposed to do anything else. The ritual was meant to be over. Godfather moved, but Clara raised a finger to warn him off.

"Clara Stole," Nicholas said, his voice low, "I swear to you on the strength of this bond that I will never use it to hurt or coerce you, to force you to act against your will. I considered it once. I admit that, and I am ashamed of it. But I swear to you I will not do it again. Not even with this bond between us. Not even if it would destroy me to refrain. Not even then, Clara. Especially not then."

Clara started at that. Could he know what she had planned, should they survive this?

He couldn't.

The words said, something ancient ripped through them, blood to blood. It rattled Clara's bones. Their bodies arched and fell, their hands clasped. A scream formed in Clara's throat, and she choked it back, hard.

A force pulsed out from them, shaking Bo's perch, rustling Ralk's hair.

Nauseated, Clara used the altar to climb to her feet. Her wounds were closed, though blood still shone on her skin. Godfather was there, wrapping the robe around her as Ralk and Bo helped Nicholas.

Overhead, the storms continued. The ground still shook, and Clara could feel it all the more sharply, as though a piece of Cane had embedded itself in her.

"Clara." Nicholas's voice. Disoriented, she turned to him, dazed in Godfather's arms.

Nicholas fumbled for her hand. "Are you all right? Are you hurt?"

"A bit." She smiled. "But it's nothing I can't handle. We two-bloods are made of sterner stuff than most, you know."

The words drained her. She slumped against Godfather, but not before Nicholas stroked her wrist. "Nothing mere about you, Lady Clara," he murmured to her, and then Godfather was leading her away, fussing over her robe.

It was finished.

Clara tossed and turned on her hard cot, the rough blankets abrasive against her oversensitized skin. She hadn't been able to sleep since the binding. Whispers in the night distracted her, things she had been dimly aware of before—leaves dying and breezes blowing and the earth groaning, and Anise's cruel magic tearing through it all like venom.

She worried her fingers over the spot on her navel where the cut had been, where Nicholas's fingers had lingered, and sighed sharply.

Might as well give in to it—she certainly wasn't going to sleep.

She slipped out past Godfather, who had a surprisingly delicate snore, through the black thicket with its rustling flowered briars, and into Nicholas's cottage across the way.

Once inside, she hesitated at the door. But then Nicholas softly called her name, and she shut the door and went to him.

They hurried toward each other and then stopped, awkward. Clara searched for words to say but found none. She heard Nicholas's careful breathing, felt the tension as he held himself back from her. Everything was new between them, or perhaps simply unveiled. She knew him, and she didn't—or she had simply discovered a new part of him.

Distrust lingered in her heart, but he had done much to counter it since finding her at the Summer Palace. She struggled with this inner war of pride and self-respect, of wanting and *need.*

"How are you feeling?" Clara said at last, at the same time Nicholas said, "You couldn't sleep either?"

They laughed, embarrassed. They were, it seemed, suddenly ten years old. Then Clara saw something that startled her. Unthinking, she hurried closer to him.

"The curse! It's—"

"Receding. Somewhat, anyway. At any rate it hasn't gotten worse."

"Oh, it looks *much* better. Do you think it was the binding?"

"Yes, I do." He paused, and there was a weight in the air as he opened his mouth and closed it, as his eyes bored into hers. The weight of *almost.*

She had to look away, her pulse coming in sharp bursts. "I couldn't sleep. You know, to answer your question. From before."

"Neither could I."

She knit her fingers together, then lowered them, rigid at her sides.

"Clara . . ."

"Tomorrow we'll discuss strategy," she said hurriedly. "We have much to plan. I think I can get everyone in with a few Doors. I'm quite good at opening Doors." She laughed. "Not so good at other, more useful things, I'm afraid. I wish I had more time. I wish I could be a better champion for everyone. Like a knight or something. Sir Clara. But then, no, I'm a Lady, aren't I?"

He found her hand, quieting her. "We'll find him, Clara. We'll get him home."

She stared at him, and the softness in his face sent her into his arms.

They were clumsy kisses at first, as they fumbled in the dark. Then Nicholas's hand threaded through her hair, and the other fell to her waist, held her in place. The kisses deepened.

Clara's blood surged through her, and she stretched up onto her toes to press herself closer to him. The heat she had felt at the fire returned tenfold. She clutched his arms, his shoulders, and when her fingers brushed metal, she felt not repulsed but emboldened. She knew that metal. It had been of her statue, and she had kissed it when no one else would. She *trusted* that feeling.

Nicholas bent lower, his kisses trailing hotly down her neck. He tugged at her collar, urgent, and they stumbled back, bumping against the wall. His hands clutched the hem of her tunic, brushing her belly, sliding sweetly up her waist, and then higher. Clara gasped and parted her lips, and Nicholas groaned.

It wouldn't stop—it *couldn't* stop, or Clara would die. Her blood sang. She couldn't kiss him deeply enough, couldn't touch him everywhere she wanted to. Only hours ago they had shared blood, shared skin, and the knowledge of that raced through her veins like a drug. *Like sugar,* she thought wildly as his fingers skimmed up her neck . . .

. . . and circled there, closing around her throat.

Her eyes shot open. "Nicholas?"

His hands tightened. Malice rippled through the room, possessive. *Clara . . .*

She couldn't breathe. Terror struck her, and fury. She reached into the night air for anchor, gathering her strength.

"Oh . . . ," Nicholas murmured, and it wasn't his voice. It was higher and crueler. His eyes glinted blue in the moonlight. "Just a bit more, sweet Clara . . ."

Clara let her power off its leash. *Do not hurt him. Only stun him.* A wave of force struck Nicholas, hurling him across the room in a burst of crackling energy. He hit the opposite wall and slid to the floor.

Shaking, she approached him. The lingering magic illuminated his dismay.

"I thought . . ." He cleared his throat. "I'd hoped the binding would diminish her."

"I had as well. Are you hurt?"

"Not terribly." He looked up at her, afraid. "Are you?"

"No. You didn't—*she* didn't get far."

They waited in awful silence. Nicholas picked himself up off the floor and put as much distance between them as the small cottage would allow. Somehow—even in such an aftermath—heat remained between them, but neither of them moved to quench it.

"I won't touch you again, Clara." His shadowed profile was tight, furious. "I meant what I said in the binding. I'll never force anything upon you. Not even she can make me."

Clara nodded uncertainly and left without another word. She did not sleep that night, just as she had thought, but for a different reason.

44

Clara awoke before dawn to the sensation of being strangled.

She jerked up, her arms tensed to strike, but no one was there except Ralk, who had frozen at the door. It stood open behind him. Half his body was still outside, and he put up his hands.

"I'm sorry to wake you."

The memory of Nicholas's face flickering into Anise's left her unbalanced and full of sadness. "What is it?"

Ralk hesitated, distressed. "There is something you must see."

She swung her legs out of bed and tugged on her boots. Outside, Godfather, Bo, and Nicholas already waited. Bo was fiddling with a bundle of thin metal, swearing under her breath; slender tools glinted behind her ears.

Withdrawn and guarded, Nicholas would not meet Clara's eyes. He kept as far from her as possible as they followed Ralk through the bracken. She was glad, for the memory of his hands at her throat was still near enough to frighten her, but it was difficult to keep this distance between them—like resisting the instinct to breathe.

They came to a strange part of the forest. The ground had grown increasingly uneven, and now the forest before them trembled like a thorny mirage. Beyond the tangle glowed a ghoulish blue-green light.

"What is this?" The sound of Nicholas's voice in the gloom startled Clara. Something was not right here. She put out a hand and felt the tension in the rippling air, and the energy of angry magic.

Ralk gestured forward. "See for yourselves."

They bunched together where the light was strongest. Clara peered out, beyond Rieden, and understood that the rippling was the magic guarding Rieden butting up against what lay beyond.

There was a city, black and teeming and . . . *growing*. Towers rose and fell; buildings tumbled into one another, and were pulled apart. Shining black strings stretched between them before snapping, sending up tiny showers of what Clara realized were spurts of clacking mechaniks. The ground shifted, hilly one moment and flat the next, jagged spires reaching high up into the sky like trees in a forest fighting for sunlight. They knocked into one another, climbing higher and higher until the height became too great and they cascaded down in dark waves. Iron bridges crossed the sky. She could not tell if it was day or night. The light here was murky, the sky thick with bulbous clouds and lightning that never ceased. A great black wall surrounded it all.

"Erstadt." Nicholas's voice was quiet and furious. "What's happened to it?"

"I think you know, Your Highness. Anise happened to it. And since you arrived, it has grown all the more ruthlessly. See there?" Ralk pointed at a swath of land past the edge of the mages' magic, a thin forest of scrawny obsidian trees. Thin metal cords wound around them, sparking blue, stunting their growth. "Yesterday that was Rieden, safe within the boundaries of our protection."

Godfather had been right. "Her magic is eating away at your wards," Clara said.

"Even now it approaches the forest."

As they watched, a shallow line of mechaniks tore at the ground. Some, overwhelmed by Rieden's wards, spasmed and fell, but the others kept coming, pushed onward by some relentless force.

"She is furious," Clara whispered.

Nicholas's eyes shot to her, but she ignored him. Part of her feared looking too closely at his face.

"We cannot delay any longer," Godfather said. "We have to leave. Now."

Yes, they had to. Urgency nettled Clara, put her even more on edge. It was her twentieth day in Cane—and five at home. *Felicity, I'm coming back to you soon. I swear it.*

Ralk agreed. "I confess, I've no guidance for you, no strategy. I've never seen the capital in such unrest." He fingered the thorns of a vine at his side nervously. "Nor have I ever seen Anise so agitated. You have provoked her mightily, Lady Clara."

Her title still sat strangely around her, but not so much as it once had. She was growing accustomed to it, like she would to a new friend. Her blood surged, chilling her, and she opened her mind to it gladly.

"Anise will be expecting stealth," she said. Nicholas's attention was still sharp upon her, and she glanced at him. "You realize you can't be privy to our planning, Nicholas. She might hear our every word."

If her matter-of-fact coolness hurt him, he hid it well. He nodded curtly. "A word, before I leave you?"

They walked a little apart from the others. Clara noticed that he kept her at arm's length, but the look on his face was anything but distant. "Clara, you know I'll fight at your side. Curse or no curse."

She longed to draw him to her, to take and give comfort. Instead she said, "Certainly."

"And you know what you'll do if it does get the best of me. If I can't keep up, if she breaks me, or if I become too dangerous." He took her hand, fingers light on her palm. "You know, don't you, Clara?"

"What are you saying?" She knew, of course.

"You'll stop me, no matter what it takes. The important things are finding your father and destroying Anise, if we can. Whoever sits on the throne after that is less important."

"Don't act as though it doesn't matter," she said sternly. "Not to me. Tell me to kill you for the greater good if you must, but don't pretend you're indifferent."

She paused. The word "kill" hovered crookedly between them.

With a searing intensity, Nicholas studied her face as if to memorize her. Then he turned and left her.

Clara watched him go. When she returned to the others, her face was a mask of coolness. She would not let them see how he had shaken her. "Here," she said, "is what we'll do."

They began at dusk, that same day.

"It's crude," Bo said, slipping a tiny headset over Clara's ears and hiding it beneath her hair, "but it'll do."

The device crackled, a mechanized growl.

Bo grimaced, her nose crinkling as Felicity's did when she saw something unseemly. "Wasn't kidding about it being crude, was I? Sorry, Lady."

"Please," Clara said, watching as the others gathered before her," call me Clara."

"But you *are* a Lady, you know." Bo winked at her over her own tangle of thin black wires. Bo's voice came to Clara both in the air and at her ear, distorted. "Might as well get used to it."

"I don't feel like a Lady. I feel like a girl."

Bo shrugged. "All Lady mages were girls at one point, weren't they? And I bet few of 'em ever planned any assassinations."

Clara winced at the word.

Godfather came up and took her elbow. "You owe Anise nothing, Clara. Don't doubt yourself. Don't doubt this."

"There were moments," she whispered, too low for the others to hear, "when she was kind to me. Treated me as I've never . . ."

She trailed off. It felt silly. Silly and dangerous and shameful. Anise's magic was eating away at the very world. She was dangerous, destructive, vengeful. She was not a person to feel kindly toward. Clara would remember that. She *must* remember it.

"I know, dear heart," said Godfather. "But it was a manipulation. You see that, don't you?"

Yes, she was all too used to manipulation. In the wake of her mother's death, every aspect of her life had been a bargain, a careful maneuvering. Evading Dr. Victor, guiding her father through his grief, ushering Felicity through a thinning path of safety. Navigating Patricia Plum's web—not to mention Godfather's own, much as his deceptions might have been for Clara's own good.

But there had been moments, almost too fragile to acknowledge, when Clara had seen something in Anise's face—something worth giving a second chance.

Our mothers made this moment between us, Clara, this moment in time.

And what a moment, she thought bitterly. *It could have been a better one, Anise, if you'd had the guts for it.*

"Don't worry about me," she said to Godfather, and adjusted her earpiece. "Is everyone in position?"

Another crackle, a stutter. Then Ralk spoke: "Yes, we're here. We await your signal."

Clara closed her eyes and drew the structure of their attack in her mind. At first she did nothing but imagine the capital's layout, as Godfather had sketched in the dirt—at least, what he had once known of it. With Anise's magic so pervasive, anything could be awaiting them now.

"I'm here," Godfather murmured at her side. His presence was a comfort. For Clara's protection Nicholas was positioned elsewhere. Bo had stepped back into the trees. Her meager army gathered in clumps along the shifting line between Rieden's magic and Anise's encroaching mechaniks. Without Godfather steady beside her, she would have felt rather alone in the world.

No, not entirely alone—even if Godfather had not been there, she would have still had her magic. It pulsed steadily within her, waiting for instruction. As she urged her power into readiness, preparing it for their most extreme experimentation yet, she felt the land responding to her, the air accepting her. She could sense it, and it was overwhelming, even frightening—a tremendous, sentient entity recognizing the newness of Nicholas in her blood. Sensing it, and bowing to it, and saying, *Welcome home.*

Protectiveness seized her, a possessive thrill that she had not felt for a long time back at home, save for in Godfather's shop. Perhaps *this* could be her home now. Or maybe it already was, or always had been.

"Clara," Godfather whispered urgently. "Not to rush you, but the longer we delay . . ."

She shook herself. "Of course." Without further hesitation she held the half-formed picture of Erstadt in her mind and opened a Door in front of her, palm thrust into the air. The first wave of soldiers—some of the Prince's Army, and the mages with their sizzling arrows—began pouring through. As soon as she knew the Door was stable, she ran over to the next waiting group, which included Erik, and opened another Door. Right before Erik slipped through with his team, he clapped her on the back. It was, she suspected, the only endorsement she might ever receive from him.

Three more Doors, in rapid succession, and when the last person was through, she looked back at the shimmering seam of magic that marked the first Door, where Godfather stood waiting for her. He looked younger, as though the approaching fight were giving him new life, and so ferocious in his ragged clothes—was that still his favorite striped cravat, tied now around his neck?—that Clara wanted to run to him and plant a kiss right on his ruined metal eye.

Instead she nodded at him, and together they leapt through their Doors.

"Good luck!" Bo called out behind them, and then the Doors swallowed them away.

On the other side they emerged into chaos—a black road littered with faery bodies, and human slaves collared with iron spikes running in a panicked frenzy, their chains severed. Mechanized horses with infected, rancid flesh drew canopied carriages that might have been fine had they not been streaked with filth. The Summer Palace had been glamorous and bright, polished and sumptuous, but the capital was a mire of ironwork and teetering buildings with shattered, half-built walls. The black filth of constant destruction coated every surface, dusted the skin of every being; the sky was thick with it.

And the *faeries* . . .

Suits of iron and metal plates covered them like second skins, with patches of frayed wiring hanging loose in their long white braids. Some of them sported swiveling blue knobs for eyes, lit by inner mechanics like that of a kambot, and mottled skin gave way to haphazard clumps of black bone and spinning metal gears. Long metal teeth lined their mouths. They rode loks, whipping them with long iron rods that sparked blue.

Clara emerged into the mess of it, aghast. Anise had gone mad enough to curse and torment her own people. Or perhaps, came the sickening thought, they so idolized her that they had done it to themselves. Automaton soldiers with ruined flesh jumped down from the walls, pistons in their legs whirring. Pain made their eyes bright, but they wore their half-made parts like proud ornaments.

The mages and the Prince's Army fought side by side through the fray, white bolts raking into the sides of buildings, axes slashing across the plated torsos of faery soldiers caught completely unawares.

Clara was still trying to get her bearings, with the Doors snapping shut behind her, when she felt Anise's anger.

It struck her through her link with Nicholas, whipping through her blood in a shock of pain. Even Godfather staggered, for some of his bond with Nicholas remained, corrupted though it was.

From somewhere in the frenzy came a howl more savage and furious than the others.

Nicholas, and Anise. Their voices mixed in a ghostly chorus.

Godfather tugged her on. "We have to get you out of here, before he finds you."

She dodged a faery soldier's blue spear, throwing up her arms to create an unseen shield. The spear's bolt hit it and scattered, dissolving. Godfather ducked them both into an uneven alleyway. Jagged gear edges thrust up out of the grimy cobblestones, as though the contents of Godfather's shop had spilled across the world.

Clara leaned hard against a shuddering wall. A stray mechanik popped out of the ironwork and nipped at her boot. She kicked it away.

"Where's Ralk?" Godfather muttered.

"Clara," crackled a tiny voice.

She adjusted her headset, squinting into the murk. "Ralk?"

"Clara, there's a problem. It's Nicholas—"

Screams of rage cut him off.

Clara started back the way they had come. "We have to go to them."

Godfather grabbed her. "Clara, without you we stand no chance against Anise."

"What shall I do, then? Leave them for dead?" She pulled away from him. "Stay close to me."

They darted through screams, mage and faery and human, natural and mechanical. Soldiers shot their spears, and the mages their white arrows. The Prince's Army brandished their crude swords with as much courage as any knights, and she was suddenly, immensely proud of them. They had no magic, and still they fought.

A hand grabbed her leg, almost tripping her. She looked down to see a desperate human crouched in the rubble. Yellow pus crusted his wide eyes.

"You're like her," he rasped. He stared wonderingly at her crackling white hands.

She kicked him off, spooked. "Only somewhat."

They found Ralk and Kora at a bend in the road beneath a scorched metal sign. Faery symbols glinted on its surface; torn wiring sputtered and kinked.

Nicholas crouched beneath it, hands in his hair.

Kora trained her bow on him. "He's gone mad."

A gash of silver bisected Ralk's cheek. "I fear he may be lost to us," he said, panting.

Nicholas lifted his head. One side of him was a gleaming mass of steel rods and metal plates. Wire trailed down his belly, following the lines of his muscles. Tiny metal plates circled his neck, inching up over his jaw, dangerously close to his eyes.

Godfather swore.

"Clara, no," Nicholas said as he got to his feet, as if he would run from her, looking at himself in horror. "Get away."

She went to him without hesitation. The others called her back, and she ignored them. Explosions rattled the roofs; crackling wires littered the ground like eels. The faeries were gathering their artillery. Unpredictable booms shook the road.

Nicholas scrambled away, but Clara caught his arm and held fast. Immediately he shuddered in relief, let his eyes close. Some of the curse receded, sinking back into the wounds along his flesh.

A distant anger emanated from him, but it was not his.

A building down the way collapsed with a groan, sliding beneath the earth in a cascade of shining metal sheets.

"I'm here now," Clara whispered to him, though the world quaked around them. "You'll stay with me from now on. All right?"

"Clara," Godfather warned.

She rounded on him. "I know the risks! I can handle him. We have an agreement. Don't we?"

Nicholas laughed ruefully. "Better dead at your hands than at hers."

How romantic, a tiny malicious voice hissed from the metal cord at his throat.

Godfather led them down the road, Ralk and Kora flanking them with bows drawn.

"Which way?" Ralk said.

Clara paused, the warm weight of Nicholas pressed against her side. She felt along the veins of the earth, letting the binding's strength stretch her magic's awareness down the road, around the corner, north a ways, turning left and then right, delving deep, deep down beneath metal and steel into stone and ground. There was a drain, barred and encrusted with thick waste.

The foundations of the castle Wahlkraft.

She pointed at the corner ahead. "Turn there, then straight until I say otherwise."

The way through the capital was nearly impassable. They could hardly take ten steps before having to fight their way past some scuffle or other. In the wake of the ambush, it seemed the entire citizenry—such as it was—had taken to the streets. The chaos of warring magic in the air tore through each roadway and railway trestle with earthquakes and random eruptions. Constant lightning surged from a sky that seemed to be slowly sinking, enveloping Erstadt in a stormy mire.

Human slaves with blue-tinged lips attacked faeries, mages, the Prince's Army, one another. A human man leapt from the corrugated metal roof over Clara's head onto the canopied roof of a carriage propelled by spindly steel legs. Inside, a faery woman, her hair an elaborate terrace of braids and wire, shrieked and struck him. Her gloved arm was bright with jewels, and blue shot from it—but more humans followed the first, their clothes in tatters, their fingernails black with rot. They swarmed on the carriage, and the air filled with stink and hot blue sprays.

"This is mad," Kora spat in disgust. A young faery boy leapt out of the shadows and clawed at her leg, spitting like an animal. She shot him at once. Her arrow scorched his chest, and he fell, a black, icy spot over his heart. One of his eyes twitched and detached with a small click, leaving behind a bundle of charred springs in his eye socket.

"I had no idea," Ralk said, stunned, "that it was like this. None at all. That the capital had become . . ." They paused at a black bridge where a clock tower had fallen, its gears spilling into the dark water. A mass of confused mechaniks writhed like a pendulum that could not hold itself together. "Is it like this everywhere, Clara? Everywhere in Cane?"

"Much has happened," Nicholas muttered, "since you've been hiding, Lord mage."

Clara gripped his arm tight. She had heard the foreign rattle in his voice. She saw the cruel smile sharpening his face. "Nicholas, listen to me—"

He threw her aside and unsheathed his sword. "Clara, Clara," he sang, Anise's voice twisting his, "little Lady Clara, she said some words and shared some blood and thinks she's something special."

"Anise, leave him alone."

He circled her, grinning. "I don't think I shall. This is far too much fun."

Then he leapt at her, his sword flashing.

Clara unsheathed the knives strapped at her waist in one swift movement, ducked the swipe of his sword, whirled around, and caught his blade between hers. Their eyes met over the crossed metal.

His wavered uncertainly. Then with a wild shout he shoved her away with his sword. She barely dodged its tip.

Alone in the center of the bridge, he lurched to the railing and gave a short sob of pain. The muscles of his arms were so prominent, she thought his skin would burst open. "Clara, do it."

"Listen to him," Kora said from behind her. "He'll kill you and ruin everything."

Clara was calm, her grip tight on her daggers. "I won't kill you, Nicholas."

"Idiot girl!" Kora shouted.

Nicholas growled, "Before it's too late." Then another, feminine voice echoed, mockingly, "Too late, too late, before it's too late." He collapsed, gasping for air.

Clara took a step toward him. "If I kill you, our bond will no longer exist. I won't be able to match her." She took another step, kept her face hard. "You'll have to be stronger. Now get up."

He glared up at her through his hair; it was slick with oil and sweat.

She extended her hand. "Now."

He took it, and as soon as he was on his feet, Clara started pulling him along again. She was relieved but also frantic with worry. How many more times would she have to fight him? How much deeper would Anise sink her claws?

Then she saw it.

"There," she said, pointing. A drain, down the waterway at another bridge. A slimed hole into the deep of the world. Clara closed her eyes, extended her power along the water, into the darkness, and down. She sensed how the air curved as it passed around objects, how it chilled as the shaft deepened.

A ladder. An ancient stone floor covered ankle-deep in rot.

This must have been how Anise felt the world. Such an intimacy, such a terrible knowledge; Clara understood the temptation inherent in this power. Like an architect dropped into a world of infinite awareness and infinite possibilities, she felt an urge to explore and create.

"We'll climb down there," she said, "and enter Wahlkraft through its belly."

45

Kora went first, then Godfather, Clara, Nicholas, Ralk. The way was long, the ladder corroded and slick with muck. At the bottom a tunnel extended in either direction. Torch brackets draped with cobwebs dotted the walls.

Far aboveground the fight continued; tremors shook clumps of earth from the ceiling.

Godfather, Ralk, and Kora readied their bows, arrows sparking. The humming light was just enough to see by. So far from fresh air, the arrows were feeble. Clara could empathize—it was difficult to stay focused, even though her bond with Nicholas lent her strength.

"Well?" Kora looked into the darkness, finger tapping on her bowstring. "Which way?"

"She's saying things," Nicholas whispered.

Immediately Ralk trained an arrow on him.

Clara put up her hand, holding him off. "Saying what?"

Nicholas shook his head, clamped his hands over his ears. "Coming out to play . . . dances in the dark . . . I won't listen to you, you wicked, you *evil*—"

Clara pulled his hands away and held them. "You're right. You won't listen." Inspiration struck her. "You told me you felt the hate returning, since being here, since seeing what she's done to your kingdom. Do you remember?"

He stared up at her wearily. "Yes."

"And then you told me you had let go of your hate, long ago. Before. You said you'd had a good teacher. Like I did. Remember?"

Godfather made a small, strangled noise, and with that one sound Clara knew. She had been trying only to reach Nicholas, to pull him out of Anise's claws with a memory of something good, something just. And now she understood.

"It was my mother, wasn't it?" She smiled at Nicholas, trying not to cry. "She was your teacher."

Nicholas bent his head. Their foreheads touched, metal to skin. "I have so much to tell you, Clara. Such a wonderful, terrible story."

"And you will tell me, as soon as we've won the day. I'll hold you to it. Princes always keep their promises, don't they?"

"Always, to you."

"Are you better now?"

He met her eyes. "I can fight."

"And you will." She jerked her head at the others. "This way."

For a time the way was clear. Clara's power reached far beyond her, following the path of the tunnel's cool, still air, but something awaited them at the end of it—something that confused her.

When they reached it, she saw why.

Their tunnel ended where it formed a junction with another one, in a T shape. At the junction stood a steel door, ajar. From within glowed a wavering blue light.

Kora peered suspiciously at it. "And what do your two-blood senses tell you about this room?"

Clara ignored her. The air here was rank, but more than that, it *felt* rank, lined with something insidious and torpid. The wrongness of it pulled at her, insisting she investigate.

She glanced at Godfather. He nodded; perhaps he felt it too.

She opened the door.

Beyond it lay a room lined with beds. Each bed was draped with once-rich fabric gone black with mold and decay. The chandelier in the center of the room crawled with bats and their waste.

On each bed lay a mage.

Their bloodshot eyes fluttered open and shut; they wore sweat-stained robes of silk and satin. Tubes extended from the flesh of their upper arms into an elaborate mess of pipes in the ceiling, where a slow swarm of mechaniks buzzed, blue crackling between them. Pistons hissed rhythmically as bright blue liquid flowed down from the ceiling, through the tubes, and into the mages.

Ralk lowered his bow. "What in the name of the stars is this place?"

Godfather bent at the nearest bed, pulling down the skin beneath the mage's eyes. The mage groaned and twisted, as if in a dream, and when he exhaled, smiling distantly, blue foam gathered at the corner of his mouth.

"She's keeping them drugged." Godfather inspected each one, disgusted. "They're alive, but barely."

"Why?" Kora looked small and suddenly frail. "Why would she do this?"

Clara stood in the middle of the room. "She bonded with them." She could feel the bindings, stretching from the mages up into the castle, to wherever Anise was, like invisible, sinister chains. As if in response, something tugged her toward Nicholas.

Ralk was furious. "But why?"

"Perhaps she believes that the more mages are bound to her, the more control she, as a royal, will have over the land."

Godfather nodded. "The land that is rapidly spiraling out of her control."

Nicholas leaned hard on a bedpost, skin shining with sweat. "She keeps them blue and keeps them sweet, drugs their minds and drugs their meat."

Clara's hand flew to her dagger. "Nicholas?"

"I'm fine. I hear her, though. Riddles and songs. She's in a corner of me somewhere, rocking. Dancing. Digging." His dark eyes searched her face. "Clara, you must think me—"

"Brave. Yes." She took his hand. "Strong. That's what I think."

His eyes softened, and for a moment he seemed fully himself. There were tired lines around his eyes and mouth. Then a shock ripped through him. He shoved Clara back toward the door.

"Leave! Go! Now!"

Clara felt it the next instant—a disturbance in the air, the ground trembling as something rushed toward them. A door at the other end of the room swung open. Four faeries entered, in uniforms of braided leather cords and high black boots.

One of them was Borschalk.

"Ah," Borschalk said, his face tight with hatred. "If it isn't the queen's little princess."

He darted toward them, the other soldiers at his heels.

Clara readied herself to fight, but before she could strike, white light flashed to the ceiling. An electric explosion littered blue sparks to the floor; pipes of sugar burst, spewing liquid. Metal beams fell from the ceiling, blocking Borschalk's path.

"Go!" Ralk summoned another arrow.

Clara hesitated, but Nicholas pulled her on, and as they barreled back through the door they'd entered through—Godfather and Kora behind them—they heard another crash, the crack of bone, a scream.

Kora cried out, "Ralk—"

"Wanted us to run." Godfather pushed her on.

Clara led them down the dripping tunnel, trying frantically to maintain focus for navigation, but the door was slamming open behind them, and heavy splashes marked Borschalk's pursuit. She felt giddy with fear.

Up, she thought, instinct taking over. *Out of these tunnels.* She did not want to die trapped underground like a rat. But the tunnel was bending, eternal. Nicholas's breathing rattled behind her. Then she felt it, a draft from the right. A fresh wave of air.

She turned them into the dark. At the rear Kora made an arrow; it was stronger here, in the fresher air. She notched it, let it fly. It shot into the dark behind them, and a faery screamed.

Clara's headset crackled, and Bo's voice spoke in her ear, tiny and worried. "Clara? What's happening? I lost you there for a while."

"Underground." There was blue torchlight ahead, stairs, and then an archway. Clara ran for the steps, and the others followed.

"The city's gone mad, Clara. I can see everything from here. The wall's *swaying*, and the storms—"

"Can't talk, Bo!"

They reached the top of the stairs, raced into a wider hallway with bare black walls and iron sconces, and high windows near the ceiling. Power gathered at Clara's fingertips, surging out from her gut. *We need an escape*, she directed it, and it obeyed, slamming through a half-formed door that cascaded into lifeless mechaniks at her touch.

"Wait," Nicholas murmured. "I know where we are."

He pushed past them into the room beyond—a wide gallery, with tall pointed windows of dark glass webbed with iron, drapes with frayed hems, a high ceiling.

A throne, black and monstrous, glittering with blue jewels.

"They came at us here." His voice was haunted, his face drawn. "They crashed through the windows and crawled down the walls. . . ."

Then he fell, screaming. A ridge of plates erupted across his collar bones, tearing open his shirt.

Behind them Kora screeched. Clara turned in time to see her jerked back, through the door and into darkness. Her bow flew from her. Awful crunching sounds ripped through the air; the crackling blue electricity burned Clara's nose.

Borschalk leapt into the throne room, his hands dripping silver. He locked eyes with Clara and raised his spear.

"Get *back*," Godfather said, shoving her toward Nicholas, but Nicholas spun out of her grip with a savage cry and ran toward the faeries, his sword at the ready.

Clara hurried after him, barely dodging Borschalk's spear. She spun around and met it with her bare hands, shoving him back off his feet with a surge of power that surprised even her. Borschalk's face flickered with uncertainty. Clara thought, *You're right to fear me*. But then the moment passed, and he attacked.

He was strong, his bulk lean and hard, but Clara matched him blow for blow—spinning to kick his legs out from under him, launching icy waves of magic at him that he couldn't quite dodge. One caught his foot and sent him flying into a window.

Behind her, Nicholas cried out in pain.

She whirled. He fought one of the faeries, and Godfather the other, and they were both faltering. The faeries were lithe, their weapons quick. As recklessly as Nicholas wielded his sword, as many times as his blade hit faery armor, it would not be enough. Clara could see that. The curse was taking its toll on him.

And Godfather—he was trying so hard, and holding up fairly well, considering, but he was unsteady without his cane. His opponent's spear caught him under the arm. Silver blood spurted; he stumbled, but still managed to point over Clara's shoulder and cry out.

Clara turned at his warning, saw the faeries—four, *six*—spilling in through the door.

They were outnumbered.

Desperately she leapt at them and thrust her arm out, parallel to her body. The magic in the air blasted toward them, knocked them off their feet.

But Borschalk was leaping for her; she could feel his shadow bearing down upon her.

She rolled away, avoiding the crash of his body. Instantly he was up, lunging for her on all fours, bestial. Long strands of jewels dangled from his right ear, and Clara recognized them as Anise's.

Nicholas dove onto him, wild, and plunged his sword into his back. Borschalk howled, reared up, and threw him off. Nicholas skidded across the floor, metal scraping metal, and was still.

Clara stared at his prone form in terror. A cry from behind her drew her attention. The faeries were swarming on Godfather, and Clara's heart soared with pride to see him fight so beautifully, despite his wounds, despite his weakened magic. He fought with dim light and sword, his coat swirling about him. This was the man she knew, the man who had taught her everything.

But it was not enough. He was falling; the faeries were closing in on him. Nicholas was still; Borschalk, wheezing, crawled toward his fallen spear.

She closed her eyes, grabbed hold of her power, and shoved it down—past the riveted metal floor, beyond the layers of surging mechaniks ready to move at Anise's command, into the stone and earth of Wahlkraft's oldest foundations.

Once there she found the pillars and beams supporting the throne room, and delved below them into the heart of the earth. There—fresh earth and pockets of air. She could breathe again, and so could her magic. And it *hurt*, the scale of magic she was about to release; it tore at her muscles, blinding her with pain. But she forced herself to focus, and felt for the ground, and pulled.

The floor began to buckle.

The faeries paused, looking about them.

Clara found Godfather, caught the dear, lone gray eye. "Protect him."

For an instant he looked devastated, as though something had crumbled inside him. But the floor was wobbling dangerously and the faeries were yelling in panic, scrambling to get away.

A great weight beneath them snapped. Godfather hauled Nicholas to his feet and staggered with him to safety. They barely made it to the room's edge before the floor collapsed, the foundations giving way, the earth driven apart beneath them. The faeries fell, scrabbling for purchase on the tilting floor. The last one she saw was Borschalk, clinging to a beam. Her magic pulsed through the room more thickly than air, making it difficult to breathe, crusting his reaching hand with ice.

Then the beam snapped, and he slid into blackness.

Across the chasm that had been the throne room, Godfather threw himself and Nicholas to the ground. Clara stumbled back against the throne, shielding her eyes.

The impact had woken Nicholas. He called for her through the clouds of black dust. She saw his figure, his balled fists, his stricken face. "Clara, no! What have you done?"

At Clara's ear her headset crackled, whined, and settled into a low buzz. "Bo? Bo, are you there?"

Nothing. The light at her cheek went dim.

Nicholas was beside himself. "Clara, stop!"

She turned to face the throne, behind which a great curtained doorway led to stairs cloaked in darkness.

Clara, Anise's voice whispered merrily in the walls.

Furious, her eyes watering from the sting of wreckage, sugar, and sulfurous rot, Clara wiped the sweat from her palms. "Where are you?"

Come and find me.

The walls moved, undulating. Then they lit up, and a face appeared in panels on every wall—bleeding and swollen, unshaven. Netted in blue lightning.

John Stole was screaming. Magic burned angry lines across his face. Tiny black mechaniks scampered up his throat, swarming him like bees. He clawed at them; his screams became inhuman, hysterical. Behind him Clara saw a green sky and black towers.

He was twisting strangely.

She looked harder. He was in *midair.*

"The roof!" Godfather cried out from where he lay, nursing what looked to be a broken leg. Silver pooled beneath him.

She nodded. Yes. High above everyone, for all the kingdom to see. Anise could not resist putting on a show.

Nicholas reached toward her, screaming her name, begging for her to stop, but she turned away and pushed past the throne's curtains into the staircase soft with shadows. Whispers laughed at her heels. Her father's screams and Nicholas's fading pleas followed her up.

And up, and up.

The whispers said, *Clara.*

Clara.

Clara.

46

The stairs led up a tower and then out onto a network of slender walkways that jutted out from the battlements and connected clusters of towers like a lattice. Grotesque statuaries and elaborate parapets lined each walkway, and gargoyles protruded from the rounded tower walls—sea serpents, loks, monstrous stags. The castle was black and shining, and the sky was lit by a storm.

Above Clara's walkway hung a man in a burning blue net. He was frozen in place, his limbs twisted.

Father. She barely resisted calling to him.

Anise waited, pale in white furs, her hair loose, as it had been *that night*. Clara hardened herself against the thought.

"Finally," Anise said, bored, amused. Her eyes were everywhere. Kambots lined the jagged towers, silent and waiting.

Clara stepped out onto the walkway. It was stable, but around her, towers shifted and climbed, spooling and unspooling like spindles being crafted from shadows.

Everywhere—affixed to the battlements, hanging from railway trestles—chromocasts displayed Clara's image, and Anise's image, and the image of her father, like a hall of lit-up mirrors. It was as though this were a stage and she and Anise the players.

Up here, alone, with memories of Anise eating away at the edges of her courage, Clara felt suddenly unsure. But the sight of her father suspended like a demon's plaything kept her moving forward.

"Hello, Anise."

Anise smiled, her bow a mockery. "*Lady* Clara. *Lady* of the North."

Clara put up her chin. "That's right."

Lazily Anise circled her finger in the air. John Stole twirled, matching her movement. "I gather you bonded with the usurper prince. I can feel the change in you and in the air. Surprising, Clara, that you should give yourself to someone who thinks you a monster, who so utterly betrayed you."

"He doesn't think I'm a monster." Clara examined everything, noting the closeness of the clouds, the temperature of the air, the taste of oncoming snow. The treacherous incline of the roof below her and to the left, capping a squat tower. "He struggles with prejudice, and he betrayed me once, but he wants to change. He wants to do better, and he will not hurt me. I am stronger than he is."

"Oh dear. I thought you were smarter than this, Clara."

"And was I smart to trust you, to believe you? Much has happened since your bedroom."

For answer Anise laughed. She clapped her hands, and John Stole jerked and fell, and jerked still again, and then floated back up to his former position.

It happened so fast that Clara could not even move.

Anise put a delicate hand to her mouth. "Oh, how clumsy of me. I forgot to mention that at one wrong move from you, or from me—one gesture, one blink of my eye—I can send your father plummeting down into—"

"You don't need to explain. I understand. I am like you. You are like me." She paused, and there *was* a hurt inside her; she held it in place, stubbornly, so it could grow no more. "I thought you wanted to remake the world. You said we could do it together. You said we would be unstoppable." She smiled sadly. "We could have been friends."

Ah—there. Anise faltered, uncertain. There was that vulnerability from the snowy tower roof; there was the fervent hope, the terrible affection.

But only for an instant.

"I was wrong," Anise said, her voice hard, and the air teemed with vengeance. Clara felt her power building inside her in defensive response, the air bending toward her and the tiny hairs on her body rising to meet it.

She moved before Anise could, running along the walkway with the wind at her back. She gathered magic into her fingers, drew strength from the lightning in the air, and prayed that she could be strong enough to at least make a good go of it.

The first strike caught Anise by surprise, a cold thrust of air slamming into her belly and flinging her back against the opposite tower. But she fell gracefully, sprang to her feet, and recovered, then flung off her furs with a savage smile. She wore a corset of chain and curved metal, her arms bare. She cast one of them violently to the side, ripping forth sharp metal plates from the shifting rooftops beside them. They shot straight for Clara, whistling through the air, and she leapt to evade them, and landed hard on her knees.

Below her, on a terrace tucked beneath buttresses, she saw a courtyard abandoned to neglect, a tangle of old trees and black soil. Drawing upon it, gasping through the stifling iron tang in the air, she jumped to her feet and flung her arms up over her face, just as a wave of mechaniks struck her, sending her reeling back. She rolled, still clinging to the anchor of the trees below, and flew unsteady arrows of light at Anise, but the queen dodged them nimbly, leaping from the walkway to a gargoyle adorning an adjacent tower.

She landed on her hands and feet, and cut her arm through the air. One of the watching kambots flew toward Clara in a flash of blue and sharp black. Clara jumped to avoid it, then reached out and sent it back at Anise on the slingshot of the wind, but Anise put out her hand and dissected the thing as it flew, its wires and metalwork scattering.

Clara ducked beneath the flying debris; her foot caught on a crack in the walkway. She teetered and fell back, grappling for handholds on the nearest statue—a sea serpent, its fanged mouth gaping. Its scales cut her hands, embedding tiny black shards in her palms. She hung there, her legs swinging for purchase on the narrow ledge below her.

This was it, then. That had been quick. Out of the corner of her eye, Clara could see herself on the chromocasts, a hundred images of her dangling in fear, and she hoped that, wherever they were, Nicholas and Godfather would not have to see.

"Such a shame."

Clara looked up. Anise was perched above her, catlike, on the serpent's back. The wind tangled her hair; the storm lit her eyes. Overhead, kambots had taken wing and now circled, waiting to pick Clara's bones clean.

"What's a shame?" Clara said, stalling. If she could lower herself enough, traverse the narrow black eave, she might make it. The tower she had come up stood a few paces away, its metal-plated wall full of footholds and narrow windows. She could climb up it, use the serpent gargoyle there to pull herself back up to the walkway.

"I thought you'd turn out to be stronger than this," Anise was saying. "Maybe it's a good thing you betrayed me. I'm well rid of you."

It would have been convincing, had her voice not had such a childishly sulky note in it. But a sulky child could still be a dangerous one, so Clara jumped, and landed hard on the ledge below her. Pain knocked her shins, and she nearly fell, but she found her balance and pushed on, not letting herself glance down at the steep drop on her left, where the castle's lower towers roiled—or beyond the far battlements, where the capital burned.

Anise was behind and above her, leaping from parapet to parapet in what was almost a dance, flinging kambots like darts. They hit the wall against which Clara sidled, feathers flying, knocking mechaniks loose like hailstones. Clara made for the tower amid a shower of them, crying out as they scraped her face. When she reached the tower where the ledge came to a stop, she clung to the corner where the walls met, fighting for strength.

Above, Anise laughed. She perched on a parapet overlooking the very gargoyle Clara needed to climb, and the scornful, petulant look on her face filled Clara with cold fury. How *dare* she act as though this were Clara's fault? Lonely or not, the queen deserved no pity.

"I *am* stronger than this," Clara hissed, and opened a Door in the sky.

Such a simple thing, a Door, that Clara had not thought of using it until now.

She emerged behind Anise, safe on the walkway, having traveled through the Door in the space of a blink. The force of it threw Anise back, and she lost her footing. The kambots faltered too, so closely linked were they to their queen. Clara ducked to avoid the tiny cuts of their flashing wings, but Anise was dazed, clumsy. A hundred wings rushed past her, clipped her, took her balance.

There was a scream in the confusion, a terrible sound, lost and frightened. Amid the mire of storm clouds and lightning and squawking black birds, Clara saw a white figure topple from the parapet and fall. She heard a sick crunch, a choked noise.

Above her another cry sounded.

Clara turned and saw her father falling. The net holding him had vanished.

"No," she said calmly, and though fear gripped her heart, though the human in her urged her to run, the Lady in her whispered, "Softly," so she cupped her hands and let magic loose from her fingertips. It skipped across the winds and gathered below her father in a gentle curve of shimmering air. He fell into it, was cradled by it, and was eased down onto the walkway.

Only then did she run to him, and it felt so strange to see him like this—to touch his ravaged face and feel the familiar stubble under her hands—that tears filled her eyes. Exhaustion overtook her, and though he was the one unconscious and barely breathing, she longed to wake him up, ask him to hold her and tell her everything would be all right.

As if he had heard her, his eyes fluttered open.

"Father," she whispered, stroking his cheek. "You're safe now. I'm here."

"Clara?"

She nodded, unable to speak. His brow creased.

"You've . . . changed." His eyes fluttered once more and fell closed, but he was still breathing—whole and breathing and the most handsome thing Clara had ever seen. She bent and kissed his cheek, so glad, she burst out laughing.

Behind her something gurgled.

She knew at once what it was, what she would see when she turned. She gathered herself into a hard knot of resolve, of unfeeling, and turned.

Anise was pinned there, below the parapets at the opposite end of the walkway, caught on the serpent gargoyle's long coiling tail. It had impaled her, soaking her in blue.

Clara approached her with a strange sense of calm. She knelt between the parapets and forced herself to look.

"You . . ." Anise's voice was full of blood. Her eyes were vague and fading, and her body kept twitching, death pulling on the strings of her limbs. "You are . . ."

"What?" Clara took her hand. She had nothing to fear from Anise now; despite her resolve to remain unmoved, pity flooded through her, and a whole lifetime of *what if.* "What am I?"

"A Lady." Anise coughed. Her fingers tightened around Clara's, and at this last, her face was soft. "A Lady of the North."

Then she was still. Her limp body sank farther down on the sharp stone with an awful sound that made Clara turn away—but everywhere she looked was a chromocast, the image of herself and Anise's body shining down from the skies.

"You've done it!" A cry erupted in her ear. With a high-pitched whine her headset flickered back to life.

Clara winced, pulled it away from her ear. "Bo?"

"Clara, everyone saw. *Everyone.*" Bo's voice was ecstatic, peppered with whoops she couldn't contain.

"What do you mean, everyone?"

"The chromos, they showed the whole damn thing! Through the entire city, probably through the entire kingdom, knowing Anise. She would've wanted everyone to see you die, don't you think?"

Clara blinked, coming back to the world, and looked around. She heard the triumphant cries of the surviving mages from the smoking ruins of the city far below, echoed by Bo in her ear. She wondered if the whole country truly had seen her duel with Anise, if similar celebrations were taking place in the choked streets of Zarko and the opulent ones of Kafflock. What were the faeries thinking, left leaderless at their posts and in the heaps of faded party trimmings at the Summer Palace? Some would be afraid; many would be angry. Perhaps a few, the ones with any sense, would be relieved.

The wind was gentle, the ground had stilled, and the castle towers no longer shifted and writhed. The air was quiet, where moments before it had been laced with Anise's chaos. Above, the clouds were fading as abruptly as the net imprisoning John Stole had disappeared. In place of clouds now shone countless stars, their configurations foreign to Clara, and a fat, luminous moon that bathed the city in a cooling glow.

"The storm," came Bo's voice, thick with wonder. "The storm is leaving."

Clara turned back to Anise's lifeless body. Even now her slender limbs held the poise of a dancer's. "No. The storm is already gone."

Then a voice spoke quietly in her ear, cutting through Bo's. "Clara? Are you there?"

Her hand flew to her headset. "Nicholas? I'm here. I'm—" She could hardly speak for her relief. "Where are you?"

"Outside Wahlkraft, near the front doors. We were forced outside. We had to keep fighting. . . ."

Bo had fallen silent. Clara glanced at her father; he was breathing and safe. She hurried to the tower.

"What's wrong?" Clara asked.

"Come quickly," Nicholas whispered, and Clara knew, as she flew down the stairs, what she would find.

A small crowd had gathered at Wahlkraft's immense black doors, composed of mages—bloodied, battered, and significantly fewer than had entered the capital—and faeries, held at spearpoint by a grim-faced Prince's Army. The faeries left standing were terribly mutilated, for the parts of them that Anise had made were gone, leaving open wounds behind; some would obviously not survive for much longer. They looked lost, frightened, grotesque, and Clara pitied them. On the periphery, lurking in the shadows, humans watched suspiciously.

Nicholas turned as Clara ran out of the castle and down the steps. They were pockmarked with the holes of the magic that had been there, and now was suddenly not.

A figure lay behind where Nicholas stood, and Clara's breath caught in a snare of heartbreak.

"He saved me." Nicholas's voice was strange, his eyes bright. His clothes were tattered and bloody, and he leaned hard on a shattered pillar, but Clara could see that most of Anise's curse had left him. A few stubborn pieces remained, tiny and glinting. It did not surprise Clara—such terrific hate, she supposed, left permanent scars.

"Clara, I'm so sorry," Nicholas said, catching her hand. "He was wild. He fought like . . . I didn't ask him to, but he saved me."

"*I* asked him to," Clara said, and she moved gently past him to kneel on the hard ground. Blood stained her clothes silver, but she did not care. "Hello, Godfather."

His eye was calm and open, the other a lump of knotted skin where Anise's curse had hit him. The metal was gone.

Even now his face lit up to see her. He fumbled for her hand.

"My Clara." His breath was tight and irregular. "Is it done? Am I done now?"

The words seized Clara's throat with tears. She thought of the days when she had not visited, and wished suddenly, fiercely, that she had gone every day, always. So many years in service, alone in that cavernous shop, and for what?

"For you," he whispered, a sigh on the air. He had always been able to read her. "For you, Clara."

She couldn't breathe in anything but choked gulps. He was slipping, he was *leaving* her. She pressed all her love for him into his hand, willed him to feel the immensity of it. "Yes. You're done now, Godfather. You've finished."

He smiled, sagging back onto the ground. His free hand waved her close.

"Here," he said, and she leaned down and kissed his cheek. Her hair fell against his face, shielding them so when he whispered his last words to her, his final instructions, she alone could hear. When she rose to her feet, she wasn't sure whether to smile or cry, so she did both, holding tight to the Godfather-shaped place in her heart.

Nicholas watched her curiously. "What is it? What did he say?"

"He told me I should leave him be and get on with it." It was a lie, but a harmless one.

"Get on with what?"

"Pledging fealty to the new king."

Clara knelt before him but kept her eyes on his. Something bittersweet twinged deep in her heart as she saw the troubled look on his face. She longed to go to him, make sure he was truly well. She wanted to let herself cry about Godfather, about Anise, and kiss Nicholas for the first time with both of them wholly themselves. No curses, no confusion. She wanted, most of all, to collapse and rest and hear the story he had promised he would tell—the story of him and her mother, and everything that had happened here *before*.

But instead she knelt, and the others began kneeling behind her. She heard the soft shuffles of the mages first, and then, brokenly, the faeries. A bloody-eared human girl in broken chains smiled shyly and gave a clumsy curtsy.

Nicholas straightened. Something fell away from him, leaving a newness in its place, raw and heavy and ready. He stepped past Clara to address the crowd; his fingers brushed her shoulder, and warmth rippled tiredly through her.

"Friends," he began, "and enemies. Both are one and the same now. Or they must be, if we are to save the land that belongs to us all. We are three peoples, but we have one home, and it needs our help to save it."

It was a beginning.

47

"It will take many years to rebuild," Nicholas said. "The kingdom is in chaos."

Clara nodded, arms crossed over her chest. It was the only thing holding her up. They stood on the walkway where she had fought Anise. The storm had long since dissipated; the evening sky was clear and cold. It had been almost two days since she'd led the attack on Erstadt, two days of tending to wounds and mourning the dead, of establishing a makeshift hospital and clearing what rubble they could from the streets. They had worked without cease, and Clara's body was stiff with strain, but this was only the beginning. There was so much more to do—a ludicrous amount, in fact—and the enormity of the task Nicholas had before him made Clara tired even to think about.

He stood beside her, cloaked, the sleeves of his tunic rolled up to his elbows. He looked industrious and worn-out, beautiful in his solemnity. She longed to draw her to him, to tuck them both away into a quiet spot to rest, but she held herself back and gazed at the horizon, ordering her thoughts.

"Anise's magic linked everything," Clara said. "The chromocasts, the trains. And now that it's gone . . ."

"Communicating with the districts is the most important thing." Nicholas began pacing, his brow furrowed with the sort of clear concentration Clara had never seen him wear. The look suited him, though it left her feeling newly shy in his presence. So much of what she had known about him was now gone; so little of her childhood statue remained. "They need to know there's nothing to fear. Although, with no way of sending them news . . ."

"Fighting has undoubtedly broken out," Clara added. "Any economic structure will have collapsed. Not to mention the physical structure of things—the trains, the *buildings* . . ."

"The walls keeping Mira's Ring closed off from the rest of the country. The walls separating districts from one another." Nicholas sighed. "The sugar addicts, may Zoya be kind to them."

"People will be uncertain, confused. Anise's soldiers will try to keep order—"

"And they will have trouble doing so, with the fear on the streets. They will be afraid themselves."

Nicholas paused at the parapet above where Anise had died. Her body had been removed from the gargoyle just below, but blue remained on the stone, a dark stain. He stared at it thoughtfully. "The magic surrounding Rieden will have to be removed. Easy travel and communication to and from the capital is essential to reestablishing order."

"The mages won't like that," Clara pointed out. "Many of them may view this lull as tenuous at best. They may think that another faery will rise up in Anise's place, rally her people to war once again."

"And those mages we freed from the sugar cellar downstairs . . ."

"They may harbor bitterness toward the faeries more than anyone, considering Anise's treatment of them, and try to stir up discontent among the mages. They may not want peace, and they will not be alone."

Nicholas chuckled ruefully. "Well. Doesn't that sound like tremendous fun?"

Clara looked out over the ruined city.

Smoke still rose from fires that had started in the battle. The air smelled of ash and singed metal and blood, and probably would for some time. But up here, where the sky was clear, Clara could see for a long distance. The towers of the capital were misshapen and deformed but still somehow grand. There was potential there for spectacular reconstruction. Past the city walls loomed Rieden, tangled and dark, and beyond that, the thinnest hint of moonlit tundra—Rosche, and everything that lay beyond. And somewhere, she knew, remembering Bo's map, were wildlands that Anise had not yet touched, where untold scores of mages, humans, or faeries might have scratched out secret lives for themselves in the aftermath of the war.

"Not fun, no," she admitted. "But possible? Absolutely."

Nicholas said nothing as he watched her. Icy breezes drifted past them, and Clara breathed them in deeply, hoping they would wash away her heartache. It didn't work.

"Walk with me?" Nicholas said softly, holding out his arm. She took it, shivering even in the bulk of Godfather's greatcoat. She had not let them burn it with his body; it held his scent, his laughter and strangeness.

Together they walked down the tower stairs.

"Your father seems to be recovering nicely." Nicholas's voice was light and pleasant, a politician's conversational tone, and it almost fooled her.

"Yes, except for the occasional outbursts when he wakes up and demands to know where he is, and to talk to Chief Greeley, and to summon George for some brandy this *instant*."

"Who is George?"

"Our butler."

Nicholas chuckled. "Fortunate that we found enough medicine in the laboratories to keep him sedated."

The laboratories where you cut open faeries. The words hung in the air, unsaid, but Nicholas's drawn face said it louder than words could have done. The wounds he had suffered went beyond the physical, and Clara wondered if they would ever heal—or if they even should.

"How will you explain everything to him, before he returns home?"

Before *he* returns home. Clara's heart twisted. *Oh, Nicholas.* "I don't think he saw enough of anything, or understood enough of what he saw, for it to be a problem. He'll no doubt wake up with a nasty hangover and wonder why he's cut up. I'll tell him he was drunk and fell through a window and be done with it."

Nicholas guided her into the throne room, where the floor gaped like a great mouth. They turned into a side corridor hung with ruined tapestries and portraits with blacked-out faces.

"You'll have to smash a window to make that story convincing," Nicholas said.

"There are plenty, back at the mansion." She thought of her family's home in shambles, of Patricia Plum and Dr. Victor and Godfather's empty shop, and of all the other broken things waiting for her that would have filled her with dread not long ago. Now she felt only an adamant determination.

They paused near the end of a long corridor at a shattered set of doors. Beyond them was a suite of once grand rooms, now black with filth. A canopied bed. A wardrobe strewn with spiderwebs.

"My parents' suite," Nicholas said drily. "Anise certainly didn't do much with it."

Clara walked into the room and fingered the bed's ruined hangings. "She hated it here. She preferred the Summer Palace."

Nicholas had followed her. His presence was warm and solid behind her, and Clara closed her eyes to memorize the feel of it. "Why do you think that is?" he asked.

"I think she was fully aware of what she had done. To Cane, to its people, and to the land itself. I think she was afraid, and being here—at the seat of her power—reminded her of it."

"You understood her."

Clara opened her eyes and turned back to him. His nearness was intoxicating. In the wake of everything, in this room full of memory, it both thrilled and steadied her. "I know what it feels like," she said carefully, "to want control, to want revenge and power, at any cost. To have your world shape you into something you'd rather not be and not know how to fix it."

"You were very alike, the two of you."

"In some ways, yes. Not so in others." She paused and ran her fingers along the ruined bedcovers. She had tucked Anise away into a secret part of herself, to be taken out and examined in safe moments; she even wanted to tell Nicholas about it, but now was not the time.

After a moment of watching her, Nicholas turned away. "You're leaving, aren't you?"

Hearing it out loud was so final, so frightening, that she considered denying it. "Yes. I am. The day after tomorrow, Father and I will leave for home."

"For New York. To right the wrongs there."

His voice was so quiet. But Clara was resolute. "To make things right."

"I suppose I could keep you here. I could order you to stay, and your blood would compel you to obey me."

She turned, indignant, power swirling automatically at her fingertips. "You won't do that. You said you wouldn't."

"No." He turned back to her, his face resigned. "I won't. You aren't mine to control. And besides, it wouldn't be very princely of me, would it?"

"Indeed, it would be utterly villainous."

His sad smile turned rakish. "*Wicked,* even."

Clara approached him slowly. "I never will be, you know. Yours to control." It felt strange to say it, to *know* it. The ghost of that night, of listening to him betray her, lingered in her heart—it would take some time to fade completely. But his face was tender as he reached for her, and the answering pull in her heart outweighed her fear.

"And thank all the gods, everywhere, in all the worlds, for that." He drew her close. "I like my women with backbone."

She punched his arm. "*Your women?*"

"Well, woman. Singular."

"I'm not your woman." Though it was a startlingly enticing thought. *His* woman. Certainly that wasn't a thought any self-respecting Lady would have.

"No. You're no one's woman." He kissed her fingers, and then her palms. "But you would be a magnificent queen."

The meaning of his words sank into her. "I could perhaps return someday," she said, appalled to find herself crying, "when everything in New York is as it should be."

Nicholas bent low and brushed his lips across hers. "I would wait for you."

"Time passes more quickly here than Beyond. You'll be older, you'll be courted by everyone from here to Mira's Ring—"

"Yes," he agreed, taking her face in his hands, "but I want *you*."

Then he kissed her, slow and deep, and this time there was nothing in the room but them. No faeries watching, no curses or danger, but instead a sweet fullness, a sense of careful discovery—and then, when they had moved unsteadily to the bed, Nicholas's lips hot against her neck, his hands sliding up into her hair, a sense of wanting and *need*. Clara gasped with the pleasure of it, turned into his chest and melted into the shaking cradle of his arms, let him pull her atop him and met his kisses joyfully. His hands slid up her back, beneath her shirt, turning her, and then he was above her, and Clara could no longer think. She could feel only the scorching thrill of his body against hers, the care with which he touched her, the *rightness* of being loved by him.

"Clara," he murmured against her ear.

"Hmm?" Oh, was he *talking*? Whatever for?

found her bottom lip, nipped it gently. "I just have to say . . ."

Well, be quick about it!"

That this bed . . ." He stopped kissing her for a moment to meet her es, his expression somber. "Is disgusting."

She pulled away. "*What?*"

"I mean, really, look at it. Dusty, horribly out of fashion . . ."

"Are you out of your mind?"

"Not sure what that patch is over there. Maybe something *growing* . . ."

Outraged, she found a pillow and pummeled him with it. "I don't care about the bed," she tried to say, but the pillow had released a cloud of dust, and it sent them both into coughing fits.

Nicholas collapsed beside her, laughing. "Oh, the look on your face!"

She sneezed, disgruntled. This had been so *nice*—a kiss, and she'd been able to enjoy it and not be afraid or ashamed, or worried for her life, and he had ruined it. "What about my face, you idiot?"

"It looked like it used to when you'd be in the shop with old Drosselmeyer and couldn't get a punch right." He wiped his eyes. "You'd be so furious, and your face would scrunch up like that—yes, like that—and I'd think to myself, *Oh, I would give* anything *to be able to laugh right now.* You always made me want to laugh. You brought me such rare joy, Clara."

Touched, Clara leaned over him, cherishing how his eyes softened at her nearness. "My face made you want to laugh? That's . . . mildly insulting."

"Not the most gallant of observations, is it?"

"Not in the slightest."

"And what if I said that your face was a gift? That it saved me?"

"That," she said, "is much better."

As he slid his arms around her, gathering her down into a kiss, a gentle wind shook the windows behind them and brought with it a light whirl of snow.

* * *

Later they lay in contented quiet. Snow was falling steadily now, and though the bed *did* leave something to be desired, it wasn't so bad, with Nicholas's cloak beneath them and Godfather's greatcoat draped over them. Clara closed her eyes and snuggled deeper into Nicholas's arms.

"You promised you would tell me a story," she said after a long while, lulled almost to sleep by the rhythm of his thumb caressing her shoulder. "About everything that happened before. About you and Mother."

"So I did."

She looked up at him fuzzily. "Tell me now?"

"Demanding, aren't you?" He smiled down at her.

"Please."

"Anything for my Lady." He twined her hair around his fingers. "I suppose I should start at the beginning. You may know some of it already, but there's something to be said for hearing it in the right order." He breathed in and out; his hand settled at her waist. "Our oldest stories say that when the human world was first made, not all of it fit. . . ."

The first time you noticed me, you were tiny and quiet—a serious little thing with red hair and sharp eyes that noticed everything. You held your mother's hand, and you wore a ribbon in your hair, and when Leska sat with the old man to chat in hushed whispers over tea, you wandered the shop.

Your skirts and boots and miniature lace gloves were so prim, the very picture of propriety. But your face was more curious than any I've ever seen as you looked through the shelves of trinkets and toys, delicately fingering the curved dancer figurines and the goblins' sharp tails. You puffed out your cheeks and blew the wooden pinwheels into a frenzy; you stood before the wall of clocks and watched them tick.

Then you found me.

I think I startled you. You paused midstep and stared. You looked to your mother and your godfather, as if to make sure they weren't watching.

Then you came to me.

I was so glad for company, I could have danced. But of course I didn't. I could only watch, and as I did, the faery queen's voice that curled insidiously in my ear seemed to vanish.

I wanted to bow before you and tip my hat. I wanted to act ridiculous and make you smile.

But of course I couldn't.

You stood before me for a long while, frowning. Your eyes traced every inch of me, from the jagged mockery of a crown on my head to my ribbed metal armor down to my spiked boots. Then you found a stool, nearly as tall as you were, and struggled to drag it over to me without drawing the others' attention.

Laughter lodged in my frozen throat, unable to escape.

You climbed onto the stool, so close I could see the freckles on your skin. You put out your hand and touched my face with one finger. You touched my forehead, my cheekbones, my chin.

You traced my lips.

Then you smiled, Clara, and cupped one hand around your mouth, and leaned close to whisper, "Hello."

PART FIVE

THE LADY

She heard a strange singing and whirring and buzzing, which ebbed away in the distance. Higher and higher she rose, as though on mountain waves—higher and higher and higher.

48

Clara awoke in a room of dark rosewood and lace curtains. A mahogany vanity stood nearby, upon which rested a porcelain frame with a photograph of her mother's face inside it.

Her bedroom. Her bedroom at *home*.

She bolted upright and scrambled from the bed, wobbly as if on new legs.

The hearth was dark, the wood floor covered in plush floral rugs. In the corner next to the open window hung the mobile Godfather had made for her.

Only now did she recognize the creatures dangling from it for the symbols they really were.

Or had it all been a dream?

The memory of Nicholas's hands on her body and his lips on her skin told her that it was anything but, and the words of his story—of him and of Godfather and her brave mother—were still fresh in her mind. And yet she felt entirely normal, entirely as she had been *before*. Before the battle in the ballroom on Christmas Eve, before Cane and the Summer Palace, before her time in the broken black city.

Before Anise.

Before *Nicholas*.

She put her fingers to her lips. If she closed her eyes, she could hear him whispering her name as they'd moved together. She could remember the surge of magic in her blood when she opened the Door that had helped her defeat Anise.

But when she tried to summon that same magic now, when she moved to the open window and stuck her head out into the cold and breathed deep, she felt nothing. No answering pull at her fingertips, no vitality in her blood other than the knowledge that she was breathing and alive.

The loneliness of it tore at her. She put her cheek to the frozen pane and remembered the Door that had carried her here. The effort of creating it had been so intense that the other mages had had to help her. An oppressive darkness had tugged her through, throwing her against unseen boundaries that had resonated through her like thunder. She remembered falling into her bedroom with her half-conscious father in tow, helping him down the hall to his own room, and then—weak, heartsick—pulling herself to her own bed.

She looked around frantically. Yes, there it was—the tangle of wires on her bedside table.

Bo's headset.

"You never know," Bo had said, grinning her cheeky grin and shoving the thing into Clara's hands. "You might want to visit someday."

As they'd embraced, she'd looked over Bo's shoulder at Nicholas and blushed at the look on his face. There'd been no need to say goodbye out loud, not now. There'd been only one heated kiss, a lingering of his fingers at the small of her back. A low murmured, "Good luck, Clara Stole."

Footsteps racing down the corridor outside brought Clara out of her memory. She hurried for the headset and shoved it into a drawer just as the door opened.

"*Where* have you been?"

Clara turned. A choked sound burst from her. She hurried toward her sister and threw her arms around her. "Felicity. Felicity, oh God, you're all right."

"And no thanks to you." Felicity shoved Clara away, her face scrunched up in fury. "I don't know what you and Father have been up to, but first he turns up with scars and scabs all over him, and then I hear this giant crash and come in here to find you sleeping away like you'd never left, and—and you both *left* me here alone for this entire week, with Mrs. Plum and Dr. Victor breathing down my neck, and I can't even find horrible old Godfather, and—" She broke off, dissolving into tears. "Clara, I don't understand what's happened!"

Clara pulled her close, wiping her face. "I'm sorry, so sorry, darling, about everything, but Father got scared, you see? Big, dangerous things are happening in Concordia, and—"

"Oh, *hang* Concordia!" Felicity cried.

Clara smiled a secret smile. "Soon enough."

"What . . . what do you mean?"

"Just know that Father got scared and went off to try to make things better, but it didn't work, and I had to find him and bring him back."

Felicity sniffed. "And now you've returned for good?"

Something bittersweet stabbed Clara's heart. "For good."

"And where's Godfather? Not that I blame him for not showing his face here after that embarrassing display at the party. But he could have at least stopped by to make sure I was all right, for goodness' sake."

"He's . . ." Clara looked away, fighting through a wave of sadness. "He's gone away now. He finished what he needed to do."

"You mean he's closed his shop?"

A thought struck Clara and filled her with swift, unexpected joy. "Well, not quite. It's complicated."

Felicity was watching her strangely. "Clara, what's happened? You seem different. Odd, somehow."

"I'm odd now, am I?" Clara teased, suddenly nervous. Would her transformation be noticeable here?

"Oh, I don't mean that. I mean . . ." Felicity shook her head. "Never mind. Come have breakfast with us, will you? George brought it up to

Father's room, and we've got to get ready soon. The ceremony's tonight, and positively *everyone* will be there."

Clara grabbed her dressing gown from its hook and followed her sister down the familiar corridor, with its dark panels and wainscoting and rich red wallpaper. "The ceremony?" she said carefully.

Felicity pursed her lips. "The New Year's Eve ceremony, Clara. Honestly, you and Father have both lost your senses."

"Of course. How silly of me." But Clara knew very well what tonight was, and what it would bring.

John Stole's bedroom was warm and dark, with forest green walls and thick burgundy curtains. He sat in his high bed with a tray of food beside him, deep in thought. Someone had tried to shave him and had left various nicks on his face; those combined with the traces of injuries from Cane made him look frightful.

Felicity climbed up onto the stool beside his bed to comb his hair. "His hair won't lie straight anymore. I don't know where you went, Father, but it seems to have disheveled you completely, inside and out. Did you know, Clara, that he won't eat his toast? He says it leaves a strange tang in his mouth!"

John Stole looked up with relief. "Ah, Clara."

She came to his bedside. "Hello, Father."

"Fear not, Father," said Felicity. "I've already reprimanded Clara quite forcefully about how the two of you left me here, and even if it *was* to do something to hang Concordia, I don't much care at the moment. I bet if you thought about it for the rest of your life, you couldn't understand how frightened I was."

"Something to hang Concordia?" He looked at Clara, a keen, cutting look in his eyes as he examined her head to toe.

She swallowed hard. "Oh, a joke I had with Felicity."

Felicity harrumphed and took a rag from the washbowl. "Your arms are filthy, Father. What did you get yourself into?"

"A good question," John Stole said. "Tell me, Clara, what are these cuts on my arms? And these bandages on my face? Do you know?"

Clara drew in a deep breath. "When I found you, you had gotten drunk and fallen through a window. You were unconscious. I bandaged you and tended you myself, and brought you back here last night, very late."

His brow furrowed, as if he were trying to remember. "And . . . where did you find me, exactly?"

"In some hideout of yours or other, uptown. I shouldn't say specifics; we wouldn't want innocent ears to hear." She gave him a calm smile. "Would we?"

"Indeed not." He frowned even more deeply. "And what was I doing there? In this . . . hideout?"

"You were in the midst of documents and papers. I couldn't make heads or tails of them, but you kept babbling on about some great plan to leave Concordia forever." She shrugged. "Don't worry. I collected your things and put them in your study. They should be right where you left them."

He rubbed his chin, his eyes never leaving her. "Indeed."

She turned and said lightly, "Well, I should go check on the household, see what havoc the servants have wreaked in my absence."

"Fine, fine," her father muttered, and as Clara passed out the door, she heard him say, "Felicity, pet, I believe I have had the strangest dream. . . ."

"And I'd like to hear all about it someday," Felicity said briskly, "but right now it's time to get dressed. After Christmas Eve, you've simply *got* to make a good impression."

49

At the bottom of the stairs, their butler, George, saw Clara hurrying down and nearly dropped the coats in his arms. Behind him Mrs. Hancock let out a great bubbling cry.

"Miss Stole," George gasped. "It's true. You have returned!"

"Yes, George, I've returned, and I must apologize for all the confusion." She walked along the room's perimeter, noting that the servants had done much to clear away the wreckage. The windows had been boarded up to keep out the cold, presumably until new glass arrived. The torn drapes had been disposed of, leaving the room looking as though it had lost its hat. Great clawed slashes marked the floor, and in the corner, where the Christmas tree had stood, sat the ruined grandfather clock, in pieces. Clara shivered, remembering.

George was aghast. "Miss Stole, I assure you, we've been working day and night to—"

She smiled to comfort him. "I trust you have taken stock of the damage, ordered new furniture?"

"Well, of course, but—" George hurried close, his eyes afraid. "Miss Stole, I should warn you, now may not be the best time to discuss it. They've been here every day—"

"Ah. Clara. There you are."

The voice was unmistakable, the anger within it palpable, but Clara noticed as she turned to face it that she was not afraid. Not after what she had seen, and not with Godfather's last words lingering in her mind.

She smiled meekly. "Mrs. Plum. How good of you to call."

Through the ballroom doors, their fringed drapes askew, glided Patricia Plum, hair pinned up with jewels glittering as coldly as her eyes. She wore a silk gown, a smart coat of deep burgundy, and a shawl trimmed with ermine. Dr. Victor, lean and tall in his dark coat and hat, was right on her heels. Snow dusted their shoulders.

Clara curtsied. She did not have to delve far to find the remnants of fear from Christmas Eve, when Dr. Victor had gripped her so cruelly on the dance floor. She hoped it showed on her face.

"You don't fool me with that demure facade, Clara," Patricia Plum hissed, and when Dr. Victor grabbed Clara by the elbow, she let it happen, let her body go limp and allowed tears into her eyes.

"You're hurting me." She trembled for good measure.

"It's nothing compared to what I will do to you tonight," Dr. Victor whispered, his cold lips at her ear. George and Mrs. Hancock had hurried out. Clara was alone.

"Where have you been?" As Clara struggled in Dr. Victor's grip, Plum's face was impassive but her eyes were furious. "Clara dear, you nearly missed our deadline."

"Yes, Mrs. Plum," Clara said, "but we're back now. Father, too. He's upstairs with Felicity, eating breakfast and preparing for the ceremony tonight. You can see him for yourself."

Plum jerked her head at Dr. Victor, who released Clara to hurry upstairs. The Concordia glove glinted on his left hand; it had left indentations in Clara's skin.

Once they were alone, Plum floated closer. "Let's try this again. Tell me, Clara, where have you been this past week?"

"Father was afraid." Clara looked up, biting her lip, wringing her hands. It occurred to her that no one in Cane would believe this timid front for an instant. The thought cheered her. "He knew how terribly angry at him you were. He ran off, went into hiding. But I know him well. I know all his little hideouts."

Plum smirked. "The coward."

Clara ignored her. "I found him, told him that he had a responsibility to his city, to me and Felicity. He couldn't hide and hope his troubles went away. It was easy to guilt him. He was so horribly drunk."

Plum relaxed; Clara could practically feel the woman accepting her story, reveling in the sense of it.

Dr. Victor returned, his expression sour. "She's right. He's back, with the girl. When I walked in, I thought he would piss himself."

"Please, Dr. Victor, such crude language," Plum reproved. She considered Clara carefully for a moment, and then gave a delicate shrug. "I suppose, then, we're finished here and should leave you to prepare."

Dr. Victor seized Clara's wrists and yanked her back against him. She cried out piteously, though inside she longed to scream, to free herself from his grasp and attack him. Were it not for what she intended to carry out tonight, she would have.

She no longer feared his brutish hands, his stinking medicinal breath.

Patricia Plum tilted up her chin. "We'll see you tonight, Clara. And don't forget our bargain, at least for Felicity's sake, hmm?"

Behind Clara, Dr. Victor chuckled; Clara felt his wet breath on her neck.

She nodded, the tears in her eyes entirely genuine. She was furious.

Plum smiled. "Very well. Happy New Year."

George hurried to her once they had gone, his face pale. "Oh, Miss Stole. Are you quite all right?"

Clara hardly heard him. She was staring at the front doors, which Dr. Victor had left open. Snow swirled in, frosting the parquet floor. She wiped her cheeks dry and smiled.

"Yes," she said, "I'm fine."

And soon, with Godfather's help, they all would be.

50

At eleven o'clock that evening John Stole exited his carriage at Wall Street and Broadway to ring in the New Year.

Clara stepped out behind him, Felicity firmly in hand. In her other hand, tucked inside her fur-lined glove with the cunning satin ribbons, was a small vial, chilled against her skin.

Their carriage was lit with lamps and strewn with holly garlands. The stamping horses wore bells at their necks, and red ribbons at their tails. John Stole was resplendent in his top hat and smart silk shirt, his red vest and scarf, his dark overcoat. He raised his hands to greet the crowds, and a searchlight on a rolling cart illuminated him, turning the snowfall into a glowing curtain.

Overhead, the spires of Trinity Church stretched into the cold black night, and bells rang joyously. Throughout the crowd citizens in patched coats and frock coats, in leather gloves and frayed knitted ones, shouted and cheered, giddy with the night, giddy with drink, their cheeks red and their voices hoarse. From the trees boys threw wads of confetti that mixed with the snow and turned it colored. The air was thick with noisemakers and whistles, clapper bells and toy horns.

A tremendous clock had been wheeled to the wooden stage,

constructed especially for this event. Clara remembered when it had been commissioned, years ago. She had sat on Godfather's lap, his fingers over hers as, together, they'd molded the faces of the clay figurines that would encircle the clock face.

When the Stole family had finally worked their way through the crowd, where her father shook as many hands as he could and Leo Wiley forced him to answer a few questions from shivering reporters—centering primarily around his recent rumored disappearance and reports that the old toymaker Drosselmeyer had gone mad on Christmas Eve and ransacked the mayor's mansion—they climbed up the stairs and onto the stage.

Clara was jittery with anticipation. She ran her gloved fingers along the clock's rim, down the curve of a serpent's tail, up the wing of a nightbird, and thought of home.

She started. Home? But home was here, in New York.

Or perhaps, she thought, *it is both.* New York and Cane. Human and mage. A child of two worlds, and of two bloods.

The thought filled her with a comfort that slid from her head to her toes, strengthening her. She passed Felicity on to Mr. Wiley, who patted her absently on the head. Felicity glared back at Clara from beneath the brim of her ribboned felt hat, but Clara shooed her along. Patricia Plum was coming up the stairs at the other end of the stage, in a dark gown and coat trimmed with lace and pale fur and glittering white jewels. The crowd quieted a bit at her appearance. Dr. Victor appeared behind her, his bowler hat rimmed with snow.

"Clara," Felicity whispered, indignantly edging away from Mr. Wiley, but Clara shook her head.

Believe me, dear sister, Clara thought, watching Plum with what she hoped was an appropriate amount of resigned grief, *you want none of this.*

She glanced at the clock. It was eleven forty-five. Time for her father's speech, and nearly time for his death—at least, as far as Patricia

Plum knew. Clara met the smug blue eyes across the stage and let her face constrict, let her eyes fall.

Mr. Wiley bustled forward and muttered into her father's ear. John Stole nodded and raised his hands to the crowd.

"To the good people of New York City," he called out into the snowy night, "welcome to the first night of a new beginning."

Clara stared at her father, nonplussed. So too, she noticed, did Leo Wiley, who glanced at the planned speech in his hands before coughing loudly and waving it about with no small amount of nervous bluster.

That, Clara knew, was not how the speech began. She had rehearsed it with her father that afternoon.

Across from her, Dr. Victor shifted, his hands in his coat pockets and his eyes on the crowd. Clara followed his gaze and saw a hard-looking man with greased hair and a pockmarked face, muffled to his nose in a dark scarf.

His right arm was stiff, his hand obscured.

The gunman.

Clara clasped her hands at her waist and bowed her head, as though pensively listening to her father's words. She pulled out the vial from her glove.

It was filled with silver. Her recently bandaged palm stung to look at it.

". . . it has been a hard few years for us," her father was saying, "and for some more than for others. There has been injustice in our city, a great number of injustices that have left many hardworking citizens poor and cold and hungry, while others luxuriate by their fires. Crime runs rampant, the economy is poor, the courts are corrupt and full of greed, and as your mayor . . . I must assume responsibility for this. For your hunger, for your cold and your weariness, your anger and fear."

The crowd was silent, shifting, but their eyes were on John Stole, whose image burned brilliantly in the snowy light. They stared at him—uncertain and angry, yes, but hopeful most of all.

"My wife," he continued, "was a woman of great integrity who believed in fairness and generosity, both of bread and of spirit. She worked tirelessly for you, for every one of us, and I think she would be . . ." His voice broke; he had to pause. The wide-eyed crowd swayed closer. "She would be ashamed of what I have let happen since her death. Of how I have behaved. I have not done right by her. I have not done right by my daughters, who remind me of her whenever I see their faces."

He turned to Felicity, who looked caught between mortification and delight at the attention, her cheeks glowing bright pink. She put a hand to her mouth and bobbed a perfect curtsy. Then John Stole looked to Clara, and their eyes met. In that moment, with the memory of her mother surrounding them, Clara realized with a shock that perhaps he remembered more of what had happened in Cane than he'd let on. His eyes upon her were too knowing.

"They have taught me more than I ever thought possible," he continued, "especially you, Clara." He blew her a soft kiss. "Your mother would have been so proud of you."

For a moment, as the crowd murmured approvingly, Clara was thunderstruck. But then she saw how Patricia Plum fumed, how Dr. Victor's eyes were intent on the gunman.

Clara nodded at the crowd, smiled, and uncapped the vial, spilled two drops of her own wintry blood onto the skin of her wrist.

Perhaps she could not access her magic so easily, now that she was not in Cane, but it was still in her blood. Godfather had used his last breath to tell her that with a small tithe—a spot of pain to create focus and bring her blood out into the open—she would still be able to use her power. That had been his own solution, the awful night he'd cast his own special breed of mechaniks across the ballroom, doused in silver.

So Clara focused on that spot at her wrist, on the pain of her stinging palm, and used the pain as an amplifier to extend herself outward, awareness flooding her. The sky was a darker black, the snow colder and brighter, and somewhere, so distant she thought it might be a trick of her mind, she felt the line of another's blood, coursing thin but steady within her own. It pulled her ineffably toward a world unseen.

As if he were there beside her, Clara could hear Nicholas's voice say, with that easy confidence, *Well, go on. You know what you have to do.*

She pointed her attention at the gunman, who was moving forward in the crowd, readying his arm . . .

". . . so it is with solemnity, humility, and most important of all, a promise, that I ask you to help me ring in this new year, this new century, dare I say this new *age* . . ."

Across the stage Dr. Victor had begun to sweat; Clara could see it on his brow. Patricia Plum, however, was unflappable, her cold eyes trained on John Stole's profile.

Clara readied herself, her magic poised, with the anchor of her blood—*Cane's* blood—steadying it. She drew a picture in her mind of what would happen next, and held it there.

". . . with a resolve to better ourselves, better each other, and better our city."

The crowd began to applaud. Dr. Victor jerked his head. The gunman pushed his way forward to the front row and lifted his arm.

Clara raised a finger, sent a wave of magic out from her core through the blood on her wrist. It gathered power from the frigid air, happy to be released in this strange new environment, and raced toward the gunman with a tiny white flash too fleeting for anyone to understand.

It burrowed into the gunman's pistol and ignited.

There was a brief, sharp explosion, the acrid smell of gunpowder.

The gunman screamed, falling to his knees. His hand was a bloody stub, the gun a smoking metal tangle at his feet. The crowd nearest him leapt away, shouting. Two police officers dove from their positions at the stage stairs to throw John Stole to the ground and cover him. Others grabbed Felicity, Leo Wiley, Clara herself.

She hardly noticed. The crowd was a sea of chaos, and across the way, Patricia Plum's eyes flashed blue fury. Chief Greeley tried to hurry her away, but she slapped him.

"Leave me be, you fool," Clara heard her say.

Behind Plum, Dr. Victor was rustling in his long dark coat. A flash of silver glinted in his hand, and it was not the Concordia glove.

Clara shoved at the police officers. They grabbed for her. Her skin felt tight with fear, but she did not falter as she spilled what remained in the vial onto her wrist, thrust her fingers at Dr. Victor from the safety of her coat, and let her magic fly sharp and true.

In that instant, as a sharp white light cracked open the stage and the crowd screamed, Clara's breath caught. Would it be enough?

A shot was fired. Everyone ducked. But in the swarm of black uniforms and frosted police caps, scarves and snow-soaked skirts and holly berry brooches, one figure did not move.

Patricia Plum lay on the stage floor, limbs askew. Darkness pooled from a wound on her belly, and her eyes stared, unmoving, at the stars.

Dr. Victor could not move as he took in the sight of her, his pistol still in the air. His astonishment could not have been more complete.

"But I aimed . . . ," Clara heard him mutter. "I aimed right at him. Not at her."

"Murderer!" someone screamed.

Chief Greeley shouted at his men, and they rushed at Dr. Victor, restrained him. When the gun was ripped from his hand, he seemed to awaken.

"But I wasn't aiming at her!" His eyes were wild. He struggled to break free, but the officers held fast. They wrenched his arms behind his back, locked him into chains. "Something jarred my aim, right at the last . . . It was you, wasn't it?"

He jerked his head at Clara, the force of his hatred pointing at her more than any hand ever could have. "She did it. *She* did it. I don't know how. . . . Get off of me! The little devil-bitch . . . There's always been something off about her. Listen to me. Listen, all of you!"

Chief Greeley took out his club and struck him in the stomach. Dr. Victor went limp.

"Get him out of here," Greeley said, disgusted, and his officers dragged Dr. Victor away, his boots making dirty tracks in the snow.

"Clara, are you all right?" Her father was there, within the protective circle of police coats. Immediately Felicity latched on to him. They were being herded down from the stage and into their carriage, where two officers held the spooked horses by their bridles.

Just before the door shut, Clara looked past her father's shoulder. There, looking lost and furious and even, Clara thought, a bit frightened, were the Merry Butcher and the Proctor brothers.

"Father," she whispered, nodding at them, "go to them. Say something now, or someone will reach for Plum's power. Assert your authority. We aren't safe yet."

He shot her a queer look but went without another word. Clara watched him from the carriage window, Felicity shivering in her arms. He clapped his hands on the Butcher's back, shook Hiram Proctor's hand. The police standing guard at his back, the sympathetic, bright-eyed hands reaching for him in the crowd, did not go unnoticed. A certain light went out of the Butcher's eyes. He nodded, tugged his coat tighter around him, and melted into the crowd. The others followed suit.

Clara smiled. It was not the end of Concordia; it would take long months, even years, to cut the many strings of Patricia Plum's web. It might become even harder now, with Concordia's most powerful figures fighting to control the fractured pieces of the empire. But it was a beginning, a step in the right direction. At least now, she hoped, her father would have more conviction to do what must be done.

"Clara?" came a small voice.

"What is it?"

Felicity frowned up at her. "You've got something on your wrist."

Clara laughed lightly and drew down her sleeve. "Oh. An ink stain, I expect. You know I was helping Father draft his speech earlier."

"*Silver* ink?"

"Don't be silly. There's no such thing as silver ink."

Felicity looked entirely unconvinced, but then the door opened, admitting their father and a gust of snowy wind. The door shut, and the carriage began to move.

"Father!" Felicity cried. She went to him and sniffed prettily in his arms as he smoothed her hair. "Oh, how awful that was, Father. Were you very frightened?"

"It happened too quickly for me to be frightened, sweetheart. Not to worry."

Clara kept her eyes fixed on the world passing outside her window, but even then she felt her father's attention upon her.

"You are remarkably calm, Clara dear."

"I suspect I'm in shock, Father," she said, letting her voice waver.

"Indeed." He was quiet for a moment, shifting Felicity under his coat to warm her. "Or perhaps it is that you also had a strange dream last night?"

Too stunned to think better of it, Clara whipped her head around. His face was pensive, his eyes distant, and it occurred to Clara that perhaps John Stole knew more about his wife's past than Clara had assumed. A chill came over her as she thought of the sum of history and memories and secrets that she had yet to uncover.

But now—with the church bells chiming midnight behind them and the new year with its work looming ahead of them—was not the time to ask.

Instead Clara said, "Happy New Year, Father," and kissed him lightly on the cheek.

51

One more hour—a photo or two, a clever quote for the reporters, and the carriage ride home—and Clara Stole could finish packing.

She turned away from the shabby gray building behind her and back to the crowd, in their winter coats and fur muffs, their scarves billowing in the sharp wind off the Hudson. The air smelled of winter; it would be the first snow of the year, and Clara could hardly keep still for her excitement.

Excitement—and, if she were honest with herself, apprehension.

Would it be the same, after all this time? Two years here; *eight* in Cane. After carving out a place for herself here, would she be able to do the same *there?*

Her blood surged in eager affirmation.

Not yet, she scolded it, and somewhere distant, an answering, patient tug stirred warmth deep in her belly.

"They say that a civilization can be judged on how it treats its defenseless and unfortunate, its young and its old," she said, raising her voice to the crowd. The faces that stared back at her were so different from the wary, pinched ones that had watched her at the Bowery Hope Shelter two years ago that, for a moment, it took her breath away. Much had happened in that time.

In the wake of Patricia Plum's death and Dr. Victor's incarceration, and most especially given her father's upsurge in popularity after his near assassination, Concordia had fallen. It still existed, of course, as pieces of its former whole, and it was not a danger to be dismissed. But its members had scattered into the shadows like roaches, and though their relative dormancy might be temporary, it was something. There was hope on the streets again, and money in the collection plates at churches throughout the city, and the holly they had put out on the park lampposts to usher in the holidays was fresh and green.

Under Clara's close supervision, Trifles & Trinkets had reopened with a new toymaker in residence, a Mr. Peter Hoffmann, who had so delighted in seeing Godfather's fantastic inventory for the first time that he had had to be administered to with a fan and cool cloth, like some simpering debutante.

Pangs of loss came to Clara every time she paid Mr. Hoffmann a visit, and every time she stood beneath the mobile in her bedroom and spun it, letting the shadows of dragons and nightbirds flit across her skin. But she knew Godfather would have been proud of her—*had* been proud of her—and that, though it pained her to think it, he had probably been glad to die, after those long, lonely years of being so near her mother and yet never near enough. Several times since hearing Nicholas's story she had tried to muster up anger against Godfather—for loving her mother so blindly, for betraying Leska not once but twice. But Clara could not manage anger for long; he had suffered enough by his own doing, and so she kept the memory of him close and dear and free of blame.

Clara snapped the shears closed. The bright red ribbon floated away on either side of her, and applause rippled up from the crowd.

Beside her, plain-garbed, rosy-cheeked Mrs. von Meck grabbed Clara's hand and shook it. She was to be the headmistress here, and was without doubt one of the most pleasant and intelligent women Clara had ever met. The girls would be in good hands.

It was one less thing for her to worry over, one less thing to feel guilty about leaving.

"This," Mrs. von Meck gushed, "is the most remarkable day, Miss Stole." There were tears in her eyes. "This will be a place of hope for many."

Clara smiled up at the imperious gray facade with its marble pillars and the words HARROD HOUSE etched severely into the stone. It still unnerved her somewhat, to think that this place had once been Dr. Victor's, that the classrooms now gleaming with polished wood and lined with books had once been cells holding bloody cots and shivering girls.

No longer. Now it would be a school, and those girls would not be cowering in their cots but rather huddling in them late at night to study for examinations or share the latest gossip. It would be open to any who wished to further their education, who looked to university and beyond. Their classes would keep their minds sharp, and their exercises would keep their limbs strong, and none of them would have reason to be afraid.

Clara squeezed Mrs. von Meck's hands. "It already is a place of hope for me," she said, and turned to smile for the photographer.

Later Clara stood in front of her mirror, her bags at her feet, and raised her chin.

"I have done what I said I would do," she told her reflection. "I have put Father back on his feet and on the path to righting Concordia's wrongs. I have looked after Godfather's work, ensured my family's safety, and helped rebuild my city . . . and I have flourished doing it."

She paused, stepped closer to the mirror. Her nose almost touched the glass.

"So, you can try to make me feel guilty any moment now," she said firmly, "but it won't work. I have nothing to feel guilty about."

She waited to feel it, some lingering sense of responsibility that would keep her here, but none came. Her reflection was calm.

She had finished here. It was time.

"What are you doing?" came Felicity's sharp voice from the doorway.

Clara immediately returned to her packing, tucking her mother's portrait beneath a layer of underthings. "Packing, of course."

"No, I meant before." Felicity sat primly at the vanity, arranging her skirts. "You were talking to yourself in the mirror."

Clara smiled. She had rarely been able to truly fool her sister, and that ability had lessened even more in the last two years. If Clara had flourished during that time, then Felicity had done so tenfold. She still enjoyed her pretty things—the lace on her skirts, her silver hairbrush, her favorite ribboned hat—but she was constantly at her father's side, learning politics, learning government, and everyone who met her whispered to John Stole, "Watch out for that one; her mind's twice as keen as yours," and every young man who met her grew flustered and tongue-tied, much to John Stole's dismay.

"I was giving myself courage," Clara said, tying the bag shut. "It's a hard thing, leaving home for the first time."

Felicity was quiet, watching as Clara went about her room, straightening things that didn't need straightening.

Finally she said, "Clara, are you really going to university?"

Clara turned at the window. The biting air outside pulled at her, insistent.

"Of course I am," she said, laughing. "I'm boarding a ship this afternoon. You know that, you silly thing."

"Yes, going abroad to school. To see the world and find adventures. To stretch your legs."

"You'll want to do the same yourself someday."

"Perhaps." Then Felicity leaned closer, thoughtful. Clara had never seen her so serious. "Will you come back?"

"I'll visit often." Clara kissed her cheek, then teased, "Perhaps I'll even bring a husband back with me!"

Felicity burst out laughing, and with that the moment had passed. "You? Clara Stole? The day you bring home a husband is the day I sprout wings and fly."

Clara threw a pillow at her, and Felicity squealed and rushed out the door, her ribbons streaming behind her.

Alone, Clara waited until she heard Felicity's voice mix with her father's down the corridor, then grabbed her bags and hurried downstairs. They would be upset with her for leaving without a formal good-bye, but even though her blood was ringing like bells in her ears, and she could hardly keep the nervous smile from her face, she feared that seeing them and being wrapped in their embraces would stall her courage.

She hurried out into the oncoming winter and shut the mansion's great doors softly behind her.

As she turned the corner onto Sixty-Sixth Street, a coach-and-four splashed muck onto her skirts and a group of boys raced past, tossing a ball between them. The daylight was dimming, washing the city in shades of cold pink and gray. When she reached Trifles & Trinkets at Twenty-Third and Sixth, Clara paused at the window and let her fingers touch the glass.

She closed her eyes and let the sounds of the city wash over her—the streetcars and the clomps of horses' hooves, the bells of shop doors and the laughter of passersby and the deep barge horns from the river.

Then she took one last look at the familiar shopfront and its curling gold letters, and turned into the nearby alleyway.

She set down her bags and took out the headset from the folds of her coat. Hands trembling, she placed it on her head, beneath the ribboned brim of her hat, and switched on the mechanism at her ear.

"Hello?" She sounded uncertain, and younger than she had felt in a long time. "Is anyone there? Bo?"

A pause. A heavy, unbearable stillness. She heard nothing but a dim crackling noise, thin and spotty. Then a high whistle and the sound of someone clearing her throat noisily.

"Well," said Bo, "it's about time."

Clara heard the familiar grin in her voice, though it was older now, and she went weak with relief.

"Bo, I—"

"Not to worry. I'll patch you over to him right now."

"What?" Sudden panic struck her. She wasn't ready; it was far too soon. "Bo, wait—"

A snap, a change in the silence, as if whatever magic connected the two worlds had tilted, shifted.

Then a voice said, "Clara? Are you there?"

It was different, this voice. Older, richer, lined with the passage of several years and the wisdom that came with it.

Clara pressed her fingers to the headset, bringing his voice closer. Her vision was hot with tears. "Yes. It's me. Hello, Nicholas."

His name sat strangely on her tongue, although she had said it many times over the last two years, alone in the intimate safety of her bedroom. She found herself laughing. Her heart swelled, lifting her.

He let out a slow breath in her ear. "I've missed you, my Lady," he said after a moment, and his voice was thick. She wondered what he would look like now, if his hands would feel the same, if his kisses would be as irresistible, and how beautiful it would be to learn to know him, finally, as two people who had done what they needed to do and survived to celebrate it.

"Come home to me," he murmured, and it was like arms enfolding her. "I'm here."

Clara closed her eyes, slipped the glove from her bandaged palm, and emptied the vial's contents onto her fingertips. Then she let it fall. The glass shattered on the cobblestone. Somewhere on the road, bells jingled merrily. She focused her senses, tasted winter on her tongue, and reached out into the cold. A sense of going home filled her, and she whispered: "Take me *home*."

When the Door formed, she felt its light without opening her eyes. She smiled, took hold of it, and stepped through.

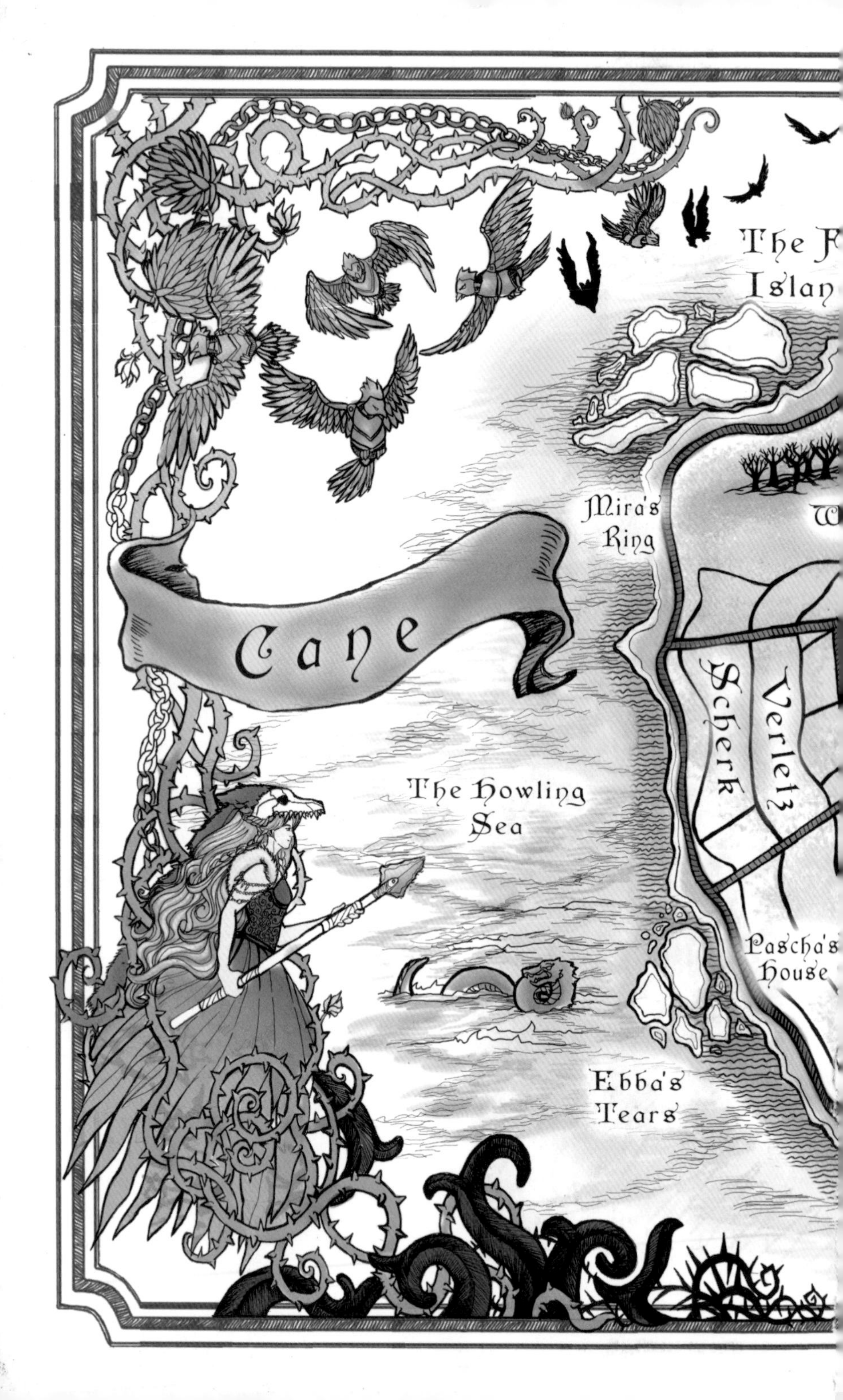
Mira's
Ring
Cane
Scherk
Verletz
The Howling
Sea
Pascha's
House
Ebba's
Tears